I0819167

THE INSOMNIACS

ALSO BY ALLISON WINN SCOTCH

Take Two, Birdie Maxwell

The Rewind

Cleo McDougal Regrets Nothing

Between Me and You

In Twenty Years

The Theory of Opposites

The Song Remains the Same

The One That I Want

Time of My Life

The Department of Lost & Found

THE INSOMNIACS

Allison Winn Scotch

BERKLEY
NEW YORK

BERKLEY
An imprint of Penguin Random House LLC
1745 Broadway, New York, NY 10019
penguinrandomhouse.com

Book design by George Towne

Library of Congress Cataloging-in-Publication Data

Names: Scotch, Allison Winn, author.
Title: The insomniacs / Allison Winn Scotch.
Description: New York: Berkley, 2026.
Identifiers: LCCN 2025013961 (print) | LCCN 2025013962 (ebook) |
ISBN 9780593817926 (hardcover) | ISBN 9780593817933 (ebook)
Subjects: LCGFT: Fiction | Novels
Classification: LCC PS3619.C64 I57 2025 (print) | LCC PS3619.C64 (ebook) |
DDC 813/.6—dc23/eng/20250602
LC record available at https://lccn.loc.gov/2025013961
LC ebook record available at https://lccn.loc.gov/2025013962

Printed in the United States of America
1st Printing

The authorized representative in the EU for product safety and compliance is Penguin Random House Ireland, Morrison Chambers, 32 Nassau Street, Dublin D02 YH68, Ireland, https://eu-contact.penguin.ie.

For my fellow insomniacs,
bright beacons in the night,
keeping watch until dawn

Hope begins in the dark,
the stubborn hope that if you just show up
and try to do the right thing,
the dawn will come.
You wait and watch and work:
you don't give up.

—ANNE LAMOTT

THE INSOMNIACS

PART ONE

PROLOGUE

BETTY

December 13th

BETTY DIDN'T MIND working the dead shifts while the Columbia students were all huddled in their libraries studying for finals. Graveyard slots meant she got paid time and a half, and frankly, she liked being unbothered. Also, she planned to quit next week, with the money she had earned from the laundry detergent commercial safely in her bank account. It had been a risk, the commercial, but she could dye her hair, get some colored contacts, find a way to blend into the New York City masses now that it aired, and the paycheck had been worth it. It was nearly time to move on. She'd been here for two years, too long really, and she knew she'd probably been lulled into a false sense of security. Not that there was any other sense of security for her. But she had to admit, even if it was just to herself, how comfortable her new little tribe had made her; how maybe this was something akin to happiness, not being so entirely on her own, not being so wholly anonymous.

Tonight, she sent the line cook home at one thirty A.M. because he had a kid who would wake him up in about five hours, and if anyone came in and ordered something she didn't know how to make, she'd just lie and tell them they'd sold out tonight. She preferred being alone anyway, even if that, too, like the commercial, was a risk. But with four years behind her since she left, she'd learned to rely on her instincts, and in this diner on the Upper West Side of Manhattan, where her bleached blonde hair and hipsterish clothing helped her blend in, she felt safe. Well, safe enough.

She grabbed the Lysol spray and a rag from the supply closet and wiped down the tables. She worked in silence, eschewing the Christmas music that they had to start playing the day after Thanksgiving when the diner was busy because she hated Christmas music and barely tolerated Christmas. Growing up, her mother decorated the outside of their house as if she were Michelangelo and their ranch home were the Sistine Chapel. Not that Betty had ever been to Italy. Not that she had ever studied art. She thought of her brother Levi, how he had traveled the country from tip to toe, and felt a palpable pang at the distance between them. Anyway, back then, the exterior of their home sucked up enough electricity to nearly blow the local power grid. Of course, no one within the community would dare complain to Betty's dad. They probably didn't even bill him. Or if they did, he probably never paid it. Everyone was in his debt in one way or the other. Ironically, his church, not their house, did indeed eventually blow. No one decorated Betty's childhood home now.

It had started to snow, so Betty eased into the booth she was cleaning and allowed herself to appreciate the beauty of the fat flakes illuminated by the streetlights, of the way that the city actually felt still, silent. She'd come to New York after a stint in Baltimore, then Philadelphia, without a plan, without much of anything, and it was nice, she thought, to have a quiet moment to appreciate that she was still on her feet. She checked her phone to see if Caleb had texted, but he worked around the clock and usually turned his phone off while doing so, so she couldn't be disappointed. Low expectations. Betty had settled into those.

She jolted at a loud clatter coming from the alley behind the back door where the line cook went to smoke. Her heart rate accelerated out of habit, but she reminded herself that it was probably just the rats who were on a nightly buffet schedule by the dumpsters. She pressed her palms flat against the table and pushed herself up. She knew she shouldn't feed them, but part of her pitied the family of rodents who dwelled back there. In this weather, the least she could do was give them some left-overs. There was expired bread in the pantry that the line cook would toast to seem less stale for customers, so she grabbed the bag.

Betty unbolted the back door, and the frigid air blew in, her entire body turning to gooseflesh. She'd expected to see the garbage cans knocked over or some wee rat footprints in the snow, but the trash cans were upright, and the flakes hadn't yet stuck back here, so that was no help. She slipped outside, then crouched down, looking for the little family. But the alley was hushed.

She laughed aloud, because not a creature was stirring, not even a mouse.

A memory of her sister easing out of her own bed and into Betty's one Christmas Eve—how old was she? Eight? Patience, then maybe seventeen, still lived at home, so Betty couldn't have been older. She remembered the two of them listing all the things they hoped to unwrap under their tree the next morning. A delusion. A fantasy. But at eight, Betty hadn't yet stopped dreaming.

Patience wanted a science kit, one of those make-your-own-battery things, because she was a closet nerd and, in a different life, aspired to go to college to become a doctor. Betty wanted some jeans and hoodies from a boutique at the mall, clothes that the other third graders were wearing, because she resented having to always wear woolly, itchy dresses. Neither of them would find such gifts the next morning.

She reached into the bag of bread and grabbed a slice, tearing it into morsels and scattering them on the concrete.

"Bon appétit," she said to the nonexistent rats. They'd come out eventually.

Maybe she could go to Paris next, she thought. Though she needed a passport for that, so it was probably out of the question.

Her phone vibrated in her pocket. Sybil.

"Hey, Sybil, still up?" Betty watched the mist from her breath disappear into the air. Of course Sybil was still up. Betty angled her neck, heard a vertebra pop. Her body felt about a hundred years old from the lack of sleep, slow and creaky and worn down, all an injustice upon her youth.

"Betty," Sybil said, her voice serious and shaking. Betty had never seen or heard Sybil anything less than stalwart, less than unflappable.

A long pause hung between them. Betty wondered if the line had been disconnected.

"Hello? Sybil? Are you still there?" She squinted down the alley. Where had the rats disappeared to?

"Something's happened to Julian." Sybil's voice cratered.

Alarm rocked Betty's gut, and her fingers clutching the phone began to tremble. She held a hand up against the exterior of the building as if she were propping herself up. She breathed in, breathed out. She could handle difficult things. She'd *handled* difficult things, but that didn't mean she had the spine to handle any more. She was so tired. Just so fucking exhausted. It didn't seem fair, this weariness at twenty-two.

"One second," she said finally. "Just give me a second to sit down, before you tell me. Let me get inside."

"Take your time, honey. I'm here."

Betty spun around to head back into the diner, the chill from the air or maybe Sybil's forewarning tone seeping into her bones. She'd been here for two winters now; you'd think she'd be sort of used to it, but she wasn't sure she ever would be. Georgia had gotten cold but never like this.

And that's when she saw it.

Tacked against the back door, a sign that could be meant only for her.

RUN

If she stopped breathing, she wouldn't have been surprised. She allowed herself three beats for her ears to ring, her mind to spiral. She knew she was lucky to have been warned, though how they'd found her, what mistakes she had made, she didn't know those answers yet.

It didn't matter.

It doesn't matter, she reminded herself.

She had to move, and she had to move quickly. She raced into the kitchen, pulled on her parka, flipped up the hood and tugged her backpack onto both shoulders. Then she unlatched the back door and stepped out into the snowy dark alley. She'd be out of the city by dawn.

1

NIGHT ONE

SYBIL

October 11th

WHEN SYBIL FOSTER rolled over, the other side of the king-sized bed was empty. Of course it was. She blinked several times and allowed her eyes to adjust to the darkness and chastised herself. She didn't know why she expected otherwise: that Mark would be here.

When would she stop expecting otherwise?

Sometimes, he surprised her, true. He'd slip in after a long night in the OR and fall asleep without disturbing her, which was different from not waking her. Because Sybil was nearly always awake these days, even when her husband would flop on the custom-made mattress and be out in less time than it took Sybil to count five sheep. She had to hand it to him: He really did not disturb her, which at this stage in their marriage was no small thing. Still, on those nights when he made it home, she'd lie there on the right side of their bed, unmoving, frozen, as if greeting him after a sixteen-hour hospital shift violated some unspoken agreement between them.

To be fair, nearly everything between them was unspoken these days.

In the blackness of their suburban bedroom, Sybil pushed up to her elbows and flung their white duvet to Mark's side of the bed, her feet swiveling to the floor. She tiptoed to the bathroom, until she remembered that her children were no longer home, either—an adjustment that five weeks into their freshman year at college she still hadn't made peace with. Empty-nesting. Everyone rattled on about how this was the chance for her to reclaim her life. To get a grip back on her *own* time. Was she traveling? Had she taken up pickleball? What about a part-time job? Like Sybil was interested in opening up an Etsy store or exploring the wine pairings for the lunch specials in town.

Sybil sighed and flipped on the bathroom lights, then took a glimpse at herself in the mirror on her side of the marbled vanity and recoiled. She quickly dimmed the lights to something softer, something more suitable for two A.M. and the back half of her forties. How was she only four years away from *fifty*? She pulled her hair into a bun and stared at the fine lines that were etching themselves around every millimeter of her eye sockets. Her fingers tugged the skin tighter, then released it, then tugged it again. Maybe she should do that eye lift that a few of her friends had whispered about. Maybe she should just blast off the entire layer of her face, actually. Not that Mark would notice, but wasn't this the time to do things *for herself*? That's the other thing that everyone kept saying: The kids are gone, isn't this a wonderful time *for yourself*?

Sybil turned sideways and raised her chin, considering if she should vacuum off the double chin that had planted itself on her jawline about a year ago. Not a double chin exactly. Jowls? Excess skin with a little fat? Her own mother had remained beautiful right up until the day she dropped dead six years ago at seventy-two in her desk chair in her corner office, so Sybil couldn't call her now and ask if she had any family secrets to pass down, inquire about just what she was doing wrong. If her mother were here, she suspected her list of grievances about Sybil's choices would have been long anyway. Better not to consider it.

Sybil flipped the lights back off and padded over to her side of the bed, yanking her phone from the charger on her nightstand and reaching for her reading glasses but discovering she must have left them in the kitchen. She'd abandoned them alongside her laptop on the island earlier in the evening having read multiple articles that implored her to get off her goddamn electronics a few hours before bedtime. Then, these articles promised, she would sleep like a newborn.

As if newborns didn't wake up shrieking every ninety minutes.

Now, of course, she couldn't see anything on her phone because her body was betraying her, but since she was wideawake, she plodded down the upholstered steps to the open kitchen and living room, where her dog, Pluto, named by the twins back when they were obsessed with astronomy, snored so loudly, slept so deeply, that Sybil took it as a personal affront to her own sleeplessness.

"*Pluto,*" she whispered, then louder, "Pluto!"

The dog, an oversized mutt of undetermined ancestry, jolted his snout up and leapt off the custom couch that Sybil had paid too much for because she had nothing else to do than spend weeks working with an interior design shop in town that took a hefty commission. Sybil was once the top of her class at Harvard Medical School. *Harvard.* Now she roamed her empty house in the bleak hours of the night while her twins were at college and her husband scrubbed into the OR but more likely was scrubbing into one of the on-call anesthesiologists. Sybil had known about it for at least a year. She simply hadn't decided what she was going to do about it. What she cared to do about it.

Pluto parked himself at her feet and panted.

"No, it's not time for breakfast, buddy," Sybil sighed, opening her laptop and waiting for it to power on. He swatted her with a paw, hard enough that it hurt, but Sybil barely flinched. Maybe she deserved it. She'd be pissed if someone decided to wake her just for a little company too.

"Okay, no, you're right," she said, pushing back the counter stool and moving toward the ceramic treats container that she'd bought some other night off a fancy pet site when she couldn't sleep. Pluto raced around the corner of the island, his feet sliding on the wood floors, the stain of which she'd spent at least six days fretting over but that she probably couldn't pick out of a lineup anymore.

He sat obediently, his eyes wide, a smidgen of drool foaming on the right side of his bottom lip. She tossed the salmon square in a beautiful arc, and he opened his mouth and caught it with immaculate timing. Sybil smiled. At least some things could still be counted on.

Pluto waddled back to the couch and settled in, so she grabbed her laptop and plopped next to him, her feet resting on the coffee table, a habit that Mark hated, but well, Mark wasn't here, was he? Mark was still at the hospital. What couldn't Sybil do when left all alone? Sleep.

She used to listen to true crime podcasts when she was up all night. Incessantly. She'd joined message boards for unsolved murders; she read old news articles and watched *Dateline* reruns. Indeed, she'd thought she was pretty close to solving a dead-wife case in Ohio before she realized, as an unlicensed medical professional, that maybe her fascination with the macabre was part of what was keeping her up at night. So she googled and googled, looking for cures or suggestions, and frankly, had spent too much money trying all of them to no avail, and now, here she was. There were sixty-seven people online in the forum. All Sybil needed was one, it didn't even matter who. Just one person to keep her company until dawn broke through her kitchen windows.

The group, the link, was called THE INSOMNIACS.

Her laptop dinged with a notification nearly instantaneously.

Beartown: Mama2Twins, hey, you awake?

Sybil cracked her knuckles, dopamine coursing through her cerebral folds. A friend. A conspirer. Someone who understood exactly just how bleak life could be when your body refused to give itself the one thing it needed: rest.

Mama2Twins: Totally. Wide awake. Just like always.

Sybil always used to tell the twins that nothing good ever happened after midnight. It was a shame, she'd think later, that she didn't heed her own advice.

2

NIGHT ONE

ZEKE

ZEKE RODRIGUEZ KNEW the pain in his elbow was going to rouse him even before the pain shot up his arm and through his shoulder and straight down his side, so what was the point of sleeping? He had physical therapy tomorrow, and he'd have to put in a half-ass effort if he pulled an all-nighter, but what choice did he have? Sleep for five minutes before his fucking pitching arm rebelled on him? Pop another Percocet and risk becoming a cautionary tale in the tabloids? What he did instead, instead of sleep, instead of the pain pill, was replay over and over again the moments that his major league career went out the fucking window, as if his mind were caught in the spin cycle of a washing machine.

Why had he thrown that pitch fast and low to Brian Schmidt's sweet spot? When he saw the ball ricochet off Schmidt's bat, why hadn't he moved quicker, higher, lower, *anything* to prevent the hundred-mile-an-hour line drive from careening right into his elbow, shattering just about every bone nearby, destroying his pitching arm, landing him on the IL right at the peak of the season, just when his team needed him? Possibly ending his career.

Zeke had watched the actual replay enough to know that he could have moved. *He had time to move.* But he froze. He stood there like some motherfucking third grader who was about to pee his pants in dodgeball. Now he didn't need to watch the tape. He could simply mentally rewind the moment again and again until it was all he could think about. It was on all the time, the highlight reel in his brain. It kept him from sleeping; it nearly kept him from breathing.

The lights of Manhattan twinkled thirty stories below his bedroom window. When he landed his twenty-seven-million-a-year contract, everyone told him not to buy a place in the city. *Get a compound in the suburbs, dude,* his teammates had advised, as had his financial guy. *You'll be hassled everywhere you go.* But they hadn't grown up in the middle of bumfuck Oklahoma. They didn't know that the silence of the suburbs would kill him, that pleasantries while squeezing cantaloupes at the grocery store or filling up the gas tank would bore him to the point of near oblivion. Even now, with his arm plastered and bandaged and sutured, the electric pulse of the city below made Zeke, well, happy. He pressed his forehead against the floor-to-ceiling window and stared down. That ridiculous interior designer his Realtor had hooked him up with begged him to get blinds—*The primary bedroom faces east, so you'll be woken up at the crack of down every day!* she'd said—like Zeke wasn't up anyway. Even before the injury and the two surgeries with one more to go, and the pain and the instant replay running through his memory, he'd been an early riser. He trained every morning before dawn, or at least he used to. Why would he install window treatments and miss out on the very reason he'd spent seven million on this apartment in the first place?

He'd bought a big-screen TV and an oversized couch, an extra firm mattress and called it a day. He hadn't expected to spend all that much time here anyway, what with eighty-one games a year on the road, spring training in Arizona, the occasional visit back home to his parents and his younger sister, who still lived in the middle of goddamn nowhere.

His sister, Lani, told him that he needed a girlfriend. Like really really needed one. Tell him something he didn't already know, he'd texted her back a few days ago. The problem was that the girls who hung around the team bus weren't the type of girls he was interested in, and he was too famous to date someone normal. He couldn't just, like, go on Bumble and swipe right. A celebrity, Lani had suggested then. But he wasn't interested in a celebrity either. *That shit is stupid*, he'd texted her back.

So no one normal and no one not normal, she'd replied. *Cool. I'm sure it will work out for you.*

Zeke started to respond that he hadn't asked her for any dating advice so why was she getting testy, but he realized he didn't really want to fight with one of the few people outside of his physical therapist he actually had contact with these days.

Tonight, he checked the time on his phone. It was almost two A.M. There wasn't much point in getting back to bed now. He'd try to nap this afternoon because he had nothing better to do after physical therapy. The team had wound down the season a few weeks ago when they went out in the NL wild card round, and technically, they were mandated to stay in shape starting now through spring training in March, but Zeke couldn't do much. Swim some boring one-armed laps with a kickboard like a toddler, do some stupid excruciating exercises that pushed his pain tolerance to levels he thought were reserved for squeezing oversized baby heads out of a woman's pelvis.

He found his laptop on the chaise of the humongous couch, reached for the remote of the equally humongous TV and fired up ESPN on mute.

He'd discovered this forum a few weeks ago when the sleeplessness had begun—The Insomniacs. His whole life he had slept like, as his mom used to say, he'd been kissed on the ass by God. Maybe he had been. Athletic, handsome with broad shoulders, an arm that threw a fastball like an artillery cannon, well-liked enough to win homecoming king. You already knew his story before you even met him. So sleep, no, that had never eluded him. Even on the team bus. Even on the team plane. Through time zone changes and after-hours parties and nightclub hopping in Ibiza and through the South of France, though Zeke rarely partook in nightclub hopping.

Zeke Rodriguez had never had a singular worry in his conscious world. Even on game day, even the night before game day.

Now it felt like this forum was a life jacket holding his head above the water before he was pulled under and drowned. Someone was always online, ready to chat like they were all old friends, like they didn't know that the man behind the screen name *Beartown* was named Rookie of the Year, was an All-Star nine seasons in a row, was one of the top ten highest-paid players in the league. They didn't, of course, know. Here, he was just a kid from Oklahoma who couldn't sleep like the rest of them. He squeezed his eyes closed, reopened them, his left lid spasming from fatigue. Even if his arm were decent enough to throw right now, the rest of his body never could. The precision required to hurl exactly the right spin or exactly the right placement or exactly the right velocity meant every single thing had to be in perfect working order, create a synergistic harmony. He couldn't even control his left fucking eyelid right now, like the lid was a cry for help, a representation that the rest of his body was breaking down too.

Yeah, no fucking shit, he wanted to scream.

He pressed his fingers against his eyelid, then spotted a name he'd been chatting with the past week—*Mama2Twins*—and clicked on her handle.

Beartown: Mama2Twins, hey, you awake?

Mama2Twins: Totally. Wide awake. Just like always.

Zeke felt his shoulders soften. He liked her company, liked the way that they'd started chatting about Sudoku a few nights ago, which Zeke had never played before, so she sent him a link and they raced each other to see who could finish the puzzle first. Zeke had always thought Sudoku was for, like, senior citizens, so he had typed without thinking:

Beartown: do I need to join the AARP to play this?

Mama2Twins: how do you know I'm not 75? Maybe I'm a card-carrying member, you know. Is that ageism?

Zeke had turned the hue of a nuclear detonation. He wasn't used to being judged solely by his words. Zeke Rodriguez had always been protected by the fact that he was Zeke Rodriguez.

Beartown: Shoot, good point. Are you 75? If you are, I apologize. And if it helps, I still love my grandma.

Mama2Twins: No, omg, I'm not 75. Though I'm not trying to be ageist! Of course!

Beartown: This is new for me, talking with strangers, I'm sure I'll say something idiotic every night. So I apologize in advance.

Zeke liked that, that he was telling her that he was in this for the duration. That he was hinting at, asking her really, not to leave him stranded here.

Mama2Twins: Well, if it helps make you feel better, the AARP has started mailing me letters. Aggressively. Maybe that's why I can't sleep. Staring down the back half of your life seems like it could do that to a person. Maybe I should blame this all on the AARP.

Zeke laughed, and his eyelid spasmed twice as quickly.

Beartown: Ok, so then Sudoku. What's the prize for winning? I'm a virgin, I should add, so go easy on me.

Mama2Twins: Well, I mean, I guess I don't judge? Your private life is your private life.

There went Zeke's ears again. In person, the models who flirted with him, who left their palm too long on his forearm, would tilt their heads back and laugh. Fuck. Why was he so bad at this now?

Beartown: No, no, shit, sorry, a Sudoku virgin. See? I told you. Words have never been my thing.

He searched his emojis to emphasize his mortification but worried that might only make things worse.

Mama2Twins: What's been your thing then?

Beartown: Long story.

Mama2Twins: Technically, we have all night, but I get it. We probably all have long stories.

Zeke thought: His wasn't even that long of a story. *Prodigal child, eggs all in one basket, carton dropped, eggs shattered, now what?* He could tell her all of that in under a minute. How despairing, that his whole life could be summed up in fewer than twenty words.

Mama2Twins: Anyway, we can share our sad stories another time. Tonight, we play for pride. Isn't that what we're always supposed to play for these days since everyone always gets a trophy?

Zeke rested his head on the back of the couch cushion and considered it. *Pride.* That sure as shit sounded nicer than the bells and whistles that he'd gotten used to over the past decade. The five-star hotels. The endorsement deals. The interviews and photo shoots and hot actresses whose publicists slipped him their numbers. Zeke wasn't complaining. He knew he was breathing rarefied air. His dad was a middle school principal, and his mom taught third grade. Lani was a dental hygienist. He hadn't grown up with any of this, and he appreciated—he really did—how lucky he was to have earned it. But still. Pride. Yes, remember when he used to play for that? In Peewee League? In Little League? In travel club? In the Youth Nationals?

Pride. He didn't have much of it anymore.

So Sudoku might be the best place to start. Zeke held down his eyelid again, trying to deceive his body that it wasn't as depleted as it was. And anyway, nothing could go wrong playing a little Sudoku. Low stakes, no skin in the game. That's what Zeke was all about right now. That's exactly what he needed.

3

NIGHT ONE

JULIAN

JULIAN PACED FROM his living room into his bedroom then back into his living room again, trying to find the goddamn cat. Felix liked to play this game in the middle of the night: cause some sort of alarming crash, then scurry under the furniture or on top of a bookshelf when Julian came to check on him. Often, he was skulking around the fish tank in Julian's home office, as if he were only one lucky break away from a snack. Other nights, he was as elusive as sleep was to his owner. Julian once spent forty-five minutes searching for him only to discover him in the dryer, which he had left slightly ajar earlier in the day.

Julian was not actually a fan of cats. Nor was he a fan of fish, but four years after Robin died, Simone moved out for college, and his boss suggested he get a pet. When it became obvious that Julian was going to ignore his boss's suggestion because he was both pigheaded and fastidiously devoted to his routine, the boss, always one for protocol and hierarchical command, had the tank—and sixteen different fish—delivered on a Saturday when he knew that Julian wasn't on the road. When Julian complained to Simone, she suggested a cat as a joke. She probably said it because she was only half listening, not because she wanted the cat to eat all the fish and resolve Julian's problem, but he remembered that Robin had a cat when they first started dating, and he figured maybe that would be nice. Maybe Robin would approve.

"Felix!" he shouted into the kitchen. Nothing.

"Felix!" He checked the bathroom and opened the under-the-sink cabinets. Nothing.

This was how Julian was going to die. He knew it. Alone, looking for a cat, up all night loaded with regrets. He took a deep breath, felt the air rattle in his chest, which was happening more frequently these past few months, and sank onto his couch. He fought his impulse to retreat to his office and review old files; once he did that, he'd never make it back to bed. He opted instead to text Simone—she'd still be awake. He knew that she didn't really want to hear from him all that much and that he needed to do more to bridge their gap than send her late-night texts. But it was at least a start.

Julian: Hi Simmy, you up?

He had to retype it three times because his fingers were tingly and felt a little disconnected from his body.

He imagined her phone buzzing on her nightstand, her reaching for it, rolling her eyes.

Simone: Dad, not really. Can we talk another time?

Julian double-tapped her message and gave it a thumbs-up, masking the slap he felt from her dismissiveness. He knew to expect it. He thumbed over his screen and logged into the forum he'd found a few months ago when it became clear his sleeplessness had embedded itself into his life as much as breathing had.

His phone vibrated within seconds.

Mama2Twins: hey buddy, just checking on you and saw that you're online. Another night staring at the ceiling?

Initially, Julian had wondered how secure the forum was, if it were smart to use his real email, to forge connections with strangers. He ostensibly knew better. He wasn't your typical clueless elderly dude, as Simone liked to tease when she felt like they had a relationship where she could tease him. He was up on technology and online security and wasn't about to be duped by, say, an email telling him that he had been gifted ten million dollars by a Nigerian prince. But *Mama2Twins* had greeted him so kindly when he first logged in that his hackles softened, his edges blurred. *Dad, you run a candy store,* he could hear Simone say. *Just relax, okay? No one is looking to, like, steal your identity.*

KingofQueens: Spent the night looking for my cat (don't ask). Now, yes, staring at the ceiling long enough to draw you a diagram of the paint peeling.

He rolled his wrists, trying to limber up, loosen his joints. He was going to have to speak with his doctor about his meds.

Mama2Twins: different night, same problems. Want to join us for Sudoku?

Julian didn't know who "us" was, and he honestly didn't want to join any sort of bigger group discussion at all, but he didn't want *Mama2Twins* to hop off their chat and abandon him. Soon enough, he and *Mama* and *Beartown* were in a heated race to pair up numbers into empty boxes. An absolute ridiculous waste of time, but it's not like any of them had anyplace else to be. The game dwindled after an hour, and Julian found that he didn't want to log off. He was used to being alone without Robin and postretirement, but being alone in the interminable stretch of predawn hours was a different sort of emptiness. If he hopped off the forum, he knew he would indeed find his way into his office and drive himself crazy with would haves, should haves, could haves, with micromanaging all the small screw-ups that led to an avalanche. Not that he had many doubts, but yes, there was one.

KingofQueens: Hey, long-shot but any chance you guys are on the east coast? Educated guess because we're up at the same time.

He had always been excellent at putting clues together.

Mama2Twins: I'm just outside New York City. First suburb on the train.

Beartown: No shit! I'm actually in the city. Right by the park.

Julian felt a pang of nostalgia for when he would take Simone to the carousel on crystal-clear spring days and let her ride as many times as she wanted. Or trek through the zoo and watch the seals. Or buy ice cream from the truck on the 72nd Street Transverse and race to see who could eat it before it dripped down the outsides of their hands. Robin was still alive; he was still a semipresent father; the job that consumed much of his waking hours was his.

The idea tumbled out of him before he could realize what he'd proposed.

KingofQueens: I'm right near both of you actually—in Queens. Sorry, it's a stupid handle. Feel free to say no since meeting strangers from the internet is probably ill-advised and I should say, I promise I'm not a serial killer, but . . . wondering if you guys would like to meet? There's an all-night diner on the Upper West Side I used to go to, near Columbia. Maybe this would feel less lonely if we did it face to face, like our own little Insomniacs club. Any takers?

4

NIGHT TWO

BETTY

October 15th

BETTY HAD BURNED the coffee at the diner again, but since there were no customers and she was the only employee present, barring the line cook who was asleep in a folding chair by the grill, she stared at the swirl of brown sludge until she lost track of time. Eventually, she snapped out of her trance, and then she dumped the coffee down the industrial-sized sink drain. No one had bothered to ask her if she had any culinary skills when she applied for the job, and if they had, she would have lied. She lied so quickly and so easily now that sometimes she hadn't even realized what she was spinning until the words were out of her mouth. But the trust-fund kid who owned the diner hadn't delved into her work history and pretty much offered her the gig on the spot. The last girl had quit; he was desperate. Desperate meant easier to manipulate.

Betty had learned that from her dad, actually.

The kid, not too many years older than she was, had been surprised but not particularly interested that she wanted only the overnight shift. But barring a few hours on the weekends, when the drunk Columbia students packed the booths and paid with their parents' credit cards, she could always have a decent sense of who was coming and going during her shifts, always felt like if she needed to simply walk out the back door and leave, she could.

"So it's ten P.M. to seven A.M. five nights a week," he'd said. She saw his eyes coast over her mousy brown hair, over her curves, which she was just learning how to flaunt. She'd been taught to cover them for so long that a V-neck sweater felt nearly pornographic.

"I don't sleep much," she'd replied, forcing a smile because she knew young men liked that sort of thing. She needed a job after ditching her gig at the perfume counter at Bloomingdale's. The main floor there was too hectic, made her feel claustrophobic, like she had no idea who was approaching.

"No one will mind that you're not available for overnights?" He was flirting now, but she also knew he was harmless, completely toothless really.

"They'll only mind," she said, "if I can't convince you to give me two dollars more an hour." She flashed a grin at him again. Like hey, maybe this is a possibility, you, me, sex in the stock room. It was absolutely absurd, which was the only reason Betty felt comfortable with it. Betty had only had sex a handful of times, mostly to get it out of the way so something about her was normal for her age.

He laughed and said, "I should call your references, but what the hell, sure, why not. I like you, Betty. You're hired." It was better that he didn't call her references, all of whom were invented, so Betty really lucked out. Desperate always did as desperate does.

She'd almost never seen him since, so it wasn't much of a risk, the flirting. She had the sense that the kitschy diner was more of an afterthought in his portfolio, like a sports car that sat in his garage that he could show off to his other rich friends to impress them. He could have turned into a predator, sure. But in the years since Betty had left home, she'd gotten a feel for who was dangerous and who just liked to think of themselves as dangerous. Those were two very different things. If she were another girl in another life, maybe she would have actually slept with him. She had to use everything available to her; she wasn't under any illusions about that.

Tonight, she replaced the burned coffee and started a new pot. The line cook was snoring now. When the bell at the diner's front door clattered, it took her a few seconds to register that she actually had a customer. Wednesdays tended to be dead, and they could go nearly a whole shift without seeing anyone between about two A.M. to five A.M. So when she popped out of the kitchen, she was even more surprised to see a trio slide into the corner booth, one of whom she thought she recognized, though she couldn't initially place him. She grabbed three menus and made her way to the table.

"Evening, folks," she said. She was trying something new these days, a lilt of a Midwestern twang, elongating her vowels for emphasis. Something to practice in case she needed it when the time came. "Late-night meal?"

An older Black man turned his attention toward her and rested his arms on the table, which wobbled under his weight.

"One sec," she said, fishing two packets of sugar from her pocket and dropping to the floor to wedge them under a metal leg to level the tabletop.

Also, she needed a second to compose herself.

She was pretty sure, no, she was definitely sure, that one of these customers was Zeke Rodriguez. Betty wasn't even a sports fan but now that she'd gotten a good look, his face was impossible not to recognize—he was advertising razors on the sides of buses; he was on television selling low-calorie beer. Zeke Rodriguez could leave her a tip big enough to cover a month's rent. Zeke Rodriguez was an opportunity.

"Sorry about that," she said, righting herself, knowing her cheeks were flushed, hoping it came off under the guise of hard work. "You guys chose the one table that's a troublemaker."

"Do you have coffee?" the woman who looked to be somewhere between mid-thirties and mid-forties asked. In New York, so many women kept such good care of themselves that guessing their age was akin to throwing a dart at a bull's-eye with a blindfold on. This woman had immaculately highlighted blonde hair, a soft pink manicure and skin that screamed expensive night cream, and even though she was probably just a few years younger than Betty's own mom would have been now, Betty could find nothing superficially alike in the two women: This woman seemed like a mom who packed her kids' lunches and used fabric softener on their sheets and bought brand-name Halloween candy for neighborhood kids. Betty's family didn't even celebrate Halloween. The woman must have felt Betty's gaze linger, so she smiled kindly at her, like she was sorry to be asking about the coffee, as if it weren't Betty's job.

"No, not for me," the older Black man said. "I'm off coffee. I would just love an ice water. And if you do a fruit salad? Or something fresh. Just nothing with sodium, please."

"You're off coffee?" the woman asked. "To help with the insomnia? I should do that, too, but honestly, I'm not about to cut one of the few pleasures of my life."

"You haven't tried ours yet," Betty said. "Don't set your expectations too high."

At this, Zeke Rodriguez threw his head back and howled, and Betty felt a bubble of pride rise up from her belly. She'd gotten good at identifying what turned people on in the four years she'd been on her own. She stowed this away in case he became a regular.

"What do you recommend for food?" the woman asked. She'd put on reading glasses and was examining the plastic menu with a scrutiny better reserved for a legal brief. "Or, Julian, you suggested this place, you've eaten here?"

Julian was lost in a thought and didn't seem to hear her.

"Okay, well, then I'll take an order of pancakes," the woman said. "I probably shouldn't be eating in the middle of the night given the state of my own midlife metabolism, but oh well." She handed the menu back.

"How'd you end up on the night shift?" Julian asked, reengaged. Betty wasn't wild about his penetrating gaze, but her fight-or-flight response was well honed, and she suspected he was harmless. Just an inquisitive dad who probably saw his own kids in her.

"I've always been a night owl," she said. "I can't ever remember sleeping. Thought I may as well take advantage of that, you know? Though the tips are lousy, it gives me more time in the day, actually."

Zeke clapped his hands together. "A fellow insomniac! What are the chances?" Then he thrust out his hand that wasn't in a cast. "I'm Zeke. And none of us ever sleep anymore. Welcome to our club."

"This is a club?" Betty said. She very intentionally didn't do clubs.

"I'm Sybil," the woman said. "I have two kids about your age," she added as if they were going around and saying a fun fact about themselves. "And this is Julian . . . actually, I don't really know much about you."

Julian pressed his lips together like he wasn't all that

interested in revealing cute details about their lives to the graveyard-shift waitress. "I own a candy store," he said.

"Ooh," Sybil said. "Now that sounds fun."

"Really just a small business like any other."

"Okay, but favorite candy?" Sybil said. "I love Good & Plentys. I could literally live off them if I had to."

"Chocolate," Zeke said. "All day every day. Though I can't really do a ton of sugar when I'm training."

"Oh, and I *love* marzipan," Sybil added, looking to Betty as if she would nearly bathe in it if she could.

"I'm actually not much for sugar either," Julian said. "Again, it's just work."

Sybil deflated like her Willy Wonka bubblegum dreams had been pricked with a sewing needle. She tried to stitch herself back up.

"This is actually the first time we've met in person," Sybil said to Betty. "The three of us met online." She paused. "That sounds creepier than I meant. This is not, like, a sex cult."

Betty nodded passively like the mere mention of *cults* didn't spike her cortisol levels.

"We met online when we couldn't sleep," Zeke clarified. "And now there are four of us who are up all night. So sit. Have some pancakes with us."

"Oh, I don't think I can sit, but let me put the order in," she said. "I have to wake up the line cook. So give it a few minutes." What she didn't say was that she also needed a few minutes to google Zeke, to see if she could google the others. How common was the name Sybil? She could probably find her in less than two minutes. Julian who owned a candy store? Easier than shoplifting a Hershey bar.

"The fruit plate," Julian said. "Don't forget."

Betty didn't have the heart to tell him that it would be cantaloupe too pale to be edible and some canned peaches. Maybe a sliver of pineapple if there were any left over from the dinner shift. He was still glaring at her, so it was easiest to say nothing anyway.

"And some coffee for me," Zeke added. "I have physical therapy in five hours, so I may as well just power through."

"And when you come back," Sybil said warmly, as if she needed a child to mother and maybe Betty was her surrogate, "you'll sit?"

They looked so harmless tucked in the booth by the window.

A small allowance for friendships with old people and a celebrity, Betty thought. Innocuous. Safe. Nothing that could throw off the delicate house of cards she'd worked so hard to construct. So she nodded yes. Because if an All-Star and his friends were offering her an opening, she'd be a fool not to take it.

5

NIGHT TWO

SYBIL

THE PANCAKES GAVE Sybil a stomachache, but it could have also been her nerves. They'd gotten the pleasantries out of the way before they went inside the diner, and Sybil was mortified to realize about fifteen minutes later when Julian and Zeke were talking sports that she had been completely clueless about Zeke. *Beartown.* She didn't mean to be a stereotype, but she had left the sports to Mark. She had been team mom, of course, every season—club soccer, club baseball, club swimming (Eloise still held the freestyle record in the state for fourteen and unders). And though Sybil was an exceptional team mom—snack sign-ups went out as soon as rosters were made, no one ever went without oranges and Gatorade—she did not follow professional sports. While she thought Zeke looked familiar, it wasn't until he and Julian were chatting about contract negotiations and Julian was making inquiries about Zeke's injury that Sybil connected the dots.

She choked on the rancid coffee when she realized. Mark had been rabid about the end of the season and absolutely lost his shit when Zeke Rodriguez got beaned by a line drive right on his pitching elbow, ending both the Mets' and Zeke's season nearly on the spot. She'd been on her third glass of wine, slightly tipsy, thinking maybe this was the night she would confront Mark about the anesthesiologist, but he was so grouchy about the loss that she knew she had to pick a better moment.

Betty whisked away their dirty dishes, and Zeke grabbed the check, and Sybil wondered if maybe she wasn't always waiting for a better moment. She didn't used to be this way, but like so much about her life in her forties, she'd either lost control or given up on it. Those weren't the same things, and in her more truthful moments, she knew it.

"Well," she said, "I should probably get home." It was three in the morning, and she didn't actually have to get anywhere. But she decided right then that she was going to be the leader of the group, organizationally-speaking. Sybil did not like people to be uncomfortable in any sort of social setting, so didn't want Zeke or Julian to feel as if they had to linger.

"Betty," Zeke called toward the kitchen. "If we come back here next week, will you join us? Turn this triangle into a square?"

Betty popped out of the swinging door, wiping her hands on a dish towel. Sybil wanted to leap out of the booth, embrace her and take her home with her. Betty was too thin, Sybil thought, with purple crescents under her eyes. Not that any of them looked their best, because sleeplessness will do that to you. Though to be honest, Zeke actually did look his best. He was so handsome—huge dark moony eyes, poreless tan skin, a thick head of espresso hair, the exact right amount of stubble to weaken your knees—that Sybil had a hard time making eye contact. But Betty wasn't much older than Eloise, not old enough to be considered a full adult. Maybe Sybil could find her a better-paying job? Maybe Sybil could rescue her? Though maybe Sybil needed a project more than Betty needed any fixing.

"I'll be here next week," Betty said. "And if you tip me well enough, I'll be happy to join you." She beamed at Zeke, which for reasons Sybil didn't understand, reddened her own cheeks. Like Betty's flirting meant that Sybil was flirting too. Sybil hadn't flirted in so long, she wasn't even sure if the muscle still worked. Her stomach turned over, the pancakes sitting like a brick. She was desperate to undo the top button of her jeans, which weren't particularly flattering to begin with. If she'd known she was meeting Zeke Rodriguez, she would have picked a better outfit.

"Sit for a minute," Julian said to Betty while Zeke signed the bill. "So that next week, we have less to catch up on."

Betty hesitated.

"There's no one else here," he added, gesturing to the deserted restaurant. "If you're going to join us, then join us properly."

"You seem like someone who likes rules," Zeke observed to Julian.

"I think all three of us probably like rules one way or the other," Julian replied, accurately sizing up Sybil within just a few hours of meeting her. And to Sybil's mind, accurately sizing up Zeke too. He was a professional athlete after all.

"Touché," Zeke said. He pressed his good hand to his eyelid. "This fucking thing has a mind of its own." Then to Betty, "How can you make ends meet when you don't have any customers?"

Betty smiled. "I rely on generous tips from the ones I do have," she said, then frowned. "I think that sounds like I prostitute myself."

"Honey, *no*, don't even imply that," Sybil said, her tone maternal but her internal joy sky-high. Because she knew it. *She knew it!* Here was a girl who needed mothering, and Sybil was a woman who knew how to mother. “Zeke, are you leaving her a generous tip?”

Zeke, so easy and gregarious, so unlike Mark, who was a tight-ass with money, said, “Can I pitch a fastball down the middle with my eyes closed?” And when no one spoke, he said, “Well, obviously.”

“Thank you, kindly,” Betty said, and dipped her head. “Anyway, I should probably check on the line cook.”

“Blowing off us old folks?” Julian asked. “I have to admit I’m a little curious why someone your age can’t sleep. The rest of us, well, I guess the older you get, the more problems you have.”

“I’m not that old,” Zeke said, and Sybil was reminded that she must look like a perimenopausal troll sitting across from a man who, if she wasn’t mistaken, was once on *People*’s Sexiest Man Alive list.

“Maybe next time,” Betty said. “If you come back again, maybe I’ll tell you then.”

6

NIGHT THREE

ZEKE

October 21st

SIX NIGHTS LATER, Zeke was *pumped*. Hadn't been this pumped up in ages. Certainly not since his injury, so give or take about six weeks. It was one of those perfect fall New York City evenings, so he decided to walk to the diner. The days between their first meeting and now had felt interminably long—there was physical therapy, there were calls with his team to discuss the road back for next season, and there was nightly Sudoku with Sybil and Julian—but there was very little sleep. He wanted to suggest that they meet more often, but he didn't want to sound desperate, like these two—three, if you included Betty—were the only thing he had going on.

He spotted Sybil on the street corner in front of the diner with her back toward him. She was doing some sort of stretching exercise, rolling her spine down, touching her toes, rolling back up and reaching toward the sky. He lingered for a beat, not wanting to be the interloper. She straightened out and raised her eyes to street level. How fascinating, how mesmerizing, Zeke thought, to watch her spine stiffen in real time.

Sybil turned and spotted him and raised both hands, shimmying them as a sort of wave.

The crosswalk light was still red but it was midnight, and the streets were deserted, so Zeke stepped off the curb toward her. He heard a car peel around the corner and felt the headlights on him with no warning.

"Zeke!" Sybil shouted.

He couldn't much move his injured arm, but his legs worked fine, and in three leaps, he was planted next to her, the car's engine revving as it cruised past and turned north.

"Oh my god," she said, her hand over her heart. "Jesus Christ on a stick. I thought you were about to die. Then I'd never sleep again." She pursed her lips, blew out her breath. "Seriously, you should feel my heart right now."

Without thinking, Zeke placed his left palm over hers, then she slipped her hand down to her side, and indeed, he could feel the vibrations of her racing heart. They stood there for how long, Zeke wasn't sure. Long enough that he could have dropped his hand, but she didn't pull away, and so his palm stayed. Sybil's gaze wandered up toward his, and for a moment, neither one of them blinked, and Zeke had the oddest feeling: that by intuiting the pounding of her heart, somehow she had resurrected his. Then he averted his eyes, embarrassed that something in him turned this romantic. No no, that couldn't be right. He must be delirious. That must be what sleeplessness did to your brain. He was so eager for a connection with someone that he was inventing bonds out of nowhere.

"You saw me doing my roll-outs?" she asked.

He nodded.

"Sorry," she said, as if she owed him an apology for the show. "The sleeplessness. My shoulder. Those help. At my age, it's all bad."

"You can't be much older than I am," he said.

She laughed like he was kidding.

"My eye spasms," he said. "Like my eyelid is throwing a temper tantrum because it's been open for too long."

"Maybe your eyelid can have a discussion with my left shoulder blade. Agree that they both need to give us a break." She smiled, and Zeke couldn't believe for a second that she considered herself old. Or even if she was, that she was apologizing for it. She was beautiful exactly as she was.

"We should go in," he said, and his voice cracked like he was going through puberty.

Sybil nodded but didn't move.

"It's nice out here," she said. "It's not often you hear the city so quiet."

"Did you live here? Before moving out to the suburbs?"

She shook her head, something like regret washing over her.

"As a kid, I did. I grew up by the park on the West Side. I always thought I'd end up back here as a grown-up. After medical school, I was offered a spot to stay at Harvard for my residency. Mark wasn't, but his dad made some calls. Anyway, long story short, we stayed in Boston, which, I mean, is great, obviously. Who doesn't love Boston?" She sighed. "But Boston isn't New York, I guess. Eventually, he got a job here, and we had the twins by then, so had to be practical. Bought our house. A yard, a swing set, that whole thing."

"Well, you're the first stop outside the city." He remembered these details she shared, their online conversations fully three-dimensional to him. "That's not too far."

"If you throw a pitch that's half an inch outside the strike zone, it's still a ball," she replied.

His laugh sneaked up on him. "You told me a few days ago that you didn't know anything about sports."

"If I admit to doing a crash course in Zeke Rodriguez, will you agree not to judge me for it?" She cringed. "I can't help myself. I sort of always need to be the smartest person in the room."

"Do you find that it always goes that way for you?"

"Mostly," she said, and didn't elaborate. "Though my kids give me a run for my money, and I don't mean that as a brag. It's more annoying than anything, to be honest. Eloise, my daughter, won more science awards in high school than I ever could. She's premed now too. Charlie tested as a genius, but we're still waiting for him to reach his potential. As parents do."

"And Mark? Rounding out the family of geniuses?"

An aura of disappointment passed over her. "No, not him."

She started toward the diner's door, then seemed to realize he hadn't joined her. She spun back around, the glow of the streetlamp bouncing off her blonde hair, illuminating her like she was an actual angel. *What was wrong with him?* He'd met her *once*, and now he was inventing a whole thing between them.

Zeke obviously knew she was married, knew she was way out of his league, especially when it came to intelligence, and he couldn't imagine why she'd even consider it. *Consider what?* He chastised himself again. He wasn't about to proposition her on 110th and Broadway. But Zeke was used to flying on instinct, on adrenaline, and of course, yes, on strategy. You couldn't just hurl a fastball at every single batter. Some you had to deceive; some you had to outmuscle; and some, well, you'd intentionally bean them on the head just to push them back off the plate a bit. His good hand reached over and touched the arm that was still in a soft cast, a reminder that even when you thought you were the one in control, you could find yourself in plenty of trouble.

"You coming?" Sybil called to him.

He squeezed his eyes closed and considered that just as he had a game plan for every batter, every batter had a game plan for him. He replayed that moment again in his brain, the playback always running, even when he tried to press pause, wanted to delete the tape entirely.

Why didn't you move?

You could have moved.

You had time to move.

"Zeke!" Sybil called again. "Are you okay?"

Another cab peeled around the corner, and his eyes flew open at the sound of the tire squeal, his learned response from just a few minutes ago already keener, already more honed.

That was the thing, he realized. Anything could be a danger once you paid attention: a cab, a fastball, a line drive. Probably a million other things, too, that Zeke just hadn't woken up to yet.

7

NIGHT THREE

JULIAN

WAS IT A risk, this whole thing? Absolutely. But Julian had gotten comfortable with assumed risk, weighing the odds, weighing the outcomes. Tonight, on the train into the city, he used the time to keep his brain sharp, to assess who was in his subway car, where they were headed, if they posed any of those risks, which were nothing, he knew, compared to the overarching one of the larger chessboard he was stepping onto. Robin used to say that he couldn't shake the training or maybe the training couldn't shake him. He missed his wife all the time now. When he had his heart attack, he almost welcomed it, thinking at last he could be put out of his grief. But then he didn't die, obviously; he instead retired at Simone's insistence, like that meant living a more relaxing lifestyle. Like that meant that he didn't stare at the ceiling all night replaying how much he wanted to fix what he'd gotten wrong, make up for the things that slipped through his fingers. As the subway careened around a turn, he asked Robin to forgive him for sticking around for so many years after she was gone, for needing a little more time to get some things right.

Julian intentionally arrived last at the diner. He wanted a chance to observe them all as a unit, take mental notes. He couldn't help it; his brain was just wired this way, always looking to solve a puzzle, even with three strangers. He was better at Sudoku than he let on; in fact, he nearly always finished it well before Sybil and Zeke but took his time filling in the final squares by chasing down Felix or dropping in some fish pellets. It felt important that they lowered their expectations of him. Julian had long manipulated outside expectations; it was his way of managing people without them knowing it. Robin used to laugh and laugh and laugh about it. How other parents at Simone's school thought he was a mortgage broker or insurance salesman or something so boring, no one could even remember when it came up in conversation.

Tonight, Julian's body ached, his fatigue permeating on a literal cellular level, and through the window he watched Zeke throw his head back and laugh at something Sybil said, and he hated him for a moment. How effortless his life must be. How fortunate he was, even with his injury, even with the questionable road back. Julian didn't know what kept Sybil up at night, and honestly, he liked her company well enough, but he wasn't all that interested in her milquetoast problems either.

Betty. He was mostly interested in Betty.

He stepped off the curb and opened the door to the diner, his muscles crying in protest as he went. He resented that his body, at sixty, was betraying him again. He resented that he hadn't screwed up the nerve to call his doctors. He resented that Robin left him so soon.

"Julian!" Zeke called from the back booth, waving him over with his good arm. Julian forgot his resentments and compartmentalized, took notes, took stock. The diner had a few more patrons this Tuesday night, mostly college students who looked like they were either on their way to hungover or already hungover. Julian did a quick scan of the area: an innate habit, a sixth sense. Robin used to give him shit about how he couldn't ever relax, couldn't just walk into a movie theater and enjoy an extra-large buttered popcorn and a Coke the size of his head—because he was constantly on alert, constantly high-strung. Was it any surprise that his daughter didn't particularly like his company now? Was it any surprise that he couldn't sleep? Was it any surprise he'd had a heart attack at fifty-six?

"Julian," Betty said as he slid into the booth next to Zeke. "What can I get you?"

"I thought you were joining us tonight," he said, gazing up at her from his seat. "No offense to these two, but I've had enough of them this week. I could use some fresh company."

"Don't be mad because I beat you at Sudoku every night," Sybil said, then reached for her reading glasses to check something on her phone.

"I think you're cheating," Zeke offered. "No one can be that good at Sudoku."

"Or she's just a genius," Betty said.

"Or we're just morons," Zeke replied.

Julian started to interject but actually sort of thought that Zeke was a bit of a moron so stopped himself.

"If it's not Sudoku, it's true crime," Sybil shrugged. "And listening to podcasts about women turning up in rivers really doesn't do much for my sleep. I swore off them. Or I tried to." She set her phone on the table, screen down. "I've sort of started up again. I swear, it's an addiction. Like it actually triggers a dopamine hit in my brain, which maybe is why it's an addiction, because I'm so goddamn tired all the time that I feel like I can't think straight. Like, I need to be put in a clinical trial or something." She shrugged, then grimaced and reached around to massage the nape of her neck. "Anyway, yeah, my name's Sybil, and I'm a true-crime addict."

Julian felt his gut rumble. Sybil, he considered, could be useful. Or problematic. Sybil was obviously very smart and well educated, a bored middle-aged empty nester who thought she had the skill set of a detective. He wondered how she would react if she really did have to examine a bloated dead body pulled from a river. Probably not as well as she expected.

His gaze returned to Betty. "Come on, sit down, tell us about yourself."

Betty glanced around to the other diners, who had all been served.

"Okay," she said. "I have a few minutes. But I can't blow off the other customers. Unless, Zeke, you wanna tip me like you did last time."

Her face illuminated into a wide grin, and Julian sized her up: He didn't quite buy the smile, but also didn't find it totally disingenuous. She was slippery, he thought. His favorite type of company. A puzzle needing to be solved.

"So," Sybil said, and Julian let her take the lead because it came naturally to her. "Betty, tell us everything important we need to know about you."

Betty raised and lowered a shoulder. Julian didn't believe the performance. You don't end up on the graveyard shift at a diner in lower Harlem if you don't have a story.

"Moved here from North Carolina. Thought I could be, like, an actress. Turns out that being cast in your high school musical in your small town of ten thousand people does not qualify you for Broadway."

"Oh, you're an actress?" Sybil looked delighted. "My best

friend is a casting director. Can I help?" She aimed her phone at Betty. "Can I take a quick pic? I know she's casting something right now. And she's always looking if that doesn't pan out."

Betty held up a hand abruptly, blocking the camera. "No, no. I'm actually not much of an actress, as it turns out. I'm a better waitress than an actress, which pretty much tells you everything."

"So this is the plan? Overnight shift until something better comes along?" Zeke asked.

"Overnight shift until I save enough to move out of my apartment. My roommate's a psychopath." She flopped that shoulder again. They all looked at her expectantly, and she just said, "Don't ask. It's a nightmare."

"Zeke, isn't your apartment about as big as the White House?" Julian said. He remembered reading about it in the *Post* when the sale had gone through. Some gargantuan penthouse that was ridiculous even for a family of five, much less a thirty-four-year-old bachelor. The *Post* had claimed the co-op board had a heated debate over his application approval. No one in New York really wanted a celebrity in their building, but also, the diehards kind of wanted Zeke Rodriguez in their building. Such was the blessed life of the golden boy.

"I mean," Zeke said. "It's not small, I guess." Now it was his turn to shrug.

"Maybe Betty could crash with you?" Julian suggested.

"Oh," Zeke replied.

"Oh no," Betty said over him.

"That is a *great* idea." Sybil beamed, and Julian knew that her endorsement would sway Zeke. He'd seen the way that the All-Star's eyes lingered on her for approval, how even when they were just talking about mundane stuff in their group chat at three A.M., Zeke always tapped a heart on Sybil's text. "Betty, you're a young woman in New York City, and I know you're not my daughter, but it wouldn't be so bad if you had a roommate."

"I have a roommate," Betty said.

"A psychopath," Julian offered.

"You know what?" Zeke said. "My apartment *is* ridiculous. And I actually wouldn't mind the company. Want to try a trial run?"

"You're basically a stranger," Betty said. Her tone was clipped, and Julian suspected that Betty had plenty of reasons to be wary of strangers.

"How'd you meet your current roommate?" Julian asked, because he already intuited that the answer would tilt in his favor.

Betty pursed her lips. "Craigslist."

"Betty, no!" Sybil said. "Your parents are okay with this? That doesn't sound like a safe scenario at all."

"My parents are dead," Betty said flatly, and then they all looked a little apologetic. Sybil looked particularly mortified.

But Julian watched Betty slump against the back of the booth, her face downcast, her posture a curve. And though he didn't say a word, the thing was, he was pretty sure that she was lying. It was a masterful performance, he thought, and he suspected they were in for an encore.

8

NIGHT THREE

BETTY

BETTY WASN'T LYING. Mallory was a nightmare. She ate Betty's yogurts. She had an absurd collection of cacti. She played weird bohemian music with an annoying bass that gave Betty a headache. She had very loud sex with her boyfriend at least twice a night, which was part of the reason Betty tried to accrue as many work shifts as the trust-fund diner owner would allow. Arguing with Mallory about any of the above meant drawing attention to herself, and Betty preferred to go unnoticed, to be as unintrusive as possible.

As a child, she had this down to an art.

It really wasn't all that hard to go through life nearly invisible. She had an unmemorable face, average brown hair, average brown eyes, average though skinny in a malnourished way build, average height. When she'd bleached her hair blonde, she'd emerged from the bathroom to find Mallory's boyfriend on the couch with one hand on the remote and one tucked under the waistband of his sweatpants, and he said, "Holy shit, Betty, you're actually fucking hot," and Betty wanted to spin on her toes and undo it.

She wasn't interested in being hot. She was simply interested in getting by.

"I think this is a great idea," Sybil was saying. "Betty, I know that we don't know each other well, but I have a daughter—"

Betty knew she had a daughter. All Sybil talked about was her kids. Betty could already tell you more about them than she could her own siblings as of late. Betty had four of them. Three brothers. A sister. She'd ghosted them all but Levi when she left Georgia, and now she and Levi swapped an email every few months, a phone call even less so, mostly for emergencies or when Betty really missed him so palpably that she had to hear his voice to ground herself. Betty knew that Sybil had twins, that this was the first time they'd been away from each other, choosing different colleges. She wanted to dislike Sybil. The upper-middle-class highlighted blonde, Pilates-toned, Range Rover–driving woman was so not her type. But Sybil had a warm heart and also, Betty thought, a stone-cold disposition when she needed to. Which maybe meant the two of them weren't all that different.

Tonight, Betty decided to be agreeable. She thought it might be useful to stay with Zeke, and certainly, it would be more peaceful than her current arrangement. Also, importantly, he seemed harmless, the exact right level of clueless about the world around him and narcissistic about his own needs that it took to be successful in his sport.

"Sure, Zeke, thank you for the offer," Betty said. "I guess, well, sure, I'd love to move in with you. On a trial basis."

"Of course," Zeke said. "No pressure. I have another surgery coming up next month, so it would be nice to have someone around."

He struck Betty as someone who, surprisingly, did not have many friends. If he did, he wouldn't be here in this shitty diner with strangers he had met online. Something they had in common.

"I can help!" Sybil offered. "Betty, you're young, you should be out exploring the city. Meeting young men. Or women. My Eloise likes both, which I totally support, by the way. But you should be out having fun! Doing what young people do."

Betty didn't reply because she wasn't interested in sharing anything personal, so Sybil clapped her hands together. "I feel like this is the thing, the thing that we all need. We need each other to help solve each other's problems."

"Who said I have problems?" Julian asked.

"Well, you don't sleep, my man," Zeke said. "So there's gotta be something."

Julian emitted a cough at that exact moment that sounded like a train engine. When he caught his breath, he said: "Sorry, I do feel like my body is falling apart from not sleeping."

"Ditto," Zeke said.

"Tritto," Sybil said, then her cheeks flushed and she added, "Sorry, Eloise says that sometimes . . . it sounded cuter in my brain."

"It's the perfect amount of cute," Zeke said, and Julian raised an eyebrow toward Betty, like they shared a secret. Betty kind of liked that too. She was used to secrets, but only her own, and it was a balm, a relief, to be in on someone else's.

"Maybe this was preordained." Sybil's cheeks were bright pink now, like she was really amping up to something big. "What are the odds that the three of us met on an internet forum—"

"That sounds like the start of a horror movie," Betty said.

"Or porn," Zeke replied, then his eyes went wide like he'd

forgotten that they didn't actually know one another all that well. Betty watched his face blanch and marveled that someone so famous, with so much clout and power, could still be a bit of an idiot. Didn't he have a filter? Betty's filter was so rigid that she never said anything without thinking three beats down the line. This is why she was still on her feet. She thought about Levi again. Wondered if he were still on his feet. She couldn't remember the last time they'd connected. Where had he been last? Seattle. Maybe he was still in Seattle.

"Sorry," Zeke said, mostly for Sybil's benefit, Betty thought. "I'm still on pain meds. They make me loopy. That was a joke . . . about the porn." His eyelid spasmed like it, too, was crying out in apology.

Zeke turned to Betty as if he still had to plead his case. "I swear, I'm a feminist. I'm best friends with my sister."

Betty didn't care about his politics. She honestly was just thinking about living in an apartment the size of the White House.

"I would never, *ever* put you in a position where you were uncomfortable," he continued, rambling now. "It would just be nice to have the company. And if it helps you out, um, financially, then I'd feel less selfish in offering."

"So we agree!" Sybil said, tapping her palms on the table, like that was that. "We will lean on each other until our problems are solved."

"I'm in," Zeke said.

Julian wheezed again, which the table took as a concurrence.

Later, Betty realized that she had never really agreed to anything. So as far as she was concerned, if she ever needed to break the terms of the deal, she could, no questions asked. She'd learned that from her father too. Her terms, her choices, her freedom. No matter what the others thought she agreed to, she well understood that she would abide only by her rules, by what served her needs, by what kept her safe. After that, it was every man for himself.

9

NIGHT FOUR

SYBIL

October 26th

SYBIL AND MARK had a pied-à-terre on the Upper East Side that Mark used when the hours got away from him at the hospital or when he was on call but needed a nice mattress to sleep on for a short stint. She'd texted Mark that she'd be using it tonight—they mostly communicated via text these days, other than when he called her for advice with a case—but he'd never responded.

The first thing she noticed once she turned the key to the apartment was the silence. Mark wasn't there. A relief. She hadn't actually seen him in several days. With her nocturnal schedule and his few hours at home before returning to the hospital, she'd managed to dodge him. Or he her. At this stage in their marriage, it was equal-opportunity avoidance. She wondered if this could go on interminably: being married without actually having a partner. It wasn't so bad, really. It wasn't so good either. But there were worse things, she knew. Her best friend, Natalie, the casting director, had left her ex-husband half a decade ago when it turned out he had gambled away her children's college funds and most of their savings too. That was a worse thing.

Sybil closed her eyes and flattened herself on the living room couch, allowing the quiet to seep in. But then it felt too quiet, too isolating. So she popped up, pulled her phone from her pocket, and though she should have tapped her music app, she went right to the podcasts. She was deep into an unsolved mystery of a man who had disappeared in Florida gator country, and she was pretty sure she was one Google discovery away from finding new evidence.

Back on her feet, the second thing Sybil noticed tonight was the scent. Sybil had been cursed with an oversensitive sense of smell since childhood. It was no good walking around with a nose that detected everything. In medical school, she had to lull herself into a type of semihypnosis not to gag at formaldehyde, and once Charlie hit puberty, her own home was a near nuclear site. Mark himself had a specific sweat smell that in their early days turned her on. In recent years, maybe his hormones shifted or maybe hers did (hers definitely did), but sometimes she'd walk by him in the hallway, and she could almost taste the acridity. When Sybil told Natalie about it, her friend had suggested that maybe Mark was rotting from the inside out. She'd meant it metaphorically, but Sybil then thought about all the medical diagnoses in which this was possible and envisioned Mark afflicted with each and every one. She really did need to decide what to do about Mark and the anesthesiologist.

Tonight the pied-à-terre did not reek like Mark's maleficent odor, but instead had the very slight lilt of an expensive perfume. It was probably two days old, nothing that Mark thought would linger. But Sybil was a bloodhound, and here was the evidence. Mark obviously did not wear perfume, and ostensibly, Eloise could have ditched college for a night or two and come to the apartment, but Eloise wore cheap Brandy Melville body spray. This stuff was straight-up Parisian. Also, Sybil had Eloise's location on her phone, so surely she would have noticed if Eloise had driven to the city from DC for the night.

She opened the fridge, as the podcast narrator broke down the science of how an alligator could eat a dead body, and she saw a half-drunk bottle of Cabernet.

Fuck you, Mark.

She slammed the door closed.

She moved to the bedroom, the narrator's voice growing distant. The bed wasn't made, and the perfume was even stronger in here.

I want to murder you, Mark.

She made her way back into the living room and sank into the couch, then bounced back up, wondering if Mark and the anesthesiologist had fucked on the couch too. She grabbed her phone, paused the podcast—as interesting as the science was of how long it takes a gator to digest human flesh—and punched in Natalie's number. It was ten P.M.; she had an hour to kill before heading to Zeke's, and Natalie's household would still be buzzing.

"Thank god," Natalie said on the first ring. "Save me from my children. They are animals. Absolute lunatics. How did you make it through the teenage years?"

Most of Sybil's friends were older than she was: She had the twins still in her late twenties, so she was considered the "young mom" at preschool; many of the women were on their first child at their mid-thirties after a slog of a career and finding their husband along the way. Natalie was the exception. They met when Eloise started babysitting Natalie's kids in eighth grade because Natalie, newly divorced, had a life outside of them. *Imagine that,* Sybil thought now, wishing that it had occurred to her back then too.

"On a scale of one to ten," Sybil said, dipping down, touching her toes, trying to stretch out her back, which continued to be furious at her for her lack of rest, "how much would it scare you to see me naked?"

For some reason, in the heady swirl of the anesthesiologist's perfume, she'd thought of Zeke. But once she said it aloud, the idea felt preposterous, absurd, nearly humiliating. She knew that she used to be pretty in a buttoned-up sort of way. Mark, obviously, in med school, couldn't get enough and used to tell her that she was *edible*. Edible! But good god, her breasts after two kids and at the age of forty-six? Her cesarean scar? The way her body had recently begun feeling less and less in her control, like she was going through reverse puberty—the periods that looked like massacres, the hot flashes that left pit stains in under ten seconds, the way the brain fog drifted in like she was on the edge of the San Francisco Bay.

"Oh. My. God," Natalie screeched. "Are you finally leaving him? Please, please say you are leaving him."

"I'm not leaving him," Sybil said, righting herself, then rotating a shoulder until it popped. "But I guess . . . I'm thinking about leaving him. But . . . I mean . . . do men actually want to sleep with women . . . of a certain age?"

"I'm coming over," Natalie said. "I think this is my chance to finally convince you." Then: *"Jesus Christ, Truman, if I have to tell you to brush your teeth one more time, I'm going to post about your hygiene habits on TikTok!"* Then: "Sorry. I don't think Corey makes them shower the entire weekend when they're with him."

"You'll miss them when they leave you though," Sybil said, and she thought of Charlie and Eloise. God, what she wouldn't do to have them back, to have kept the status quo forever. What would happen if she murdered Mark, chopped him up and fed him to alligators? Would anyone blame her for going mad and reinventing herself at midlife? Men did it all the time.

"You keep saying that, and yet I can't wait to prove you wrong."

"Well, you can't come over. I'm in the city. At the apartment."

"On a Sunday? You're in New York City at your apartment? And you're calling me asking if someone will want to sleep with you? Girl! What are you not telling me?"

Sybil hadn't told Natalie about the insomnia other than occasional comments about fitful sleep, jokes about the bags under her eyes. She wasn't sure why. Natalie wasn't yet perimenopausal, and maybe Sybil wasn't ready to admit that she was rocketing toward elderly, or maybe it was that if she verbalized it—how heavily her life weighed on her, how desperately she missed her children, how she'd lost so much of *everything* to a man who she saw now hadn't deserved to be given anything—she knew that it would be time, finally, to do something about it. She certainly wasn't ready to tell her best friend that she'd met several strangers online and now was meeting them a couple times a week at midnight, like they were a group of newly befriended vampires. Natalie wouldn't judge her for it, but Sybil wasn't sure that she wasn't judging herself.

"Nothing nearly as sexy," Sybil said. "Have an early mammogram. Made sense to stay over."

"Well, at least someone is feeling your boobs," Natalie said.

"Oh, shut up," Sybil laughed but very acutely and unavoidably thought of Zeke.

10

NIGHT FOUR

ZEKE

THEY'D AGREED TO meet at Zeke's apartment since Betty had taken the overnight shift off to get settled there. Zeke was nervous as shit. One, because he'd probably gotten a little over his skis at inviting Betty to move in, and two, he hadn't hosted anyone other than his sister and parents in the four years that he'd lived here. His agent, Timothy, made a habit of showing up unannounced, but he didn't care about impressing Timothy, who bought his beach house thanks to Zeke's last Nike contract.

He'd asked his assistant to order some platters from Zabar's, and now it looked like he was hosting a wedding in his kitchen. He surveyed the spread and moved too quickly, forgetting for a moment that his elbow had split in two. Jolts of sharp pain radiated up to his shoulder.

"Motherfucker!" he yelped, his voice bouncing off his cabinetry and reverberating back to him. The kitchen was the size of some New York City one-bedroom apartments, and he'd had the entire place soundproofed anyway, so it's not as if Betty could hear him. And he didn't even really know her well enough to expect her to come running. He opened the fridge with his good arm, grabbed a can of Bud Light (he was sponsored so they sent it by the case), popped it open one-handed and leaned against the wall to try to steady himself. His fucking eyelid spasmed again.

The truth was that Zeke well knew that he was good at only one thing in life, and it wasn't making new friends, as he was feigning with Betty, and it wasn't being an excellent group thinker, like he was feigning with the others. He was good at throwing a ball. That was it. If he died—and he thought more and more about this when he couldn't sleep—his entire obituary would be about his arm, about his velocity, about the no-hitter he threw two years ago to clinch the playoffs.

"Hello?" Julian's baritone cut through the hall into the kitchen. Zeke stitched himself back up.

"Julian!" Zeke sauntered through the maze of his apartment and found Julian standing in the foyer, his hands tucked into his black jeans. It had been less than a week since they'd last gotten together, but there was something different about him, Zeke thought. Maybe he looked a little thinner? Maybe his exhaustion was just catching up to him? He was delirious with his own insomnia, and he'd never been particularly intuitive, so he'd ask Sybil. Sybil would see it. Sybil would know.

"You live here all by yourself?" Julian asked, his eyes roaming the space, his incredulity obvious.

"Well, not anymore," Zeke said. "Betty lives here now."

The door swung open behind him, and there was Sybil. She also looked a little different, though again, Zeke was terrible at these things. At details. At keeping track of the details. It wasn't that he was dumb—he did well in high school, though he had to work harder at it than Lani. Besides, he was the anomaly who got called up to the majors right out of senior year, so his grades didn't matter anyway. But details, unless it was memorizing every single thing about a batting lineup or the feel of the leather or the rotation of his arm, none of the rest of it was his thing.

Still, though, Sybil looked nice tonight. Pretty.

"What have I missed?" she said.

"All-Star lives like a goddamn king," Julian said.

"Well, that's not really accurate," Zeke answered.

"Want to swap with me? Live in my two-bedroom walk-up?" Julian said. "Anyway, where's Betty?"

"Unpacking. I haven't wanted to bother her," Zeke said, then used his left hand to wave them into the kitchen. "Come on, I have midnight snacks though."

"I'll grab her first. She should join us, right?" Julian peered down the hallway, then another. Zeke hated that he thought Julian was judging him for his extravagance. He was just a normal guy from Oklahoma, he wanted to tell him.

"Third door on the left. The hallway to the right," Zeke said.

Then he and Sybil found themselves alone in the kitchen, staring at the platters that could serve a party of thirty and strand him with leftovers for days. Because he could barely train right now, he had to be careful with what he ate. As it was, it would take a miracle to get him back on the mound for spring training. The platter of black-and-white cookies and little gooey brownies felt like an offense.

"I'd say that we shouldn't eat the sugar because it will keep us up all night but, well," Sybil said.

"It can't be sugar," Zeke said. "I never have it, not on my training regimen."

"I should cut it out," Sybil said. "But honestly . . ." She sighed. Didn't have to explain. When you stopped sleeping, so many of life's pleasures were dimmed. If you wanted a cookie, you gave yourself a cookie.

"Can I get you a drink? Would you like a tour? Are you hungry? Want to sit?" Zeke gestured toward the breakfast nook with six chairs, none of which were ever occupied because no one ever came over.

"You sit," Sybil said. "I can take care of myself."

She moved past him and found a Bud Light in the fridge, examined it like he imagined she did a patient back in medical school, her lips pursed, her brow furrowed, and then popped it open.

Zeke wanted to tell her that it was just a sponsorship, that he had an entire wine fridge of fancy bottles, but honestly, he didn't really know one from the other anyway, so. He started to ask her how she'd been sleeping these past few nights, but he already knew. They'd been intertwined on text every night since last week.

"So your surgery next month," Sybil said. "Tell me all about it."

"It's boring."

"Nothing about surgery is boring. The capacity to open up a human, fix them, then sew them back up? The sexiest thing ever. I just spent an hour googling how an alligator digests human flesh and bone, so trust me, all of it is fascinating to me."

"Do I want to even ask?"

"No, you probably don't." She dropped her head, then raised it. "So fill my head with surgical lore, distract me."

"Why didn't you see it through?" Zeke didn't even know Sybil all that well, and he already thought she would have made an excellent surgeon. "The doctor thing?"

"Another story for another time." She took a long pull of her beer and burped with her mouth closed. Zeke felt something stir in his belly.

"Doesn't your husband share his surgery stories? To include you? Share the sexiness?"

Sybil made a face like nothing about her husband was sexy, which pleased Zeke immensely.

"Actually, he calls me for help all the time." She said it with disgust. Zeke was practically levitating. "Though he's an ER doctor, so less surgery, more emergency."

"And him calling you . . . a bad thing? Also, isn't that a HIPAA violation?"

"No, I mean, yes. Mark isn't one to abide by rules." She didn't elaborate. "Anyway, he and I both know that I should never have been the one to quit." She raised and lowered a shoulder, then rotated the same shoulder around in circles a few times. Zeke fought the urge to reach over and massage it. "But I did. And that was that. Now tell me all the juicy details about what they intend to do to you."

"Well, it's the third surgery. They have to remove the pins—some, all, I'm not sure—see if I can get the rotation back, see if my movement is the same or what my pain threshold is without them. See how much scar tissue is in there, see if the bones healed properly."

"Hmmm." Her eyes narrowed. "And if they can't, if they haven't?"

And if they can't? If they haven't?

He didn't reply because they heard Julian's footsteps nearing, and they each swiveled toward him. Which was just as well, his nonreply. Because that was also another story for another time.

"You said she was in her room?" Julian lingered in the doorframe.

"Yeah." Zeke nodded, relieved for the change of subject.

"Third door on the right?"

Zeke glanced at Sybil, the mother hen, and the lines on her face were all pointed downward.

"Well," Julian said, "she doesn't appear to be here." He paused and something about his tone, his face, his posture shifted. Like Zeke was looking at someone he didn't recognize. "I think," Julian said. "I think that she's gone."

11

NIGHT FOUR

JULIAN

WHAT DO YOU mean, she's gone?" Sybil asked, suddenly on her feet.

It was sweet, Julian thought, but naïve, that Sybil assumed she could tame a child who didn't want to be tamed. He suspected that both of Sybil's kids were straight-down-the-middle children. Kids who didn't push curfew, and when they did, it was because they lost track of time sipping White Claws; kids who had private tutors for their SATs; kids who had private coaches for their club sports.

Julian hadn't been a particularly good father since Robin died so he didn't judge Sybil for any of that, but he'd always had an uncanny ability to size people up immediately. It's probably why he'd been recruited out of the University of Delaware; probably why his unit had been so bereft when he retired. He'd been the best bloodhound of all of them. But without Robin to balance him, he found himself obsessing, spiraling over a botched case, and then one mundane day, his heart seized while having his morning coffee at his desk, and the doctors all told him he was lucky to be alive. Simone had just graduated college and moved back home for two weeks to mind him and refused to leave until he called his boss and quit. He knew Robin would want Simone to start her adult life in peace, so he did. He still had the passive income from the candy store, and for a while, he accepted it. Like the universe had handed down its decision, and the least he could do was respect it. Until that period passed, and he found himself running through all the loose ends, all the work he still hadn't completed.

"Third door on the left is empty. I checked the other rooms too." He looked at Zeke. "Did you spook her?"

"What? No!" Zeke yelped.

"Well, she obviously hasn't *gone*, like run away," Sybil said. "Let's not be dramatic. Wait, Julian, are you implying that she's run away?"

Zeke pushed his chair back, and they strode down the hall as if Julian had maybe just overlooked Betty, as if she were hiding under the bed. He wanted to tell them that he was a professional, but it was easier, *better*, if they thought he was just a candy store owner, so he said nothing. He already knew enough about Sybil to assess that she would get her nose bent out of shape if she knew about his past employment.

Betty's room, as Julian had told them, was empty. The bed untouched, the white towels folded atop the mid-century modern bureau.

"Maybe she's just at her old place," Zeke said. "Getting some stuff."

"At eleven o'clock at night?" Sybil asked. Her brow was furrowed in genuine worry.

"Well, we're awake," Zeke said. "Also, she *is* an adult."

"We're *always* awake," Sybil replied. "It's just odd, that she wouldn't say anything. I'll text her."

"She's fine, I'm sure she's fine," Zeke said, and Julian thought it was pretty incredible, this golden boy's rosy view of the world. He hadn't seen what Julian had; he didn't know what Julian knew.

"So you're not worried?" Sybil looked toward Zeke. "It's a little weird, isn't it?"

"We don't really know her that well. I don't want her to feel like I'm monitoring her. Also, no, I don't think it's weird that she, an adult, left the apartment without issuing an all-points bulletin," Zeke said.

"And you *didn't* do something to scare her?" Julian asked.

"What? Julian, I think you have the wrong impression of me."

"What impression do I have of you?" Julian felt a little acceleration of his heart rate. This was just like an interrogation, only Zeke wasn't aware. It had been so long since he'd felt that invigorating thrum.

"Like I'm like some idiotic lecherous jock."

"I don't think you're lecherous," Julian said.

"Just the dumb jock."

"Come on, you guys," Sybil said. "Let's focus on being positive."

They'd retreated to the kitchen, Zeke pulling the plastic wrap off the platters. *How many people did he expect to feed?* Julian wondered. Everything about Zeke was almost cartoonish—this apartment, for one. The ceilings were nearly two stories high; the kitchen was expansive enough to be a subway stop; the living room was goddamn palatial, like Zeke was Louis XIV and required his own personal Versailles.

"Honestly, Jules," Zeke said, as if Julian had ever told him that he had a nickname (he did not), as if they were old friends (they were not). "My entire life has always been about my game.

I just want to help Betty out. Keep each other company, I swear. I have the room, and it feels like good karma."

Sybil looked up from her phone, the whoosh of her text going off into the void. She nudged her head at his soft cast. "I texted her."

From Betty's bedroom they could hear the very distant ding of a text being received.

"Shit," Sybil said. "She left her phone. Okay, now maybe I can be worried?"

"She wasn't kidnapped from the apartment," Zeke said. "Like, she wasn't taken against her will and left her phone behind."

Sybil sighed. "You're right. You're right. I really need to cut off those podcasts."

"Come on," Zeke said. "Please, let's eat."

He put three different types of sandwiches on a plate and passed it to Julian. Julian wasn't hungry, but he knew that he needed to be collegial, so he nodded a thank-you and rolled up his sleeves, a habit from boyhood when he had to tuck a napkin in. Zeke gestured to the table, and Julian was relieved to sit. His ankles were swollen, he'd forgotten his compression socks, and he needed a break. He was good at stony-faced but must have winced as he sat down.

"You okay?" Sybil asked.

"Just tweaked something. The price of being sixty, I guess."

Sybil gave him a long stare like she was used to seeing through liars, but maybe he was imagining that, because right then, the front door unlatched in the foyer, and then squeaked open and slammed shut, and Sybil jumped from her seat, her demeanor changing entirely. She rushed into the other room, with Zeke and Julian trailing.

To Julian's great surprise, Betty had returned.

He watched her from across the foyer, his hackles rising, his eyes narrowing. She was back; hadn't gone or at least hadn't fled. If he didn't see it with his own eyes, he wouldn't have believed it, because Julian, in a moment of rarity, had gotten the facts wrong. And Julian knew, deep in his bones, that he never got anything wrong. At least nothing like this.

12

NIGHT FIVE

BETTY

November 1st

BETTY HAD GOTTEN used to being a fully functioning island. Even when she was living with Mallory, they were two circles that never overlapped on a Venn diagram, other than when Mallory would occasionally eat Betty's Chobanis. So she'd forgotten what it was like to have people expect to know where you were, what you were doing. Everything felt easier, albeit lonelier, but easier nevertheless, as an island. She was safer this way; she could see all the exits; she had no blind spots. Every turn was a horizon. It had been an adjustment at first, of course. Growing up in a house with five kids, being part of a thousand-person church. Back then, she was never alone. But once she left, isolation became a necessity.

So last week, when she came back to Zeke's after slipping out, she hadn't expected a full interrogation. It made her so twitchy that she almost packed her one bag and fled. But she knew that was counterproductive, and she'd trained herself to ignore counterproductivity.

"Betty!" Sybil had rushed to her that night and wrapped her

in a tight hug. In another lifetime, it would have felt like a comfort instead of just a violation. "Julian made us think you'd . . . left. Left us."

They both turned toward Julian, who was standing in the archway that divided the foyer and the kitchen, his arms crossed, his brow knitted. Zeke was right behind him, looking like a man who had intended to throw a party that the cops busted before he even tapped the keg.

"I needed some air. I was just out for a walk," Betty said. A lie. They weren't entitled to know everything about her just because they'd befriended her. She practiced doing this sometimes—disappearing without her phone, being untraceable, slipping around corners in the city in case she needed to do so at a moment's notice. Maybe she was overly paranoid, she couldn't tell anymore. But it wasn't worth risking, letting her guard down.

"Your phone was still there," Julian said. "I got . . . worried."

"If I ever disappear, Julian, trust me, I'll take my phone," Betty said. "You know my generation. Addicted to technology." She smiled. He did not. Julian was hard to charm, that was an unavoidable truth.

"Are you planning on disappearing? On leaving us?" Sybil had said as she untangled herself and rested her hands on Betty's shoulders with a look of maternal concern. Betty worked extremely hard to relax. She didn't really like people touching her, but she didn't want to freak anyone out, either, cause a scene.

"No." She shook her head and took the time to meet all their eyes. "I am not planning on disappearing. Besides"—she glanced around at this palace that Zeke thought was a normal apartment—"how could I possibly leave this? *Why* would I possibly leave this?"

"I thought maybe we were smothering you," Sybil said. She

shook her head and added, “I’ve been guilty of that with Eloise and Charlie.” She lost herself to a beat of something that she didn’t share with the rest of them.

Betty didn’t want Sybil to think she wasn’t appreciative, so she forced herself to meet Sybil’s gaze and said, “No, I can’t imagine how you could ever smother me.”

She could though. Certainly.

“We need you in our square,” Zeke said earnestly. He loved this metaphor, the equality of the four-sided shape, as if Betty didn’t wield the least power, the least importance in their quartet.

“Happy to be included in the square,” Betty had said, which seemed to satisfy both Zeke and Sybil, though she couldn’t ignore Julian’s unrelenting gaze. But they’d dropped it. They’d eaten sandwiches and meted out details of their lives in Zeke’s kitchen that could be the germs that infected their insomnia, hoping for cures to resolve such illnesses by putting their problems out into the world. Zeke and his arm. Sybil and her empty nest. Julian and, well, Julian didn’t share much. Sybil complained about her back. Zeke complained about his eye. Julian just said he was old so everything hurt anyway. Betty muttered that she could crack her neck from three different angles when her body was tired, but the truth was that insomnia wasn’t nearly as debilitating for her as it was for the rest of them. Insomnia, for Betty, was nearly a choice, a way to stay attuned to the world, a way to protect herself with one eye, literally, always open.

Tonight she’d left the apartment early before her waitress shift to check on her locker at Grand Central. She had a ritual. On the first of every month, check. Even though it was silly. Even though she was the only one with the locker key. She’d gotten panicky last week and had slipped out to check it again, even though it wasn't on the schedule. This was what she had been doing when she told them she was out for a walk. The best way to snuff out panic, Levi used to tell her, was to be in control, to take back control.

Now fall had blown in quickly after a last gasp of summer in mid-October, and the November air shocked her system. Her parka was left over from high school, for the rare days when Georgia turned cold enough for a winter coat, and feathers poked out of the sleeves. She should upgrade, but that was an expense for another time. Sybil had offered to buy her a new one when she was leaving Zeke's apartment tonight, but Betty had declined. She'd kept almost nothing from that time, her old life, but for some stupid reason, this was one of the few mementos she chose. It had been a hand-me-down from Patience, so that was probably it. A reminder of a time when Betty still believed her sister loved her, believed her sister would save her.

Grand Central was busy on a Saturday night. Betty preferred to come down to her locker when the station was less frantic, but her excuse that she was leaving for work early was the only cover. Mallory never noticed when she came and went, and though there were many reasons why Zeke's apartment was a significant upgrade from their shitty walk-up with questionable plumbing and most definitely mold in the walls, her privacy wasn't one of those improvements. Zeke was almost always home. His physical therapist came to him. His massage therapist came to him. His team of agents and managers came to him. Sometimes Betty eavesdropped on their conversations and wondered what it would be like to have Zeke's problems, which really weren't problems at all.

What an absurd life he has, Betty thought as she turned the corner from the main thoroughfare of Grand Central and kept her head low, tucked under the hood of her parka. No wonder

Zeke was desperate to get it back. His third surgery was scheduled for next week; she'd taken the shift off that night so the three of them—Sybil, Julian and her—could be there when he was in recovery.

She fished the locker key out of her fanny pack. It slid in, clicked, and she opened the iron door, touched the bag with her fingertips, exhaled, closed the door and locked it. That was all she needed. A quick reassurance.

She slipped the key back into her bag and headed back from where she came.

Her phone buzzed:

Zeke: Sybil decided to sleep over. Can we convince you to ditch your work shift?

Sybil: Let's have a sleepover!

Betty sighed. She knew how hard Sybil was working to take her under her wing. Sybil just didn't realize that Betty wasn't born to be part of a flock anymore.

She started typing with both thumbs, face looking downward. So she didn't see the body she collided with. She felt her balance tilt and landed backward on the concrete, her lower back already forming a bruise. Her phone skittered across the ground. All around her, the sea of commuters parted, and a few people stopped to glare. She glanced up and saw a generically attractive investment banker type reaching for her arm.

"Oh my god," he said. "I'm so sorry. I was reading an email, not paying attention. My bad."

She allowed him to pull her to her feet because if she hadn't, she would have drawn even more attention to herself. *Fuck,* she thought. *Fuck fuck fuck fuck fuck.*

"It's fine," she said. "I'm fine."

He took a few strides to grab her phone, wiped it off on his suit jacket, and handed it back to her.

"Someone is begging you for a sleepover." He smiled.

"My mother," she said, her breath short in her chest, her pulse a bass drum in her neck. "Less fun than it sounds. She can't stand that I've grown up, moved out. You know, the whole classic thing." Some of these things were actually true once. Or nearly true anyway.

"Well, I'm sorry again," he said. "I'm an idiot. Could I—would you—have you eaten? Can I buy you a granola bar or . . . trail mix or . . . M&M's from Hudson News?" He grinned a million-dollar grin, expensive orthodontia, probably some cosmetic whitening.

"As tempting as that sounds, I'm actually busy," Betty said, but she felt a smile cresting at the corners of her mouth, like her facial muscles were doing things her brain hadn't yet approved. He was cute, yes, but she was an island. And she already had new small outposts with Zeke and Julian and Sybil. She didn't need another complication.

"Sleepover with Mom," he said.

"Sleepover with Mom." Betty willed herself to turn and run, to point herself as far from this stranger as possible, but inexplicably, her feet remained grounded.

"Okay, well, I'll let you go on your way unobstructed. If you decide to file an insurance claim, just for, you know, like, an injury, here's my card."

He fished a card out of the inside pocket of his jacket.

"Who still carries business cards?" Betty asked.

"This guy." He looked utterly delighted.

He really was very cute, Betty thought. Dark hair, long lashes. Dangerous.

She read his card. "Caleb."

"My parents were Bible-thumpers." He shrugged like this was just casual information he shared, which, maybe it was.

Betty never had the luxury of casual information. If she had, she would have shared that they had this in common, the parental religious zealousness. Her siblings: Patience, Levi, Noah, Jacob. She'd adopted Betty full-time when she left after eighteen years of Elizabeth, which her dad liked to remind her meant "God is my oath." Only Patience and Levi called her Betty back then, and only when their dad wasn't around. Now Caleb felt slippery, treacherous; this whole thing did. She needed to get out of there.

"I'll think about it, Caleb."

"That's not a no."

She shook her head and started on her way.

"That's not a no," he called after her.

She grinned over her shoulder, then refocused and pointed herself in the other direction. And that's when she realized that Caleb wasn't the only one who had noticed her. She was nearly certain that someone had a phone pointed at her, filming her as she walked away and rounded the corner. She picked up her pace to catch them in the act, but when she reached the main hall, whoever it was, was gone.

She spun on her toes and raced toward the uptown track, putting as much distance as she could between whoever it was and her anonymity.

13

NIGHT FIVE

SYBIL

SYBIL STILL HADN'T gotten used to Zeke's easy handsomeness, to the way that she felt like maybe he was flirting with her. But wasn't that a ridiculous thought? She was probably mistaking kindness for flirtation. She'd given in to his proposal for a sleepover. She'd boarded Pluto with their dog walker because Mark was allegedly working an overnight shift (again), and since this was a night for an Insomniacs gathering, she thought why not, what the hell. Sleeping alone in the perfume-scented king-sized bed in their pied-à-terre had already lost its appeal. She'd spend the time listening to another bleak murder-y podcast or watching some gruesome documentary—*Death on Cruise Ships* or *Rocky Mountain Horror House*, and wondering if she could make Mark's body disappear.

Betty had left early for her shift, and Julian texted that he had something come up, so it was just the two of them. Zeke had greeted her in his sponsored tracksuit and fleece slippers, and Sybil felt a little foolish in tapered jeans and a cashmere sweater, but she didn't know how to be casual in front of him yet. She was always too aware of her age, of the fact that she needed tinted moisturizer to get her skin to look normal, that if she slipped on Eloise's sweatpants, she wouldn't have the luxury of looking like she hadn't just given up. The cliff between chic and dowdy was a steep one in your forties.

It was midnight now, and she decided to make them baked ziti.

She'd gone to the organic co-op in her town and shown up with a full bag of groceries, even though Zeke said his assistant could just as well pick them up. But she needed to stay busy. She needed to *be* busy. Eloise had called and said she regretted not taking a gap year, which spiraled into an argument about Sybil pressuring her to go right to college and pressuring her even more to become a doctor. Like Eloise hadn't been the science star all through high school! *Forgive me,* Sybil had shouted, *for supporting your interests!* Charlie never called, which made her wonder if he missed his mother at all, and if not, what she had done wrong such that he hadn't. And Mark? She sighed as she sliced a perfectly round, perfectly red tomato. She'd sharpened her knives last night, and the cut was incredibly satisfying.

"At what point," Zeke was saying—he was lounging in his breakfast nook, and Sybil had a hard time meeting his eyes—"do you think our bodies will just break down, just collapse from never sleeping?"

"Mine sooner than yours," she said, then regretted it because she didn't want him to think she was fishing for compliments.

"I don't know," he said. "You seem to be holding it together."

"My back disagrees."

"Have you seen my eyelid?" he countered.

"Sometimes when I stand up too quickly, I think I'm going to pass out."

"Sometimes at PT," he said, "I get so angry that I feel like I'm having an out-of-body experience."

"Sleep does control your mood," Sybil said.

"You learned that at Harvard?"

She dared to look at him now, and he was smiling.

"You know that I learned that at Harvard," she said, smiling back. "Anyway, how are things going with Betty?"

"Fine? I wouldn't say she's particularly expressive."

"And you don't have . . . anyone else in your life to keep you company?" Sybil was digging, obviously. She hadn't worked up the nerve to ask him about his love life yet, but when she wasn't thinking about true crime podcasts late at night and wasn't playing Sudoku, she was googling Zeke's ex-girlfriends, creeping onto gossip boards to see what sort of partner he was rumored to be.

"You're the only girl in my life right now."

Sybil felt her eyes go wide, and her knife stopped in midair.

"Oh shit," he said, his own eyes wide. "I didn't mean . . . I mean, obviously, there's Mark. I wasn't implying . . ."

"There is indeed Mark," she concurred, and slid the knife cleanly through another tomato. He hadn't meant anything by it; she needed to get a grip.

Mark had been charming at first. Of course. More than at first, if Sybil was being honest. They were each assigned to assist in a clinical oncology study, and it was immediately clear that he thought she was brilliant. She loved this about him. She loved this about herself. It helped that he had a curated stubble, a swimmer's build and, honestly, he wasn't dumb. He just wasn't Sybil. He kissed her one night when they were trying to get a few hours of sleep in the break room, and then when their shift was over, they stumbled home bleary-eyed and took off each other's clothes. Had she thought they would get married and have twins? She wasn't sure she was a reliable narrator in her own story anymore. But if she hadn't gotten pregnant during their residency, she suspected they would have fizzled out. Her heading off to a prestigious fellowship at Stanford or Hopkins; him landing at some midtier hospital where his dad, a retired but important cardiologist, had pull.

Sybil sighed aloud, and Zeke, popping a handful of supplements he'd read might alleviate the sleeplessness, sat up straighter.

"Okay, well, if you insist on cooking, how can I help?"

"You are down to one working arm," she said. "Let me do this. Really, I enjoy it."

"That's a lie," he laughed. "You know you're very type A, right?"

"Eldest daughter. Workaholic parents. Tale as old as time."

"So what happened?" he asked.

She set the knife down.

"What do you mean?"

"What happened with the doctor thing? You . . . I mean . . . you mention it . . . a lot? Maybe that would help, with the sleep. A job."

Sybil angled her body so she was sure he couldn't see the rush of blood to her cheeks. *Obviously, that would fucking help, Zeke.*

"I didn't mean . . ." he said, then stuttered. "I just meant that you seem supercompetent. That's all. Like, I happen to be good at one thing. And only one thing. But I think if we were in a foxhole, you'd be the person I'd want by my side."

Now she turned toward him with a smile. This was exactly the sort of compliment that charged Sybil Foster's battery. Her love language was appreciation, and Zeke unknowingly realized that. She couldn't say that she wasn't at least a little turned on.

"I basically raised my siblings," she said. "My brother's a state senator. My sister runs a tech company in Palo Alto."

He rose, and for a brief moment, Sybil imagined that he was going to cut the distance between them into nothing and kiss her. He instead made his way to the refrigerator, opened it and tilted over, looking for something or other while Sybil admired the way that his T-shirt clung to his back muscles.

He righted himself. "Okay, so what are you going to do now with all that competence? I don't think, um, er, I assume that you can't still be a doctor?"

Sybil shook her head. If she knew what else she could do with her life, she'd be doing it.

"I guess I like helping people."

"Well, that's not nothing. That's actually a very big something," Zeke said.

"I'm not sure about that. It's sort of already factored in when you have kids. The caretaking."

"Okay, but they're gone now. What about, like"—he stared up at the ceiling—"like a life coach?"

Sybil burst out a staccato laugh. "I don't even have my own life together. In case you haven't noticed, I'm making ziti at midnight and have circles under my eyes that they could measure the diameter of in geometry classes."

"Well, (a) that's not true, I've never even noticed the circles, and (b) isn't that a thing with therapists? Doesn't everyone say that they are the most screwed up?" Zeke smiled.

"No, I don't think everyone says that."

"Well, you haven't met mine. The one the team insists on." He smiled wider, pleased to be entertaining her. Sybil found herself staring at him and he back at her, and she could hear the blood pounding in her ears, which is why—she realized later—

she must not have seen or heard Betty slip back into the apartment and announce herself in the kitchen.

"Hello?" Betty said. Then repeated herself, only louder—a sharp bark that punctured the thick air in the kitchen.

Sybil was so startled that she jumped at least a foot in the air at the surprise, shouting *"Jesus Christ,"* and knocking the newly sharpened knife off the counter with the small of her back. Then watching in horror as gravity plunged it directly into the vortex where her big toe met the top of her foot.

If Sybil Foster had been listening to the scene on one of her podcasts, she would have known right then that this was an omen. Instead, the only thing she did was scream.

14

NIGHT FIVE

ZEKE

ZEKE DIDN'T REALIZE for at least a solid minute that Sybil was bleeding or that she had a chef's knife jutting perpendicularly out of her foot. Instead, he was staring at Betty, who was sheet-white and glassy-eyed when she stumbled into the kitchen.

"Betty, are you . . . okay? Aren't you supposed to be at work? Did something happen there?" He took a step closer to her, surprised at how much he wanted to protect her. It was an unfamiliar feeling for Zeke—wanting to look out for someone else.

"I—" she started, then stopped. "I—had to run an errand by Grand Central and I thought I saw . . . but I'm not sure . . . I don't—it doesn't matter." Her eyes shifted to Sybil, like Sybil would understand, which naturally made a lot more sense to Zeke. Zeke followed her gaze, and that's when he noticed that there was blood pooling on his kitchen floor and Sybil was frozen, mouth half open, staring at her sliced sneaker, like she couldn't believe it either.

"You're bleeding!" he shouted. An obvious observation.

Sometimes, he really was the dumbest person in the room. "Sybil! There is a knife in your foot!"

That seemed to startle Sybil out of her trance, and she jolted.

"Shit! Shit shit shit." She allowed herself one beat to freak out, then got steady. He watched it happen in real time. "You need to take me to the hospital. Now."

"We need to remove the knife!" Zeke shouted again. Jesus, was he not the person she'd want in *her* foxhole; he was making that abundantly clear.

"No," she said, and this time, he could see why she would have been a world-class surgeon. A total pro. Calm. Cool. A veritable cucumber. Good god, he hated himself, but . . . it was a turn-on. Maybe if they slept together, then they would actually sleep? His mind would finally find the balm it needed? "If we remove it here," she said like she was on *Grey's* fucking *Anatomy*, "we run the risk of being unable to stop the bleeding and increase the chances of infection." She looked toward Betty. "Can you drive?"

"I can drive," Zeke said.

"You can't. You're already down one arm," Sybil said. Correctly so. How was she the one thinking so clearly in this situation? She had a knife jutting from her foot. He hoped that when she thought back on this moment, she'd attribute his inadequacy to his sleeplessness.

Betty swallowed, then Zeke saw her spine stiffen, color returning to her face, as if she was happy to be useful, to prove that she could be as helpful as Sybil was so often helpful to the rest of them.

"I can drive," Betty said. "I also know first aid. I mean, it's self-taught, but can I help?"

"No, thank you, Betty. I just need you to drive." Then: "Zeke," Sybil shouted, as if she were the head surgeon in the

OR. Zeke wanted to rip her clothes off. "Call the garage, have them bring your car around. We're going to Mount Sinai. Mark will be working."

"Mark, your husband?" Zeke asked. Now this plan immediately grew less appealing.

"He's not a particularly good doctor," she said. "But we'll be seen quickly, and I can tell him what to do."

"Remind me not to have an emergency at Mount Sinai," Betty muttered as Zeke punched the phone number for the garage.

"Do you have crutches?" Sybil asked.

"How are you not, like, dying?" Betty said as Zeke scrambled to his gear closet where he did, indeed, have crutches from the time he came down wrong on his ankle in spring training.

"I nearly gave birth to twins without an epidural," Sybil said, and Zeke almost got a hard-on. "Until Eloise, naturally, decided to be stubborn. But right up until the C-section, I was good to go. I was *fine*."

"Here." He eased the crutches underneath her armpits, and she winced, but that was the only ounce of pain she betrayed.

"What about the blood?" she asked, meeting his eyes. "It will stain your floor."

"Oh god, Sybil, fuck the floor," he said, and he was delighted, if one could be delighted in such circumstances, to see a hint of her smile.

They managed to get her down to the garage where the car was waiting. Betty floored the gas as they turned the corner from his building, and the tires spun out.

"Holy fucking shit!" Zeke yelled. "Betty, can we get there in one piece?" He grabbed the handle above the back window with his good arm, feeling slightly emasculated that he couldn't be the hero. He glanced at Sybil, but she had her eyes closed, her head tilted back against the headrest.

Betty drove like she'd grown up as a professional Formula One driver. If Zeke hadn't been so terrified, he would have been impressed. She dodged taxis and late-night dog walkers in the Central Park Transverse, and she pulled an absolutely insane move where she went around a city bus on the wrong side of the street. Zeke was certain he foresaw his own death. By whatever miracle, Betty bounced right up to the curb by the ER, and Zeke—having texted his agent, Timothy, that he needed someone waiting for them at the Sinai ER with a wheelchair, only to get into a tedious back-and-forth with Timothy that he was not the one who needed it and no, he couldn't get into the details now, and no, there was not going to be a lawsuit—waved down the nurse. Sybil was wheeled away, and Zeke looked for a nearby bush by the curb because he thought he might throw up.

"Are you okay?" Betty asked.

"Where'd you learn to drive like that? And no, I'm about a minute away from vomiting."

She pursed her lips together into a flat line, as if debating what to tell him.

"I drove the tractor a lot on my family's farm."

Zeke couldn't help himself. His staccato laugh erupted so loudly that Betty jumped away from him.

"What?" she said.

"Betty, I know that I'm not Sybil, and I know that I'm not even Julian, but seriously, I'm not that dumb. If you're going to lie to us, you're going to have to learn to do it a little bit better."

15

NIGHT FIVE

BETTY

TECHNICALLY, BETTY DID not have her driver's license. Not technically. Actually. She wasn't allowed to drive back home, and once she left, she was wary about giving identifying details in a government database. Which she knew sounded paranoid. Bananas, really. But Levi used to tell her all sorts of things about the way the government put its finger on you without you even being aware of it—sounding exactly the same as their father, ironically—and even though she hadn't spoken to Levi in months, she couldn't just shed his voice in her brain. So what she didn't tell Zeke is that she'd learned to drive that way because she worked at a pizza place that doubled as an arcade as her first job outside Baltimore. She always took the latest shift, and after she closed for the evening, she played *Pole Position* until the early hours. Armed with the key to the machine, she just unlocked it and reused the same quarter over and over again. Like a lot of things in life, Betty was self-taught.

At the hospital, in between trying not to gape at the knife jutting from Sybil's foot and not draw attention to herself, she replayed the scene from Grand Central. Not just meeting Caleb, the thought of whom fluttered her stomach, but if someone had snapped her picture. If someone was on her tail. She worried that maybe her mind was playing a trick on her, that she hadn't seen what she thought she'd seen, because if she had, then she needed to execute plan B and fast. But if she hadn't—maybe it was just someone holding their phone up trying to get better reception—well, she didn't want to spin this into a problem. Her brain was doing this more often with its lack of sleep: Sometimes, she felt like she was unable to distinguish between the real and the imaginary. Like she was in a prolonged fugue state that had become her life.

"Where is Dr. Foster?" Sybil demanded at the nurse's station.

Betty was seeing Sybil in a whole new light tonight. She'd written her off as an overbearing maternal type, but now she was thinking that Sybil was someone who shot to kill and didn't miss. Betty's own mom had been overbearing but not particularly maternal, a much less desirable equation. Occasionally, Betty thought she saw her mom's face in the crowd, on a subway platform, on a clogged New York City sidewalk, and even though that *was* just her mind playing a trick on her, she always panicked, always fled by pointing herself in the opposite direction.

"I believe that Dr. Foster is resting in the lounge," a nurse said.

"Well, someone rouse my husband from his beauty sleep," Sybil snapped. "I'm about to lose half my fucking foot, and god knows that man owes me a few things."

Betty and Zeke exchanged a glance. Betty was pretty sure that Zeke's cheeks were flushed in that horny way she'd unwillingly grown to recognize in men. The first time she saw it, she was thirteen, and it was from an elder in her father's congregation. Her dad was making introductions, like a barely pubescent girl had any interest in conversing with a man who had flecks of gray in his sideburns, like Betty had the emotional sophistication to fully entertain what the implication could or would be. Patience, then nineteen and already married and pregnant, had swooped in, taken her hand and ushered her into the refectory before Betty had truly processed what was happening. It was one of the few times Betty could remember that Patience, since marrying Matthew, had taken an interest in looking out for her.

The nurse hesitated for only a flicker of a moment, then ran down the hall.

No less than twenty seconds later, a boyishly cute middle-aged man emerged. His hair was sticking up in the back as if he'd been sleeping hard, which, Betty figured, of course he had been. She disliked him on the spot. The offense of deep sleep in the middle of his work shift was enough, but also, Betty had developed a radar for duplicitous men since that time at thirteen, and the casualness with which he approached his wife, the round handsomeness of his face, the demeanor of bravado, all signaled the same thing: This was not a man to be trusted. She felt a firework of anxiety, could still feel the clutch of Patience's hand, and reminded herself that she was safe here, that sometimes she was just too tired to sort the red flags from the white ones. Besides, this man was Sybil's problem to deal with, not hers.

She inhaled deeply, blew out her breath and clenched her fingers into fists so no one saw them shaking.

"Jesus, Sybil!" Her husband dropped to the floor to examine the situation. "What the hell?"

"Get me to a room," Sybil said. "I'm worried I'm going to lose the toe if we don't deal with this immediately."

Mark jumped to his feet and only then took notice of Betty, his eyes lingering on her for a beat too long. *Skeevy.* Then his jaw loosened when he recognized Zeke.

"Are you—" he started, then stopped, then looked at his wife. "I'm sorry, I don't— Did you come in here with Zeke Rodriguez?"

"Mark!" Sybil barked. "Focus! Do you want me to bleed out in the waiting room or are you actually going to do your job? Or do I have to do everything around here?"

Another doctor approached. Betty thought she looked like she could be Sybil's younger sister. A little blonder, a little thinner, fewer lines around the eyes.

"Mark, is everything okay?" She reached her fingers toward his arm, then took notice of Sybil, not just Sybil's foot, and yanked her hand back as if Mark were a live wire threatening electrocution.

"Oh my god, *of course*," Sybil said, her voice a full octave lower now. "The anesthesiologist."

"I'm sorry?" the woman, whose fair skin was now beet red, said.

"Your perfume," Sybil hissed. "I might have a knife in my foot, but my nose works just fine."

"Sybil, I think you're going into shock," Mark said.

"If it's shock that I came to this ER for you to treat me and instead, I'm meeting your *lover*," Sybil said, "then you are correct."

Now the nurses were all paying attention. Betty saw one move her hand to cover her mouth, and the other two looked like they were either going to live-tweet this or possibly pee in their pants. She glanced to the corner and noticed the security cameras clocking this as well. Just a precautionary measure for the hospital, but there was no denying that Betty was well exposed now. This was why she had always been an island. This was how she got into trouble, by softening and actually caring about people. She'd learned to drive that way because Levi had taught her that she needed to have every available resource at her disposal to stay safe. *In case you ever need to get away quickly,* he'd said, *better to be prepared.* So *Pole Position* wasn't exactly traditional driver's ed. It was emergency driver's ed.

"Syb," Mark said, then Zeke took a step forward, and Mark shut up.

"Can you please treat her like you would any other patient?" he said, his voice booming, and Betty was certain that Mark's testicles curled up nearly inside of him. This was absolutely incredible. She wanted to take notes. She wanted to film it. She wanted a mother who stood up to her husband like this. She wanted to be a woman who had the courage to do the same. She wanted to be a normal teenager who didn't practice driving at a dingy arcade/pizza place and instead had parents who paid for a driving instructor or gave her the freedom to drive herself in the first place.

"Not like any other patient," Sybil said. "He's really not a very good doctor. I let him cheat off of me through medical school and had to hold his hand through our residency." She started to say more but seemed to think the better of it.

"I don't think—" the anesthesiologist started.

"I don't care *what* you think," Sybil said. "But if someone doesn't get this knife out of my foot in less than two minutes, I will not be held responsible for my actions."

"Do I need to call security? Mark, should I call security?" the anesthesiologist stuttered.

Betty watched Mark grow increasingly rattled, his eyes darting from his wife to his mistress. It was almost enough to distract her entirely from Grand Central—*had that really just been an hour ago?* She tucked her hand into her pocket and felt Caleb's card. That part she hadn't been imagining. She let herself drift for a moment to another world, another time, when she was just a normal girl who collided with a normal boy, and they would go on a normal date and have normal drinks then normal sex then maybe some normal months or years together.

Betty had never had a real boyfriend for a variety of reasons.

Zeke inched closer to Mark. "Do not call security, dude."

"I can't believe . . . are you two *friends*?" Mark really had a problem focusing. No wonder Sybil didn't seem to like him very much.

Zeke placed a hand on Sybil's shoulder, and she tilted her head toward it. It was a master class move, Betty thought. Enough of a hint to worry Mark; enough of a threat to maybe make him panic.

"We are," Zeke said, though he may as well have said that they were fucking, given the look in his eye. Betty wondered if something wasn't brewing between the two of them, which she would endorse because she genuinely liked them both—and also, maybe it might divert Sybil into less mothering. Betty did enjoy her doting, but she suspected that Levi would disapprove of her having any parental figures in her life. She made a mental note to track him down. They'd gotten good at checking in every few months, but—she tried to rewind the calendar—it felt like it had been longer than that by now.

"How do you know each—" Mark started, but Sybil cut him off with a guttural howl.

"My big fucking toe is dangling from my fucking foot, Mark! If you want a goddamn autograph, he'll do it afterward!"

The blood drained from Sybil's husband's face. How easily she emasculated him in front of the staff; how sharply she cut him down to size. Betty absolutely loved it. She tried to memorize everything about it. She tried to picture her saying these sorts of things to her father, to Noah, to Jacob, to Patience once she made herself over in her husband's image. *Fuck all of you. Fuck the patriarchy!* She never did, never would. But she enjoyed thinking about it all the same.

"Right, right," a nurse said as she rushed over. "Dr. Foster, I'm taking her into room 305. If you aren't up for treating her, please let me know immediately so I can page the on-call resident."

"Don't be ridiculous," the anesthesiologist said. "Of course we can treat her."

"If you even think of working me up," Sybil said to her, her voice so calm that Betty thought she might be an actual sociopath, "I will take this knife out of my foot myself, and then all bets are off."

The anesthesiologist stiffened. "Is that a threat? Are you threatening me?"

"No," Sybil said as the nurse began to wheel her away. "The threat is that when I walk out of here, Mark is all yours. You wanted him? You got him. Good luck."

16

NIGHT FIVE

JULIAN

JULIAN CHECKED HIS phone again. No one had texted him all evening. Not to check in, not to play Sudoku. He didn't want to read too much into it, but he worried something had gone wrong. Mostly, he worried about Betty. From a distant corner in his apartment, Felix meowed. Julian had given up on finding him tonight.

He slunk to his bathroom, and a pain, a sharp bubble, rose up in his chest. He froze, worrying it would escalate and maybe he would drop dead right there on the tiles with graying grout, but he took five deep breaths and slowly, the pain ebbed out of him. Probably gas. He shook his head, reached for the Tums in his medicine cabinet. He needed to call his doctors. He should tell them that he was having recurring symptoms, that it had been four years since the heart attack and maybe it was time to fine-tune his valves again. He made a mental note to take care of this in the morning. He wouldn't do it, he knew, but he was very good at pretending.

Julian peed, washed his hands and examined his face in the

mirror. He didn't think he looked too bad for sixty, for a man whose job had caused enough stress to induce his first heart attack, for a widower who hadn't relieved himself from his grief for a decade.

He made his way to his office, sat in the chair that had the back that squeaked and had done so since he bought it. There was a lot you could learn to live with. He opened his filing cabinet, pulled out his old cases. Maybe there was nothing to solve here, he told himself. Maybe he needed to just let it go. Run a candy store. Look after his heart. Build a relationship with his daughter.

He massaged his temples, eased back. *Squeak squeak.*

But also, maybe all of that was wrong. If he'd missed something, maybe there was something left to be done.

17

NIGHT SIX

SYBIL

November 8th

IN THE END, maybe a knife through her toe was exactly what her marriage needed. Or exactly what she needed, even though they had to suture her toe back together and Sybil was already concocting a story to tell the twins about the situation when they came home for Thanksgiving break in two weeks.

Back home in her too-big, empty-nesting house, Sybil yanked the sheets off her king-sized bed, wobbling a little uncertainly in her foot bootie. She refused crutches and said absolutely *not* to a cane or a walker, so the boot, an eyesore, it was. But the knife had cut straight down to the bone, and even in her stubbornness to carry on as normal, she wasn't dumb enough to tempt risking a toe. Toes, she thought, as she gave the top sheet another yank, were undervalued. Lose the big one, and it's way more than just a horrendous look in sandals in Turks and Caicos. Your entire balance would be destabilized, your entire gait obliterated. Goodbye to what babies learn as second nature: how to walk, how to stay upright. She suspected she was now talking to herself in analogy. Something about losing

Mark. But honestly, she thought her toe was more critical to her future than her husband. So that was a pretty strong indicator.

Sybil dumped the fitted and top sheets on the floor. She hadn't been home for the past few nights, having camped out at the pied-à-terre since the accident, and while she didn't detect the scent of the anesthesiologist's perfume, she didn't trust that Mark wouldn't have invited her for a sleepover, despite blowing up her texts telling her that she had misunderstood at the ER. She wondered if it would be too extreme to haul the bed to the front lawn and burn it. She liked the imagery of that, the metaphor there, but then, well, someone would surely post about it on Nextdoor, and she didn't really see how she could keep a bonfire in her front yard a secret from the twins. She did have a fire pit in the back, so maybe if she chopped the mattress up into itty-bitty pieces, she could incinerate it there. But, she thought, as she gave the pillowcases a hard tug, that wouldn't be nearly as satisfying.

"Sybil?" A voice from downstairs, then footsteps ascending, and Natalie burst through the bedroom door. She was breathing heavily and looked like she'd just come into contact with the surface of the sun. She was too young for a hot flash, Sybil thought.

"Are you okay? Your cheeks are maroon," Sybil said and threw a pillow, *hard*, against the headboard.

"Why did Zeke Rodriguez just let me into your house?" Natalie hissed, quiet enough not to be overheard a story below but loud enough to be extremely dramatic.

"Oh."

"Is this why you asked me about your boobs a few weeks ago?"

"No—"

"Oh my god, are you sleeping with Zeke Rodriguez?!" This time, Natalie couldn't help herself, and her voice rose to a quite

audible level. There was a clattering downstairs, and Sybil's eyes went wide, then Natalie's eyes went wide, then Betty's voice called out, "Sorry! I was just giving a treat to Pluto, and he knocked over a plant."

"Who are these people downstairs, and why are you sleeping with Zeke Rodriguez and haven't told me?" Natalie whispered.

"I'm not sleeping with him. And that's the girl I mentioned a while back, the aspiring actress. She's a waitress. I told you?" Sybil couldn't remember if she had actually told Natalie anything. She thought she'd sent Natalie her picture, but that could also just be something she imagined. She was so tired that nothing stayed in her brain for long anymore.

Natalie ignored the second part of Sybil's statement and gestured to the bed, raising an eyebrow. "Changing the sheets?"

"I kicked Mark out."

Natalie's palm flew to her chest as her jaw loosened. "You didn't lead with that? You didn't call me immediately?"

Sybil shook her head. "Sorry, I'm ahead of myself. I haven't *kicked* him out. I told him that I *wanted* to kick him out."

Natalie planted her hands on her hips.

"When?"

"Last week."

"*Last week?* Does your phone not work? Does my phone not work?"

"It's complicated."

"No, it isn't," Natalie said. "You married a man who turned out to be a disappointment. Also"—she dropped her voice—"*you want to show Zeke Rodriguez your boobs.*"

"I *don't* want to show Zeke Rodriguez my boobs," Sybil said. "That's the problem! Do you have any idea what sort of boobs he's seen?"

"Yours are spectacular," Natalie said, with the bravado of a best friend and not that of an objective observer.

"Well, now I know you're lying."

The bed was stripped bare now, and Sybil sat on its edge, dipped her chin to her chest. Natalie sat next to her and placed a hand on the middle of her back, which ached all the time now.

"Okay, but for real, are you going to explain why Zeke Rodriguez is in your kitchen?"

"I never sleep," Sybil said. "We met online."

Sybil felt Natalie's gaze on her, so she raised her head to meet her delighted grin.

"So this *is* about your sex life. Are the other two people downstairs—" Her eyebrows pointed downward as if to say, *I didn't know you had it in you, but I'm not disappointed.*

"Oh my god," Sybil laughed. "We're all just friends. We're friends who don't sleep. And we're trying to help each other fix our problems. Zeke is injured; he has surgery next week . . . I'm not even sure he *could* sleep with me if he wanted to."

"Girl, he *could,* even with you in . . . this." She gestured at her foot. "Totally naked but for a medical boot. Hot. All sorts of weird shit turns people on, you know."

Sybil had texted Natalie that she'd injured her toe but hadn't told her how. There were too many details to explain in a text, honestly. A thought occurred to her.

"Actually let's just . . . can we focus on Betty, the actress? Can you help get her some work?"

"I can probably help anyone," Natalie said, because she had the exact type of confidence you needed from a sidekick in moments like this.

"Come on, let me make introductions. I worry about her. She doesn't have any family."

"You worry about everyone but yourself," Natalie said but trailed her downstairs.

Betty was in the backyard, despite the nippy temperature. Sybil had hung fairy lights last spring for the twins' pre-prom party, which she had naturally agreed to host (she hated hosting), and she was surprised they hadn't yet fallen. Still sparkling like nothing had changed. She and Eloise had a huge fight before the party about Eloise wanting to turn down Georgetown for a gap year, but if you looked at the pictures from that night, you'd never know. Mark had worn a tuxedo and served the kids mocktails, though a few surely sneaked the cocktails designated for the parents. Charlie certainly had. He was already tipsy by the time the bus pulled up to take them to the dance. When the house was at last empty, she and Mark got into it because she needed to be mad at someone after the fight with Eloise and witnessing Charlie's delinquency. And she had plenty of reasons to be mad at Mark. He ended up claiming there was an emergency and had to go into the hospital. So she sat in her backyard under the fairy lights and got drunk enough to fall asleep in a chaise lounge by the pool.

At least, she thought ruefully now, she'd managed to sleep.

"Betty," she said, hobbling closer. "This is my friend Natalie, and I'm pretty sure she can change your life."

Looking back, it never once dawned on Sybil that Betty hadn't asked for such a thing, that changing Betty's life might be the very thing that ruined it.

18

NIGHT SIX

BETTY

BETTY DIDN'T KNOW how to tell Sybil's friend that she really wasn't super interested in being cast in the laundry detergent commercial Natalie was working on. No, not just super uninterested. Like, not at all interested. She couldn't be. She didn't have that luxury.

"So what sort of experience do you have?" Natalie asked while Sybil lit the fire pit on her back patio and offered Julian and Zeke some spiced cider. It was so exactly like Sybil to have spiced cider on hand.

"Oh, just some high school stuff," Betty said. "It's okay, you don't have to feel obligated."

"No," Natalie said, like that was the end of the argument. "I like your look. You can play young, which is always a huge advantage, and you don't look like all the other girls I see."

Betty didn't know what that meant, if it was a compliment really.

"Also," Natalie added, "Sybil wants to help. And in my experience, when Sybil wants to do something, it's better to just get on board because eventually she's going to wear you down into doing it anyway." She seized Betty by the shoulders and steered her over to better lighting by the sliding glass door, and before Betty could protest, snapped a few pictures.

"Oh no, please don't—" Betty started, but then she heard the clack of Natalie typing and whoosh, her pictures were shot into the ether. A burst of wind blew through, and she zipped her jacket tighter.

"I told them you can ride a bike. You can ride a bike, yes? We need someone who can play high school who can also ride a bike."

Suddenly Zeke was by her side. "If she can't ride a bike, she can *definitely* drive a stunt car." He thrust out his left hand, which wasn't his dominant hand, and he looked like he was still adjusting to learning how to use it. "Let's make her *famous*! Also, hi, I'm Zeke."

Betty watched Natalie raise an eyebrow, while Sybil limped over because she seemed to always be where Zeke was these days.

"Zeke, this is my best friend, Natalie," Sybil said.

"I already sent her pics over to my agency. We're getting you your SAG card and health insurance, Betty, don't worry."

"I wasn't—" She wasn't worried before, but now she was very worried. Betty had taken meticulous care to blend in so well that she was nearly invisible, and now this well-intentioned but extremely pushy woman wanted to cast her in a commercial? Betty allowed herself to imagine a different life, one in which she really could become a star, one in which she could arrive at a premiere with Caleb, the subway boy, on her arm. She still had his card in her pocket; she still thought about reaching out every day. She still knew better, so she didn't.

"I don't actually want to be famous," Betty said. She wasn't used to being steamrolled recently, having spent her childhood being steamrolled and having worked hard to break the habit. But in trying to flex that muscle now, she discovered that it had atrophied.

"Ah, I see, an actor's actor," Natalie said. "Well, everyone has to start somewhere; this is just a regional commercial, nothing high stakes, but we can get it in your reel, get some actual headshots and start to send you out from there."

There were so many things in that sentence that Betty didn't understand that she opened her mouth, then closed it, then opened it again, but nothing came out.

"Natalie," Sybil said, with the tone of a woman who decided they were moving on from the subject, "I also want to introduce you to Julian."

Julian was looking even more exhausted than usual tonight, purple pillows under his bloodshot eyes, a curve of his shoulders that looked like it might topple him.

"You okay?" Betty asked him, once Natalie, Sybil and Zeke had retreated inside because the November air had enough bite to seep into your bones. She liked the steely chill, though, like she had something in common with the elements.

It was still fall weather back in Georgia, and if she were there, it would have been her favorite season. Her parents had always mandated that Betty and Patience cover up, though no such rule was made for the three boys of the family. So summer was excruciating: heavy dresses, long sleeves, sweltering humidity, sticky clothing. Fall meant a respite from that. She could semi-blend in with the other kids; she could stop feeling faint from the heat as her body temperature sizzled underneath all the layers. Her dad would speak about God's magnificence being reflected in the beauty of the leaves, in the snap of the air, in the season of life, but all Betty could do was think: *Thank you, God, for dropping the temperature below eighty.* She and

Patience used to whisper at night about moving to Canada, where they figured it was always cold, but then Patience turned eighteen and got married that same week, as was customary in their church, to a man their dad picked out, and then she had a baby, and soon, it was clear that Patience was never leaving. And in fact, had maybe never wanted to, not with the way her husband was rising in her dad's ranks, in the way that Patience stopped whispering with Betty at all. She nodded to her at church on Saturdays and smiled, of course, when they passed each other in the halls and the rectory, but by twenty, Patience wasn't anything like Betty had remembered her to be. Maybe she was just pretending for her little sister's sake, telling her fairy tales like other kids read them at bedtime.

Julian sat on a chaise lounge by the pool and stretched out, crossing his arms and closing his eyes. He rotated his ankles, and they cracked loudly enough for Betty to feel his satisfaction from the *pop*.

"Do you want to be an actor?" he asked, avoiding her question. He was shivering a bit, so Betty grabbed one of the chenille blankets that Sybil had draped over her outdoor couch and laid it atop him.

"I don't know what I want to be," she said, resting on the chaise beside him.

He turned to her and met her eyes, his glare serious, but then Julian was nearly always serious.

"If you're ever in trouble, I want you to come to me."

Betty felt worry rise in her. She worked to steady her voice. Why would Julian think she was in trouble? How would Julian think she was in trouble?

"Oh, I'm fine. You mean because I don't sleep? Or because I don't know what I'm doing with my life? Don't you have kids my age? Isn't this part of growing up?"

"I do have a kid your age-ish. Simone is twenty-six."

"And does she come to you when she's in trouble?"

Julian smiled at this. "Simone wouldn't dream of getting in trouble."

"Dad owns a candy store," Betty said. "Picture-perfect fairy tale?"

"Something like that," Julian said.

Betty wondered if it wasn't something totally different, and Julian just didn't want to say.

"So what you're saying is she's gotten arrested for larceny?"

"No," Julian said.

"Murder?"

Julian laughed. "I doubt she's even gotten a parking ticket."

"Oh," Betty said, almost disappointed. She would have liked to know that Julian could prove it, back up the claim, that he really could be there for her if shit hit the fan. "Well, it's nice that she has you if she does decide to pull off some light larceny."

"Fathers aren't always what they're cracked up to be," Julian said, and closed his eyes.

Betty stared at the stars and had the unnerving feeling that he was talking about hers.

19

NIGHT SIX

JULIAN

JULIAN PRETENDED TO sleep on the chaise while Betty flipped through her phone, leaving the clatter and sociability to Sybil, Zeke and Sybil's friend. He was trying to be delicate with Betty, rely on his instincts and not push her. He didn't come off like a people person, he knew, but that's what often lulled people into a sense of security with him: He was like white noise in the background of their confessions. It wasn't until they stopped oversharing that they realized they'd overshared at all.

He fluttered his eyes open just a crack to watch Betty. She dug her hand into her pocket and retrieved a business card, then rested it on her lap and chewed the side of her lip. Suddenly, she sat up straighter, typed furiously into her screen, and he heard the swish of the sent text.

"Shit," she whispered, and he pressed his eyes closed so she wouldn't think he'd been spying. "Fuck," she said louder, and now he pretended to rouse.

"You okay?"

She startled like she'd forgotten he was lying on the lounger beside her. Exactly as Julian had expected.

"What? Oh. Um. Yes."

"Want to go inside? My bones are getting chilly."

"How did your wife die?" Betty asked instead. It was blunt but not surprising coming from her. She hadn't been raised attending cotillion.

He took a sharp breath in.

"Cancer," he said. "How about your own parents?" He watched her carefully.

"Oh." She paused and then looked appropriately bereft. "Farming accident."

"That couldn't have been easy."

"I had four older siblings to raise me," she said. "At least I wasn't alone."

"And where are they now?"

"Other than my brother Levi, I think they are all still in the exact same place I left them. North Carolina." She fidgeted with her hands.

"Too cold?"

"A little." Her phone buzzed and she grabbed it and concealed a grin when she read whatever had come in.

"That looks like good news," Julian said.

She shook her head like she already regretted it. "A boy. Something dumb."

"They usually are."

She laughed at this and then so did he.

"Your siblings, are you guys in touch?"

She caught herself for a moment. "Maybe like you and your daughter are. Not like you should be, but not like you aren't at all."

It was a masterful answer, Julian thought. Betty was very good at this; probably had a lot of practice over the years. Her fatigue hadn't made her brain any less sharp, which was important to keep in mind.

"You get home often?"

She fixed her smile so she looked perfectly tranquil, perfectly unbothered.

"It's expensive to travel. Until Mr. All-Star came along, need I remind you that I was living in an apartment that may or may not have been declared a hazardous site by the government?"

"Hopefully next week's surgery fixes Mr. All-Star up and he can get back to it," Julian replied.

Her face dropped. "Oh, do you think he'll ask me to leave once he's better? Back with the team?"

"No," Julian said plainly. "I think Zeke is lonely, like all of us, and having the best arm in the National League isn't going to change that, even if it's back in working order."

"I don't want to look like I'm overstaying my welcome," Betty said. "I really am okay on my own."

Julian wanted to tell her that she shouldn't have to be. Instead, he said, "No, this gives you the chance to save up. To visit your family."

"Well, Natalie thinks I'm an *actor's actor,* so maybe I'll be rich and famous one day. Have my private jet on standby." She grinned. She was so talented, so adept, so agile. It was hard to knock Julian's socks off but consider his knocked. "I actually don't even know what an actor's actor is."

"It's someone who takes her craft seriously. In it for the art, not just the dazzle."

"Oh." Betty's face went pensive, her mouth a frown, her eyes thoughtful. "Actually, you know what, maybe that's exactly what I am."

"I need a cider refill," he said, pushing to his feet. He felt his right knee pop into its socket on his way up. "But for what it's worth, I agree. I suspect you are a better actor than anyone gives you credit for."

20

NIGHT SEVEN

ZEKE

A Week Before Thanksgiving

THE LAST THING Zeke remembered was counting down on the surgical table as the nurse gave him anesthesia, and now he heard Sybil's voice before he actually registered it was her voice, his grogginess a cloud over his cerebral synapses. He kept his eyes closed and tried to center himself. He was aware of the steady beep of some machine nearby and that the right side of his upper body was elevated and immobilized, but the fatigue kept dragging him back under. He'd listed her as his emergency contact, as his medical proxy, but he didn't know why he was surprised that she was here, waiting. Maybe it was because other than his parents and his sister, Lani, he didn't expect much from anyone in terms of loyalty. The rest of it was all contractual. And yet here she was, as promised. A joy in a joyless time.

"Hey, it's me," Sybil was saying. "Just checking in on Betty. Wanted to see if you'd lined up any auditions yet? Don't tell her I called. I'm at the hospital so might not pick up but call me back." She paused. "I'm at the hospital with Zeke. I didn't mean to imply that something's wrong or that I've killed Mark."

Zeke liked that: *I'm at the hospital with Zeke*, and he must have been more conscious than he realized because he saw her face shift and their eyes met, and then she said, "Oh my god, I have to go. Call me back." She dropped her phone on the chair opposite his bed and was beside him.

"Good morning," she said.

"Is it morning? Have I been asleep all night?"

"Actually, no, it's nine P.M."

She gestured to the window where blackness had fallen. They were so comfortable now, being awake in the dark, that rousing when others were preparing for sleep felt entirely normal.

"The surgery took longer than expected," she said. "You've been in recovery for a few hours. Betty and Julian are outside too. Waiting."

"Mmm," he managed. He fought to keep his eyes open, an irony for an insomniac.

"Here." She put a cup of water with a straw in front of his lips. "Let me get your doctors. They'll want to know you're up."

"Wait," he said, and forced his eyes open again. Though they'd been friends for only six weeks or so, Zeke had come to believe that he could read Sybil as well as he could read anyone. She blinked under the weight of his stare, and Zeke knew, acutely, that whatever the medical team was going to say was not the news he needed to hear. "Just . . . can I just have a few more minutes before they tell me?"

"Yes," she said, then slid the chair in the corner over to his bedside.

His phone was buzzing relentlessly on the side table by his bed. What a joy it had been to be knocked out and unreachable. Zeke considered how much he would like to take his phone and hurl it out the glass window. A fastball straight into the East River.

"Want me to get that for you?" Sybil asked.

"I'm sure it's just media," Zeke sighed.

"What about your parents? Shouldn't you let them know you're in recovery?"

"I never told them the exact date," he said. "Of the surgery," he added in case there was any confusion.

"But Zeke," Sybil said, astonished, "surely they'll read about it? Surely they'll worry?"

It was sweet, he thought, that she took it so personally. Like one of her own kids could leave her in the dark. No wonder she was nosing around Betty's business.

"That's why I tell them after the fact. When there's good news, so they *don't* need to worry."

Sybil pressed her lips together, and Zeke thought this was her tell. He was decoding her in a way that he never even figured out the women he was sleeping with or dating. His phone vibrated again, and she raised her eyebrows.

"Fine, okay," he said. "You can look."

She reached for her glasses tucked into the neck of her sweater and scrolled.

"No, no, hmmm, I think this is your agent? No, no, delete, delete." She rested his phone back down. "You're right. Busywork."

"You're extremely efficient."

"Have you met me?"

"Yes." Zeke smiled. "Type A plus plus."

"A compliment," she said, and smiled.

Zeke laughed, and his entire body hurt. "Ow, fuck."

"Okay, you're my patient now," Sybil said, jumping to her feet. She adjusted his pillow, and he sank his head back on it. For a brief moment, he was too aware of the rise and fall of his chest, the way that she distracted him from his pain. He stilled and stared at the wall, and she tucked him into a little burrito swaddle with the sheets.

"Just tell me how the surgery went," he said. "Rip off the Band-Aid."

A long silence bubbled between them.

"Sometimes I think—" she started, then stopped.

"It's okay," he said. "Whatever you need to say, I can handle it. I realize I may have to come up with a plan B."

Sybil's eyes welled, like his pain was her pain, or maybe that she didn't want to deal with her own plan B. Both probably. He reached his good arm toward her to grasp her hand. She interlaced her fingers into his and squeezed, and he squeezed back. Like they were drifting so far from where they'd imagined they'd be in life right now, but if they were knotted together, maybe they could survive the undertow.

"Sometimes I think," she said, her voice catching, "that we don't believe we're capable of difficult things because we've never been tested. And no one wants to be tested. Why would we ever want to be tested? But if you tell yourself you can't, you really don't know until do you do it."

"You would have made a very good doctor," he replied. "You have an excellent bedside manner."

"Two things are true: One, I would have made an exceptional doctor. But two, you're going to be okay, Zeke. Whatever happens next, you're going to be okay." She cleared her throat. "Plan B sometimes ends up being so much better than plan A, you know?"

"Sybil Foster, you definitely do not believe that."

"I'm working on believing it," she said.

"The only way through is through," Zeke said, which reminded him of his high school coach who used to say that all the time. When his arm was throbbing from relentless practice, when he couldn't throw a strike to save his life, when he got so nervous for the MLB scouting practice that he sat on the toilet the entire twenty-four hours before.

"I'll be right back," she said, patting his leg.

"Don't go," he started, but then she disappeared anyway.

It was hard to feel like that wasn't a sign.

21

NIGHT EIGHT

BETTY

Just Before Thanksgiving

IN THE WEEK since Zeke's surgery and the weeks since meeting Sybil's casting director friend, Betty hadn't really thought much about Natalie until she got a text telling her that she'd booked a commercial. If she *had* thought about it, she never would have agreed, would have told Natalie no before the yes even came in. But she was tired; even with the better housing, sleep rarely found her, and the fog of that fatigue sometimes clouded her thinking, like a notion would be in her brain and then poof, it was gone. So maybe Natalie was just a poof, or else Betty would have mounted a better protest.

"They loved your look," was Natalie's only explanation in her text, and before Betty could write her back and decline, Natalie followed up with a second text with a monetary figure that would mean that Betty could quit the diner for good or at least pare her shifts down to a couple of nights a week. Betty had been so prudent, so meticulous for the past four years, but also, she was sick of constantly being poor. To confidently lock in a permanent exit plan, she needed more money than what she had in the storage locker at Grand Central. That was the foundation, but to build the walls, tack on a roof, she needed *more.*

Betty so rarely allowed herself to be greedy, which was her only excuse for agreeing to finally meet Caleb for a drink after a string of back-and-forths in the two weeks since she'd impulsively texted him that night at Sybil's house. She'd already be in midtown for a hair and makeup test for the commercial; it felt easy, it felt convenient, and unfortunately for Betty, it felt safe. Betty never trusted safe, but she *wanted* to. She really really wanted to put her full faith behind *safe.*

Zeke had been moored on the couch, painkillers coursing through his veins, when she left in the late afternoon for the shoot. More or less where he'd been in the week since his surgery.

"Betty," he said, his eyes glassy, his arm elevated, his jaw loose. "It's almost Thanksgiving. What should we do for Thanksgiving? Why don't you invite your family? We'll make a feast of it. Like the Pilgrims. Like we just got off the boats."

"Oh, my family couldn't come," she had said. She wanted to correct him that he meant *ships,* not *boats,* but Zeke wasn't in any state for fact-checking. But Betty had been a reader—sneaking into the school library as a child, and of course never checking out a book and bringing it home because there were consequences for disobedience, but still. She'd made that mistake only once—Judy Blume. She could still envision the cover, as well as the punishment. Now she reminded herself that at least she knew the difference between a ship and a boat. That even if she was just a high school graduate with no discernable life skills, she knew the difference. Also, she reminded herself, she did have life skills. She was still here.

"Didn't I hear you say you have *four* siblings?" Zeke asked as

Betty searched the living room for a stray mitten. “Can’t I meet one? Couldn’t you invite even one to stay with us?” He dipped his head back on the couch cushion. “Betty, I would like to meet *just one.*” He quieted, and Betty thought he may have fallen asleep, but then he jolted his head up and said, “My sister, Lani, is coming. Did I tell you that? Don’t worry, you’ll love her. I bet you guys will be best friends. My mom and dad too.”

Betty didn’t have the heart to tell him that she almost never made friends easily, and she was highly doubtful that Lani would break that streak. Growing up, her father had told her that with so many siblings, she didn’t *need* friends. But once Patience was married off, she’d really just had Levi.

“Sybil worries about you, you know,” Zeke said.

“Sybil doesn’t need to worry about me.”

“She told me that she thinks it’s weird that you have such a big family but never talk about them.” His eyes were closed, and it was possible that he was making all of this up in a fever dream. But it was also possible that he wasn’t. And Betty didn’t want Sybil asking questions.

“Oh,” she had said, “I do talk to them. We email. And text. We just aren’t really the phone types. You know how it goes.”

Zeke had hummed something that sounded like a concurrence, but Betty didn’t think she had convinced him.

“Actually, maybe my friend Caleb can come to Thanksgiving,” she had said. “I’m sort of seeing someone.”

Zeke’s head sprung up from the back of the couch. “Yes! Yes!” he said. “Bring Caleb to Thanksgiving. Then Sybil will shut up.”

Betty hadn’t actually meant to suggest that Caleb would come to Thanksgiving. But she spoke before she could think it through. She hadn’t even gone on an official date with him yet. But if Sybil was talking, then Sybil was plotting, and that meant she was going to roll up her sleeves and dive headfirst into Betty's life with or without her permission. Maybe Betty could find a way to ask Caleb and not make it weird. For obvious reasons, she hadn't been allowed to date in high school. The assumption was that her father would match her with a suitable boy and that would be that. When he turned out to be closer to a man than a boy, Betty wanted to protest, scream, fight. Her dad, as if sensing her rebellion, her need to turn and flee upon an introduction to Silas, squeezed her upper arm so tightly that she was bruised for a week. Patience had been paired with his brother, Matthew, who Betty always thought looked like he would endorse cannibalism if God told him to, but Betty no longer spoke with Patience, so she didn't know what God did or didn't say to them anymore.

Now, after three hours of test hair and makeup and wardrobe, Betty spotted Caleb at the bar, scrolling through his phone with a scowl on his face, and she forced herself similarly not to turn and bolt. Her nerves rose up in the form of bile in the back of her throat, and everything about the situation screamed *run*. But before she could, Caleb looked up and saw her, and his entire face shifted from scowl to delight, and well, what was she going to do then? Even an expert runner had to time her escapes carefully.

"Oh wow, you look really pretty."

And she allowed herself to blush because she had wanted to look pretty for him.

"Thank you," she said. "So do you." She slapped her hand across her mouth as soon as she realized, but he laughed.

He ordered them two beers, and then they moved to the back, where she slid into a booth next to him and let her stomach feel fluttery when their legs touched. She decided right then, even if it was just for a night or even if she just needed him as some sort of proof, an offering of normalcy to Sybil, that she could permit herself this. She could take something that she wanted. And she wanted the money from the commercial, and she wanted Caleb. She liked who she was when she was being greedy, even if she also knew that greed could end up eating you from the inside out.

Her father had always liked to preach about greed—and, as he eventually learned, greed could end up being the thing that giveth, but also taketh away. Betty knew that lesson too.

22

NIGHT EIGHT

JULIAN

DAD," SIMONE SAID, poking her head into his office. "What are you doing? This is not what we agreed to." Julian startled and shut his laptop too quickly. A child caught with his hand in the cookie jar. Simone was back in town for the night for work and had gone out for a drink with her high school friends, and Julian hadn't realized she was home already.

"It wasn't work," Julian said, swiveling his chair around to face her. "I promise."

After the heart attack, he'd sworn to Simone that his retirement meant just that: that he was out. He took over Robin's candy store business full-time and lived a quiet life that didn't involve extra stress to his heart. But that didn't mean that he couldn't dip a toe in to test the water temperature every once in a while. That didn't mean that he could just stop thinking about the loose ends he still felt compelled to tie together. He still had friends in the game, still had contacts he was waiting to hear back from. Recently, things had gotten more urgent, and it could have been that he felt like his heart might literally stop at any time, but also, Julian's instincts almost never failed him, and for the past few weeks, those instincts had been flashing red. He'd been rereading a LISTSERV on the unmarked, untraceable parts of the internet—he would know what he was looking for when he saw it—when Simone surprised him.

"Don't tell me what my eyes didn't see," Simone said.

"Really," he said. "I was just reviewing some of the budget for next year for the store."

"Ummhmm," Simone said, but dropped it because her point had been made, and Julian was rightfully chastened.

"Did you eat?"

"I did, but that doesn't mean I couldn't again." She smiled and looked so much like Robin that Julian's heart nearly stopped right there.

They settled on Greek food from Simone's favorite takeout place from high school and then sank into the couch, Simone watching some reality dating show, while they waited for delivery. He wanted to ask her if she could stay longer, more than just the one night for business, but theirs was not a relationship where asks like this came naturally.

"Dad," she said during a commercial. "You know I am just trying to look out for you."

"I know, but I'm an old man, I don't need a babysitter."

"Sixty is the new forty," she said. "Don't call yourself old. But also, maybe you do need a babysitter, because I don't for a second believe that you were tallying invoices. Don't make me call Richie and rat you out."

Richie, Richard. Julian's best friend from work. He already knew that Julian couldn't just let things go; they used to argue about it in the office all the time. "Your gut is not enough to waste more resources, Julian," he would call out to him at least once a month as he passed him in the hallway.

"Really, Simmy," Julian said. "I know that work nearly killed me. And I have no interest in dying anytime soon. Okay?" He had a headache building from his restless night; he had to pretend to inhabit normal human hours while Simone was staying with him, so he hadn't even had a chance to rest today.

His phone buzzed on the coffee table, and he reached for it only because he assumed it was the delivery guy. It wasn't.

"Hey, Zeke," he said, not particularly enthusiastically. Zeke had taken to FaceTiming him when Zeke was home alone, like he couldn't possibly bear the weight of his own thoughts. Sybil usually kept Zeke company in the hours when Betty had to work her shifts or when he wasn't in PT or being harangued by his management team, but Julian didn't know where Sybil was tonight. Betty was at the diner; Julian did know that.

"Zeke," Julian said to his screen. "My daughter's here, we're watching . . . what are we watching?"

"*Love Island*," Simone said without shifting her gaze from the TV.

"*Love Island*. So can I call you later?"

"Oh, your daughter the spiker?"

Julian couldn't believe that Zeke remembered Simone's college volleyball career. He was not the type Julian thought of as remembering details.

"Who's Zeke?" Simone asked, and since he had her attention for once, he made the mistake of tilting the screen toward her.

"Hey, Simone." Zeke tried to wave, but since he was holding the phone in his good hand, mostly, the screen shook.

Simone knitted her eyebrows together then moved closer to the phone, resting her hand on her dad's leg, giving him an abrupt glance, which Julian knew meant that she felt how skinny he had gotten. "Are you Zeke Rodriguez?"

"I am!" Zeke sounded delighted.

"Wait, why is Zeke Rodriguez calling my dad?" Simone grabbed the phone and was holding it with both palms now.

"Your dad didn't tell you that we are friends? Not just friends, we are *tight*."

"You and my dad are tight," Simone repeated. "Is this . . ." She glanced around. "Is this some sort of prank show?"

"Simmy," Julian said. "Zeke and I really are friends."

Her jaw slackened. "What? Come on. No you are not." She stood and spun around, truly looking for cameras.

"What can I say," Zeke said. "Your dad is awesome." For a very brief moment, Julian fell in love with Zeke and forgot why he generally found him solipsistic and annoying. "Wait, I have the best idea," Zeke continued. "You must come to Thanksgiving. I'm putting together a big feast, and Simone, your dad has told me all about what a superstar player you are, and so I insist that you come."

"You told Zeke Rodriguez about my college career?" Simone reminded Julian now of who she was as a teenager. The edges of her mouth tilted up, as if she didn't want to smile in her father's presence, but also, she couldn't help it. Also, she had perfectly straight, perfectly white teeth, a smile that Julian had paid through the roof for, and his heart levitated every time he saw it. His headache was nearly forgotten just at the sight of her happiness.

"Did he tell me about your college career?" Zeke bellowed. "I can't get your old man to shut up about it."

Now Zeke was exaggerating, but Julian wasn't about to stop him. They'd had three conversations about Simone, and certainly, yes, of course, Julian was proud as hell about her spiking record and her senior year undefeated streak. But mostly Julian always preferred to listen, found that you learned much more about things that way.

"Can you rewind?" Simone said to the both of them. "And explain to me how my father, candy store proprietor of Queens, suddenly gets FaceTime calls from the best pitcher in the MLB?"

"I have to say," Zeke said, "I'm a little offended that your dad didn't tell you that he's friends with the best pitcher in the MLB. Though I have to be honest and say that my career might be over."

"Oh, your career isn't over," Simone said. "And my dad has a lot of secrets. So maybe I shouldn't be surprised actually."

"Well, you can't just say that and not tell me," Zeke replied. "You have to share at least one of his secrets."

"Zeke, can I call you Zeke?"

Zeke cackled on the other end of the FaceTime. This man got high off attention, Julian thought.

"Well, Zeke, if I knew what his secrets were, then they wouldn't be secrets, right?"

Right then, thank god, Julian's buzzer rang.

"Food is here, Zeke," Julian said. "We gotta go."

"Wait!"

"What?"

"Simone," Zeke said. "Promise me you'll come to Thanksgiving. I'll tell you all the ways your dad is cooler than you give him credit for, and you can tell me all of his secrets."

Simone raised her eyebrows and beamed.

"Okay," she said. "That's a deal."

Julian disconnected the call, an uncertain pit planting seeds in his stomach. On the one hand, he was flush with gratitude that Zeke had managed to find a way to get Simone to stick around for the week.

On the other hand, he did indeed have plenty of secrets.

23

NIGHT EIGHT

ZEKE

ZEKE HUNG UP with Julian and was thinking about it again, the moment that ruined everything. His team told him that he was a champion, that he was going to make his way back, but he suspected they were just panicking at the thought of their moneymaker hanging up his glove, and trying to keep him calm so he devoted himself to his physical therapy. But for the first time in a long time, Zeke was starting to think he was just a specimen, there for everyone else to examine, to put in a bottle and stare at. He used to love the game, the adrenaline of a perfect pitch, the high of a strikeout, the rush of a pennant series. But now he'd allowed himself to care about something other than the zip of electricity at the stadium when he took the mound, about the thirst for winning, the thirst for being the best. Now he cared about Sybil. And Julian. And Betty.

Timothy wanted him to start seeing the sports psychologist again. He'd proposed it earlier that morning under the guise of being altruistic. They were sitting in Zeke's kitchen drinking smoothies prescribed by his nutritionist, and Zeke was thinking about Sybil, who occupied the better part of his brain these days, and also if he could tame this motherfucking eyelid spasm before Timothy noticed and insisted on another medical appointment. He had pressed the top of his eye with his good hand, and Timothy had not said a word.

"Please cut the shit, Timothy," Zeke had said. "It doesn't matter if my head is on straight. My arm isn't."

"Buddy—"

Zeke suddenly realized how much he hated being called *buddy*. He and Timothy weren't buddies. Timothy worked for him. Timothy profited from him. This didn't mean that Timothy wasn't on his side. Most of the time he was. But they weren't *friends*. Timothy's retirement was fully paid for thanks to Zeke's last contract deal. There were strings attached; there were conflicting interests.

"I don't want to meet with a psychologist," Zeke said. "I don't think anything's wrong with me."

"No one said anything is *wrong* with you. That's not what she's there for."

"I don't even know if I *want* to go back, Timothy. Okay? Forget if I can. I don't know if I want to."

The blood had drained from Timothy's face. Which was precisely how Zeke knew they weren't *buddies*.

"Zeke, come on—"

The conversation came to an abrupt end when Betty rounded the corner and screeched at seeing them sitting there.

"Shoot, sorry," she said once she had settled herself. "I thought I was here alone. Not that I—I mean, it's your place, of course." She squinted at Timothy, sizing him up, then made her way to the Nespresso machine.

Timothy bugged his eyes at Zeke like he hadn't realized he was interrupting a next-morning tryst. It dawned on him just how little Timothy knew about his life. Not his game life. His *life* life. Once Timothy was out the door, Zeke apologized to Betty, in case she intuited what Timothy had been implying.

But she had just shrugged and said, "We're all just projections of what we want to show other people and what they decide to think of us, so it doesn't really matter." Which, Zeke realized later, was just a very fancy way of saying they were all liars. He didn't know what Betty was lying about, and he didn't want to consider what Sybil could be lying about. He knew he was a liar, but he hadn't pinned down about just what yet either.

"You're okay?" he had said to her. He'd noticed she was jumpier, a little more fragile, but he didn't want to pry. Didn't actually know how to pry. Zeke had gotten used to everyone asking questions of *him* but was terribly out of practice in doing it for others.

"Tired," she had replied. "Just tired."

But she'd been tired since the day they met, and Zeke was beginning to suspect that maybe Sybil was right about Betty; maybe there was more to her story. Which he didn't mind. Didn't even find all that odd. But the question that circled around him was: What was so important to Betty that she had to keep up the ruse around *him*? He wanted her to trust him. He didn't want to be to her what Timothy was to him.

Tonight, with Betty at work and Julian having disconnected the FaceTime, he felt an urgent need to convey this to Sybil. She was already so many steps ahead of him on just about everything, and he wanted to let her know that maybe he couldn't keep up at her speed, but also, he was trying to keep pace. That he was a partner, an ally, ready to stand shoulder to shoulder with her in her pursuit of solving and helping Betty.

He tugged his cell phone out of his back pocket with his left hand and texted his car service. Sybil was in the suburbs for the night, so he would just have to go to her.

24

NIGHT NINE

SYBIL

The Night Before Thanksgiving

SOMEHOW, ZEKE ENDED up staying for four days. When he first showed up on her doorstep last Friday, no small part of her felt like she was finally the heroine in her very own rom-com. She'd been watching *Unsolved Mysteries* and had just put on an anti-aging seaweed mask, which she knew, medically-speaking, did nothing to stop the onset of aging. And there was Zeke, looking too striking for his own good, with an overnight bag and a five-o'clock shadow, and yes, Sybil felt a stir of lust that she thought had disappeared from her repertoire entirely.

He said, "Hey, Syb, I need some company, can I stay the night?"

She'd raced to the bathroom to wash off her face, then dabbed on some mascara and blush because, let's be real here, and then they watched the rest of *Unsolved Mysteries* while Sybil offered her theories—"It's always the boyfriend or the husband, Zeke, always" or "The DNA match wasn't reliable back then, why haven't they rerun it, that makes no sense, maybe it's an inside job." It really never turned out to be an inside job and truly was almost always the boyfriend or husband, but Sybil liked to narrate along all the same.

"By the way," he said, "I am starting to think you're right about Betty."

She tucked her knees into her chest and turned toward him on the couch.

"That she is too alone? That she doesn't have support from her family?"

Zeke shrugged. "I can't . . . I don't know what it is. But I wanted to tell you that you looking out for her, well, I think that's a good thing." He paused. "You're better at this stuff than I am. But you're definitely right about something."

Sybil didn't think he was issuing a warning. She thought instead that he was encouraging her hands-on approach. This was a girl who needed a mother. And she was a mother who could help this girl. Still, though, you don't binge-watch four days of true crime without darker elements wedging their way into your mind. But maybe Sybil needed some fictionalized drama in her life so she could forget the real drama—her lousy husband, the empty-nesting, the extremely horny feelings she was having for the man on her couch sitting close beside her—in her life.

Indeed, there was a moment on the second night when fatigue had turned to absurdity, when Zeke said he didn't mean to stay, to take up her time if she had other things to do, and she replied, "Zeke, you're the only thing I want to do," then thought she might die—actually *die*—from her idiotic candor, but he had laughed, and said, "Don't worry, I know what you meant." Which he obviously did *not*, or else he would have either peeled off her clothes right there or made a run for the front door, depending on his own feelings. Then later, the following day, they took a walk with Pluto through the neighborhood, Pluto trouncing through fallen red and yellow leaves, the air scented with fireplaces and pinecones, and Zeke looked at her and said, "Honestly, Sybil, if I never had to go home, I'm not sure I would." Sybil had disposed of the medical bootie and was in thick-soled sneakers she thought were for retirees in Florida, but Zeke didn't seem to mind, so she laced her elbow into his good arm, and Pluto zigzagged all over the road like he was dancing and that made them both laugh, and she thought: *Maybe? Possibly? Is this something?* But he never tried to kiss her, never made a move, even that night when she was dizzy from two glasses of wine and in an apron, and he, sober because of his rehab, said, "I think I could watch you cooking a Thanksgiving meal every year for the rest of my life." She froze and found herself unable to look in his direction, and then Pluto barked at a squirrel in the backyard, and Zeke pushed back his stool at the island to investigate. They spent the next half an hour playing fetch (Zeke was a naturally good pitcher, even with his left arm), and by the time they returned, Sybil was elbow-deep in stuffing prep, and the moment had well passed. But she thought again: *Maybe? Possibly?* And tucked it away to revisit.

As the first night of his stay turned into four, Sybil made a point to check in with Betty in his absence, but she was *fine*, she kept saying over text; she was *busy*, she promised; she had a *date with a boy*, she admitted, at which Sybil immediately FaceTimed her, but Betty didn't pick up.

Zeke had shuffled out the door yesterday morning, a car service idling at the edges of her front walk, because his own family was descending for Thanksgiving. He'd said they should all come to his apartment for the holiday, but in her attempt to say no because Thanksgiving was Sybil's favorite family holiday, she unintentionally invited Zeke, and therefore Betty, and then they couldn't exclude Julian, to join them.

Tonight, just before Thanksgiving, Mark had met the twins at Penn Station, and the trio was on their way home. Sybil had reluctantly taken three Benadryls last night to finally just get a little rest so she could be composed, the mother the kids needed, for the weekend. Now she busied herself in the kitchen while she waited for them, feeling less weary but not at all rested. While she was chopping the ends off green beans with a new knife she'd ordered after the old one sliced her toe in half, the front door swung open. Pluto yelped and skittered out to the foyer. Sybil set the knife down, more careful now, and flattened her palms against her marble counter as if to ground herself, and reminded herself that honestly, she could get through anything. She was Sybil Bowman Foster, though she was thinking of dropping the Foster. She'd raised her two siblings. She was the top student at Harvard Medical School. She could make nice with Mark for a few nights while her children were home so their worlds weren't obliterated on their very first college break.

She squeezed her eyes shut, then opened them again.

Her bones were so exhausted. If she told the children the truth, if Mark permanently moved to the pied-à-terre, if she slept with Zeke Rodriguez, if she figured out what she could still do with the rest of her life, would she finally sleep?

"Hello?" Charlie called.

"Mom's probably in the kitchen," Mark said, and his voice alone tripped her nerves. She thought she wanted to kill him, but then she reconsidered and realized that actually, she didn't care enough to murder him, bury the body. Natalie had offered to help, of course, if she changed her mind.

Mom's probably in the kitchen.

Just like she always was.

Sybil eyed the knife on the counter, considering all the ways she could have instead wielded a scalpel in the operating room, or all the ways she could carve up Mark, end up on her very own episode of *Dateline*. For some reason this made her think of Betty, and a tingling portent of warning ran flush through her. She dropped the knife into its slot in the butcher block and thought, for the first time in decades, that she could still be the heroine in her own story, that she could be done with total reliability. For once, she wanted to be wholly selfish, to detonate everything before thinking it through.

Hugs were exchanged, and Sybil noted that Charlie seemed to still be growing but also could use a shower. Then, once they were settled in the kitchen and Mark had ordered a pizza and no one offered to help Sybil with tomorrow's Thanksgiving preparations, she said simply, but to the point:

"Guys, your father has been fucking his anesthesiologist. We're getting a divorce."

25

NIGHT TEN

BETTY

Thanksgiving

BETTY DIDN'T KNOW what to expect when she trudged out to Sybil's house for Thanksgiving. Growing up, her family hadn't celebrated Thanksgiving, and it wasn't like she had been invited to anyone's home for the feast in the ensuing years since she'd left. Caleb had gone to his parents' place in Maryland for the holiday, but she hadn't expected him to invite her and would have turned him down even if he had, despite promising Zeke she'd extend an invitation. They were sleeping together now, not Betty's first time, but she wasn't exactly a pro, and full admission, if Betty had been another type of girl in another type of life, maybe she would have begun to wonder what the future had in store for them. But she wasn't, so she didn't. Betty could live only from moment to moment, other than the bag of cash at Grand Central and being aware of all of her nearby emergency exits. She had to be willing to pull that lever at the first sign that she needed to.

Betty could hear voices that sounded heated through Sybil's front door, so she hovered her finger over the doorbell out of habit, trying to eavesdrop. She hadn't grown up in a house of yellers. Her father's word was the final word, and Betty couldn't dream of her mother challenging him. Levi got in his face once when he was a teenager, but that ended quickly when Levi was kicked out. But her other two brothers and Patience, no, never. Patience was the one who taught her: Avoid eye contact, keep your head low, speak softly, say yes when spoken to. Betty always assumed that Patience hated it as much as she had, but then Patience married Matthew and had no problem being a fully subservient wife to him and keeper for her father's ever-changing rules, so Betty, it turned out, had entirely misjudged her. That realization was more devastating than Patience's about-face.

Betty pushed the doorbell, and Sybil swung the door open, and for a flicker of a second, Betty thought her face was all shadow. Then there was the Sybil she knew, a smile full of teeth, cheeks perfectly blushed. Betty couldn't be sure, but she thought Sybil had gotten her highlights done in the past few days. Whatever it was, was working, like she'd shed her veil of fatigue just in the nick of time for the gathering.

"Well, don't you look gorgeous," Betty said, an entirely different person from just a few seconds ago, and stepped inside. Maybe she *was* an actor's actor. The commercial shoot had gone well; it would be airing starting next week. Natalie wanted to send her out for more. Betty had declined, but Natalie was pushy, and the money was life-changing.

"That's what happens when you leave your husband," Sybil whispered, leaning into Betty's ear. Betty could smell alcohol on her breath. "I hope you didn't hear me yelling just then. I've found that since I've stopped caring, I just say whatever the fuck I want." She pulled back and smiled. "It's wonderful. Betty, I'm telling you, it's *wonderful*."

"I thought maybe you'd started sleeping."

Sybil paused, considering it. "No, not really." She shook her head and her highlights shimmered. "But this has given me a totally different sort of comfort."

The house itself smelled delicious, like rosemary and apple cider and crackling turkey skin. Exactly what Betty imagined a bustling Thanksgiving should smell like.

"I'm sorry I didn't bring you a gift," Betty said, because she only just realized that she was empty-handed. "Also, I'm poor."

Sybil threw her head back and laughed. Something rose up in Betty again, pride, at how good she was at being a chameleon.

"I wanted to introduce you to Charlie, but since you were on a *date*"—her voice dropped low and conspiratorial—"you are going to have to tell me all the details." She reached for Betty's shoulders, hugging her tightly, which Betty had learned was part of Sybil's demonstrative display of maternal affection. So she leaned into it, absorbed it. She was playacting, yes, but also, she really did think Sybil was rooting for her. It was so highly rare that Betty had people rooting for her. She again thought of her own mother, of how when Betty's father mocked her for not knowing an immediate answer at Bible study or when he sent her home from church because she didn't look tidy enough or when he excused her from the dinner table because she didn't wait for him to be served to start eating, her own mother never said a word in her defense. Never put her daughters first. She leaned into Sybil's embrace for another second; it was something for Betty, even if it couldn't ever be everything.

Julian was loitering in the kitchen deep in thought when they made their way inside. His eyes, heavy with bags, wandered toward Betty's, and everything about him perked up.

"Betty!" She stepped toward him, and he tapped a striking young woman on the elbow. His daughter, Betty could tell just by her eyes. "This is Simone."

"Hi, Simone," Betty said. "I'm Betty. Your dad has been very kind to me." It was important to be cordial here, to blend in with the gregariousness of the spirit of the holiday. Also, much like Sybil, Betty had taken a shine to Julian, who had indeed been very kind. She could tell the truth and still keep her wits about her.

Simone raised an eyebrow and made a face as if to say she couldn't believe it, but then she smiled and said, "My dad has told me so much about you." Which made Betty's hair stand on end. She never wanted to be the star of any story.

"I heard you just shot a commercial?" Simone continued.

"Oh yes," Betty said, now itchy and claustrophobic, though surely Simone was just making conversation. "Well, yes. But I really just did it for the pay. I'm not the next . . ." She had to stop and think of a movie star, but none came to mind. "I'm not the next big thing."

"She's an *actor's actor*," Julian said with a wink.

"Is your family far?" Simone asked. "Not close enough to head home for the holiday?"

"My parents have both passed," Betty said. She always let a beat of silence fall after this admission. A proper mourning period for the conversation. "And my siblings . . ." She waved a hand. "They're all over."

Some of that was actually true. Betty didn't know where Levi was these days, though she'd tried to track him down these past few weeks. His radio silence unnerved her, and if she weren't already not sleeping, the worry probably would have kept her up all night. Early on after their dad kicked him out, they'd stayed in touch as much as was possible. She set up an email account to use at the school library's computers just for him, and he'd also left her an emergency way to reach him. But only if things were dire. They used to message back and forth every few weeks. Levi was a nomad, and he assured her she was ready to do the same, ready to leave when the opportunity arose. He was the one who taught her to be overly cautious, to look not just over her shoulder but out front and to the left and right too. **Once you leave,** he said over email, **you have to be sure that you are never dragged back.**

But once she fled Georgia in a hurry and determined to leave no trace of where she'd gone, their correspondence became even sparser and more coded. He told her in another email that she couldn't be too careful, even if it meant leaving him behind too. And she told him she never would, but it had been a few months now, and she had no idea where he was in the world, and he certainly had no idea about any of what had happened to her. Zeke, the commercial, Caleb, all of it.

Sometimes, now, at night when she couldn't sleep, she thought about Patience. What she would say to her if their paths ever crossed, what she would ask of her and if her sister's answers would ever be enough. Patience's betrayal—how easily she abandoned Betty when she bound herself to Matthew—was still the most acute. An open oozing wound, and so it really was her sister's face, not her father's, not her mother's, that Betty envisioned when she envisioned returning home, saying her piece.

"Anyway, my family is too scattered, and we weren't big on holidays," Betty said to Simone. Only Christmas, and even that was all for show for her father's benefit to gin up money for the church. Which mostly went right into his own pocket.

"Oh, well, that's too bad," Simone had said. "Though family can definitely be complicated."

"We're not complicated," Julian said, and Simone rolled her eyes, then huffed air through her nose.

"You two are lucky," Betty said. "I was never close with my dad."

She thought of being called to the altar a week before her eighteenth birthday. The empty auditorium. How her footsteps echoed as she made her way to him. Her dad telling her he'd decided that Silas, Matthew's odious brother, was meant to be her husband. God had told him. God had sent him a vision.

Maybe God forgot to tell him that everything was about to go up in flames not even a week later. Maybe God forgot to tell him that it was only a matter of time before your luck ran out.

26

NIGHT TEN

JULIAN

JULIAN SHOULD HAVE mentioned to Simone to keep things close to the vest, but he was so happy that she was willingly spending time with him that, in a rare lapse of foresight, he'd forgotten. He didn't want or need any of these people to know the dynamic of their relationship or really any of the pertinent backstory unless he was offering it himself.

"Simmy," he said in the kitchen while she and Betty were exchanging getting-to-know-yous. "Could you run to the car and get the gifts we brought? I forgot them in the back seat."

She swiped his keys and nodded. He'd taken great care with the basket for Sybil—imported chocolates, rare German gummies, marzipan flowers—though he doubted she had passed a piece of candy through her lips in decades. The other one was just a hodgepodge for the rest of them to enjoy over dessert because Julian had always hated pie, even Robin's. Even on Thanksgiving. Also, it was important that they saw him as a laconic candy store proprietor. He hadn't spent decades of his life learning how to be deep undercover without paying attention to all the smaller details of how people sized you up.

The front door swung open again, and Zeke strode in with his parents and sister, Simone trailing them, a gift basket in each hand. Zeke toted an enormous bottle of Veuve Clicquot under his good arm, resting it on the kitchen island, and proceeded to disappear into Sybil's dining room and emerge with as many champagne flutes as one hand could carry. It was interesting, Julian thought, how Zeke knew exactly where to find those. He wondered how much time the two of them were spending together and what else he didn't know.

Introductions were made, Zeke hugging Simone like they were childhood friends, so he left her in Zeke's company, to find Betty sitting in the backyard on the same chaise lounges they'd lain atop a few weeks back. The dog curled up at her feet.

"How are things? It's been a bit since we've really had a chance to catch up."

Julian hadn't seen Betty in person in over a week, too long for his liking. He'd wanted to check in, make it to the city and swing by the diner, but then Simone showed up and stayed, and he spent the time duping her into thinking everything was normal. That he was healthy, that he was sleeping, that he didn't open and close his old files several times a day, looking for any questions he'd forgotten to ask, looking for the answers he hadn't known to seek.

"Well, you know, life is absolutely wonderful. I won the lottery, met the man of my dreams, am now a major philanthropist."

"You want to be a philanthropist?"

"That's what you took from that, Julian?" Betty sighed. "No, it's fine. My life is fine."

Julian knew that she had met a boy, but Betty wasn't aware that he had kept further tabs.

"Speaking of dating—"

"Is this the part where you pretend to be my dad?" Betty stretched her legs out, and Pluto reoriented himself to rest his head on her shins.

"Well, with no family to speak of, would that be so bad? To have someone?"

"No," she said, and to her credit, Julian thought, she didn't even hesitate, didn't even flinch. She was as good as he was.

"Come on, aren't you freezing?" he said, nudging his chin toward the house.

She ignored him. "Do you think," she started, then trailed off. "Well, do you think that all of this is helping? That we'll ever actually sleep again?"

Julian thought he might literally die before he slept through the night again, but he knew what she wanted to hear. And so, with so many lies already between them, he said, "Yes, Betty. Absolutely yes."

Then before he could assess if she believed him, there was a commotion, followed by loud shouting in the living room, and they both darted up and ran inside.

27

NIGHT TEN

ZEKE

IN ZEKE'S DEFENSE, if he had full use of both of his limbs and had been better rested, he would have punched that motherfucker back. He would have dodged his fist in the first place and then flattened him onto the fancy hardwood floors that Sybil had told him, a few nights ago over chamomile tea while they were both in their pajamas, she had taken two weeks to select and now had grown to resent.

"Two weeks," she had said flatly. "Do you know how bored I must have been to obsess over such things?"

"And you were top of your class at Harvard Medical School," Zeke had said. He liked that they now had this inside joke, something only the two of them shared.

"That's going to go on my grave. My highest achievement."

"You're a very good mom," Zeke had said.

"That's true," Sybil had acknowledged, and blew on her mug. "But they're gone. And Charlie never calls, and Eloise seems to hate me even when she does call. I worry . . . I worry I may have pressured her into becoming me."

Zeke had grown too fond of her to tell her what his first coach always told him: That no one takes anything from you that you don't give them. That you don't lose a game unless you're the one who makes a mistake, and even if you're flawless, they might still get the better of you. Years later, he didn't think his coach was quite right, but also, he didn't think he was entirely wrong. Instead, Zeke reached over as she sipped her tea and squeezed her knee. When her smile met her eyes, he let his hand linger. She did that thing again: reached around, rubbed her shoulder that he knew ached, and he was close, so so close to inching nearer and offering to work the knot out, but then she stood to pour more water from the kettle. But he liked his hand there, on her knee, maybe up her back, too, as if it was something solid to hold on to when everything else around him felt so tenuous.

Tonight, Mark, the taker of what was hers, had literally just punched him in the jaw. Simone had gasped, "Not Zeke Rodriguez's face!" like that was the important part. She and Zeke had been discussing women's college sports when Zeke felt a blow and stumbled back into the stainless steel refrigerator, which, thankfully, broke his fall. Because if he had fallen on his throwing arm, already so damaged, he would have strangled Mark with his left hand alone.

"Jesus Christ, Mark!" Sybil yelled. "What is wrong with you?"

Mark was staring at his fist like he couldn't believe what he'd done, like his fist had a mind of its own, completely separate from his brain. From what Sybil had told Zeke about him, maybe this was true. Or maybe this was Mark's excuse about the whole mess he'd created in general.

"Dad! Oh my god," Eloise said.

"Holy shit," Charlie muttered, and started to leave the kitchen but then reconsidered, as if maybe he didn't want to miss his father taking another swing at the pitcher whose baseball cards he used to collect.

"Okay, okay, let's all calm down," Zeke's dad said. Zeke hadn't even introduced them yet to Julian or Betty, who had been outside. They'd barely been there for five minutes when Mark had walloped him. "I'm Daniel, Zeke's father."

"Dad—" Zeke started. He didn't need his father to treat this like a scuffle on the middle school playground, even though in many ways, that's exactly what it was.

A timer went off, and Sybil, who Zeke only now noticed was the hue of an extremely ripe eggplant, said, "Oh fucking shit, that's the turkey!"

Eloise said, "Oh my god, Mom. Dramatic?"

So Sybil snapped, "You're an adult now, Eloise. You can handle me saying 'fuck.' I say it all the time. *Fuck fuck fuck fuck fuck.*"

And Charlie started laughing so hard that Mark, who had started all of this chaos, said, "Charlie, maybe you should excuse yourself until you have calmed down."

"I don't think *he's* the one who needs to calm down," Lani interjected. God, Zeke loved his little sister.

"I don't know what got ahold of me," Mark said.

"That's not an apology," Sybil said. "That is not even in the ballpark of an apology." She was now trying to wrestle an enormous turkey out of the oven, and Zeke moved to help her out of instinct until he realized that with only one arm, he was impotent. The turkey was perilously close to teetering toward the floor when Simone stepped in. Julian had mentioned that he thought he'd been a pretty absent father, but from what Zeke could tell, he'd done a better job than he gave himself credit for.

"Well, this is an extremely exciting first Thanksgiving for me!" Betty said. Zeke hadn't even noticed her there, but Betty had a way of slipping into rooms and into conversations unnoticed.

"Wait," Eloise said. "You've never had Thanksgiving? Are you, like, not from here?"

"It's a long story," Betty said, and Zeke wondered how long a story it could actually be. Then he wondered why he didn't know this about her, how she'd been living in his apartment for over a month now, and actually, he still knew so very little about her.

"Can you two sit at a dinner table amicably?" Daniel said to Mark and his son. He really was a middle school principal. "Or is there something we need to discuss further?"

Mark was flexing his hand like he'd broken his knuckles, which, Zeke thought, was absurd. He hadn't hit him *that* hard, not that Zeke had ever been in fistfights before and not that Zeke would have minded if Mark *had* broken his knuckles. Sybil could probably swoop in and cover all of his surgeries, though Zeke was well aware this wasn't actually how it worked. But he thought it should have worked that way. There wasn't much that he thought Sybil couldn't actually do.

"I can," Zeke said. "Though I think I am owed an apology."

"Well, I just have an issue with the fact that Zeke Rodriguez is sleeping with my wife," Mark said, and this time, whatever Sybil was holding—it turned out to be a tureen of gravy—landed on the floor.

"What the actual fuck?" Charlie squealed, but not with any sort of rancor.

"Oh my god," Eloise said.

"I'm not—" Zeke started, but Sybil cut him off. He wanted to defend himself because, of course, they weren't sleeping together. But also? It's not like Zeke hadn't thought about it. It's not like Zeke hadn't thought about it *a lot*.

"Mark Foster," she snapped. "Zeke is a friend. A dear friend.

And he has been here for me while you have been busy getting *anesthetized*"—she said this like he had been getting dipped in venom—"and I won't even dignify your comments." She shook her head, and only then seemed to notice the gravy all over her seagrass runner. Her entire body slumped.

"I can make an excellent gravy," Zeke's mom said, and he smiled at her, grateful, because she could. "Don't worry, I'll take care of it."

"Oh," Sybil said. "No, I can—"

"Syb," Zeke said, knowing full well what he was doing, baiting Mark. "Stop. Let her. You've done enough. Come on, let's go sit outside, let everyone else take care of this for once."

As if on cue, Pluto bounded into the kitchen and began cleaning up the gravy with his tongue.

Zeke watched Sybil soften, relax under his gaze, even with the surrounding chaos.

"Okay." She nodded at him, then opened the freezer and grabbed a bag of peas for his jaw.

"Okay," he replied.

They slipped out the sliding glass doors as the rest of them, or at least Zeke's family and Simone, got to work doing everything that Sybil had put on herself. Zeke pulled out a chair at the outdoor table for Sybil.

"Thank you. That was very chivalrous," she said.

"You know me, ever a white knight," he replied, pressing the bag of peas against his chin.

She looked at him for a long beat and then erupted in high, staccato laughter. She laughed so hard that she had to double over to stave off a cramp, and when she finally got ahold of herself, her cheeks were tear-streaked, and then she started up all over again.

"Oh my god," she said. "I don't know if I am so tired that I'm delirious or if this is actually the funniest thing that has ever happened to me."

"This is definitely just what our forefathers envisioned at the Thanksgiving meal," Zeke said. "Chaos and fistfights."

"They all died at like, thirty-five," Sybil said. "That made marriage much easier."

"I'm thirty-four. Jesus," Zeke said. What if he'd lived in a time when he had only a year left? What if the only thing his obituary said about him was that he was once a Hall of Famer, but now all of his records had been surpassed by someone younger, better, harder-throwing, harder-working? He swore to himself that as soon as Thanksgiving was over, he was going to actually try to give a fuck about his rehab, about returning for spring training.

"And I refuse to tell you exactly how old I am," Sybil said.

"Whatever it is, I like it."

"It's old."

"It's not."

"It is." She held his gaze and heat grew in his chest.

"Did you know that Betty had never celebrated Thanksgiving?" she said. "That makes me sad. But also, isn't that . . . I don't know, odd?"

"It does seem like she's not telling us . . . everything," he replied.

"And you know that I don't do well with loose ends."

"Aren't all your unsolved true crimes loose ends?"

"Precisely," she said. "That's probably why I'm addicted. That's definitely why I can't let them go."

28

NIGHT TEN

SYBIL

AT LEAST THE night was salvaged, Sybil thought, when she, Simone and Lani were doing the dishes. Julian and Zeke were on the couch with Zeke's parents, Mark was upstairs in their bedroom, packing a suitcase since Sybil had told him she was planning on changing the locks tomorrow. Betty was at the table scowling at her phone, then abruptly stood up, still scowling, and started pacing. Sybil dried the serving plate, placed it back in the china cabinet, then moved to the dining room.

"You didn't like dinner?" she said to Betty.

"What?" Betty dropped her phone, then flipped it over so the screen faced down. "Oh, oh no, it was wonderful. Thank you so much for including me. Really."

"You just looked . . . unhappy."

"Oh, that's my face in general," Betty said, though Sybil knew this wasn't true.

"You'd tell me if something were wrong?"

"I would tell you if something were wrong," Betty said. They locked eyes, and Sybil waited for her to pick up her phone, flip it over, but she didn't. And Sybil was well aware that she had watched too many shows, listened to too many podcasts, but also, she felt certain that Betty didn't want her to see what she had been reading or typing. Based on nothing. *Nothing!* Sybil reminded herself. She had no reason to be suspicious of Betty or think she was in trouble. She just, she told herself, needed someone to mother, and Betty was someone who needed to be mothered.

"Okay, well, here if you change your mind," Sybil said, and retreated to the kitchen. She felt Betty's gaze as she went, then pretended she'd forgotten something in the pantry and noticed Betty still staring, her phone still down, as if she was waiting to be sure that Sybil really was intending to leave her alone. Or maybe Sybil was just seeing what she wanted. Maybe Sybil was tired of the mundanity of this house, of washing the dishes, of making the green beans, of worrying about her children, of all of it. Maybe this whole thing, The Insomniacs, her crush on Zeke, her suspicious curiosity of Betty, was all just a midlife crisis of boredom.

She wandered to the back patio, where the late fall air smelled like damp leaves and woodburning stoves.

Eloise's and Charlie's heads were dipped together on a shared lounger by the far side of the pool, excavating the candy basket Julian had brought.

"Can I join you?" she asked, then pulled up a chair before they answered.

"Charlie ate all the gummy bears," Eloise said, because those had always been Sybil's favorites.

"I probably deserve that after I dropped a bombshell last night—about divorcing," Sybil said. "And I'm sorry that your dad punched Zeke."

"I wouldn't say our first twenty-four hours at home have been uneventful," Charlie said.

"I'm not sleeping with Zeke," she said.

"I mean, obviously," Eloise said.

Sybil winced.

"Mom, he's Zeke Rodriguez," Charlie said.

"Well, anyway. I'm also sorry that you had to come home to this. To Dad and me. I think . . ." She felt both of them staring at her, undivided attention, like they were toddlers again, and it was story time. And her heart so acutely seized, for how much she loved them, despite the simultaneous fact that their arrival upended everything. "I think that Dad and I were a good match for some things and a less good match for other things, and we did a really good job parenting you. But it shouldn't have exploded at Thanksgiving."

"If we're saying truthful things, I should probably tell you that I went to the registrar and dropped premed," Eloise said.

"You *what*?" Sybil jumped to her feet.

"Oh shit, El," Charlie said.

"You knew about this?" Sybil turned to Charlie.

"Well, yeah. But so did Dad." He was unwrapping a Tootsie Roll and at least had the humility to stop and rest it in his lap while Sybil nearly detonated.

"Your father knew about this?"

"Mom, calm down," Eloise said. "I have a plan. You don't get to control my life. Or my choices. Or like, yeah, any of that."

Sybil wanted to scream that if she could just, like, calm down, then she would. *About everything.* But she couldn't. She hadn't been calm for forty-six years. How exactly was she expected to act calm now? Did Eloise think that pointing out that Sybil couldn't control her own children at this stage actually *calmed her down* at all?

Before she could say any of this—threaten Eloise with withholding her college tuition or guilt her over lost potential—Betty slipped out the back door and glanced around. Then she held her phone to her ear and disappeared around the side of the house.

"One second," Sybil said as she stood. "And, Eloise, we're not done with this conversation."

"I mean, we are, but okay. You're not in charge of me anymore."

Sybil huffed and trailed the rim of the pool toward where Betty had gone. She didn't want to be a snoop, but there was something so furtive in Betty's body language that Sybil told herself that she was just . . . curious. If Betty was weathering a crisis that Sybil could help with, well. She slowed and tiptoed as she got closer.

"Levi, hey, it's me. I'm know I'm not supposed to use this number, that I'm breaking a rule, but I haven't heard back in a while. Did you get my message a few weeks ago? I don't even . . . I don't even know where you are."

Sybil could see Betty in the half-light of the side lantern. She was pacing and chewing on a fingernail, and she looked so young but also so hardened. It wasn't fair, Sybil thought, that both parents had died before Betty had a chance to rely on them as a young adult.

"I had my first Thanksgiving tonight. At my friend Sybil's. I guess I was wondering if you had Thanksgiving too," Betty was saying. "If you get this, please call. Anytime. I don't sleep, so even if it's late your time. I'll pick it up. I just . . ."

Sybil stepped on one of Pluto's squeaky toys, and Betty paused. Sybil panicked and raced toward the twins, arriving at the back of the pool just in time to sink into a chair and see Julian pop his head out of the back door. He scanned the yard slowly, cocking his head like Pluto when he was really trying to decipher what Sybil was saying.

When he heard whatever he was listening for, he straightened out, then headed toward the side of the house where Betty had absconded to. Sybil watched him in the muted patio lights stand exactly where she had just moments ago, clearly eavesdropping. Why would Julian eavesdrop on Betty? Maybe Sybil had been pointing her suspicions at the wrong person. Maybe Betty was just Betty; maybe Julian was the one hiding something.

She could almost hear the narrator's voiceover leading into the commercial break.

Julian turned around quickly and scurried back inside, and not a moment later, Betty emerged. She took a deep breath and stared up toward the black November sky. Then she composed herself and dipped back into Sybil's house, while Sybil tried to convince herself that she wasn't witnessing her friends trying to prevent their secrets from spilling over.

29

NIGHT ELEVEN

JULIAN

December 3rd

THE APARTMENT WAS so quiet without Simone. The filter from the fish tank bubbled, somewhere from atop a cabinet Felix meowed, and the rest of it was a silent dead void. She promised to return for Christmas, and in exchange, Julian promised to leave his old work alone.

"Dad, you quit for a reason," she had said as she was zipping up her suitcase.

Yes, he had. Because after thirty years, the stress of the job literally seized his heart. But four years later, he was finding that the boredom of ordinary life was its own sort of death. Was he meant to run his late wife's candy store for the next decade until he retired to a condo near Simone in Chicago?

"Stop worrying about me," he had said, and hugged her too tightly by the front door. "It's my job to worry about *you*."

"But if I don't," she said, "who will?"

"Sybil and Zeke and Betty."

"So you're telling me there's a reason to worry?"

Julian had laughed, a distraction, and ushered her down to a taxi.

Now it was midnight again, and he was doing the exact thing that he'd promised Simone he wouldn't. He closed out of one tab, then another, pushed his shoulders back in his chair and stretched. He was missing something, his gut told him that much. But what it was, he had no idea. He needed to start over at the beginning.

He opened his desk drawer, pulled out a file that he'd taken with him when he retired.

He didn't even need to look at the pictures taken from the fire; they were embedded into his brain. He ran his fingers over the glossy shots, going inch by inch in case there was some detail that he misremembered or never initially saw. The fire department had been well over thirty minutes away, and the sprinklers in the building never activated. When he and Richard, his partner, asked around, it turned out the sprinklers had been broken for two years—everyone in the senior ministry knew about it—but no one bothered to fix them. *We thought we were protected here,* he remembered a parishioner, in a head covering and a long dress despite the heat of the summer, saying. *We thought God would protect us here.* The man she was standing with looked toward her, his eyes glazed, his mind filled with nonsense, Julian thought, and the man said, *Maybe he did, maybe this was just God's way of showing us a different path.*

He and Richard were in the anti-corruption unit, so they were called in when something went awry with a case they'd been watching from afar. And they had been watching Pastor Aaron from afar. The air that night had been still so thick with ash residue that it nearly choked Julian, and later Richard suggested maybe whatever they were inhaling had led to Julian's heart attack. Like an Erin Brockovich situation, he had said. It was a naïve thought, no different from what that woman's husband had said. Julian's heart had been giving out for years, since Robin died.

He reread his notes from the scene.

> Pastor Aaron Jones presumed dead—last seen on-site. Recovery of his wife's body confirmed. Explosion from unknown source started in the boiler room near the kitchen and raced out of control (*Accelerant? Arson? Electrical issue?), taking down the chapel, then half of the main building, within minutes. Several unidentifiable bodies at morgue. Too charred, waiting on dentals. Youngest daughter, Elizabeth, has not been located.

He reviewed the asterisks. They'd never pinpointed what started it. The church wasn't up to code and hadn't been subjected to an inspection in years. There weren't any obvious signs of arson, but then the executive board of the ministry wasn't particularly interested in answers to begin with. Richard argued that a dead Aaron Jones was honestly better than an alive Aaron Jones.

"Seriously, come on, man, you know that," Richard had said, running his foot through the soot by the coroner's van. "These doomsday cultists, I mean, one fewer of them in the world isn't the worst thing."

"Right," Julian had said, nodding. "But that doesn't mean that murder isn't murder. Arson isn't arson. We still do have jobs to do."

"You know that they basically marry women into enslavement, right?"

"I do, but does that mean that we just condone murder?"

Richard shrugged. He'd always been a little less by the book than Julian, which was actually what made them a great team. "Maybe it was. I don't think I'd blame someone. From what I've gleaned, they were about one step away from that Nike cult who all took a permanent nap. You know, Heaven's Gate." He cleared his throat and spit on the dirt. "Or Waco. Take your pick. Good riddance."

Regardless, no one was talking, and within a week, there were three dead bodies in the Hudson River, and Julian and Richard were told to focus their energies there since it was a suspected mob hit, and they'd been shadowing the ringleader for the better part of a year. Their report on the church fire cited electrical issues, and Julian pretended to make peace with the loose ends. But Julian had never been someone who made peace with loose ends.

He flipped to another photo.

Aaron Jones with his wife and five children.

They found his watch, his wedding band, matching DNA at the scene. It wasn't unreasonable that he was burned to ash and dust like 60 percent of the building; they'd seen that before in fireballs. But it also wasn't unreasonable to think that he hadn't been. And Julian believed in his bones that he hadn't been.

He held his thumb and pointer finger in a loop, moving from face to face to face.

He stayed there for a long time, his fingers circling Aaron Jones's youngest, who was unsmiling, discontent.

He couldn't believe his luck when he tracked her down a few months back, so close to him. At a diner on the Upper West Side. Elizabeth. Betty.

What had she been thinking about when this photo was taken? What was she thinking about now? And more important, when should he tell her what he knew?

30

NIGHT ELEVEN

BETTY

BETTY STILL HADN'T heard back from Levi despite leaving him another message after Thanksgiving. She'd tried emailing him, but it had gotten bounced back. In the past, whenever he had dumped an email address, he'd always let her know the new one. That he still had the same phone number was a miracle. The old phone they used to communicate was dead on her end; she'd lost the charger in the move to Zeke's, hadn't had time to track one down at some outdated electronics store somewhere in the outer boroughs since she didn't trust ordering from the internet. So she had to keep hoping *hoping hoping* that he would answer her calls from her cell.

Her phone buzzed in her back pocket, so she wiped her hands on a dish towel after bussing a table and grabbed it. Every time it vibrated these days, her cortisol skyrocketed. She had to find a way to calm down. She had to find a way to calm down even if she didn't hear back from Levi. She just didn't know how to do that. Maybe this was what your body just did when it hadn't gotten the rest it demanded; maybe it just stopped differentiating between the red flags and the white ones. Levi had been the first of them to get out, and when she fled two years later, when she was given that very small window of time to run in the backdrop of the chaos of the fire, she'd always felt protected because he'd been able to do it too. Now? Everything felt unsteady. Everything was a bright blood-red flag.

The text was from Natalie. False alarm for panic. A link to the cut of her laundry detergent commercial. Betty pressed play and watched a different version of herself bike down a Manhattan street and get splashed with fake mud. She wondered if anyone who knew her before would recognize her now. Maybe not. Maybe she could pull this off unscathed.

Looks amazing!! Natalie had said.

Then: Next Wednesday at 3:30pm. Tampon commercial audition. She'd included the address. Pay will be 25k+.

Betty's heart nearly stopped right there by the diner's dishwasher. She knew that she couldn't keep risking exposure, but twenty-five grand meant that she could disappear forever. To a nice little island in the Caribbean where she could subsist off mango and coconut and work at a fish shack. It was beside the point that she didn't know how to swim, or that she had never boarded a plane before. Permanent freedom was so close she could feel it at her fingertips. She was well aware that she was growing increasingly attached to Zeke, to Sybil, to Julian and even to Caleb. She thought that would just be sex, inexperienced as she was, but it turned out that she actually really liked him. But the really-liking-him part was the problem. Really liking all of them was the problem, the problem that Levi had always warned her about. **If you're going to do this,** he'd written over email a few days after she'd thrown a few necessities into her backpack, grabbed the secret stash of money from their pantry and raced through the woods on her bike to the next town over, **everything but staying undetected needs to be disposable.**

For the past two months, she admittedly had grown used to her setup with Zeke. She liked his apartment for obvious reasons—its thermostat set at a very pleasant seventy-two, the way the fridge was always restocked seemingly by a genie, the cotton percale sheets that felt like she was at a five-star resort. If she'd ever been to a five-star resort, which she had not.

Her parents had once hosted a retreat at the Greenbrier in West Virginia. She hadn't been invited, though Patience, her husband, and her oldest brothers, Noah and Jacob, went along because they were adults by then and part of the whole thing. Patience's husband, Matthew, had wormed his way into her father's inner circle, possibly the heir apparent, despite Noah and Jacob being the obvious picks. Betty thought her dad liked the sick thrill of the three of them fighting harder and harder for his approval. But anyway, the Greenbrier. For a long time, Betty thought maybe she imagined the memory of her mother packing her father's suitcase while he read her the agenda of the retreat—something about loyalty tests, charitable donations, baptisms and blood oaths, which Betty thought she must have misunderstood. But in the ensuing years, she'd digest that she heard everything exactly correctly. She'd just been taught to question herself so often that she doubted her memory in so many ways. Once she got to New York, a coworker at the Bloomingdale's perfume counter went on and on about a boy she'd been dating who was a "*total gaslighter*," and Betty, in her naïveté, had thought this meant that he, like, blew things up. Which set her hair on end for obvious reasons. When she asked her coworker if that was okay, someone who was into arson, her coworker had giggled and explained what she actually meant.

Oh dear, Betty remembered thinking, *that was my entire childhood.*

Tonight, she sighed and put the audition into her calendar. *Twenty-five thousand dollars.* Even Levi would agree that some risks were worth taking.

Awesome, thank you for thinking of me! she typed back to Natalie. I won't let you down!

The bell clanged from the front door, and she hastily tucked her phone into her apron, grabbed some menus that weren't too sticky and pushed out to the front.

"Surprise!" Caleb was standing by the hostess stand, wrapped in a gray scarf and navy pea coat and looking like an actual L.L.Bean model. He didn't know that of all the things Betty hated in life, surprises were number one. "I skipped off of work early, grabbed a bottle of wine and thought I'd join you."

"It's midnight," she said, and hoped her voice wasn't shaking. Her blood was pounding furiously in her ears. Betty had trained herself for no surprises, *ever,* even innocuous ones like this.

"Exactly! Do you know how rare it is for me to ditch work by midnight on a Wednesday?" Caleb worked in finance in some sort of job that Betty didn't even pretend to understand. She knew he made boatloads of money and worked grueling hours, which meant he was available only in limited gulps and for expensive meals. It suited Betty perfectly.

The diner was totally empty, so she couldn't think of a reason he shouldn't stay.

"We only have screw-top wine," she said, gesturing at the bottle. "I don't think I have anything to open that."

"I was a Boy Scout," he said, and pulled a corkscrew from his pocket. "I always come prepared."

Something about her look must have given her away, that she had no idea what he was talking about.

"That was our motto," he said. "Boy Scouts always come prepared. Your brothers weren't ever scouts? Or you were never a Brownie? Oh my gosh, my sisters were so competitive over cookie sales."

"No," she said, and she heard herself. Clipped, tense. "They were never Boy Scouts."

"Oh, well, all right, it actually was pretty nerdy. Don't judge me."

She liked this about Caleb, how he defused her live wire of tension. She thought about how in elementary school, a few girls in her homeroom were Brownies. How envious she was when they wore their uniforms, when they had badges on their sashes. She asked Patience about it once, if she had gotten to do that when she was Betty's age, and Patience looked horrified.

"Don't ever mention that to Mom or Dad," she'd whispered when they were in bed that night.

"Okay but—"

"No, just don't, okay? I asked once. It's not worth it."

Patience didn't have to elaborate. Betty was only seven or eight, but she well knew by then that her dad was mercurial, nearly dangerous. For a period back then she thought her mother could protect her, but later she'd learn that was as delusional as thinking she could join the Girl Scouts.

"Anyway, there's that girls' group at the church," Patience had said, before rolling over and turning her back on Betty. "That's why Dad started it. To give girls something like that. But for our own kind. He lets me lead the baking classes now, which is sort of like science, so it's not so bad, it's pretty good."

Tonight, Betty seated Caleb at a booth by the window, the

one that Zeke, Sybil and Julian had opted for the very first night she met them.

"I'll go get some mugs," she said. "We don't really have wineglasses."

"And bring me your very best saltines."

Betty had once told him the only thing she'd trust to eat there were the soup crackers. That he remembered this felt like a small gift. Almost no one remembered anything about Betty, which was exactly as she designed it, and she knew, she really did, that she couldn't want more. But what if she did?

She thought of Levi. Of Patience. Of Noah. Of Jacob. Of how she hid her bike in the woods because it was pitch black out, then walked into town and bought a bus ticket to Charleston with cash. Of how she lingered on the edge of the tree line for a long minute, standing in the shadows, and watched the fire grow from something terrifying to something beautiful. From Charleston, she made her way to Charlotte, eventually settling for a beat in Baltimore.

What if now she wanted more?

No, *no*.

More was dangerous. More was reckless.

If only that were enough to stop her from wanting it.

31

NIGHT ELEVEN

ZEKE

ZEKE WAS SO sore that he couldn't move off his (ridiculously oversized, he could see now) couch. He understood grueling, but he hadn't really understood *grueling* until he started physical therapy in earnest with his three surgeries out of the way. His trainer's neck was the size of Zeke's thigh, and that was pretty much all he needed to say to Sybil to give her an indication of what he was up against.

"And he has a tattoo of a tiger on it, on his neck," Zeke moaned. "In case you need a clearer picture."

For the first time since high school, he'd gotten semi–out of shape during the off-season, and now the team and *his* team were determined to rehabilitate him in time for spring training. No matter that the doctors were no closer to promising him that he'd make the comeback. But surgically, there wasn't much else to do. Either he got it back or he didn't. Modern medicine wasn't going to be the answer. No matter that sleep was literal recovery time, when his body was meant to stitch its seams back together, and without it, he simply couldn't heal in the ways his team anticipated.

Sybil was straightening up the living room, though there really wasn't much to straighten. But Zeke knew her well enough now to know that she needed to keep her hands busy, needed to keep her mind busy actually. She moved on to the couch cushions holding a Dustbuster that Zeke was pretty sure she'd brought from her own house. She lifted one pillow, zoomed under it, lifted another. When she got to the last one, she stopped, hunched over and picked up something small and silver.

"Is this yours?"

"What is it? I can't see it from here." Zeke could have scooched closer, but honestly, his whole body was screaming. He envisioned his fibrous muscles wrestling with his tendons, all of them squabbling while being flooded with lactic acid. Why had he chosen this as a profession again? *Because it was the only thing you were ever good at,* his brain replied.

Sybil walked around the coffee table and stood in front of him. She was holding a small silver key.

"No, that's not mine," Zeke said. "I've never seen it before."

"It looks like one of those diary keys that Eloise had in middle school."

"Yeah, I don't keep a diary," Zeke answered. "So definitely not mine."

"Maybe from a locket?" Sybil sat next to him, and the pillows shifted to accommodate her. She was wearing just a lilt of perfume tonight. Enough so that his olfactory nerves caught the scent and nearly made him feral wanting more. Wanting to inhale it, wanting to inject it straight into his veins.

"I don't have a locket either," he laughed. "Wait, maybe it's Lani's? Let me text her."

Lani had stayed for a few days after Thanksgiving to make

sure that he was steady on his feet. It meant that he had gone the whole weekend pretending that he slept through the night and wasn't as emotionally wrecked as she had suspected. It also meant that he went the whole weekend without seeing Sybil. When she showed up tonight shortly after Betty left for her shift, he relaxed, uncoiled, as if she infused him with joy in the same way that his nutritionist infused him with a vitamin IV. Sybil was a type of vitamin IV.

He snapped a picture and texted it to his little sister.

She wrote him back within a minute. Not mine.

Then: You get your head on straight?

They'd had an argument before she left—Betty was out so she couldn't overhear, and they used their full voices—about how privileged he was, to be born with a rocket of an arm, to make boatloads of money, to take all of it for granted. He'd snapped at her that he didn't take it for granted, not a single second. What he wanted to say was that it was the opposite: *He resented that this all came so easily to him.* That he hadn't ever considered another option. But now, with the air diffused from their fight, maybe she was right. Maybe he didn't have it in him anymore to fight for his career. Not just his career. His legacy. Maybe all he needed was to sit on this couch next to Sybil. Forever.

"It must be Betty's," Sybil was saying. She stood and turned to wait for him.

"I don't think I can get up."

She offered him a hand, and he held out his good one, linked their fingers, and she hoisted him to his feet. He groaned like a wounded bear, but she just said, "Come on, we're snooping in her room." He liked that about her too: She was soft when she needed to be but also knew that Zeke couldn't be coddled. Not if he was going to make a comeback. And probably not if he wasn't going to either.

Betty's room was neat as a pin. The bed was made with nary a wrinkle, all the throw pillows aligned symmetrically. Zeke noticed she'd bought a candle that was still in the box on the bureau, but there were no other personal touches, nothing to differentiate the room from how it had been two months prior, before she moved in. Not a picture frame of her family; not a discarded scarf or glove on the accent chair in the corner.

"Wow," Sybil said. "I'd kill for Eloise or Charlie to be this neat."

Now that Zeke thought about it, Betty never left a thing out of place. Her water glass was handwashed and placed back in the cabinet, her coffee mug the same.

"It's as if she doesn't want to be a disturbance," he said. Sybil clicked her tongue in either agreement or disagreement, she didn't say.

Sybil opened the top bureau drawer.

"Oh, I don't think we should—" Zeke said, but she waved a hand, cutting him off.

"I'm just poking around."

"And you think we need to find her diary? Or her locket? For . . . ?" His voice tilted up in the form of a question.

Sybil closed the top drawer, opened the middle. Closed the middle, then opened the bottom. She spun around, glanced at all the corners of the room.

"Sybil, you can't read her diary, you know," Zeke said.

"I know," she said. "She just won't answer any of my questions. I just want to *know* her. So I can help her."

"Maybe she has her reasons," Zeke said. "And maybe she thinks she's telling you enough."

Sybil sighed. "You're right. You're right." She shook her head. "I think I've watched too many *Datelines*."

"Well, that is definitely true," Zeke said, grinning. "Come on, how about Sudoku? I'll let you win."

"I win anyway."

"Okay, but we can pretend that I'm letting you win."

Sybil laughed and made her way to the living room. Zeke lumbered behind her. The only distraction from his pain was when he noticed when Sybil tucked the key into her front pocket, as if she had claimed it as her own.

32

NIGHT TWELVE

SYBIL

December 10th

SYBIL KNEW SHE had seen a key before like the one she'd found in the couch last week. She just couldn't remember where. It was infuriating, she thought on her way home from Zeke's the next morning, that her brain was so muddled. She could take more Benadryl, numb herself to sleep, but that wouldn't fix the root cause, and Sybil, unlicensed doctor, needed to uncover the root cause. Back in suburbia, she'd tried the key in all of Eloise's jewelry boxes—why did her daughter have so many jewelry boxes?—then went into the garage and found Eloise's old diaries, and it wasn't the right fit for any of them. She could have just asked Betty if it were hers, and if so, of course just returned it no questions asked, but honestly, she didn't want to. Here was another puzzle to solve. Here was *her* puzzle to solve.

Tonight, she, Zeke and Julian had decided to decorate the Christmas tree in Zeke's apartment. Sybil had grown up with parents who didn't believe in religion though they were technically Jewish, so didn't have a tree in her house regardless.

When she married Mark, she made a big show of the holiday for the kids—wreaths on every door, a tree so tall they needed a ten-foot ladder for the star, Christmas music starting on December first, a menorah and latkes the first night of Hanukkah, which then tapered off by the fifth night because eight nights felt like a lot, even for a supermom. But this year, for obvious reasons, her heart wasn't in it. After the Thanksgiving debacle, Charlie was going skiing with some fraternity brothers, and Eloise was coming home, albeit begrudgingly, and albeit at the very last minute just a few days before Christmas. Mark? Well, she'd hired Natalie's lawyer, and they'd communicated only through her at an ungodly expensive hourly rate.

"I've never actually done this myself before," Zeke said as he stepped back to assess their work. "I've always just hired someone, and I'll leave for the day and return, and it's done." He cringed as he said it, and Sybil started to reassure him, but he said, "God, that sounds awful. Maybe I used to be awful. Holy shit, I think I actually was awful."

It had been Sybil's idea for the three of them to gather. Four, if you included Betty, but something grave washed over Betty's face when Sybil proposed it, like decorating a tree was bringing up the grief of losing her parents, and besides, Betty said, she had to work. Sybil thought of the key, which she had placed on the kitchen counter earlier that evening, and she wondered what else Betty had locked away. She noticed that when she returned to the kitchen to mull some cider, the key—unsurprisingly or maybe surprisingly—was gone.

"Did you have a favorite ornament growing up?" Sybil asked Betty before her shift started. Sybil was attempting to untangle the tree lights that she'd found in a box that Zeke's assistant had delivered from storage. She should just leave it alone with Betty, not scratch the itch that there was something, maybe a lot of things, that Betty wasn't telling her. Perhaps it was simply the residual pain of being an orphan. Whatever it was though, Sybil felt an urgent, compelling need to know. She frequently told Natalie not to be a town gossip, and yet once Natalie started sharing all the lurid dirt, Sybil would pour herself a coffee and pull up a chair. This really wasn't any different. The knowing she shouldn't and the doing it anyway.

Betty shook her head. "No, I was the youngest."

"The youngest doesn't get to have a favorite ornament?"

Betty shrugged before making an excuse that she had to get ready for work. "The youngest of five doesn't really have much say at all."

Zeke's arm was beginning to heal, so Sybil put him to work, hanging the ornaments on the top half of the tree. He moaned a bit and complained—he was too tired, too sore, and wanted to plop on the couch, but Sybil knew he needed a nudge. Besides, they were *all* tired; you couldn't just stop your life for that, give in to fatigue like it was gravity. And as much as she wanted him for herself, she worried that he was getting too complacent, too easily willing to abandon a Hall of Fame career because the road back was arduous. She'd mentioned it last night, and for the first time since they'd met on the Insomniacs forum, an undercurrent of disagreement ran between them.

"Sybil, I'm not one of your kids," he had said. "I don't need you to push me into a direction. I have plenty of other people who are already doing that." She saw his eyelid spasm and wanted to tell him that she noticed these things, she saw him in ways that others didn't.

"I'm not—that's not what—" she stuttered. Because that was what she was doing. But also, he needed it. He just didn't see that he needed it. But she did! "I just don't want you to sit around with me and piss this recovery away."

Her ears burned red as soon as she said it. He wasn't just *sitting around with her.* Like she should flatter herself. Like he was giving up a career to hang out on his oversized couch with Sybil Bowman Foster. She knew he enjoyed her company, and she very well knew that she more than enjoyed *his* company, but they hadn't discussed that yet, if they were ever going to discuss it at all. Sybil felt like a middle schooler, trying to read his signals, trying to send her own signals back, uncertain if any of it was being decoded correctly.

"Sybil," he sighed, then started to speak, then stopped. She wanted to retract it, to say of course he wasn't just sitting around with her, but she was worried she would say something even dumber. Sybil almost never said spectacularly stupid things—in fact, it was her specialty, always knowing just what to say—and yet with Zeke, it happened all the same. If he mentioned it, she would blame *her* exhaustion. It was a perfectly reasonable excuse. Finally, he said, "Sybil, I know that you mean well, but the choices I'm making here . . . the decisions . . . I don't mean to be rude, but they're mine to make. Okay? It's much more complicated than just doing the physical therapy, just grinding it out. I might do all of that and still not recover. I might do all of that and recover and never be as good as I once was. I might be as good as I once was and not want it anymore."

"I know but—"

"Actually, you don't know, okay? You don't."

"Zeke, I'm just trying to help."

"But you're *not,*" he snapped. "You *can't.*"

He stood up and went to his room, closing the door. Sybil waited for him to emerge, but eventually, when he didn't, she made her own way to the guest room, tried her usual stretches to soothe her weary back, and was still awake when she heard Betty come in from her shift. This morning, they had each pretended that it never happened, Sybil organizing the tree trimming, Zeke stumbling out to physical therapy with Timothy yammering his ear off about endorsement deals.

Tonight the tree was nearly done, and it was spectacular. Gold and silver and swirling white lights. Just before Zeke did the honors to illuminate the room, Julian's phone buzzed. He swiped at his home screen, and a scowl washed over his face.

"Excuse me," he said, then disappeared around a corner.

"Should I—" Zeke asked, his hand on the remote control.

"Let's wait," Sybil replied. "It's sort of a miracle that we got him to participate, right? Let's not blow the big moment without him."

Zeke nodded, and so they waited. Minutes ticked past, and eventually, Zeke dropped the remote on the coffee table and flopped onto the oversized couch, and Sybil wanted to sit right next to him, to fold her feet—her pierced foot now fully healed but for a scar—onto his lap, to rest her head on his shoulder. Instead, she sank onto the opposite side, placed her socked feet up on the coffee table.

"This couch is so comfortable," Sybil sighed. "Maybe we need to try sleeping out here."

"Oh," Zeke said. "I used to. I mean, not sleep. But I'd try. Nothing helped."

Sybil dipped her neck back against the cushion and closed her eyes. Maybe Zeke was wrong. Maybe the couch could be the answer to everything. Maybe she was delirious though.

"You think we should check on him?" Zeke asked, breaking their silence.

Before Sybil could rise to go do so, she heard a door open down the hall, then Julian was in front of them, looking, well, Sybil had never seen him quite like this, looking a little frantic.

"Are you okay?" she said. "Here, come sit."

"I have to go," he replied, clipped, sharp.

"You can't stay for cider? We haven't even lit the tree up yet."

"No," he said, turning his back toward her, heading to the foyer in search of his coat. "Something has come up."

Sybil jumped to her feet and trailed him.

"Is it Simone?"

"No."

"Can I help?"

"Sybil," he said to her in a tone she had never heard. Serious in a way that was even more serious than Julian usually sounded. "I say this respectfully, but you cannot help. You cannot fix everything, you cannot roll up your sleeves on every matter. Okay? Do you hear me?"

Sybil's cheeks flushed. She didn't dare meet Zeke's eyes either. She nodded. "I was just trying to be—"

"I know what you were trying to be," Julian said. "Not all of us need to be rescued."

He spun the door handle, and then he was gone.

33

NIGHT TWELVE

JULIAN

JULIAN HADN'T MEANT to rip Sybil's head off, but he didn't have time to worry about her, and he certainly didn't have time to protect her feelings. He was in work mode, despite his promises to Simone, and fuck it, the adrenaline coursing through him made him feel alive. The best he had since his heart attack. Everyone got it wrong, he thought. He shouldn't have retired and become a genteel candy store proprietor. That was actually doing him more harm than the Bureau had. He'd been good at one thing his whole life, and it was chasing leads and closing cases. He was a fool to think that idling for the past four years was the key to a healthy heart.

There wasn't any service in Zeke's elevator, so he waited and waited as he ticked down the twenty-nine floors, stopping twice for two different dogs and their owners. As soon as they hit the lobby, he raced outside, his jacket still unbuttoned, his hands and head exposed to the elements. The temperature had dipped precipitously since he'd been inside. The wind was kicking up, the air smelled of snow. He turned uptown to flag a taxi, and his fingers were nearly numb within a minute.

The streets were dead, as if everyone had heeded the incoming storm warning but him and those few dog owners making a last-minute run before the snowdrifts piled up.

"Shit, shit, shit," he said to himself, his breath a foggy plume around him. The CVS on the corner was open, so he ducked inside, the artificial heat an immediate reprieve. He should call Richard. But it was midnight, and Richard had remarried, had stepped into a different position within the Bureau, and now had little kids at home. Julian had given him such hell when he became a father again in his fifties. Richard had given him hell for having a heart attack at the same time that Richard was learning to swaddle a newborn all over again.

He'd call Richard tomorrow, first thing.

The cashier was eyeing him, probably wondering what this worried-looking Black man was doing loitering in the front of the store. He nodded at her, then made his way through the aisle. Grabbed a few necessities and a Coke because it might be a long night. He needed to be delicate about what happened next. He didn't know who might be watching. But he did know that there was a tipping point between being careful and being paranoid, and he would step right to the precipice and not tilt over it.

He paid, the cashier not making eye contact, and wished her a wonderful evening. Outside now, the snow was dumping like God had turned on a hose. The sidewalks were damp and turning slippery, and he nearly landed on his back more than once, stopping his fall by grasping a parking meter. There was a man in a heavy parka, hood up, right behind him, and Julian froze for a moment, wondering if the man was too close, wondering if he had gotten sloppy. He'd been meticulous in the years since retirement, obscuring his name on internet forums, being sure to leave no fingerprints anywhere he went. He knew how dangerous this dance was. But then the man passed by and rounded a corner, and Julian eased his grip on the parking meter and blessedly dipped into the subway station on the corner unscathed.

The train was delayed because the trains were always delayed. Fifteen minutes later, the red line screeched to a stop, and he stepped into a mostly deserted car. A few people loitered at the other end, but Julian sat in the far corner and opened his phone one more time. Just to be sure.

There was no doubting it: There, in his text, discovered in a forum in the dark bowels of the internet, was a photo of Betty at Grand Central. In the months since he had tracked Betty down, Julian had paid a source to keep an eye out online, suspecting it would be money well spent. *Slow and steady, have patience*—he'd learned that at Quantico. And here it was: Someone was looking for her, someone was hunting her. Julian was pretty sure he knew who. He pulled out a pad of paper from the CVS bag, uncapped a Sharpie pen with his teeth. This was the most he could do for now, until he figured out more. Until he figured out not just the who, but the why. Until he could tell Betty who he really was, why he was really watching. He couldn't spook her now, not when he had finally gotten close and earned a small bit of trust. This would have to do.

In dark black permanent ink, he wrote: ***RUN***.

34

NIGHT TWELVE

SYBIL

IT WAS PAST two in the morning when Sybil's phone buzzed. She and Zeke had abandoned Sudoku to watch *Home Alone*, "the greatest holiday movie ever," according to Zeke. Sybil had popped popcorn, and they were sharing a blanket on his couch with their feet touching. The Christmas tree lit up the darkened room, and it was, well, perfect. Everything about it was perfect, or would have been if they had been better rested. Still, Sybil felt a little bit like she was in high school, though she hadn't dated all that much in high school because she was so type A and also busy micromanaging her siblings while her parents ascended the corporate ranks. Then her phone rang.

Zeke hit pause. "You can take that."

She glanced at her screen. The only people she would interrupt this moment for were Eloise or Charlie. Possibly Betty too. She didn't recognize the number. A 312 area code.

"Middle-of-the-night unknown number? No, that feels like the start of a horror movie."

Zeke laughed, so she laughed and dipped her head onto his

shoulder, then he hit play, and her phone quieted but then started again.

"Go on." He nudged his chin just as Kevin McCallister was setting his first trap for the thieves.

"Sybil?" The voice, high and quaking. Sybil's heart rate spiked so high, she would have checked herself in for observation overnight if she were an actual doctor.

"This is she, speaking."

"It's Simone, Julian's daughter. I'm sorry to call so late—"

"No, Simone, don't apologize, I'm up." Sybil looked at Zeke, their expressions matching concern. "Is everything okay?"

"It's my dad." Her voice broke again. "I'm sorry, I don't know who else to call. I tried Richard, but he didn't pick up. I don't know who else my dad is in touch with anymore. And we just met at Thanksgiving so I thought—"

Sybil was on her feet now, pacing in front of the floor-to-ceiling windows with a view of the city. "No, you called the right person. Is your dad okay?"

"No," she said, and now she was really crying. "No, nothing about this is okay at all."

"Did something happen?"

"I'm back in Chicago," Simone said, a non sequitur. "I can't get there until late morning at the earliest."

"Simone, honey, what can I do to help? Why do you need to come here? I'm sure I can take care of something with your dad." Zeke pointed to himself and mouthed, *Me too.* "And I'm with Zeke actually, so we can both help."

Simone breathed in and out on the other end of the line, and Sybil took the beat to put the phone on speaker.

"Hi, Simone, it's Zeke. I'm here."

Sybil sat right next to him on the couch, pressing her legs into his so there was no space separating the two of them. She clutched her phone in her palm while they stared at the screen and waited.

"Honey?" Sybil said. "Are you still there?"

"Yes," Simone said finally. She audibly exhaled like she was screwing up the nerve to spill whatever she needed to. "Okay, right. I just need to say this because I don't know what else to do. My dad—" Her voice caught again. "My dad, he was brought to the hospital a few hours ago—"

"What? No, sweetheart, he was with us a few hours ago," Sybil said, like Simone wasn't calling with verifiable facts.

"Well, after he left, I don't know." Simone hiccupped. "It was a hit-and-run near our apartment."

"It was a hit-and-run?" Sybil said, like all she could do was mirror tidbits of information back to her.

"It was a hit-and-run," Simone repeated, her voice slower, dropping in both volume and tone. "The police found my number in his phone."

"Where is he? What hospital?" Sybil was back on her feet, like she could fix this. She *could fix* this.

"No, you don't understand," Simone said. "It was a hit-and-run, and he, oh my god I can't believe I am actually saying this, but he died. My dad is dead."

35

NIGHT TWELVE

BETTY

SYBIL HAD CALLED Betty while she was feeding the rats behind the restaurant, the snow beginning to fall, and in a literal instant, everything changed.

Betty hung up the phone and sank into the back booth of the diner. Then she jolted up, raced to the front door and bolted it, then raced to the back door and bolted that too. She needed to think. *She needed to think.*

"Something's happened to Julian," Sybil had said, and Betty was entirely unprepared for what came next. Julian? Curmudgeonly but sweet Julian? Betty was not a stranger to death, but nothing about this made any sense to her. Her brain couldn't compute the news. She glanced down at her hands and saw they were shaking, and then she glanced down at the table and saw the single sheet of paper that had been tacked up on the back door of the diner by the garbage cans.

RUN

Bile rose up from her stomach into her throat. She tried to swallow it back down, but she gagged and tilted over toward the edge of the booth so she didn't vomit on the tabletop. She hadn't eaten in hours so it was mostly just stomach acid, and her clothes were soaked in a cold sweat by the time she was done.

"Right, *right*," she said aloud.

She had prepared for this; she had essentially trained for this. She knew she was lucky to have been warned, though she couldn't imagine who warned her, what mistakes she made. Well, the laundry commercial for Natalie for one thing. But it was regional, and she didn't think anyone from the church would ever see it in the tri-state area, much less so quickly. Maybe she shouldn't have trusted Caleb, who was so roundly wonderful that maybe it had just been part of a long con.

It didn't matter.

It doesn't matter, she reminded herself.

She had to move, and she had to move quickly. She folded the sheet of paper and made her way to the back to tuck it into her backpack. She pulled on her parka, flipped up the hood and tugged the backpack onto both shoulders. Then she unlatched the back door and stepped out into the snowy dark alley. She would slip away from this life before any more mistakes caught up with her. She'd done it before, she'd do it again. In the end, Betty would do anything to survive.

PART TWO

36

NIGHT THIRTEEN

ZEKE

December 13th

ZEKE OPENED THE door to find Simone nearly unrecognizable from when they met at Thanksgiving. Bloodshot eyes, jutting cheekbones, splotchy skin. Sybil appeared at his shoulder—she'd gone home to pick up Pluto from the dog sitter and hadn't left since returning—and swept past him, tucking Simone against her shoulder like they were old friends. Zeke waited for them to separate before giving the best hug he could manage, but his right arm was aching from the day's workout, and he wasn't used to comforting others in the way that Sybil seemed attuned to. Pluto woke up from sleeping on the couch and bounded over to lick Simone's leg, then yawned and retreated back into his slumber.

"Honey," Sybil said, her hand on Simone's back. "Come in. Come sit. Come tell us what we can do to help."

They sat on the couch, Simone in a daze, Sybil resting her palm on Simone's knee. Zeke, feeling helpless, retreated to the kitchen to get them all water. He still hadn't processed it, that Julian was gone. How could someone be crossing the street on the way home and suddenly be taken like that? Zeke had spent the past two nights staring at the ceiling trying to make sense of it, remembering how early on, a car had turned the corner as he crossed the street to the diner, and all of this just as easily could have been him. Last night, Sybil knocked on his door and asked if he were still awake, which he obviously was because they were always awake, then asked if he wouldn't mind if she lay down next to him. Pluto jumped on the foot of their bed, and they stayed there, Sybil curled up in the crook of his left arm, the dog snoring, and Zeke wondering why the universe felt so doomed, until the sun came up. Sybil took Pluto out for a walk around six or seven, and Zeke thought he might never find the energy to get up. He canceled his physical therapy, told Timothy and his team he couldn't take their calls, and sat on that same foot of the bed with his head in his working hand until Sybil got back. The relief he felt upon her return, like maybe they were the only two stuck in this nonsensical spin cycle, was incalculable.

Zeke made his way back into the living room with three bottles of water. Like water could fix anything. Simone startled, like something just occurred to her.

"Is . . . is Betty here?" She glanced around.

"No," Sybil replied. "But I called her. She was devastated."

"Will she be back soon? Or I mean . . ." Simone drifted, looked around again as if she couldn't take them at their word or as if she needed to worry.

"She hasn't been back in a few nights," Zeke said, and Sybil's eyes found his. "She has a boyfr—well, I don't know what he is but she has someone in her life. She was upset, and I assumed . . . I think she's at his place?" He looked to Sybil for reassurance.

"Would it be better if she were here?" Sybil asked. "For the three of us to support you?" She reached for her phone. "I'm sure she's at work right now, but let me text her. I think she was about to quit anyway. She's doing commercials now."

"No, *no*," Simone interjected before Sybil could even swipe her lock screen. "I wanted this to be . . . just us."

"Actually," Zeke said, the thought only just occurring to him now. "Sybil, have you heard from her since . . . then?"

Sybil frowned, and Zeke loved the way her face shifted when she was really considering something. He knew this wasn't the time or the moment, but he liked this so much about her: that when she took you seriously, *she took you seriously*, and you never doubted it. So many people in his life were part smoke, part mirrors. Not her. Never her. She could be overbearing, sure, and he felt guilty that he snapped at her last week, but that was his shit, not hers.

Sybil unlocked her phone and checked her texts.

"No, now that you say that . . ." She met his eyes again. "I think we've been so wrapped up in our shock these past few days that it didn't occur to me." She paused. "Also, early on, remember, Zeke? She left that one time. But she came back. And I don't think she liked us, well, monitoring her. She's an adult, after all."

Simone exhaled, long, exhausted, uncertain.

"Right, I don't think my dad was actually honest with you guys," she said. She reached into her bag and placed a manila folder on her lap, then ran her hands over it as if it were precious to her.

"How so?" Sybil asked. "And even if he wasn't, that's okay. We met him because we were all awake in the middle of the night with our own problems. He didn't have to share them all with us."

"My dad didn't really run a candy store."

"What?" Zeke said.

"Well, that's okay too," Sybil talked over him. "What you do for a living isn't the gravest of lies."

"No," Simone said, firmer now. "What I mean is my mom did own the candy store. It was her thing. When she died, my dad couldn't bring himself to sell it, which was just as well."

"I'm confused," Zeke said. Sybil raised her eyebrows at him as if to perhaps hush him up and let Simone speak. She reached over, placed a hand on his forearm and let it rest there. He stared at it, hoped she never retracted it.

"Sorry, I'm all over the place," Simone said. "What I'm trying to say is that my dad was former FBI."

"Oh," Sybil said, a line forming between her brows. "But, I guess, I mean, that's still okay, I don't mind that he didn't tell us. He was entitled to tell us whatever he wanted."

Simone sighed out of what Zeke took to be exasperation. She opened the folder on her lap.

"My dad had to retire four years ago. He had a heart attack. I don't know what he told you, probably not that either. The stress of the job and maybe with my mom gone, I don't know, it was too much. And he promised me that he was done with his casework, really *was* moving on and managing my mom's store, putting the investigative stuff behind him. But he didn't. Or he wasn't."

She pulled out a glossy photo of a family, handed it to Sybil, who held it between her and Zeke, who pressed himself closer to examine it. There were seven of them, dressed in what Zeke thought of as religious clothes, something like what the Amish would wear, if he remembered correctly. Sybil reached for her reading glasses from the coffee table and pulled the photo closer. Then Zeke heard her gasp, and her hand flew over her mouth. Of course he didn't see what she was seeing.

"Is that—" Sybil turned toward Simone.

"Yes."

Zeke was too embarrassed to ask what *it* was.

"Four years ago, their . . . I'm not sure what the exact definition was, but their cult? Their church? It burned down. My dad had been investigating corruption, or, I don't really know, abuse or maybe money laundering; I'm sorry, I didn't live with him then and am only figuring out what I can now."

"Her parents—she said it was a farming accident. It was a fire?" Sybil said, already putting together jigsaw puzzle pieces while Zeke was still staring at the picture on the front of the box. Betty. Were they talking about Betty?

Simone shook her head. "I really don't know the details. I know that they never solved who did it, and I remember my dad refusing to let it go. Richard, his partner, forced them to close the case because there were other fish to fry. I can still hear my dad arguing with him about that. *'Richard, I don't give a shit about frying other fish!'* But—" She paused, gestured to the picture. "I don't think it's a leap to say that he never did."

Sybil placed the photo on her lap and turned toward Simone. "You think he knew who Betty was?"

"I'm sorry," Zeke said. "Which one is Betty? I don't mean to be slow but—"

Simone reached for the picture. "Right here—" She jabbed her finger at a girl maybe around ten or twelve standing at the edge of the rest of the family. She had a mop of brown hair and sad eyes and posture like she wanted to make herself curl up and disappear.

"That's her," Simone said. "That's Elizabeth Jones. And there is zero chance in a million universes that my dad wasn't onto that, that anything about this"—she flung her arm into a circle—"could be a coincidence."

37

NIGHT THIRTEEN

SYBIL

SIMONE HAD LEFT them with Julian's files. Sybil wasn't quite sure what to do next, but Simone was too overwhelmed with the logistics of what she was dealing with in the wake of her father's death to handle anything more.

"We'll take care of this," she had said to Simone as she was headed out the door, back to Julian's apartment for the night and the foreseeable future.

"I'm going to try to, I don't know, see if my work will let me move up here," Simone said. "I have to deal with the apartment. And, just, all of his stuff. A memorial. The cat. And I didn't know what else to do with this. I thought you might—"

"Honey, really." Sybil placed both hands on Simone's shoulders, which started to shake. "This is ours now. Don't even give it a second thought. But text me as soon as you need help with anything else, okay?"

It was all awful, wretched, horrific. But at least Sybil could be put to work. That's what she did best after all.

An hour later, they were sitting at Zeke's breakfast nook. Sybil felt as if the world had just been tilted off its axis, not just with Julian's death but with Betty too.

"I didn't even ask her," Sybil said with a start. "About the hit-and-run. If they found the guy."

Zeke ran his hands over his face. His right arm was bending now in ways it previously couldn't, and Sybil made a mental note, even in this chaos, that he was improving. That he could make his way back by spring. He didn't see it, his progress, because he was so disinterested in actually embracing it, like his brain wanted his body to stay stagnant, and his body, a miraculous work of art, was healing itself anyway.

"I'm worried about Betty," Zeke said. They'd each tried her twice since Simone left, and their texts were marked as delivered but unanswered. "Should I go up to the diner? Or . . . I mean, I don't even know Caleb's last name. Do you?"

"No," Sybil said. "Fuck. He works at Morgan Stanley though."

"Don't ten thousand people work at Morgan Stanley?"

"Let me text Natalie. Her ex-husband used to work there. He owes her."

Sybil shot a quick text off asking if her ex could search the bank's directory, and surprisingly, Natalie wrote her right back, even though it was nearly three A.M.

Natalie: I'll make him. Why?

Sybil: We want to make sure Betty is ok.

Natalie: Did something happen? I didn't want to say anything but she didn't show for the audition I had set up.

Sybil: WDYM?

Natalie: Huge national audition. They loved her look. Set for today at 3:30. Never showed.

Sybil: She didn't let you know or cancel?

Natalie: Nope, not a word. I covered for her bc I think she could still land it but she hasn't returned my calls.

Sybil: ok thanks, why are you awake?

Natalie: why are you?

Sybil: life

Natalie: exactly

Sybil handed her phone to Zeke, so he could read the exchange.

"Zeke, I think Betty could be . . . missing." She didn't want to be dramatic, but none of this felt right, and she'd listened to enough podcasts to pay attention to her intuition.

"Missing?" The color drained from Zeke's face as he reread

the texts. Her phone buzzed again, and his cheeks flushed as he handed it back to her.

> **Natalie:** are you with that hot piece of ass

"Oh shit," Sybil said, her own cheeks pinkening.

"I don't assume that was about—"

"No, right, anyway." Sybil batted a hand around like she could bat away her embarrassment. "Absolutely, let's just—"

"Let's focus on Betty," Zeke said, and Sybil nodded *Yes absolutely*. She was very good at multitasking, but this was too much for even her.

Something occurred to her. A puzzle piece already fitting into a slot. "That night when she went out," Sybil said. "And Julian panicked, thinking she had gone—I didn't really get why he cared at the time."

"Holy shit," Zeke said.

"Do you have any Scotch tape?" Sybil stood, made her way to the kitchen counters, started opening the drawers beneath.

"I don't think so," Zeke said, just as Sybil pulled out a roll triumphantly.

"When all of this is over, we need to familiarize you with your own life," she said, moving back toward him and grabbing the folder off the table.

"What are we doing?"

"We're building an evidence wall."

"Sybil—"

"I know, this isn't an episode of *Dateline*," she said, and she did really know that. These were two people who were real to her, whom she had come to love. She wasn't solving a sensationalized television bit, and this wasn't some morbid podcast.

"If we think Betty is gone, we need to call the police," Zeke said.

"Absolutely, but . . ." Sybil chewed on it before she said anything. She flopped over, touched her toes, tried to do those stupid stretches as if that would ensure that the blood was flowing to her brain and she wouldn't sound like a conspiracist who had consumed too much real crime. Even if she had. She righted herself. "What if she left by choice?"

"You mean what if she's avoiding us?"

"Maybe yes. She could just be with Caleb, and her phone is on silent. That would be logical." Sybil needed to believe that Betty was okay, even if it was naïve, even if on one of her shows, this would be when the baritone voice said, *Betty Jones had not returned home in three days.*

"But the audition," Zeke said.

"Right." Sybil dropped her chin to her chest. "The audition." She resented that she was so exhausted that her brain was already forgetting critical facts.

"And Julian *knew* her," Zeke said.

"But she didn't seem to know him."

There was a rhythm now between them, like they were volleying tennis balls back and forth.

Zeke paused, then pulled out his own phone. "Wait a second."

Sybil slid into the seat next to him, like they were two middle schoolers working on a science project. He scrolled until he found what he was looking for, and his eyes widened.

"I knew I was remembering this right."

This time, he passed his phone to Sybil. It was the chat from the first few nights they met on the Insomniacs board.

"Oh my god." Sybil put her hand up over her mouth.

"He set us up," Zeke said.

Sybil reread the back-and-forth. It was undeniable now, what Julian had done. He'd been the one to suggest that they meet in person that first week. He'd been the one to suggest the diner.

He'd been watching Betty all this time.

38

NIGHT FOURTEEN

ZEKE

December 15th

THEY'D DECIDED LAST night to check the diner, just to be certain. Sybil made the relevant point that if Betty were anything like Eloise, it was entirely possible that she was aggravated with them over something they were unaware of, and she was just ghosting them for a bit. Zeke didn't really believe that, and honestly, he didn't get the impression that Sybil did, either, but they had to check anyway. He was so tired that he trusted her instincts more than his own.

They arrived at four A.M., in the pitch black of night like they were vampires, which it almost felt like they were by now. They found the diner closed. A handwritten sign was posted to the inside of the glass door.

> HELP WANTED: LOOKING FOR AN OVERNIGHT SERVER AND HOSTESS.
> CLOSED BETWEEN 11PM–6AM UNTIL FURTHER NOTICE.

So that was that. Their first dead end.

By the time they stumbled toward their day in the late

morning—a few fitful hours of sleep finding them each—Natalie had tracked down Caleb.

"Caleb Drucker," Sybil read aloud as she tied her hair into a bun atop her head. She was still in her pajamas, a matching cotton set that wasn't too dowdy and wasn't too alluring, a combination that Zeke couldn't help but find absurdly sexy. He knew he needed to stop with this fantasy right now, that they were mourning Julian and worried about Betty, and his growing attachment to Sybil could have been the result of all sorts of things unrelated to actually wanting to pursue something with her.

"I have to head to PT," he groaned. "But when I'm back?"

"When you're back, we'll go talk to him." She finished his sentence.

Now it was rush hour, the city streets clogged with too many taxis and pedestrians not abiding the walk signal. The forecast again called for snow, and once the sun had set, the temperatures had dropped into the upper twenties. Sybil had remembered (of course she had remembered) that Betty mentioned that Caleb worked punishing hours, so there was no point in tracking him down at his apartment unless they went in the middle of the night. Even though they were always up at that hour, they could both see why showing up at a stranger's apartment at two A.M. looking for a girl was not the best way to start their amateur sleuthing.

Zeke's driver deposited them all the way on the southern tip of Manhattan, in front of Morgan Stanley's entrance.

"What's the plan?" Zeke asked Sybil. He figured she would have one, which suited him perfectly fine. His whole life, he'd been part of a team, but the pitchers, they did solitary work. He had to trust that if he threw the ball where his brain and arm demanded, the rest of the lineup would live up to their ends of the bargain. He wasn't a batter or a base runner or a fielder. He had one single purpose, and that was to decimate the person in front of him. The rest of the Mets then had to add the runs, field the plays. No wonder, it occurred to him now as he held the door for Sybil and they were hit with a rush of pumped-in heat, that while he was part of a team, he wasn't part of the *team*. His job required complete tunnel vision on himself, a narcissist's mirror, as it were. No one could help him if he was having a shit night, no one could help him if his speed or accuracy or drop or spin wasn't working. He looked at Sybil as she marched up to the information desk and was met with a wave of gratefulness—pure, honest appreciation—that she had asked him to be part of *her* team, that she believed he had something to offer. The only thing he'd ever offered in the past was his arm.

"Hi," she said to the receptionist. "We're here for Caleb Drucker."

The receptionist's fingers flew over her keyboard. "He's expecting you?"

"No," Sybil said.

Her fingers stopped typing. "I'll need to call up."

"Right, can you tell him—" Sybil gestured for Zeke to join her at the desk. "Can you tell him Zeke Rodriguez is downstairs for him?"

So this was her plan. Zeke didn't even mind, trading his fame for access. It was a small way to be helpful. Maybe his only use.

The receptionist's eyes moved to Zeke, and he saw them widen for a beat. She reached for her headset, waited a moment, then said: "Hi, Mr. Drucker, I have a Zeke Rodriguez here to see you . . . Right. Yes. That one . . . No, he didn't say why."

"Just ask him if we can have five minutes of his time in the lobby," Sybil whispered.

"He wants you to come down to the lobby," the receptionist said.

It was amazing, Zeke thought, how fame opened literal doors. No one in this building knew him, yet everyone in this building *knew* him. What would his life look like without being born with a golden arm? How far would he have gotten on his other merits?

A few minutes later, the elevator door dinged, and a solidly good-looking, semi-tallish, kind-faced man in need of a haircut walked toward them.

"Holy shit, Zeke Rodriguez? Are you here to see me?" He held out his hand and offered Zeke a firm handshake. Up close, Zeke could see purple crescents under his eyes, a day-old stubble growing, like he hadn't been home in a while.

"Hi," Sybil said. "We're friends with Betty."

At the mention of her name, Caleb's animated face grew still.

"You guys know Betty? I'm sorry, I'm confused."

"Yes, weird, I know," Zeke said. "We're—" He glanced at Sybil to see if she was comfortable with him taking the lead. She nodded encouragingly. "We're worried about her. She's sort of . . . my roommate. And we haven't heard from her in a few days."

Caleb's eyes moved from Zeke to Sybil to Zeke again. "I don't, I'm not . . ." he stuttered. "I'm sorry." He shook his head like he was trying to clear a muddle of thoughts. "I haven't slept in a day. My brain isn't quite working."

Zeke wanted to say, *Join the club,* but the last time he had done that, they'd ended up in The Insomniacs, where a retired FBI agent was evidently using them to get closer to a young woman who, from what Zeke had pieced together from Julian's files, may or may not be a murderer and/or arsonist fleeing from authorities.

"We're just worried about her. A friend of ours recently passed away, and we haven't heard from her since," Sybil said gently.

"I thought it was me," Caleb said. "She just . . . she just ghosted me a couple of days ago. I thought I was getting too, I don't know, clingy? I surprised her at work one night, and I thought things were going really well. But I haven't heard from her either. Not since . . ." He unlocked his phone. "Yeah, four days ago."

"Four days ago," Zeke said. "So same as us."

Now Caleb looked genuinely distraught, his jaw tightening, his eyebrows darting into a diagonal. If this were a true crime series, there was a chance, Zeke considered, that the boyfriend would be a suspect, but either Caleb was the best actor disguised as an investment banker known to man, or he was truly broken up by the news.

"I guess I thought, I mean, you guys obviously know her—she likes her space. I guess I thought she was just taking space," Caleb said.

Sybil placed a hand on his arm. "She probably is. Don't worry."

Caleb wasn't a fool, though, Zeke could tell.

"But you're here. So *you're* worried. Also, I'm still confused." Caleb turned to Zeke. "You guys were *roommates*? I mean, not to get too weird, but I obviously know who you are. My younger brother has your poster on his wall."

"She didn't tell you?" Zeke asked.

"No, and now I'm starting to wonder what else I didn't know."

Join the club, Zeke thought again.

"Can I give you my number?" Sybil reached for his phone. "We can stay in touch. I'm sure she'll turn up soon, and maybe if you hear from her, you can let us know? And vice versa?"

"Yeah, for sure," Caleb said as Sybil punched her contact information into his phone, then sent herself a text from his phone.

"Now we're connected," she said, and Zeke knew she was leaving nothing to chance. His Sybil. She was really something.

"Hey," Zeke said. "How did you guys meet? She never told me."

"Oh, funny story, sort of one of those meet-cutes," Caleb said. He lit up, then realized that maybe their story wasn't going to have a happy ending. "Anyway, Grand Central, rush hour, we were on our phones and literally collided. I gave her my card, she texted a few weeks later." He sighed. "I don't know, man, I really like her."

"Did she say what she was doing at Grand Central?" Sybil asked.

"I assume getting a train? Like I was? Although, actually, I was getting on, heading home. She was getting off. So . . . come to think of it, I'm not sure. I never thought about it."

"And did she tell you anything about her family?" Sybil was good at this, Zeke thought. Kind but still pressing.

"Grew up in Colorado, not close with her parents who still live there, I think, hmmm, Mom works in a salon, Dad is a contractor. Divorced when she was little. Moved to New York out of high school thinking she could be a star? I know it sounds stupid but I really think—thought, I don't know—that she could be. I just totally believed in her."

"Right, right, that sounds about right." Sybil smiled at him. "Okay, we shouldn't take up more of your time. I know how these places grind you to the bone."

His eyes grew somber, then widened. “Her brother, Levi, maybe you could call him? Maybe he would know?”

“She mentioned Levi to you?” Zeke perked up.

“Yeah, for sure. She really admired him, seeing the world, all that cool stuff.”

“Great,” Sybil said, and squeezed his arm. “Great, this is so helpful. We’ll be sure to track down Levi.”

Colorado. Both parents alive. Dad a contractor. But also, Levi.

Betty seemed to weave truths into her fictions, Zeke thought. Maybe this was one moment of honesty they could bite into, one real thing among a spool of lies. If they were lucky enough, this lead would unravel the rest of them.

MYSTERIOUS LOCAL CHURCH BURNS, THREE DEAD, OTHERS MISSING

The Macon Telegraph

June 12th, 2021

By Annabeth Collins

Firefighters were called to the scene of the Revivalist Church last night shortly after 8 p.m. to find the building in flames. It appears, however, that the trucks arrived too late to salvage the church and its outposts, as both floors were smoldering when the trucks pulled up. According to eyewitnesses, the fire may have started in the kitchen or utility room but spread so quickly that many parishioners, who were having a Friday Sabbath meal, had no choice but to run, leaving behind their personal effects. By the time the firefighters were able to contain the fire, the entirety of the church had burned to little more than smolder. This morning, on-site, the air was still choked with smoke, and locals gathered to mourn not just the dead but also the house of worship, which had more than its share of scandal surrounding it. Local police have made several visits to the church to speak with Pastor Aaron Jones, who as yet is unaccounted for after the fire. While the sheriff refuses to comment on what prompted those visits and whether or not Pastor Jones willingly spoke with his officers, there has been years-long speculation that the church is less religious in nature and instead is a front for what some in the area describe as a cult. There have been rumored reports of abuse and forced marriage, among other allegations. Among the confirmed dead is Pastor Jones's wife, who ran the afterschool program for girls. Her body was recovered earlier this morning.

"Please leave us alone," Patience Morrow said, when interviewed on-site. Her husband, Matthew Morrow, sits on the church board, and if Pastor Jones is found deceased, is presumed to assume the leadership role. "My family is grieving the loss of our mother, along with several other church members. We are searching for my father and my sister. Have you no regard for our pain?"

Nearly twenty-four hours after the fire, Pastor Jones is still missing, and there remain multiple hot spots within the fire site that cannot yet be accessed. One firefighter was hurt on scene, treated at a local hospital and is in stable condition. This remains a developing story.

39

NIGHT FIFTEEN

SYBIL

December 17th

SYBIL HAD QUESTIONS. She had so many questions. Because try searching for a Levi Jones online, and you'll get basically nowhere. Sybil took it as a personal affront that other than Betty's sister, Patience, all of her siblings had such roundly generic names that she'd have better luck searching the haystack for a needle than googling them. Patience, it seemed, still lived near Macon, near the once-charred church, which had been rebuilt with both insurance money and congregation donations, according to the Revivalist Newsletter, which she found on Reddit. Patience's husband, Matthew, was indeed now the lead pastor, though information about the church beyond that was murky at best. A follow-up article in *The Macon Telegraph* tried to unpack the rumors about a doomsday cult, but few of the members were willing to speak on the record, and the quote that most haunted Sybil was the anonymous one in the last paragraph that stated, "Pastor Aaron always told us that we were just passing through this ground on our way to a better place, so the way I see it, this was God's way of fulfilling that promise, taking those souls. I wish it could have been me. I wish it could have been all of us."

Yesterday, Sybil and Zeke had spent a few fruitless hours trying to discern what was fiction and what was truth in Betty's stories, but the more they talked, the less they realized what they actually *knew* about her. It had been Georgia, not North Carolina, as Betty had told them, though after tracking down her old apartment, she had indeed once lived with a woman named Mallory. Sybil had gone to Bloomingdale's and shown the sole picture she had of Betty—taken at Thanksgiving, a lifetime ago, when Betty was petting Pluto and oblivious to the rest of them—and one very nice lady at the perfume counter confirmed Betty had worked there for six months or so. "Sweet girl," the woman said. "But kept to herself. I always figured she was saving for college or something. She seemed like she knew she wanted something else and was here temporarily." Sybil had bought an extremely expensive bottle of French perfume as a thank-you. When she opened it in the cab on the way back to Zeke's, she realized it reminded her of the anesthesiologist. But only momentarily because Sybil had done an excellent job not thinking about Mark at all since Thanksgiving.

"Is it possible," she said to Zeke when she returned and was unwinding her scarf, unzipping her parka, "that we're misremembering? Maybe she had said Georgia, not North Carolina?"

"I don't think so," he replied, and headed into the kitchen to make her some tea. They'd found this rhythm of domesticity in the past week, and Sybil didn't mind it one bit.

"But are you sure?" She trailed him with Pluto at her feet.

"She told Caleb 'Colorado,' which isn't anything even close to North Carolina," Zeke had sighed. "I don't think deciphering the minutiae of Betty's lies is going to help us find her."

Sybil did her fruitless shoulder stretches and stared at their evidence wall, which hadn't gotten much more detailed than when she first started it. Other than the *Macon Telegraph* article, Julian's handwritten notes, some pictures of the scene after the fire, and the photograph of the family from when Betty was ten, it was pretty much empty white space at the moment and not nearly as gratifying as Sybil had envisioned. On cop shows, the detectives stare at the boards with their hands on their hips until they're struck by genius. Mostly, in the past few days, Sybil had stared at the nakedness of the wall and felt her frustration grow at the utter lack of clues, at the complete mystery of how Betty had simply vanished.

"I'm just, I guess, genuinely shocked that she didn't think she could trust us," Sybil said.

"It seems to me, if she really was raised with a crazy father and an enabling mother, trusting us is probably the last thing on her mind." Zeke passed her the tea and sat beside her, neither of them at all clear on what to do next.

Tonight Sybil was back home in the suburbs because Eloise had been deposited by a college friend a few hours earlier. She'd walked into the house, rubbed Pluto behind his ears and said, "No Christmas tree? We're not doing Christmas?" and then marched up the stairs and slammed the door.

So Sybil ordered a tree online from a local pop-up store. It was delivered with rapid speed and she texted Eloise up in her room to tell her. What she actually wanted to say was: *Hey, nice to see you! How have you been, Mom? You look exhausted, is everything okay?* But she didn't say any of that to her daughter, of course. Sybil felt desperate to be something other than their mother, someone whom Eloise would find fascinating, someone whom Sybil herself would find fascinating, but she wasn't yet there. Maybe never would be there.

She opened Julian's folder again. In the days since Simone

had shown up at Zeke's with the folder, Simone had been in touch to say that she was having her dad cremated, so there hadn't yet been a service or funeral. Sybil didn't think she was in a position to demand anything from Simone, as much as she wanted to have a proper goodbye. The truth was that they'd known Julian for two months, more or less. Even though both she and Zeke were plagued with fits of grief—one of them involuntarily tearing up with no notice—they weren't old friends, they weren't all that close. They were brought together by circumstance—insomnia—and evidently a manipulated opportunity for Julian to either bring Betty to justice or protect her from someone else who needed to be. Sybil still wasn't sure which one it was. But the best that Sybil figured, the way that she could honor Julian, grieve him actually, was to find Betty, to help Betty. Even if Betty had been the one to light the match that led to the fire, the more Sybil delved into her father's church, the more she thought he had it coming.

"This guy was a lunatic," she had said to Zeke last night.

"Not a lunatic," Zeke said. "That lets him off the hook like he couldn't help it."

"So you think he was of sound mind?"

"I think I've met a lot of people who use other people to give themselves power."

Zeke had stood and started to pace, then ran his dominant hand through his hair, more progress toward his recovery that he seemed not particularly interested in. He rarely talked about his physical therapy and usually returned home with a scowl, but Sybil was used to teenagers and didn't mind. She liked their quiet, if pretend, homemaking; they watched the sun rise from his floor-to-ceiling windows, then tried to rest in whatever way they could, her in his second guest bedroom, him in the primary, before he rose to go repair his body with the team trainers and the private therapists, who stopped coming to him when his routine grew more rigorous and required a full gym. She spent the early afternoon hours walking Pluto and losing herself to the pulse of Manhattan; it wasn't how she envisioned herself living here, of course, separated from her husband, her children off at college, the first half of her life behind her, but it brought her peace all the same.

"Mom," Eloise said behind her, breaking Sybil's chain of thought and startling her. She flipped the folder closed quickly. "Jesus," her daughter said. "Calm down."

"Sorry," Sybil said, though she wasn't quite sure what she was apologizing for. "I'm not used to having company."

"If I want to go into the city and sleep at Dad's, how mad would you be?"

Sybil thought about saying that she would be hurt, not mad, but then a quieter voice suggested that maybe she would be relieved. She liked the lack of company, the quiet. She liked the time to focus on something other than her kids. She liked that when the Christmas tree showed up, she wouldn't have to spend the time decorating it for a holiday she didn't grow up celebrating anyway.

"That would be fine," Sybil said. "I wouldn't be mad."

Eloise crossed her arms and narrowed her eyes. She started to say something then stopped herself. Then seemed to reconsider. "Are you sleeping with Zeke Rodriguez? Because this"—she flapped a hand in her direction—"is not your normal reaction."

Sybil laughed. "I am not. I already told you at Thanksgiving."

"That was almost a month ago," Eloise said. "A lot can happen in a month."

Sybil's phone buzzed just then. Zeke.

I think I found something. When is
the soonest you can come back?

Indeed, a lot can, Sybil thought.

"Pack a bag," she said to her daughter. "I'll be happy to drop you."

40

NIGHT FIFTEEN

ZEKE

JUST TO BE clear, I wasn't trying to snoop," Zeke said.

"Why do you think I would care if you were snooping? We need to snoop. Snooping is mandated at this point. It's been two weeks since we've heard from her. I think snooping is the bare minimum." Sybil flicked on the light in Betty's room, and Pluto hopped atop her bed.

"Okay, I know you're right, I just . . . when she moved in, everyone, well, Julian, wanted to be so sure that I wasn't a creep. I don't want you to think I'm a creep."

"Zeke, I could never think you're a creep."

He knew he was fishing now, seeking her reassurance, which was new territory for him. Women in his life, well, other than his sister, tended to tell him what he wanted to hear, tended to give him whatever he asked. But not Sybil, and this unnerved him as much as it pleased him. Prior to his injury, Zeke's solitary challenge in his life had been about his pitch. Women weren't a challenge; relationships, because he never really wanted one, weren't a challenge. The depth of his attraction to

Sybil was new; if he didn't have Betty and Julian to think about, Sybil would probably be the only thing on his brain.

"Okay, uh, after you left, I had to do one more check. Of her room."

He and Sybil had obviously gone through Betty's belongings. They'd concluded that she hadn't planned to leave that night. That after taking Sybil's call about Julian and the hit-and-run, something had spooked her. Was it Julian? Was it Sybil? Had something else happened that they couldn't understand or weren't yet aware of? She'd left behind all of her clothes and toiletries, though they realized that her room was devoid of nearly any personal effects. It made sense, actually, once they connected with Caleb, once they understood that most of the stories Betty had told them were woven from lies.

"I completely forgot about this," he said, walking into the en suite bathroom. He opened the vanity door beneath the sink.

"We already looked there," Sybil said.

"Right, I know." Zeke crouched, and his knees popped. He almost lost his balance and without thinking, jutted his throwing arm down to stop him. He waited for the pain to come, to shoot up to his shoulder and down to his ribs, but he felt only a quiet ache for a moment. He really was recovering. And he had no idea how that made him feel. "But look."

He reached in and pressed his palm against the back of the cabinetry, and a magnetic panel swung open.

"What on earth?" Sybil was hunched over but crouched beside him now. "Is this like a secret passageway?"

"It's embarrassing," Zeke said. "When I moved in, I tore everything down to the studs. The decorator I hired told me this was the new thing—your housekeeper could store all of their cleaning supplies in the bathroom sight unseen. She told me how classy it was for guests, I guess. Like seeing a can of Lysol spray was only for the impoverished."

Sybil turned to him, now befuddled.

"I know, I know. I was a single guy with no clue what I was doing, so I just listened to her," he said. "Though I did refuse to let her put up shades in the living room."

"You know what they say about a fool and his money," Sybil said, and Zeke must have winced, so she put her hand on his arm and said, "I'm kidding. It's just an interesting upsell: hidden shelves in cabinets so your guests don't have to come face-to-face with extra toilet paper or Soft Scrub."

"Anyway," Zeke said, and edged the door open a little wider, "I'd forgotten about it because it was useless. But Betty obviously went looking for hiding spots, because I found this." He reached in and pulled out a rusting metal baking tin that was a green gingham pattern and said FLOUR.

"Is this . . . ?" Sybil inhaled sharply and sank from her heels to the floor, so Zeke did the same.

"Yep." Zeke tapped the lid, which was dented on top. "It's definitely not mine. Which means that it has to be hers."

Zeke held it out to her, as if she needed to be the one to do the honors, see for herself. She pried off the lid.

One photo of Betty and her family. Betty was a little older than in the picture that Simone had shared, maybe early teens. Her face had lost some of the baby fat but wasn't nearly the straight edge of the young woman they knew now. An unfamiliar man stood beside Patience, who had a round belly at least six or seven months along. There were two other new women in the family picture too. They wore dark dresses that buttoned up to their necks, their hair in French braids. At their feet were a smattering of young children.

"That must be Matthew," Sybil said, tapping the photo with her index finger. "Patience's husband. The new pastor."

"Yes, and those must be her brothers' wives," Zeke said, pointing out the other women, each with frozen smiles and hands on the shoulders of the toddlers.

"And that"—Sybil tapped twice on a young man with dark eyes, jet-black hair and a pained expression but with no wife beside him—"must be our elusive Levi."

"Well, speaking of that . . ." Zeke lifted a worn-out Bible from the box to reveal an old flip phone beneath. Now Sybil audibly gasped, and Zeke, despite the circumstances, found himself delighted. "It's dead, obviously. And I haven't had this type of charger since 1998, but I think I found one on Amazon."

Sybil popped the phone open, pressed a few buttons, then flipped it closed. Just to be sure.

"And that's not all," Zeke said.

He opened the Bible and thumbed through until he found what he was looking for.

There, in the middle of Psalms 118, Betty had written:

I CAN'T WAIT TO RUIN YOU. I CAN'T WAIT TO SEE THE SURPRISE ON YOUR FACE WHEN I TELL YOU IT WAS ME.

41

NIGHT SIXTEEN

SYBIL

December 23rd

SYBIL HAD TAPED the new family photo on their evidence wall along with the torn-out page of the Bible, which she realized was possibly evidence tampering, but it wasn't like they were about to call the police and let them know what they found. She thought about contacting Simone to see if she had any insights, but Simone hadn't replied to her last text, checking in, asking if there were anything Sybil could do. They hardly knew Julian's daughter, but she was a little stung all the same. *Let me mother you,* she wanted to say. Old habits die hard.

The plug for the flip phone—shipping from overseas—would arrive tomorrow, so for now, all they could do was wait. In the meantime, Sybil scoured the internet for wedding announcements about Betty's brothers, any information on their wives.

"You think that has anything to do with it?" Zeke asked.

It was the middle of the night again, which meant that it was almost Christmas Eve. Sybil had presents for Eloise back at the house, but she'd barely heard from her daughter since dropping her at the pied-à-terre to stay with Mark, and she wasn't interested in racing to their house in the suburbs and depositing hundreds of dollars of wrapped Lululemon gear at her daughter's feet. She thought briefly of that unadorned, naked tree sitting in the middle of her living room, and her heart panged for the way that things used to be, for the way that her life had pretty much detonated this past year.

"I don't even know what the *it* is that we're looking for," Sybil said.

"I think the *it* is if Betty burned down her father's church. And if for some reason, now, a couple of years later, that made her run when Julian figured out who she was."

Zeke picked up an elastic exercise band and started doing one of his rehab exercises. Sybil had done her stupid back stretches, but the throb of her shoulder never relented; it was just there all the time now, like her body wanted to remind her what it really needed was the thing she couldn't give it: rest. But she did her stretches all the same alongside Zeke. They'd learned to be productive in their waking hours, interminable as those hours were.

Sybil opened Julian's folder again, which still had a few scraps of paper that they hadn't made heads or tails of. "Was he actually looking to, like, charge Betty for . . . oh my god, this sounds preposterous, but was he actually looking to charge her with murder? Or was he just . . ." She flipped through some of the pages. "It seems like he was more interested in her father's corruption." She pulled a printed email out and rose to tape it on the wall, after initially thinking it wasn't relevant. "Like, I didn't really think much of this, but why was Julian so interested in the increase in church membership?"

"Read me what he said," Zeke said. He'd tied the elastic band to the door handle of the pantry and was working on his range of motion. Sybil felt like they were in an old-school cop show. This camaraderie was what she missed most after abandoning her medical career. Examining a patient's symptoms, pinpointing a cause, figuring out the fix. Maybe she hadn't really been all that interested in *helping* other people's ailments; maybe she'd just been high on the chase for the cure. If she stopped to consider this, she realized, she'd lose her equilibrium. All this time, she'd been angry, resentful of Mark for upending the career she'd thought she was rightfully owed, but what if it wasn't the career she'd needed, just the thrill of the hunt?

Sybil read Julian's email aloud.

R—

I know you think this is a dead-ender, but I pulled up their financials. The Revivalist Church was taking in well over 3.2 mill for the past two years, double what it was doing before. Which is still a shit-ton, tax free, for this sort of thing. I know we've closed this case, but come on, man, this doesn't make sense. Also, look at the enrollment rolls: Did they rope in half of the county? Are they actively recruiting? I admit that I'm not a churchgoer, but for a midsized rural congregation just a few years ago, this thing looks like a Florida megachurch. I think there are a lot of reasons Pastor Aaron Jones might have wound up dead. We shouldn't exclude any of them, in my opinion. Isn't this all a little odd?

"Jesus Christ," Zeke said. His arm was hovering in midair, like he had been too stunned to complete his rep, and Sybil noted the perfect arc of his bicep, the way his forearm was solid muscle, how his skin was a golden tan that Eloise would kill for during one of their Caribbean vacations that they used to take before Mark started fucking the anesthesiologist. "So this is a *money* thing, not a *we marry off women at eighteen and seem totally unhinged* sort of thing?"

"I want to find someone down there to talk to," she said. "I feel like whatever went on with the fire is going to lead us back to Betty." She eased back onto the breakfast nook bench, tapped her laptop awake.

"If she even wants us to find her," Zeke said, and Sybil bristled. It hadn't occurred to her that they shouldn't be looking.

"Why wouldn't she want us to help her?"

"I mean, if she burned down the church, right? She might be better off if we don't chase her?"

"But she's in trouble," Sybil said.

"I agree, probably." He dropped the elastic band on the counter and walked to the evidence wall. "But also, there's a chance that she's not. There's a chance that she doesn't want to be found. I saw her handwriting on that Bible as clearly as you did."

He stared at the old article from *The Macon Telegraph*. Then tapped his finger on it.

"Here, the byline. In my experience, reporters are almost always willing to talk, especially if it's to me. So let's start with her."

42

NIGHT SIXTEEN

ZEKE

THEY'D FOUND THE reporter's contact information, and Sybil crafted an email, which Zeke then sent from his team account, a New York Mets email address. He included his cell number, as if that might also lure her in, a personal connection to the Mets superstar. He thought his name alone would be enough to merit a reply because that was how things usually worked with a Zeke Rodriguez introduction, but it had been three hours and nothing.

"Zeke, it's the middle of the night, you have to stop checking," Sybil had said.

Of course he needed to stop checking. He was just used to, well, getting everything, having everything. Everyone adjusting their posture when he walked into the room, everyone asking what they could do to accommodate him. This was what it was like, he supposed, to have a life stripped of his fame. This, perhaps, was the change he was looking for when he froze as that line drive careened right into his arm.

"I just want to be able to *do* something," he said. "Now."

Sybil was on her phone playing one of her puzzles that Zeke had given up on. Forget that she always beat him, Zeke didn't mind that one bit. But without Julian, the whole thing felt empty, or if not empty, a reminder that maybe Julian didn't consider them friends, that Zeke and Sybil were a means to an end, not the good stuff in the middle. Zeke was almost embarrassed that Julian had used them so seamlessly. Even though Zeke was well aware that he quite often was not the smartest one in the room, he didn't need it to be pointed out either.

"You're stewing," Sybil said, and set her phone facedown on the couch. "About Betty or about Julian?" She could read him so well, Zeke thought, a sea of gratefulness washing over him.

"Both? Him? I'm not sure."

"You think that none of it was real? Our . . . situation? Our friendships?"

Zeke moved toward the couch and sat next to her.

"You don't?"

Sybil stood, and he fought the urge to reach out to her, grab her hand, pull her back beside him. She gazed up at the Christmas tree, then walked toward one side and adjusted an ornament that was askew. She turned back toward him with the glow of the fairy lights illuminating her from behind, and his heart seized. He knew she wasn't his; he knew that the bond between them could be as make-believe as it had been with Julian and Betty. But it had been so long, seemingly forever, since he'd trusted someone wholly, wanted someone wholly, the way that he did Sybil.

"I think that it seems like they each had their reasons for . . . this." She raised an arm and dropped it. "Maybe Betty was in trouble. Maybe Julian thought he could help her. Or maybe Julian was going to cause her more trouble. I don't know. But I'm not sure we should take any of that personally. Everything started a long time before we met them."

Zeke clenched and unclenched his hand. Sometimes now, his fingers went a little tingly. His PT assured him that was normal, just the nerves rebuilding their pathways. But maybe it wasn't just his nerves. His eyelid still had a mind of its own. He knew that Sybil had noticed, and he also knew that she wouldn't point it out. Their bodies were betraying them in ways they couldn't control, and it was just another thing they had in common, another humiliation of their sleeplessness.

"It's hard not to feel like we were duped," he said.

"That it wasn't real?"

Zeke shrugged.

"I think it was real," she said, then her eyes never wavering from his, said, "I think it is real."

Zeke felt his pulse quicken. He so wanted to believe that she meant him, *this*, them, that whatever was building, even unspoken, between them was important and vital and unquestionable. It was. It had to be. But he wasn't brave enough yet to ask or to articulate his own assuredness.

Sybil returned to the couch right next to him. He adjusted his body, a leg up on the cushion, to face her. "Maybe this is an opportunity," she said.

"We're not starting our own podcast," he said, and she rolled her eyes but smiled, which delighted him.

"Okay, but that would be pretty amazing, right? *True Crime with Zeke Rodriguez*," she said.

"Given how much better you are at this than I am, I'm pretty sure it would be *True Crime with Sybil Bowman and Occasional Interruptions from a Former Mets Player*."

Sybil laughed, but then her face fell. "I really hate it when you do that."

"Do what?"

"Insult yourself, like you're not valuable."

"I'm valuable," Zeke said. "To my team."

"You're valuable," Sybil answered. "To me."

That thing from before—*hope,* he realized—bubbled up again, and he was suddenly acutely aware that his breath had gotten heavier. He met Sybil's gaze, but she broke it just as quickly, then was back on her feet. *Fuck.* She moved back to the tree, stared up at the bright golden star on top.

"Do you think Betty could have killed someone?" she asked finally.

"I mean, who knows what any of us is capable of," Zeke said.

"Right, I know." She faced him. "I'd kill someone for my kids. I just would, no questions asked."

"Maybe, uh, killing her parents is how she thought she could escape? Like, the cult? Is that weird, to say that Betty was in a *cult*? I feel like that's . . . ridiculous. Like, are people actually *in* cults?"

"Do you want to hear how many podcasts I've listened to about that? Because it's upward of a hundred." Sybil shook her head. "Wow, I really have way too much time on my hands." She reached for her phone. "This is what Wikipedia told me about the Revivalist Church."

> Founded by Samuel Jones, the father of six daughters and one son, Aaron, in 1979, the Revivalist Church was a fringe offshoot of the Worldwide Church of Believers, an already extremist church that had, prior to its shuttering, hundreds of thousands of followers. An estimated several hundred parishioners followed Jones from Tennessee to his new outpost in Georgia, where he implemented even stricter guidelines than the WCB and continued to grow his following.

"Hold on, let me skip ahead, there's a lot of religious stuff." Sybil swiped her phone and scrolled. "Oh here, this is what leads me to Betty."

> Women were mandated to be married on their 18th birthdays, and their purpose was to bear children and be their husband's caretaker. While girls attended public schools so as not to draw attention from local law enforcement, once they were of age, higher education was forbidden, as was marrying outside the sect.

"Betty is twenty-two," Sybil said.

"And the fire was four and a half years ago," Zeke replied.

"Does she seem like the type who wanted to be married at eighteen?"

"No," Zeke said. "She certainly does not. So, I mean, not to sound ridiculous, but that's a motive."

"Or maybe that's justice," Sybil replied. "Because if it were me, maybe I'd do the exact same thing."

"Do you think Julian agreed? And was just ensuring that she didn't get caught?"

"He has a daughter."

"But he was *FBI*, Sybil. Granted, I've never had a face-to-face with them, but he doesn't seem like the type to just . . . overlook that. And if he just wanted the case to be closed, that had already happened, right?"

"So you think she ran because she's guilty," Sybil said.

Zeke detected a very slight twinge of judgment in her voice, the very first of its kind in any of their conversations. He didn't want to be judged by this woman whose opinion he had come very much to respect. More than respect, to crave. He *craved* Sybil's approval. If he were sitting down with the mandated sports psychologist right now, surely, she would ask him why; she might suggest that Sybil's approval was simply a replacement for a coach's approval, for parental approval, for forty thousand screaming Mets fans' approval. Then he said something that surprised him, something he knew Sybil didn't want to hear.

"I think she ran," he said, "because she doesn't want to be found. And you need to face that maybe it's okay if we leave it that way."

Sybil's head reared back. "We can't just leave it that way."

"Why? What if she left for her own reasons?" As soon as he articulated it, he realized that he believed this to be true. Perhaps Betty's reasons to blow up her life and Zeke's reasons to blow up his career weren't all that different. Perhaps they just wanted *out*. And with no other escape routes, they chose detonation.

"Zeke!" Sybil's voice was a little higher, a little tighter now. He'd only ever heard her this way when she was speaking to Mark. He didn't like it one bit, but he didn't feel like backing down. "Betty is in trouble. *She needs us.*"

He stood, took his time and stretched. His arm didn't reverberate with pain the way that it used to, and that should have made him happy or maybe that should have made him scared. When he stopped in the moment to consider it, though, it made him feel almost nothing at all.

"I don't know if she needs us, Sybil. We want to think she does. But maybe Betty knows what she's doing. Maybe she left for a reason. Maybe we don't know what those reasons are because she didn't want us to. Maybe we have to live with that."

"Absolutely not," she said.

"Why is it that your opinion simply overrules mine?" He

didn't mean to get so pissed, but actually, he was suddenly extremely pissed.

"My opinion doesn't overrule yours," she said. "But you're implying that we just leave this alone. I can't do that."

"Why? Why can't you do that? If Betty has been on her own for four years because she wants her *freedom*, why would you be the one to stop that?" He was yelling now because this was as much about him as it was Betty. "I actually don't even know what we're doing here! Don't you think, if she wanted our help, she would have *asked*?"

"Zeke!" Sybil said louder again, but he was already down the hall, heading toward his bedroom. He couldn't have explained why he was looking for a fight, but sensed that throwing a punch would be gratifying, might dissolve the hurricane of tension threatening to combust inside of him.

UPDATE ON CHURCH FIRE

The Macon Telegraph

June 19th, 2021

By Annabeth Collins

Questions remain outstanding about last week's fire at the Revivalist compound. Authorities have yet to determine the cause or the site of where the fire broke out, as over half of the building burned completely to the ground. Three bodies have been recovered, but several are still reported missing, including Pastor Aaron Jones and his youngest daughter, Elizabeth. The deceased include Jones's wife and two church elders who were among the founding members of the sect. Jones is presumed dead—as his personal effects have been recovered, as well as DNA matches—while Elizabeth, it is understood, had not been seen at the church that night and may have fled the scene. Investigators have listed her as a person of interest but concede she may, in fact, have perished in the fire, which is cited as the deadliest fire in Georgia in the past decade.

More details are emerging about both the pastor and the church, where Jones was thought of as something of a divine prophet from God. "We believed that Pastor Jones was our judge, jury and potentially executioner," one former member who wished to remain anonymous said. Those who have left the church are shunned by the remaining members and often harassed and threatened by what former members called the Task Force. There was also the death of another council member, the church treasurer, two years ago. Initially ruled a carbon monoxide poisoning, it is now being looked at in a new light. "Jones set it up such that there could be no dissension, and if there was, you were punished or ridiculed until you didn't have the desire to dissent anymore," said the anonymous source.

A different former member describes being shunned from the community for forty days and nights because he was caught going to a local bar and was seen dancing with a nonmember. "It turned me around real good," he said. "Until they picked out a bride for me, and I realized I didn't want to be married to a child, and I wanted to live my life, including going dancing at bars." This same source noted that he has not spoken to his other family members, who remain steadfast in their commitment to the church.

"Jones says that he is a disciple of God," a third member, still active in the church but who agreed to speak with no identifying details, also shared. "My parents brought me into the church when I was eight. I don't know any different. If he says that he sees God and hears God, well, you should come by one Sabbath and hear for yourself if we are blessed enough to have him return. I have prayed every day since the fire that he comes back to us. In physical form, in spiritual form, in godly form. It doesn't matter to me. I just don't know what I would do without Pastor Jones's guidance. I think all of us here at Revivalist feel the same."

Inspectors remain on the scene, and this is a developing story.

43

NIGHT SEVENTEEN

SYBIL

December 28th

CHRISTMAS HAD COME and gone, a depressing span of days that Sybil spent mostly by herself with her unadorned tree in her living room, while Eloise went back and forth between the pied-à-terre with Mark and the house in the suburbs. After Sybil and Zeke had their disagreement the night before Christmas Eve, she returned to her empty house rather than bridge their gap. She suspected she could convince him that they *had* to find Betty in order to help her, but then he made the last-minute decision to fly to Oklahoma for the holiday—he emerged from his room and said his physical therapist was on vacation so he was going to take one too.

She wanted to text him multiple times a day:

Did you hear back from the reporter?

Did the charger for the old flip phone arrive?

Do you miss me?

She flattened herself on the couch, not nearly as enveloping as Zeke's, listening to Pluto's snoring, and reached for her phone. This was ridiculous! They were adults! She didn't get into squabbles unless it was with her teenage daughter or her philandering husband! She hadn't gone this long without speaking to Zeke since they'd met in September, and she was pretty sure, with the holiday over and wrapped, he was back from Oklahoma by now. Shortly before they'd argued, she'd overheard him talking to his agent about what came next in January, amping up his training to see where he could be by February, then into March and spring training. Timothy was on speaker phone while Zeke paced in his kitchen, the tenor of Timothy's voice all business, the tenor of Zeke's the same. Sybil had been under the misguided notion that maybe Zeke's heart was no longer in it, in his rehab, in the game, but maybe she'd misread him. Or maybe he'd let her misread him so that she thought they were more aligned, not just in what the future looked like, but in his focus on Betty, on helping her, on finding her.

Her phone buzzed in her palm, and she shot up, ramrod straight, startling Pluto. She'd barely been working out lately, but all those years of Pilates evidently paid dividends. Maybe Natalie was right. Maybe at forty-six, she still had it. Maybe if she just took off her clothes for Zeke, her new doubts about what was going on with them would fall to the wayside.

No. This was foolishness, this was fantasy.

She swiped at her screen, her pulse palpable in her neck, as if maybe Zeke had been thinking of her at that exact moment too.

Simone: hi sybil, sorry to bother.
know it's late

Sybil: Simone! Hi! I'm so glad
to hear from you. I'm up!

Simone: right, my dad had mentioned that

Sybil: Are you ok?

Sybil felt a rush of euphoria. It was demented, she realized, how much she wanted to be needed, how badly she needed to be put to use. Simone was grieving, and here Sybil was, using her for a contact high.

Simone: hanging in. been better, you know? anyway, i'm going thru my dad's things and thought you might want his phone

Sybil: oh ok? You don't want it?

Sybil had no idea why Simone would want her to have Julian's phone, but if Simone was asking, then Sybil's answer would be yes.

Simone: i take it no word from betty?

Sybil: Not yet.

Simone: ok, send me your address, i'll take an uber

Sybil hadn't realized Simone had meant she was giving her the phone *now*.

Sybil: I have a car! I can come to you!

Forty-five minutes later, at 2:12 A.M., Sybil pulled up to Julian's old apartment building. Pluto had fogged up the windows in the back, and she rolled down a window to air it out for a beat before heading in. It was strange, seeing where her late friend lived, seeing where he had a whole *life* before he knew her and even during, and now that was all gone. She thought of Betty, of what her old life must have looked like. Unimaginable really. Maybe Zeke was right, maybe Betty did want to get lost. Maybe she had burned down the church, and even if she had killed those people, maybe Betty thought they had it coming. That Sybil could understand, the vengeance of retribution against people who had taken so much from her.

She thought of Mark.

It wasn't the same, of course, but he'd stripped something from her, too, over the years of their marriage.

She rolled up the window, opened the back seat for Pluto and made her way up Julian's stoop. The air was blustery, frigid, like if you weren't careful, you could succumb to the elements quickly. In medical school, Sybil had been fascinated with frostbite, how your limbs just . . . died . . . like they weren't even part of you anymore. No feeling, no blood. Attached but dead all the same.

Julian's apartment was cozier than she'd expected, a deep couch, a leather chair, a rich and ornamental patterned jewel-toned rug. Pluto immediately started sniffing the perimeter.

"We have a cat," Simone said. "Or I guess I do now. Felix. He doesn't mind dogs."

Sybil unhooked Pluto's leash and let him roam and took a long look at Simone before making the impulsive decision to hug her. Really really hug her. Like the girl needed a mother now that she didn't have a father, and Sybil was going to hug her until she felt like she had one.

Simone eventually pulled back. "Thank you." She had bluish circles under her eyes, her cheekbones so much sharper than just a few weeks back at Thanksgiving. "One second, let me get his phone."

She wandered into another room right as a cat raced through with Pluto chasing it.

"Here," Simone said when she returned, placing the phone in Sybil's palm. "I removed the lock code so you don't have to worry about that."

"And you're sure . . . I mean, I'm happy to take anything off your hands or help in any way," Sybil said. *Please please let me help in any way!* "But you don't need anything off this? Want anything from it?"

Simone shook her head like Sybil was aggravating her. "No, here." She took the phone back and punched a few icons on the phone. "I'm tired, I'm sorry, I'm not explaining things right. You need his phone. Because of this."

She passed it back to Sybil. It took Sybil's brain a solid three seconds to catch up to what her eyes were seeing.

There was a picture of Betty taken from afar on a subway platform. She was being helped to her feet, having apparently fallen to the ground, by a tallish dark-haired man in a suit. Caleb.

"I don't . . ." Sybil said. "What am I looking at?"

"It came into his texts the night of the hit-and-run."

"The photo?" It was a dumb question, and she regretted asking stupid things of Simone, but she knew her brain was dulled from the lack of sleep.

"*This* photo."

"And you think . . . that is not a coincidence?" Sybil considered herself an amateur expert in true crime, but even she didn't see where the dots were connected.

"I think that my dad was tracking Betty for a long time. From what I can tell, he found her, here in his backyard, and you guys were a good excuse to meet her. Probably less threatening as a group than a solitary Black man showing up at her place of work asking questions," Simone said. "And maybe someone else didn't like that very much, that he found her, was asking questions." She clenched her jaw. "Of course he couldn't leave it alone. Of course he couldn't just *let it be.*"

"Let *what* be?" Sybil's knees felt unsteady, and she sank onto the arm of the couch. She was obviously aware that Julian was tied to Betty, but it hadn't occurred to her that his death was somehow tied to Betty as well.

"I don't really know," Simone offered. "But I do know my dad. And if he thought that there was a loose end in one of his cases, he wasn't going to quit until it was all sewn up. It nearly killed him four years ago. And my guess is that this time, it actually did."

44

NIGHT SEVENTEEN

ZEKE

ZEKE WAS TRANSFIXED by the cityscape, working out how to call Sybil now that he was back in town. Had been back for two days actually and still hadn't figured out how to smooth things over. He wasn't used to fighting with friends, but as Lani pointed out as they drove around their town Christmas Eve because there was nothing else to do, he wasn't really used to having many friends in the first place. And maybe he shouldn't go and fuck this one up. And maybe he thought of her as more than a friend, she added, and that's why the stakes felt so much higher.

He'd told her she was an idiot, that she'd seen too many rom-coms, then turned up the radio to that Chumbawumba song that they used to play whenever he struck out a batter in high school and veered onto the highway where he could floor it.

He pressed his forehead against the floor-to-ceiling window, which was cold, a buffer from the elements outside and his extremely pleasant always-seventy-two-degree living room. Twenty-nine floors below, Sybil was out there. Yet here he was, a grown man paralyzed about doing anything about it.

Someone was pounding on his door, and he jerked back from the glass. He checked the time on his phone, nearly three in the morning. He knew almost no one who would barge in at three in the morning other than, well, maybe Timothy, and two other people, neither of whom he dared to think could be in his hallway.

He peered through the peephole. And there she was. Sybil.

"Hey," he said once he opened the door. He felt like a barely postpubescent boy, saying hi in chemistry class to a girl he'd had a crush on.

"I'm sorry I didn't call," she said.

"No, no, I was awake." He glanced down, only now realizing he was shirtless, in flannel Christmas pajamas and barefoot. Pluto sniffed his feet, then licked his right big toe, and she unleashed him and let him into the apartment. As if that was that.

"I wasn't sure if you'd pick up," she said, and then he stepped aside as if to say *Come in, please, I've missed you*. Even though he didn't say any of that out loud. He was a fucking idiot.

"I would have picked up," he said, closing the door, bolting it.

"I came right from Julian's." She sat on the couch, more like fell into it, rested her elbows on her knees and placed her head into her palms. He was beside her in half a second.

"Julian's? Why?"

She looked up at him, and for the first time that he could remember, even with all the sleepless nights between them, she looked so tired. A new line between her brows, a new weariness in the way her lips pressed together. He thought this made her even a little more beautiful than just five days ago when they'd last seen each other. When they'd had their fight. He suspected this would sound ridiculous if he tried to tell her, but it was true nevertheless.

Rather than answer, she opened her purse and passed him a phone.

"Simone wanted me to have this. There's a photo of Betty. A recent one." She took the phone back, swiped, then set it on the coffee table, as if it were a specimen that they needed to examine in a lab. Zeke tilted over to look more closely.

"Okay. And?"

"I think it's the night she met Caleb."

Now Julian reached for the cell and brought the screen closer.

"You think Caleb is part of the reason why Betty left?"

Sybil sighed, dropped her head back on the couch. He turned toward her, rested his hand—his good hand, even though now they were both working, but he still thought of it that way, good or broken, useful or worthless—on her knee. Her own hand found its way to his, and they braided their fingers together.

"I actually don't. I can't explain it, but I *don't* think Caleb has anything to do with her disappearance."

"Okay."

"But why . . . I guess what I don't understand, if Julian thought Betty was responsible for the fire, what did he need us for? He knew where she worked; he could have just . . . I don't know, arrested her or whatever the FBI calls it. Indicted her." She lifted the hand that was holding his and pressed her temples, like she was staving off a headache.

"But he didn't," Zeke said.

"He didn't," Sybil agreed.

"So then why was he following her?"

"The thing is," Sybil said, "I am not even sure that he *was*. Someone *sent* this to him. It wasn't on his camera roll."

"So he had someone else follow her?"

"Simone thinks someone hit him intentionally. She also thinks he used us to befriend her, Betty."

"Wait, what do you meant 'hit him intentionally'? Like . . . the car accident?"

Sybil nodded. Zeke felt something flare in his gut, and he thought he might be sick. He didn't want to break in front of her; he couldn't freak out in front of her. She was already so much smarter, so much *wiser,* so much more together. But he felt like he was a skein of yarn about to become totally unraveled.

"That's—" he started, then stopped. He didn't know what that was other than he wasn't prepared to put his life at risk, *their lives* at risk to take this any further.

Sybil stood, more like heaved herself off the couch, and moved to the kitchen. He found her there staring at the evidence wall.

"Betty is in trouble," she said when she heard him behind her. "And maybe Julian didn't think she had done anything wrong. Maybe Julian was trying to help her steer clear of the danger she was running from."

"Sybil," Zeke started. "I think we're out over our skis here."

"Simone already told the police. About her suspicions. After the hit-and-run."

"Right," Zeke said. "So maybe we need to leave it to them."

Sybil spun around, her face a mix of fury and disappointment. "We can't *'leave it to them,'* Zeke. They don't know Betty, they don't care about Betty!" Her tone was high and tight, and Pluto ran into the kitchen, like she needed an ally.

"Sybil, look, I know that you are a *Dateline* expert—"

"Do not say it like that. Do not patronize me," she interrupted.

"I just think that this is over our heads. Four dead in a doomsday cult? A missing young woman? A man—*our friend*—run over outside his apartment in Queens?" Zeke didn't want her to think of him as a coward, but someone had to be reasonable here. "Shit, Syb, I mean, come on, let's be honest. This is . . . not realistic."

She pushed by him, and Pluto followed, as if neither of them could tolerate his presence. He trailed them like the runt of the litter.

"Syb," he said to her back. "Please, I really don't want to fight with you. I, I mean, I missed you. I hated not talking to you. I don't want to . . . do this."

He saw her shoulders rise then fall.

"Fight with me or find Betty?"

"Both. I don't want to fight with you, and I don't think we should find Betty."

"You may not want to," she said finally, still not turning to face him, "but I have to, Zeke. *I have to.*"

Zeke stared at the ceiling, willed himself to say the right thing. His physical therapist had just lectured him this morning on skipping two days while he was in Oklahoma. Forget that his PT took his own vacation. Forget that his body didn't have the rest it needed to properly recover from his workouts in the first place. For Zeke, there could be no gasps, no gaps.

"Your life has to be tunnel vision," his trainer had said as Zeke was easing his way into the Olympic-sized pool for a quarter-mile swim. "There can be no distractions, there can be no women, there can be no days off, there can be no nothing. Then, you might have a decent shot at being ready in the spring. Anything else, it's a snowball dropped in hell."

Sybil did turn now and held his gaze.

"I have to, Zeke," she repeated. "And I'm going to find Betty, with or without you."

He inhaled because he was being asked to choose: the rehab and his career or, well, Sybil.

"Okay," he conceded. "I'm in."

45

NIGHT EIGHTEEN

SYBIL

December 31st

THEY STILL HADN'T heard back from the *Macon Telegraph* reporter, and when they shot an email to Caleb, it bounced an out-of-office back to them. Sybil was getting antsy, losing whatever fitful sleep she could manage, dreaming of dooming scenarios where Betty was in danger. She'd actually doze off for a few minutes, then jolt up, check her texts, as if maybe she were clairvoyant and Betty was trying to reach her in her subconscious. The flip phone charger finally showed up after holiday shipment delays and a lost tracking number waylaid it somewhere at a Los Angeles airport. Sybil was back at her house with Eloise when Zeke called to tell her. He promised he wouldn't search the phone until she got there.

Eloise was hosting a "small" New Year's Eve get-together with some of her high school friends, and Sybil had planned to be there, albeit tucked in her bedroom, to ensure nothing went sideways. Mark had evidently already signed off on the idea—*convenient,* since he wasn't living in the house anymore—and by the time Eloise informed Sybil, she'd already invited her high school crew.

Now she had to go into the city and trust that Eloise wouldn't burn down the house. A terrible metaphor given the circumstances but alas, the one that sprang to mind. She swiped mascara over her lashes and thought of all the things she should have said to Mark when he so blithely asked, "What's the big deal, Eloise is only home for a few more days," then got out of all the responsibility that came with hosting underage college freshmen on New Year's Eve.

Her phone buzzed again. Natalie had sent an attachment.

Natalie: They decided to run a different cut of Betty's commercial nationally. Bigger check, more residuals. No word from her? I wanted to tell her.

Sybil's heart lurched as she clicked on the link. She hadn't shared the details of the church fire with Natalie, of the Revivalist upbringing, the implications of where the facts were leading them. Like maybe if she told anyone else, outside her bubble with Zeke, she'd have to see the judgment on their faces, hear the judgment in their voices. *Wait,* she could hear Natalie say, *Betty might have burned down a church? With the congregation inside? I vouched for this girl? I need to get this commercial off the air, the client will murder me.*

Sybil wouldn't blame her.

The video filled her phone screen. Betty looked so beautiful, and Sybil thought maybe she'd forgotten her face, the crystal blue of her eyes, the tapered nose, the shimmery blonde hair. She used two fingers to zoom in on a close-up. No, it wasn't that

Sybil had forgotten. It was that Betty never looked this way around them, as if she were constantly trying to blend in, wearing her own disguise. The realization nicked another piece of her insides. That maybe Betty never trusted her at all; that maybe Betty *had* been playing them all along.

Sybil double-clicked the video to give it a thumbs-up, let Natalie know she'd seen it.

By the time she arrived at Zeke's apartment, she'd watched it no fewer than twenty times, even if it was just a slightly different iteration than the first one. At every stoplight, in the logjam on the bridge into the city. She didn't have the right to feel so betrayed, and yet, she did.

Zeke greeted her at his door with a party hat, a noisemaker and a flute of champagne.

Sybil's shoulders were up toward her ears, her jaw tight. But Zeke looked so charming, so exuberant that she didn't want to kill the vibe. Eloise had accused her of being a "vibe killer" earlier today when Sybil put her foot down at a keg delivery.

She let Pluto off his harness, then clutched the flute stem, and he tinked her glass.

"Happy New Year," he said, and she thought maybe he was already a little tipsy. Zeke didn't drink very often, especially not now when his team was laser-focused on his recovery, and even though he was a solid two hundred and thirty pounds, it might not take all that much to turn him a tad swoony. "You look very pretty tonight," he said, kissing her cheek. His hand moved to that spot on her shoulder she was always rubbing, and he squeezed, like he was letting her know that he noticed. *He'd noticed.*

"Should we go through the phone before we start drinking?" Sybil replied, though she knew her skin was flushed like she was having a hot flash, and she couldn't meet his eyes. Did she look pretty tonight? She had tried to, of course, though the sleeplessness made it a challenge. It thrilled her that Zeke noticed.

"Sure, yes, absolutely." He closed the door behind her and disappeared, then reemerged with the phone and the type of plug that Sybil probably had in a box in her garage somewhere, a leftover relic she couldn't part with from a decade earlier. "But in case it's not obvious, I already started." He shrugged one shoulder, and his mouth edged up on one side, the sort of smile Charlie, her impish son, knew exactly when to employ to get away with trouble.

In the kitchen, Sybil took a gulp of the champagne just for show, then glanced at their pathetic evidence wall and drank half the glass.

Zeke had plugged the phone in by his espresso maker. Sybil had to don her reading glasses because the screen was so small.

"The last time I had one of these," Zeke said, "I think I was a senior in high school."

Sybil didn't want to tell him that she was so old, the last time she'd had a flip phone was in her residency, already a fully formed adult and heavily pregnant with the twins, while he wasn't even legally able to vote.

Zeke pressed a series of buttons and landed on the address book.

There was only one entry.

L.

Followed by a number with an area code Sybil didn't recognize.

"Levi," Sybil said. "It has to be Levi. I . . . overheard her calling him on Thanksgiving."

Zeke narrowed his eyes. "I don't get the impression she's used this phone in a while." He clicked another button, and they returned to the analog home menu.

"Right, no. But she *did* call him that night."

"Eavesdropping?" Zeke turned to her and smiled.

"Definitely not."

"Sybil."

"What?"

"Come on," he said.

"Fine," she conceded. "Eavesdropping."

Zeke looked utterly delighted.

"You're a little drunk," she added. "We need to be serious. This is serious."

Zeke put on a stern face and clicked a bunch of buttons, and they landed on the long-ago texts. The last one came in from Las Vegas.

L: Hey, look where I am!

A photo of a young man, scruffy facial hair, a crew cut and oversized jeans and a hoodie that read *USA*.

Betty: are u in paris?????

L: Haha, vegas. but it feels like a foreign country.

"Wait!" Zeke grabbed Sybil's shoulder, then darted out of the room.

Sybil abandoned the phone on the counter and trailed him. She found him on the floor of Betty's bathroom, the flour tin between his legs. He pried off the lid, then pulled out the stack of postcards. They were blank, so neither Sybil nor Zeke had initially paid them any mind.

Zeke flipped through them until he found the one with the wide-angle shot of the Vegas Strip.

"Voilà," he said, and handed it to her.

"I didn't realize these were postmarked." She sat beside him, and they pressed their backs against the tub. The Lincoln Memorial in Washington, DC; Fenway Park in Boston; Niagara Falls; Mount Rushmore; the Liberty Bell in Philadelphia; the Rock & Roll Hall of Fame in Cleveland; the Fountains of Bellagio in Vegas; the Four Corners in the Southwest.

"A map, of sorts."

"But a map of where her brother has already been," Sybil said. The postmark from Vegas was from nearly a year back. Not so long ago, but a lifetime when you're looking for someone. The others were a scattershot of months across years. "So I'm not sure how that helps us."

"This must be how Levi told her where he was," Zeke said.

"But they had the cell phone. Doesn't that seem more efficient?"

Zeke dipped his head back, closed his eyes.

"I never snooped on her, obviously. But I can't remember ever hearing her on her phone. It's not like she really had friends, now that I think about it. So I think I would have noticed . . . if she'd been talking to someone."

"Well, she also obviously knew what she was doing, blending in, shape-shifting of sorts." Sybil pulled out her own phone now and tapped on Natalie's text. "Look at her here. She's . . . well, she doesn't look like the Betty we knew."

They watched the commercial in silence.

"Maybe they agreed to only talk every once in a while. Let's say she did burn down that church," Zeke said. "Or let's say . . . maybe Levi did."

"I think he was gone by then, right? Didn't she tell us that? That he was the only one who left, who got out?"

"Okay, but hypothetically, let's think like Julian." Zeke pushed to his feet, then held out his hand to hoist her up. He didn't realize until he'd done so that he'd offered her his throwing arm.

"Your arm!" she said, and beamed.

"Oh yeah. My arm," he replied. "We'll see."

They returned to the kitchen. Sybil pulled out Julian's file.

"Okay, so we're thinking like Julian. And one of them is the suspect?" Sybil asked. She liked this. She liked this very much. This was exactly how she envisioned it would be if she were a true crime podcast host or a producer on *Dateline*.

"Maybe Levi dropped her a postcard when he left for someplace new. Or when he got someplace new, I guess," Zeke said. He tore off a piece of tape and pressed the Las Vegas postcard on their evidence wall. Sybil didn't mean to notice that his biceps rippled when he did, but she didn't mean to not notice either.

"And maybe they had an agreement to check in only if something was wrong? Like a break-in-case-of-emergency number?" Sybil added.

"But you heard her call him on Thanksgiving."

"Check the log on the flip phone," Sybil said. "But I swear it was with her iPhone—I saw her using it that night at my dining table, which means that either she was really worried or really desperate."

"Or getting sloppy," Zeke said. He finished off his flute and poured another one, then topped off Sybil's.

"The log," she said. "And thank you." She raised her glass and drank. Why not. It was New Year's Eve, after all. And she was pleased, tickled, to see their evidence wall bloom into something like a real police case.

His thumb worked its way through the buttons, then stopped.

"Last call on this phone was in September."

"So just before we all met," Sybil said.

"But maybe before she got spooked by Julian?"

His eyes widened, and hers did the same.

"You think she ran because of Julian?" Sybil said. Her pulse was racing now; this felt like *something,* she didn't know what though. But something. *That's* what she was missing from her life. Not surgery, not medical school. But a problem needing to be solved. Her phone buzzed. Eloise. *Fuck.*

A picture of her daughter holding up a glass of water.

Eloise: I'm behaving, see?

This wasn't Sybil's first rodeo, unfortunately.

Sybil: how do I know that isn't vodka?

Three dots appeared, then disappeared.

Sybil grabbed her flute and finished it.

"I don't know why she ran," Zeke said, on his way to top her off again. "But maybe we piece together Levi's route, his map, and find his final stop. What if wherever Levi is, that's where we'll find Betty?"

46

NIGHT EIGHTEEN

ZEKE

ZEKE CONVINCED SYBIL that they needed to get out of the apartment. It was almost midnight! It was New Year's Eve! Also, he was drunk, and he was pretty sure that she was halfway there, too, and if they sat next to each other at the breakfast nook, their thighs touching, their heads angled together as they organized the postcards and looked for a pattern to predict where Levi could be now, he wasn't going to be able to stop himself from kissing her.

And kissing her was just so, so inappropriate right now. They were trying to track down their friend who was in serious trouble! Technically, ostensibly, they should also still be mourning their other friend who may have been in even deeper trouble. And here he was, trying not to stare at her pink lips, trying not to think about if he'd be able to taste the champagne on her tongue when he'd had just as much, more actually, champagne.

It was blisteringly cold outside. The kind of New York City night where your skin cried out when the wind kicked up. He was in a goose-down parka, but his elbow ached nonetheless, like he was now one of those people whose joints hurt when a storm blew in. His progress had been steady and not even all that slow, even though to him, it was a frustrating drip of molasses. He knew he could do better, be better, but that required sleep. But his trainer, after chastising him for taking Christmas off, was pleased; Timothy was pleased; the front office was pleased.

The Upper West Side was buzzing despite the windchill. They walked uptown, as if they were still headed to visit Betty at the diner. Sybil had called and called until she finally reached the owner a few days back, who said Betty simply didn't show up one day, and when he tried to contact her, she had either blocked his number or she was ignoring him.

"If you track her down," he said, "I still have a paycheck for her. She was a fucking great waitress, and she is always welcome back."

"He must have wanted to sleep with her," Sybil had concluded. "Because she was a terrible waitress."

Zeke wondered how Betty was getting by without a job, if the parachute of living with him was part of her plan, a way to stow more money for when she had to leave. After Sybil hung up, he went into Betty's room and looked through the drawers again, double-checked the bathroom vanity. Finally, he raised the mattress—and at this, his pitching arm did protest—and found a wad of cash. She left so quickly that she didn't even bring it with her. Then he remembered that key that Sybil had found a few weeks back. He'd noticed she'd returned it the next day, left it on the kitchen counter. It must have been Betty's because it was gone by that night when Betty left for her shift. The last night he'd seen her.

Zeke didn't want to walk to the diner. It was New Year's Eve; he wanted to do something *wild*. Well, wild for a professional athlete who was known for his intense discipline. So not particularly wild. He looked at Sybil, who was wrapped in a cashmere scarf, a fuzzy hat, bulky mittens. She was tucking her chin into the neck of her coat to stave off the chill. *God, he wanted to kiss her.* He wanted to press her up against a streetlamp, make out with her against the side of a brick-walled building.

He grabbed her elbow with his gloved hand.

"Should we just . . . let's take a cab to the airport and get on a flight."

She stopped. "What?"

"Let's go to Paris. Or London or I don't know . . . anywhere but here."

Her eyes were watering from the cold, and she wiped her face with the back of a mitten, smudging her makeup. He wanted to run his tongue over it. *Jesus Christ.*

"We can't just . . ."

"Why not?"

"Well for one, Pluto will poop all over your apartment."

"We'll bring Pluto."

"We'll bring Pluto to Paris?" She furrowed her brow, and he could just make out the dart of her eyebrows underneath the cuff of her poofy hat. "Also, and don't get me wrong, I *love* Paris, but what about Betty? What about Julian? And . . ." She reached out and held his arm. "Your recovery. You can't just go to Paris."

He tilted his head back and stared up at the sky. You couldn't see any stars in Manhattan. It was so odd, to think that he used to stare up at the same sky in his backyard in Oklahoma, when he was so spent after throwing and throwing and throwing after dinner until his fatigue was so deep that he just had to flatten himself on the ground. The universe was within reach in his backyard in Oklahoma. He'd raise his hand as if he could touch the stars. There was the Big Dipper, there was Orion's Belt. Everything felt within his grasp.

"We could walk through the park?" she suggested.

"I mean, it's not Paris."

"You're drunk." She laughed. He wanted to bottle up the sound and keep it on tap for whenever he needed it.

"I think you are too," he replied, but looped his arm into hers, reveling in their intimacy, and they pointed themselves east.

They walked for a block in silence behind throngs of other New Yorkers out to celebrate. No one recognized him thanks to the layers of winter gear, a glimpse into normalcy if he hadn't been born with a miracle of an arm. He'd probably still be in Oklahoma like Lani. He'd probably be a high school coach or an accountant or run a landscaping company. He probably would sleep just fine at night. He would never have met Sybil, Betty, Julian. The duality of this: How much he wanted to lean into the normalcy, how much he couldn't turn off his drive to be back at the top of his game, was splitting him in half. A wishbone being pulled at both ends.

"It's weird," she said, "that there were four of us. And now we're the only two left."

"Betty's still out there though," he said.

"It makes me sad to think she's alone."

"Maybe she's with Levi," he replied. "Maybe we were just a stop along the way."

"That makes me sad too."

"I know," he said, because he did.

Someone's phone was vibrating, and it took Zeke four buzzes to realize it was his. His phone was stuffed in the inside pocket of his parka, so he tugged a glove off his hand, unzipped and regretted it as the frigidity permeated every pore.

"Fuck, argh," he said, grabbing his phone. Sybil took off her own mitten and hurriedly zipped him back up.

"Hello?" He mouthed *Thank you* to Sybil, and she smiled.

"Uh, oh shoot," a woman's voice said. "I didn't expect you to pick up."

"Betty?"

Sybil's eyes flared, and she pressed herself against him and stood on her tiptoes so she could hear too. Zeke wrapped his free arm around her to pull her closer.

"No, sorry," the woman said. "I'm sorry, is this Zeke Rodriguez?"

Zeke shot a look down at Sybil, who glanced back at him indicating she didn't have a clue either.

"Yes, this is Zeke."

"Right, okay, I apologize, I thought I was going to go to voice mail. It's New Year's Eve," she said. "Sorry, I'm a little off my game. But this is Annabeth Collins, from *The Macon Telegraph*? Again, I'm so sorry, I honestly was just prepared to leave you a message. I didn't mean to bother you tonight."

Now he and Sybil were practically levitating together. She was bouncing on the balls of her feet; he was squeezing her arm.

"No, no, Annabeth, amazing! There's no better time."

"I just got back from vacation," she said. "And I got your email. And . . . wait, is this really *Zeke Rodriguez*?"

Zeke winked at Sybil as if to say, *I told you this would work.* He'd forgotten that just a few minutes ago, he was moored in ambivalence over his fame.

"Yes," he said. "That's me. Although there are other Zeke Rodriguezes, just to be clear."

"My dad is a huge Mets fan," she said. "God, sorry to be so unprofessional, I just had to at least say that."

"Thank your dad," he said.

"He's going to freak." Then she cleared her throat and pivoted. "Anyway, sorry, okay, with that out of the way, after I got your email, I went back through my notes, wanted to see if I had anything that could help you. Are you just curious about what happened? I heard movie producers might be interested."

"Oh," Zeke said. "Well, no, actually, I am friends with Betty."

"Betty?"

Elizabeth, Sybil mouthed. They were standing outside a twenty-four-hour Duane Reade, and she nudged her head toward the entrance. Her nose was ruby red, and her cheeks even redder. The automatic door whooshed open, and the rush of heat felt something like heaven.

"Elizabeth," he corrected.

"Oh, the youngest." Annabeth paused. "I didn't realize she had turned up somewhere."

"Well, actually, she's gone," he said. "And we're trying to figure out why. And also if she's okay."

There was a long gap on the other end of the line, and Zeke wondered if she'd hung up on him.

Finally, he heard her exhale.

"Listen, there are some rumors," she said. "They're unsubstantiated, and I could never print them, but you know they never *officially* found Pastor Jones either."

"Presumed dead, I thought?"

"Presumed," she said, and let it hang there. Then another long sigh. "Look, I'd rather not get into all of this at eleven thirty P.M. on New Year's Eve when I'm jet-lagged and maybe being catfished by a man who claims he is Zeke Rodriguez."

"I really *am,*" he said. "I can send you a selfie?

"Actually . . . look, okay, the rumors were that Jones was up to his neck with tax evasion and money laundering—his treasurer died a few years prior—and a variety of nefarious stuff—"

"Right, we've seen the FBI files," Zeke said. He and Sybil had wandered into the candy aisle, which felt like a sign from Julian.

"Oh wow, okay, you may know more than I do then," she said. "I don't know, but it was always my theory that maybe he was the one who set the fire, his way to leave it all behind." She hesitated again. "Look, this is going to sound nuts, I know, and I swear to god it's not just to get your autograph for my dad, but . . . would you want to come down here and see everything for yourself?"

47

NIGHT NINETEEN

SYBIL

January 2nd

ANNABETH DROVE HER Toyota Camry like it was a Porsche 911. The engine rattled as they flew down the highway, and from the back seat, Sybil clocked Annabeth taking sly glances at Zeke beside her like she couldn't believe this wasn't part of a practical joke. She'd insisted on picking them up at the airport and was now giving them a Georgia geography lesson, though from what Sybil could tell, they were mostly driving through rural acreage. Every once in a while, an exit sign popped up with gas or fast food, but other than that, it was mostly vast grasslands or leafless towering trees that were waiting for spring to wake them.

"So you actually *know* Elizabeth, erm, Betty?" Annabeth said. "Because I want to be thoughtful about how you bring this up."

Annabeth had stayed in touch—in a professional way, nothing church-related—with Patience. She'd called her, and Patience had agreed, hesitantly, to speak with her again. Annabeth hadn't mentioned Sybil and Zeke.

"I don't want to spook her," Annabeth explained. "It took me a long time to get her to see me as someone she could trust." Her GPS announced there were police ahead, and she slowed to something in the ballpark of the speed limit.

"We did know Betty. We *do* know her," Sybil said. She was sitting in the middle of the back seat like a child in carpool and leaned forward between the two of them. "She lived with Zeke actually."

"As roommates," Zeke said. "I was just . . . I don't know, helping her out." Sybil watched him flex and relax his fingers over and over again. She knew this meant his arm was stiff, and she knew that Timothy and his trainer were displeased that he'd taken time off to chase this wild lead down south.

"A lot of people around here thought the fire at the church meant that it would be the end of it," Annabeth said. "Or maybe that's what a lot of them hoped. They were losing family members to it, being, I don't know, one mother said 'put under the pastor's spell,' even though that might sound crazy. But I guess they were happy to see it burn."

"I'm not religious," Sybil said. "I'm not sure I get it." She thought of her parents, thankful for their Jewish atheism, her hackles rising at the mere suggestion of being under anyone's thumb.

"The Revivalist Church isn't one of those things where you just show up on an occasional Sunday, sorry, Saturday for them, or go to Christmas mass," she said. "Everything about your life becomes about serving the church; whatever salary you earn—and around here, that can mean not a whole hell of a lot—goes back toward church offerings. You can't really socialize outside of the group; you're expected to spend just about all of your free time at services or *in* service. And the women—"

A car shot by on the other side of the two-lane highway, its brights on, cutting through the blackness. Annabeth flinched and swerved to the side of the road, an overcorrection. Both Sybil and Zeke were propelled to the right. Sybil just swayed in the air, but Zeke's elbow careened into the armrest, and he yelped.

"Sorry, shit, sorry," Annabeth said.

"You okay?" Sybil said to Zeke.

He nodded, but she saw him blink quickly, trying to stave off the appearance of pain in unwillingly teary eyes. He grimaced, reached over with his left hand and massaged his arm.

"The women—" Sybil prodded Annabeth. The journalist was young, maybe late twenties. She had jet-black dyed hair that was blunt cut to her chin, a double nose ring, and unusually pale, near translucent, skin. She presented as both ambitious and disarmingly unprepared, a dangerous mix that, at least in Sybil's former profession, could end in disaster. Sybil could hear Eloise in her ear, telling her not to be so judgmental, telling her maybe this was half of Sybil's problem, as if Sybil had all *that* many problems. And Natalie's divorce lawyer was at least handling her primary one.

"Right, the women, they're basically, like, think of a draconian society where women are just there to serve men. That's the Revivalist way."

"What does that mean?" Zeke said, his voice tight, his face a wince. He was still massaging his arm, and Sybil wished she were within reach to do it for him.

"Married young, there only to serve their 'heads'—that's head of household—pop out baby after baby, definitely no birth control, their entire purpose is keeping house, no higher education, that sort of thing."

Annabeth flipped on her blinker, and they slowed, turning down an unpaved road that the GPS missed, marked only with a series of mailboxes. She'd been here often enough to spot it in the dark.

A sprawling ranch home rose to meet them at the end of the drive, a woman standing on the front porch illuminated by torch lights. She raised a hand as they approached. When Sybil got out of the car, she could see that Patience was at least five months pregnant.

"I hope you don't mind me meeting you outside," she said. "The kids are asleep. Matthew is in a meeting with the other elders."

That she was Betty's sister was immediately obvious. Patience was taller, and her hair was a rich brown, but the geography of their faces was borne of the same map. The straight slope of their noses, the perfect symmetry of their cheekbones, the shape of a heart formed with their chins. Patience, like Betty, had violet half-moons under her eyes, and Sybil wondered if she, too, never slept. Patience tugged her chunky knit sweater around her, as if the air were particularly chilly, which it was not.

Annabeth made quick introductions, and if Patience recognized Zeke, she didn't betray it.

"And I'm sorry to sound ignorant," Patience said. "But why are you here? Are you interested in becoming members?"

Zeke looked at Sybil, and Sybil looked at Annabeth.

Sybil made the decision for them. In order to get any answers, they had to be honest. She'd learned this in medical school: Don't pretend that you don't see the facts at hand, even if they're not what you want to see. Avoiding the unavoidable only delayed care. Patience struck her as a woman who had dealt with her own set of truths; you don't birth a litter of children and not at least become a little keen to *some* aspect of the world's reality.

"You have a beautiful home," Sybil said, because it was true.

She didn't know what she was expecting for a pastor and his wife, but it wasn't this, a new build, something that reminded Sybil of a Montana ski lodge that she might have flipped past in one of her magazines when they were redoing the house and she had nothing better to think about.

"Thank you," she said. "My husband and our church built it from the ground up."

"We know your sister," Sybil said, then wished she had been less abrupt, but fatigue and urgency did that to a person. "We're worried about your sister."

Patience's eyes flared and a hand, which had been cradling her belly, covered her mouth. She glanced behind her to her front door, as if Sybil had summoned something evil, and Patience was waiting to see if that evilness were about to emerge. When nothing happened, she stepped down the stairs and onto the driveway.

"You know Elizabeth?" Her voice was low, covert.

Sybil dug her phone out of her pocket. Pulled up the commercial Natalie had texted. Patience watched wordlessly, her face both pale and astonished. When it ended, Sybil swiped through her photos and showed her the photo of Betty and Pluto on Thanksgiving.

Patience's hands were shaking.

"I haven't seen her since . . ." She glanced around.

"I haven't taken them to the church site yet," Annabeth said. "At night, I'm not sure how much there is to see."

Sybil thought of the photos from Julian's files, now up on their makeshift evidence wall. The pile of ashes, that there were charred bodies underneath, a heap of burned wood planks where an altar used to stand, the top of a cross still slightly recognizable.

"Is she okay?" Patience asked, and now her voice matched her hands. Quaking, maybe terrified.

"She's gone," Zeke said from behind Sybil. "She's disappeared, and we thought you might know where she went?"

"No," Patience said, and now she was firmer. "I haven't spoken with her since the fire."

"So she wouldn't have come back here?" Sybil pressed.

"Or maybe Levi has?" Zeke asked, and Patience's eyebrows darted downward, her jaw setting.

Very suddenly, Sybil realized that it was indeed much colder than she first thought. She could see Zeke's breath; she could feel the goose bumps on her every limb. Around them, forest bloomed up across miles, animals scuttled and whined and chirped. Everything about this situation felt isolated, odd.

"We're just concerned she could be in real trouble," Sybil said again.

"I haven't seen Levi in years. I don't understand . . . you know him too?" She hesitated, looked at Annabeth. "I'm sorry, who *are* these people again?"

Just then the front door swung open.

"Steady," Annabeth whispered to them. Then brighter, "Pastor Morrow, nice to see you again."

Matthew Morrow was handsomer than Sybil had expected. She had absolutely no experience with pastors, but Matthew Morrow had a striking resemblance to a movie star whose name was escaping her but who starred in some holiday smash rom-com that Eloise had insisted they watch together. Blond, light eyes, a jawline with a hint of a five-o'clock shadow. He was in a white button-down, freshly ironed, and dark pressed jeans. If he were cold, as the night dipped even darker, he didn't betray it. He slung an arm around his wife.

"Ms. Collins," he said. "To what do we owe the pleasure of your visit?"

"Investors," she said, and Sybil was impressed with how quickly the lie rolled off her tongue. "We were waiting online together at Starbucks today; they mentioned they were curious about Revivalists. I told them I knew just the man to introduce them to."

Matthew stuck out his hand toward Zeke, squinted as if his face looked familiar, but then seemed to move past it. "Pastor Morrow," he said. "Welcome to our humble church."

"I hear it's not so humble," Sybil said. "I hear it's pretty impressive."

She caught an ever-so-slight flare of his nostrils, that he had to address her, which delighted her. She thought of Mark and how much she'd sacrificed for his career. She wondered what Patience had sacrificed for Matthew. Or maybe Patience didn't consider any of it a sacrifice. If you'd asked Sybil twenty years ago, maybe she'd have lied to herself about that too.

"Just serving the Lord," he said.

"Amen," Patience echoed.

Sybil wasn't sure which one of them believed that.

Either? Both? Or neither of them.

48

NIGHT NINETEEN

ZEKE

ANNABETH HAD DRIVEN them over to the site of the church, the rebuild. She had initially proposed that they return tomorrow in the daylight, but her editor had emailed her saying he needed her in the office in the morning, so tonight it was. It was just as well. Zeke was already in the shit box with his trainer, and the sooner he could get back, the better. His arm was throbbing, back to feeling like it had a few weeks ago, the unexpected swerve in the car bruising something that was too delicate to be bruised.

The church site was, frankly, magnificent. Nothing like some homespun churches that Zeke had driven by in Oklahoma growing up, compact brick architecture with small white steeples and crosses atop. No, this was a sprawling, multibuilding compound. The interior lights were on in many of the buildings, so they got a sense of its scope even from the blackness of the parking lot.

"Pastor Matthew likes his investors," Annabeth said dryly. "As you can see. They have a school, a church, housing for the day workers, an industrial kitchen . . . you name it, it's here. It's almost like a resort. Except it's obviously nothing like a resort."

"I'm a little confused," Sybil said. "Patience seemed aware that you were lying to him about why we were there, but also . . . she seems to be complacent with her life? Am I misunderstanding?"

"No, that's about right," Annabeth said. "I grew up in a church not that different from the Revivalists. A lot of us learn to live with the contradictions. Patience was always close with Elizabeth, from what I've learned, but simultaneously, I knew if I told her why we were coming, she wouldn't let us. I also know that she falls in line with whatever it is that Matthew demands—and Betty is essentially dead to them for having left that night. That's what they all realized eventually: that she hadn't died in the fire, that she'd fled. Sometimes I wonder if they'd prefer if she'd died." She paused. "But anyway, I figured we could get away with that space in between, walking the narrow line. I guess I would say that Patience has been defanged, but she's not toothless."

"So Betty might reach out to her if she were in trouble? Or is she aware that she's been made an outcast, that, as you said, she'd be more forgivable if she were dead?" Sybil asked.

"A complicated question without a good answer," Annabeth said. "When I left the church for good, most of my family stopped talking to me. I don't have any reason to think Patience—or the other two brothers—are any different."

"Can you spell this out for us like we're five?" Zeke said, walking toward the main building before Annabeth beckoned him back. "This looks like much more than just a church; it looks more like a commune. Is that what you're saying: that this is much more than just a church?"

His arm was screaming now; the cold was making it worse.

He wanted Annabeth to give them answers; they'd flown all this way, and he'd gotten four pointed texts throughout the day from Timothy asking him just what in the actual fuck he was doing blowing off his PT session. He needed her to spell things out, and he needed her to spell them out quickly.

"Also correct," Annabeth said. "When Pastor Jones died . . . or ran . . . whichever theory you believe, he was already going national with it. A slick website; sermons available for purchase; customized Bibles."

Zeke exchanged a glance with Sybil. The Bible in the flour tin.

"People were moving here to join up, though Pastor Jones made them go through a series of . . . I don't know, purity tests? Loyalty tests? Before they could do so," Annabeth continued. "To be honest, no one local minded at first—it was a good thing for the economy, and I think the members enjoyed being taken seriously on a national scale. The church bank accounts were certainly flourishing, though after the fire, I don't think anyone wanted to look too closely, likely because Jones had clearly been skimming off the top for himself. And if they acknowledged that, their pastor wasn't just dead, he'd have been a false god too. Easier to just eulogize him as a saint, you know?"

"So before the fire, Jones was pitching religion with a side bonus of personal fame," Sybil said. "And profit."

"Exactly. Then after the fire, Matthew took it to an entirely different level. I think his YouTube page has over a million subscribers last I looked."

"The other brothers aren't involved?" Zeke asked. He was trying to piece together where exactly Betty figured into all of this, why any of it mattered, how this helped them help *her.* Maybe Sybil saw the chess pieces on the board in a way that he didn't. Mostly, he was beginning to resent this drain of his time and energy.

"No, they are," Annabeth said. "I actually don't know the specifics of why Matthew was next in line after Pastor Jones, only that he was hand-selected to marry Patience when she was eighteen—he's a decade older and had been in the church for a while, and my understanding is that Jones did so to make him his number two. Also, the two others who died that night, along with their mother, were quite senior in the church. That probably sped his ascension along. Fortunately, none of the parishioners themselves were killed."

"But you said on the phone—that the pastor might have been the one to start the fire?" Zeke asked. Even he could hear the impatience in his voice.

"He was close to being indicted for a variety of financial crimes. Honestly, he probably could have been indicted for more—the emotional abuse, that dubious treasurer death, and the general coercion that ran deep. But anyway, enough of his DNA was on the premises that I guess the Feds decided good riddance. Since all of them who were killed were so high up, and probably complicit, and there were no obvious suspects, I imagine they decided good riddance to them all."

"Right, okay," Zeke said. "Maybe we should head back," he said just as Sybil said:

"And where does Levi fit in?"

"Oh god," Annabeth laughed. "Levi and I went to high school together. He was always the black sheep of the family. You could tell he didn't believe a thing that came out of his father's mouth. I liked him a lot. He was artistic, broody, constantly getting in trouble at home, which meant naturally, as a teenager, I found him wildly appealing in a platonic sort of way since I was already semi-out to my parents and friend group—the religion thing notwithstanding—and also, I think they all took vows of, like, purity, even Levi."

"So couldn't he have been the one to start the fire?" Sybil suggested, even though the postcards dated back for a couple of years, and it certainly seemed to Zeke that Levi was long gone by then.

"Honestly," Annabeth said, "I think there are a whole host of people who would have had plenty of reasons to burn this place down, literally and figuratively. Betty, sure, since she was just about to turn eighteen. Levi, for being shunned. The pastor, as a way to escape. Matthew, because he came into power, and you saw their house—I mean, the other parishioners don't live that way." She clicked a button on her car key, and the doors unlocked. "If you ask around here enough, you'll probably have a list of two dozen people who didn't mind seeing this place go up in smoke."

"So if Betty didn't do it, maybe one of those two dozen people knows that Betty knows much more than she should," Sybil said.

Annabeth opened the driver's side door.

"I couldn't tell you that she didn't," she said. "But if she's missing and someone thinks she does indeed know more than she should, that would be an entirely logical reason to run."

49

NIGHT TWENTY

SYBIL

January 6th

SYBIL MET CALEB at a coffee shop near his office. He was tanned from a winter vacation somewhere but still looked like he was fraying at every seam. Sybil understood. Her roots were a cry for help at this point, her skin was splotchy like a patchwork quilt, her forehead lines had returned from her faded Botox with a roar not a whimper, so pronounced they seemed there only to mock her.

She wanted to get herself together, to check into a day spa and emerge a butterfly having shed its cocoon, not least because the only person she spent any significant time with was Zeke. But a day devoted to her outward beauty felt fruitless, futile, not just because Zeke was growing increasingly insular with his laser focus on his training since they returned from Georgia, but because Sybil felt like a fraud worrying about her blonde highlights when Betty was out there, missing and in danger.

In Georgia, she'd held her breath when they checked into the hotel, hoping he'd propose they share a room. But his assistant had called ahead: separate, of course. She deflated at the reception desk, wondering how someone so intelligent—her—could be so dumb. Also, he'd never once knocked on the guest bedroom door when she slept over, and it wasn't like he didn't have opportunities. Why she had thought that a hotel overnight, while searching for answers about their missing friend, would be any different, she didn't know.

Caleb looked distressed, staring at the photo on Julian's phone of Betty at Grand Central. Sybil wanted to show it to him in person, gauge his reaction, assess if there was some sort of outside chance that he was involved. She'd asked Zeke to join her tonight, a second set of eyes, but his arm was aching, still hurting from getting banged up on the trip, and he was stewing on the couch in front of ESPN. Training that day had evidently been shit. As had training the day before. She overheard Timothy barking at him on speaker phone, Zeke replying in curt, monotone answers.

She left without asking twice.

"I definitely did not know that we—she—was being photographed," Caleb said. He was drinking coffee with two sugars because he had to return to the office even though it was eleven at night. No wonder he and Betty had worked in whatever way they did. Maybe aligned circadian rhythms should be more prioritized; maybe they were actually a sign of compatibility. Someone who understands both the joy and isolation of the quietness of a pitch-black night might also understand your soul. She and Mark were, of course, incompatible. She and Zeke, however . . .

She refocused. "But this is when you met?"

"Yes, for sure." He pointed to a packet in his hand. "I'd gone to this conference for my boss that day."

"But she didn't seem spooked?"

Caleb managed a laugh. "I mean, Betty seemed spooked half the time, and I don't think that had anything to do with much other than that was Betty." He chewed on his thumb cuticle. "I know she lied to me, about the Colorado thing. Probably some other stuff too. But if what you're telling me is true, about what she left behind, maybe she had a good reason."

"I don't mean to imply that she didn't," Sybil said.

"No, what I mean is, if she was being followed—or photographed—" He paused, and his face went pale. "Jesus, hearing it aloud is really weird, jarring. Like, if I'm freaked out by this, I understand why she covered her tracks."

"And she never talked to you about her family?"

"You think someone in her family was doing this? Stalking her?" The color returned to his cheeks like a fire.

"I'm just trying to put the pieces together."

The waitress arrived with her chamomile tea. Sybil still, all these months in, avoided caffeine, like that was going to be the key to curing her insomnia.

Caleb squeezed his eyes together, seemingly trying to remember.

"She said she wasn't close with her parents, I remember that. And she told me about her sister. And . . . about her brother. The one who had also left."

"Patience and Levi." Sybil blew on her tea. She always made the mistake of drinking it too soon and just as often burned her tongue.

"Right, yeah, them." Caleb lit up with recognition, so either he was the very best actor in the world or else he had nothing to do with the mess that Betty was in.

Sybil waited. This was a skill she had honed with Eloise and Charlie. She always had a million questions but very rarely got the answers she wanted when she was forthright; more often, they wandered into her room at night to unspool their burdens, as if giving them space drew them closer to her. Eloise had returned to college while she was in Georgia, and Sybil surprised herself that rather than lamenting that she was once again an empty nester, that this now meant she had more time to be selfish in her pursuit of finding Betty, in lingering at Zeke's, when maybe she should have been home.

"Levi, I mean, he seemed like a real one," Caleb said. "Just wanted to burn down his childhood." He cleared his throat. "Sorry, bad use of that phrase. I just mean, Betty didn't tell me about the, uh, cult stuff, but just said that he hated everything about how they grew up." He considered this. "Actually, maybe I should have realized that she didn't have a perfectly normal childhood, now that I say this aloud. Anyway, he had wanted to travel the world, I guess."

"Did she want to travel with him?" Sybil's heart sparked. Maybe the answers were as simple as Zeke had proposed. Revisit the map of postcards, find the pattern, find Betty.

"I didn't get that impression, to be honest," he said. "I know this sounds crazy given what you've told me—but I sort of think that Betty just wanted to be . . . normal. Like, yeah, now that you've filled me in on everything, maybe she couldn't be. Like, at all. A crazy dad, a bunch of dead people at her church, but I still think that's what she wanted."

Sybil's eyes suddenly welled. *Exactly*, she wanted to say, because this was confirmation of all she had wanted for Betty too. She blinked quickly, and Caleb, now rewatching the commercial on her phone, didn't seem to notice.

"And Patience?" Sybil asked, when he set the phone back on the table.

"Trickier," Caleb replied. He pushed her phone back across the table. "My parents knew enough not to fall into the real trap of their church, but there were times when they came close." He leaned back in the booth, ran his hands through his hair, took his time. "The only thing Betty ever really said about Patience was that she had thought they were best friends. You know, big-sister, little-sister dynamic."

"I do."

"Right, I got the impression that Patience looked out for her. I think she is six, seven years older? So she could sort of, you know, tell her what was coming down the pipeline."

Sybil startled, that Patience must have been only twenty-eight or twenty-nine years old now. On her fifth child. At twenty-nine, Sybil's twins were two, and she, despite being wholly consumed with how much she loved them, spent her days wishing she could unwind time to before she got pregnant.

"But Betty said that changed once she got married, once she was, er, baptized?"

"I guess, though she couldn't have a formal role in the church because, I mean, if you've ever wanted to see the patriarchy at its finest, just join a doomsday cult where they are perfectly happy just riding this life to get to the next one."

"So theoretically, her dad wouldn't have minded . . . dying?"

Caleb laughed. "Oh no, I'm sure he would have. It's hard to explain just how much bullshit is spouted from the heads. I think it's more that they have no problem asking everyone else for sacrifice."

"And Betty shared all of this with you? I guess I'm trying to figure out why she told you some real things and kept other things to herself."

"No, not all of this. Some of this, I'm putting together right now, in real time. But she did tell me that she lost a sister to the church. I just didn't realize . . . it was this sort of church, her dad's church. Like, she told me that once Patience was married, she sort of spied on her? Betty told me about how she once checked out *Are You There God? It's Me, Margaret.* at the school library—"

"Oh no," Sybil said. She reached for her tea, which was now a reasonable temperature.

"Oh yes. Patience had moved out of the house, so I don't know, maybe Betty was thirteen, fourteen? Levi was definitely still there because Betty told me that afterward he went to Patience and called her a 'piece of shit for ratting out her own sister.' It's not much of a surprise that he didn't last much longer at home."

"I think I'm rooting for Levi in this story."

"Not all heroes wear capes," Caleb concurred. He checked the time on his phone.

"I don't mean to keep you," Sybil said, even though she did.

"This is more important," he replied, and Sybil knew, inherently, that he wanted only good things for Betty, that there wasn't any chance he was part of the reason that she ran. She wanted to extend her hand across the table and grasp his, thank him for caring about her when it seemed like too many had not.

"You don't seem angry at her, about how she lied or maybe omitted the truth," she said. "That's very generous of you."

"No, not really." He shrugged. "Like I said, if you consider the stuff with Patience, and uh, yeah, her dad, it's no wonder she doesn't trust anyone, not completely. It actually makes perfect sense to me."

"It's nice that she shared as much as she did," Sybil said. What she really meant was that she was a little bruised that Betty never shared any of this with her. But what would she have understood? None of it. And here Sybil had spent her adult years thinking she was always the smartest in the room. Maybe smart and knowing were two very different things.

"Well, think about that—her older sister, best friend. And

once Patience got, I mean, I guess you could call it *power* . . . oh wait, Betty called it 'corrupt influence,' that's how she phrased it, because I remember it still reminded me of something I would hear at my own church growing up. But so once she got that, she became unrecognizable."

"I—" Sybil thought about how quickly Patience's posture shifted when Matthew emerged from the house; how her crestfallen demeanor hardened into something steely, something cold.

"So yeah," Caleb talked over her. "I don't blame her for keeping her cards close to her vest. And I check my phone about a hundred times a day to see if she's reached out."

"She hasn't, right?"

"No," he said, and fidgeted with the cuff of his sleeve.

"And you would tell me?" Sybil set down her tea and stared at him.

"Ma'am, I know you might not believe me, but you sort of scare me. You and Zeke Rodriguez? I'm on *that* team." He smiled, and she believed him.

"Okay," she said. "And you'll call me if you hear anything?"

"Absolutely." He paused. "But also, I sort of hope that we don't."

"What?"

"If you think about what would have happened, how bad things would have been for her once she was eighteen, married, submissive, all that crazy shit . . . I mean, it makes you wonder how far someone would go to escape when their life is on the line. And if she's still in the thick of it, I hope she keeps going until she's ended it."

50

NIGHT TWENTY

ZEKE

"WHAT IN THE actual fuck *is* this?" Timothy's arms were crossed, his face a scowl. He stepped forward and slapped a hand against one of Julian's photos of the fire aftermath, then squinted at the *Macon Telegraph* article before he fished out his reading glasses to get a better look. "Is this why you have been so distracted?"

"I haven't been distracted," Zeke said. "Barring a couple of days at Christmas and about thirty-six hours last week—"

"Two full days," Timothy interrupted. "You went off the grid. And to my understanding it was to *Georgia*?"

"Whatever, I don't owe you my itinerary. Do you want to know how many shits a day I take? Barring that, I haven't missed a single workout, a single *second* of my rehab."

"Not missing a single second and being singularly focused are two different things." His pointer finger jabbed the evidence wall. "Also, you *do* owe me your itinerary because you owe it to the team. I'm sure they'd be happy to monitor your shits too. So seriously, do you want to explain what in the fuck this is?"

"Not really," Zeke said. Because he didn't.

Timothy had stopped by unannounced while Sybil was out meeting Caleb, an invitation Zeke had shrugged off. He didn't tell Sybil that his arm was still smarting and that his trainer today had been snappish with him when he couldn't complete all of his reps. It wasn't that Zeke blamed Sybil for distracting him—he wanted to find Betty too. But it wasn't that he didn't blame her either. If she hadn't been so doggedly insistent that Betty was in trouble, Zeke honestly could have carried on with his life, with his physical therapy, with his team's charted course for his return.

Timothy sighed, stuffed his hands in his pockets, which Zeke knew meant he was about to get serious. He wished he hadn't told his doorman to send Timothy up; he wished he hadn't opened the door to greet him; he wished that he had stepped out of the way of that fucking line drive. Then he would sleep like a newborn; then the complications in Betty's life wouldn't be his problem. He wished that he weren't the sort of person who was so singular in his focus that he thought of Betty as a problem. He wished a lot of things, none of which he could do anything about now.

"Management is concerned," Timothy said. "They need you ready in eight weeks. And no one in the training room thinks, as of now, you will be ready in eight weeks."

"Dude, I don't know what they want from me. I already told you, I'm doing the fucking work."

"For how much they pay you, you *better* know what they want from you." The temperature in Timothy's tone had dipped considerably. "And forgive me, but this"—he pointed his thumb over his shoulder at the photographs, the printouts—"does not give me reassurance that you aren't filling your time with other bullshit."

"What I do in my off time really isn't your concern," Zeke said, which he knew was preposterous as soon as he said it. He was a brand, and as Timothy had noted, an extremely expensive one. In an alternate version of his life, he would have been consumed with his recovery. But that ignored the entire problem in the first place. All the analysts, all the sports writers, surely the entire MLB management, had watched the replay over and over again, slo-mo, slower-mo, freeze-framed, and they'd all concluded that Zeke simply got unlucky. Didn't move fast enough. But Zeke knew the truth: that he didn't move at all. How do you dig into a recovery when you aren't sure that you want to be healed?

"We want to bring you to Arizona," Timothy said. "Full rehab center on-site there, work around the clock to get you up for spring training."

"No," Zeke said.

"I don't think I phrased this as a question."

"I have some shit going on here, Timothy, and I'm not willing to just leave it next week or whatever."

"I didn't say next week. They want you out there sooner."

"So you're here to escort me down to the team plane?" Zeke scoffed, but Timothy just crossed his arms over his chest. He was actually here to escort him down to the team plane. "Well, I'm not doing it."

"Because of *this*?" Now Timothy spun around and grabbed a postcard, one from Niagara Falls, then tore down three more. He flipped through them, tossing each one on the ground after examining them. "Because you have some weird fetish thing going on?"

"Fuck off, Timothy," Zeke said, just as he heard the front door open, then close.

Sybil appeared in the kitchen doorway, still bundled in her

parka, scarf, hat and Uggs. Her nose was ruby red, her mascara pooling under her lashes.

"Holy shit, it is like the Arctic tundra out there," she said. Then, to Timothy: "Hi, I'm Sybil."

"My agent," Zeke said.

"Nice to meet you," Timothy replied, because he was nothing if not superficial, extremely excellent at playing both good cop and bad. "I was just heading out. I tried to get Zeke to tell me all these secrets"—he pointed to the evidence wall—"but that bastard was tight-lipped as usual."

"Oh." Sybil glanced at Zeke and unwound her scarf. "Well—" She noticed the postcards on the planks on the kitchen floor, inhaled sharply, then stooped to grab them as if they were precious.

Zeke rushed Timothy to the entry. He didn't need Sybil to explain anything to Timothy, lest he appear even more distracted than his agent already believed him to be. A hodgepodge wall of a paper trail, a flimsy excuse for a couple days off in Georgia, a different woman with a key to his apartment than the one whom Timothy met last time.

"Plane will be wheels up tomorrow at seven A.M.," Timothy said, and Zeke wanted to slug him across his perfect fucking veneered teeth. "This wasn't really an optional RSVP, Zeke."

"I'm an independent adult," Zeke said.

"Okay, however you want to think about it," Timothy said, his hand on the front doorknob. "But you're an independent adult who is under contract."

"What was that about?" Sybil said once the door had shut behind him.

Zeke was shaking. Anger was radiating from his pores. If he could levitate on rage, he would. He'd always known that ultimately, he was a commodity, but Timothy and his team had at least had the decency not to treat him like one.

He stared at Sybil, and he knew it wasn't fair; he knew actually that he might be half in love with her by now, but he resented her presence so purely in this moment that it was all he could do to breathe the same air as she was.

"Zeke?" Her brow furrowed. Her hair was a hive from her hat, and he fought his impulse to take three long strides toward her, smooth it down, tuck it behind her ears.

"I have to go out of town for a while."

"Oh." A pause. "Okay." Another one. "Is everything all right?"

"No, not really." He started toward his bedroom, which required brushing past her to turn down the hall of his ridiculous apartment that his stupid salary negotiated by his stupid agent had paid for.

"Did I . . ." She followed him. "I'm sorry, are you mad at me?"

He didn't know why she was apologizing to him, and that just made him angrier. She knew better than to apologize, and here she was, bringing herself down to his level.

"No," he said. "And I have to pack."

He opened the linen closet, pulled out a suitcase, unzipped it so violently that the zipper went off its track.

"Here," she said. "Let me help."

"I got it," he said, though he clearly did not. His fingers were still trembling, and the zipper would not abide and realign with the teeth. He gave up and moved to his walk-in closet, where he pulled down clothes haphazardly and threw them the distance toward the bed, even when his elbow barked. When he emerged, Sybil was still standing in his doorframe, her hands on both hips, the apology clearly a distant memory.

"How long will you be gone for?"

"Awhile. Some time. I don't know." Zeke opened his bureau drawer, grabbed a pile of underwear, then socks, tossed those on his bed too.

"I wandered around Grand Central after meeting Caleb," she said. "Did you know they have storage lockers? That require keys?"

"Sybil, honestly." Zeke paused, squeezed the bridge of his nose like she was a headache. "I have to leave. And I can't deal with this right now. We are not, like, *CSI* investigators. I have an actual job."

He pretended not to see her wince.

"So am I tracking down Betty on my own?"

Zeke stilled. Then took what he knew was an exasperated inhale, but he didn't feel like he was in control of himself, like he was witnessing this moment from the outside and would regret it, but fuck if he could do anything about it. Not the first time, he realized.

"Look, I'm sorry, but I have a real life to deal with right now. I can't spend all my time chasing down a girl who might not even want to be found. Much less might be responsible for burning down a building with people inside of it." He didn't mean to say what he said next but did anyway. When he thought about it later, he'd blame his exhaustion, even though that was lousy reasoning for being awful to people you love. "This whole thing, this was all just supposed to be *low stakes*. Not complicated, not anything that took me away from my actual obligations. I have *real* obligations, you know."

"You certainly do," she said, and he retreated to the walk-in, so he didn't have to see the judgment on her face.

A few minutes later he heard her in the kitchen, and then the front door closed, the latch clicking into place. The evidence wall was dismantled; the postcards that Timothy had tossed and she had retrieved, similarly gone.

Zeke plodded back to his room and sank onto his bed, his elbows on his knees, his head in his hands. His phone buzzed, and he grabbed it, hoping it was Sybil, hoping she'd absolve him of what an utter asshole he had just been.

Timothy: I'm not fucking around.
7am. White Plains.

He stood, and his knee popped. He suddenly felt a hundred years old. He grabbed a pile of clothes from the bed, and that's when he saw his suitcase.

While he had been tossing clothes from his closet, Sybil had fixed the zipper, and now, everything aligned perfectly. Like there wasn't a problem with it in the first place. Like it had never been broken at all.

51

NIGHT TWENTY-ONE

SYBIL

January 9th

SYBIL HADN'T HEARD from Zeke in three days. She'd thought of reaching out every night during the long stretch of hours between midnight and sunrise, but in the end she stopped herself each time. She was done making accommodations for other people. Still, she hadn't wanted to rebuild the evidence wall at home alone, in her suburban kitchen, so held out the smallest shred of hope that he would change his mind, call, apologize. He hadn't.

She hauled the Bankers Box of papers out of the car in her garage and fished out all the postcards. She snipped off one-inch pieces of Scotch tape, formed little sticky circles and pasted the postcards up on the wall by her pantry exactly in the order she had at Zeke's. She stepped back, hands on her hips, waiting for illumination, for clarity, but any flash of brilliance was interrupted by her doorbell. For a second, she thought maybe it was fate: Zeke was indeed here to make amends. Then she held out hope that it could be Betty, though it had been five weeks since she'd evaporated, and that was an even wilder fantasy. When she unlocked the door she found Mark, a disappointment amid a sea of disappointments.

"Word of warning, his stomach is upset," Mark said, unclipping Pluto's leash.

Sybil had forgotten that they were doing a canine custody exchange tonight. Mark stood on the precipice and waited for her to invite him in.

"I come in peace," he said finally, and she sighed and stepped to the side.

Mark found an old beer in the fridge, then loitered in the kitchen, glancing around like he'd never seen the place before.

"What can I help you with, Mark?"

"It feels different in here."

"Must be the lack of the stench of betrayal."

He raised both hands like he was being robbed, the beer still clutched in one. "Come on, Sybil."

"Come on, what?"

He sighed. "I ended things with her."

"Mazel tov," Sybil said.

"I hate living in the pied-à-terre," he said. "I want to come home."

Sybil didn't mean to laugh, but she couldn't stop herself.

"You don't hate me," he said. "I know that you can't hate me."

"You don't have any idea how I feel about you." Pluto sat at her feet, like maybe he was choosing a side.

"I am well aware of how you feel about me." Mark nursed the beer, then seemed to think otherwise and set it to the side. Sybil hoped he didn't think they were about to delve into a deep conversation for which he needed to be totally sober. The Bankers Box was sitting in the middle of the kitchen island, and she had plans to rebuild the rest of the evidence wall tonight, Zeke be damned.

"If you are well aware of how I feel about you, then you wouldn't show up whining about how much you hate the pied-à-terre and casually informing me that you graciously ended your affair."

"Sybil, you never cared about the affair, let's be honest." He met her eyes. She hadn't taken a long look at him in years. He was still attractive in the annoying way that some men grow into in their middle age. He'd grown out his hair so it curled around his ears, and he had about a two-day stubble, which shaved off about half a decade. She remembered why, in medical school, she used to want to peel his clothes off in the break room.

"That's not true," she said. "I cared about the affair." She didn't. But she had to at least put up a front.

He half grinned, then let it fall. "You think I'm not aware that if you hadn't gotten pregnant, you would have left me? You think I'm not *wholly* aware that if you'd finished your residency, you would have been a far superior doctor than I am?"

"I would have—"

"Yes, you're right, you would have been. You're better at most things than I am," he said.

Sybil opened her mouth to speak but decided she didn't want to interrupt him while she was on a winning streak.

"What's in the box?" He nudged his chin toward the island.

"Nothing that concerns you."

"Is this about the baseball player?" He stepped toward the island, but she got there first, her fingers curling around each cutout handle on the sides.

"No," she said firmly. She could say that without a doubt now. She placed the box by her feet. Her territory. This was not about Zeke at all.

"A new project?" He tried again. A project? What sort of project had Sybil ever embarked on outside of whatever the kids' school needed, whatever their sports needed, whatever this house needed? She didn't have the kids or school or sports or a renovation, so she had no idea what Mark thought she could do to keep herself busy anymore.

"Mark, honestly, what are you doing here? I have things to do."

"It's ten P.M. What do you have to do? That's why I asked about this project." He jutted an elbow toward the box.

Sybil huffed. "I never sleep. Okay? I never sleep so I have things that keep me busy at night." She didn't know why she was telling him this, not when she really hadn't told anyone other than the Insomniacs, which was now down to Zeke. So now down to no one.

"You never sleep? Is this . . . Did it just start? Am I responsible?" His shoulders sagged. "Shit. Fuck."

"You are not responsible, Mark."

"Okay but—"

"But you're right about the other stuff. I *am* better at most things, and I *do* hold that against you. Actually, no, I hold that against myself. I should have made different choices, and to be honest, you should have too."

"I've already apologized for Vivian."

Sybil waited for her insides to curdle at the sound of her name. They did not. They remained perfectly solid actually. The tentacles of ambivalence were too strong to shake.

"That wasn't what I meant. Before that. Way before that."

"So let me help. With that." He pointed to the Bankers Box. "I'm off tomorrow, I have nowhere to be either."

"It's *my* thing."

"I'm not trying to interfere," he said. "Just offering to keep you company if you're going to be up all night anyway. You've tried the usual things?"

He meant meds, meditation, white noise, blackout shades, acupuncture, all of it. He didn't mean finding a group of strangers online, one dying under suspicious circumstances, one disappearing, and the other one, the one Sybil trusted the most, the one Sybil had brewing, complicated feelings for, now ignoring her.

"Mostly," she said. "Don't worry, it's not your problem."

"Okay," he said. "But don't you sort of think that if we had made our problems each other's problems, your lawyer wouldn't have had to contact my lawyer this week?"

Sybil wasn't expecting this from Mark, her milquetoast husband of two decades who suddenly sounded enlightened. It wasn't that she had any interest in reconciling, but still, something about him felt like it had shifted.

"I don't want to get back together," she said.

He nodded just once. A patient accepting the diagnosis. "Before I leave, can I grab a snack? I haven't eaten since lunch."

She waved a hand since he knew the way to the pantry.

"What's this?" he said from around the corner.

She found him staring at the postcards. "Oh, just . . . nothing."

"I love this," he said. "All the top tourist attractions across the country."

"I'm sorry, what?"

"Well, yeah? Isn't that what you intended?" He looked at her, befuddled. "Although actually, why are you tacking up photos of tourist attractions? Are you going like all *Thelma & Louise*?"

She raised her eyebrows at him.

"No, I understand why you would. I didn't mean that misogynistically. Men are shit."

"You're extremely confusing to me right now," she said.

"I know. Eloise got to me."

"Our daughter convinced you that you're a dick?"

"You know she wants to be a women's studies major, right? Or has she not broken that news to you?" He unzipped his parka like maybe he was actually going to be able to stay awhile.

"She's hinted," Sybil said. "I haven't taken it well." She refocused on the postcards. "But wait, can you explain what you're talking about with these?"

"Sure." He flopped a shoulder. "There was that Wheaties contest, the list of the top fifteen things you have to do on a road trip, or I don't know, see before you die? I can't remember. You had to go to each place, grab a postcard, then send them all in with the bar codes from Wheaties boxes. After college, before I met you, remember I drove across the country? Jasper and I hit all of them. This was mostly before you could buy anything on the internet because now people would just order the postcards and cheat."

"Wait, so you're saying there is an *actual list* of places where, if someone has gone to these"—she hesitated and counted the postcards—"these twelve, that they are likely to go to next?"

"I mean, I'm not a travel agent, but it's pretty obvious."

"So if I google Wheaties contest, I'll find the others?"

"Hmmm, it was twenty years ago. Maybe not. But I'll find it for you," he said. "Although I really don't get why you have these up if that wasn't your intention?"

"It's a long story," Sybil said.

"I do have all night," Mark replied.

"It's *my* long night." She stepped into the pantry and fished out a granola bar that she had stocked up on when he used to live there and had gone untouched since.

"Syb," he said.

"I appreciate the help," she replied. "And I do appreciate the apology."

He dropped his chin, raised it. That was that. He knew her well enough to know there was no swaying her once she made up her mind. Though remarkably, in just a few minutes, Sybil had an entirely new appreciation for her daughter and how wrong she'd been as her mother, to pigeonhole her into her own dreams. Mark's apology and opinion had potentially just led to a breakthrough, and without her daughter, he wouldn't have thought to offer the apology in the first place.

"I'll email Jasper for the information. He'll know where to find it. He was the navigator; I just sat there and drove."

"Sounds right," Sybil said but smiled.

"Jesus Christ," he laughed.

"It was low-hanging fruit."

"Fucking A," he said, but laughed harder.

52

NIGHT TWENTY-ONE

BETTY

BETTY HAD ACTUALLY managed to fall asleep on the bus, lulled by the rhythm of the tires against the pavement. She was woken by her seatmate, a boy about her age dressed in military garb, who gently nudged her leg and said, "Hey, we're here." He looked a bit like Caleb, whom she was trying not to think of.

"You need a ride somewhere?" he said. "My buddy is picking me up, lives outside the city."

He was harmless, even kind. But Betty couldn't afford to trust strangers. Not right now. She grabbed her bag from the overhead bin and was on her way.

The bus depot wasn't too far out from the heart of the city. She'd been prudent with her money in the past five weeks. Staying in hostels, relying on public transport, eating only to feed her hunger, not for anything pleasurable or greedy. Sometimes, when her stomach clenched, she thought of what she had left behind: the platters of food in Zeke's kitchen, the open-fridge policy where just about anything she ever craved was on hand,

and if not, his assistant would track it down. She thought about Thanksgiving, the headiness of cider and rosemary and garlic that turned on all of her senses at Sybil's house. But that girl, the indulgences she allowed herself, she had to be erased for now.

She had never been this far west before. The outside air was chilly and dry, but not nearly as biting as New York. Tolerable, even though the temperature must have been below freezing. She hauled her backpack over her shoulders and decided she would walk to the hostel. She could have afforded a cab—a splurge, sure—but the few miles would do her legs good. Also, she couldn't be too careful. The walk would allow her to check behind her every so often, ensure that she wasn't being followed.

She'd paid a barber in Cleveland to chop her hair into a bob and dye it a muted pink. In Chicago, where her lips nearly turned blue from the wind chill, she paid someone else to color it Raggedy Ann red. Somewhere in Iowa, she couldn't even remember the town, she went espresso black. That was three weeks ago, and she stuck with it, like its harshness suited her. But also, she hadn't been given reason to think that anyone was trailing her, so she left it for now. Of course, she hadn't thought anyone was trailing her in New York either. Sometimes, she'd wake up after a few hours of fitful sleep in whichever bed, whichever town she'd landed in and wonder if she'd misremembered: the warning of *run*, Sybil's phone call about Julian. In Omaha, she'd spent an afternoon in the public library googling Julian's name to be sure that maybe this wasn't a wild fever dream, that maybe she hadn't lost touch with reality. It wouldn't be unheard of, she knew, that a child of a cult leader had distorted memories, had fits of paranoia and delusion.

Tucked in a library cube with a desktop computer and their free Wi-Fi, she hesitated, nearly googling the Revivalist Church but unwilling to stomach whatever the results now were, whatever complicity her sister was tied to, whatever conspiracy Matthew was surely involved in. How had it been four years since she'd last seen Patience? The night of the fire, her sister was in charge of Sabbath dinner, tasked with setting up the refectory, aligning the place mats and the servingware and the decor. Their dad had always been fanatical about the dinners, or rather, in hindsight, fanatical about the *appearance* at these dinners, as he welcomed in church outsiders under the guise of breaking bread with strangers. But more often than not, he used the time to recruit the more gullible into the church. That afternoon of the fire, Patience was in the main kitchen; she had her younger child on one hip and another, her middle son, who sat cross-legged at her feet, with damp cheeks, wet eyes but not making a sound. Betty and her siblings had been routinely punished for tantrums as kids, and she'd spent enough time around Matthew to know that his tolerance for outbursts was nonexistent. Children were meant to tame their inner demons, meant to act godly at all times. Anything less was disrespectful to their elders.

Betty knelt in front of her nephew. Outstretched her arms. "It's okay, buddy, come on."

His round eyes peered toward his mother before he agreed to an embrace. Patience, lost in the trail of a thought, only just saw Betty there when he did.

"Elizabeth, get up," she said to her sister, not her son.

"What?"

"Stand up, John needs to learn his lesson."

"His lesson for what?" Betty did stand but glanced toward John. "Johnny, what did you do?"

Patience rested her hand on her arm. "It doesn't matter. Matthew says that explaining yourself when you've done wrong doesn't absolve you of what you did."

"Patience," Betty said, "he's three." Her sister looked exhausted, but Betty noticed she was now allowed to wear a hint of mascara and her nails were painted a very soft pink. Progress, perhaps, in softening her father. Or maybe Patience was rebelling. Betty liked that option better.

"I like your nails," she said. "I didn't realize we could—"

Patience looked down at her own hands as if they weren't her own.

"You should go," Patience said quietly. "You need to clean up before the Sabbath."

Betty was in dark blue jeans and an itchy knotted deep forest green sweater, too hot for the June weather, that she'd taken from Levi's room, which was still untouched from when he left. Her father had lifted the onerous dress code only a few months earlier, and though she had a few new items in her closet, she often had to improvise to look even remotely normal at school. She still had to cover all of her skin, but at least it wasn't those heavy woolly dresses that suffocated every pore.

Before she could insist on helping, her father appeared, and Patience's spine shot even straighter. John bit his lip, his little nostrils expanding and compressing with each breath, but otherwise frozen in his concentrated effort not to disturb his grandfather. Her dad took a singular look at Betty, her androgynous clothing, her hair wild and matted after a day at school, and clicked his tongue.

"Disappointing," he said, and Betty's breathing quickened. A laundry list of things she wished she could say in return, a laundry list of ways she wanted to cut him down to size sprung to mind. She, of course, said nothing. Saying something meant at best a diatribe, at worst, the back of his hand. "I expect you to be my very best one, Elizabeth," he added.

"I told her," Patience replied. "I told her to go home." Then she turned her back toward Betty and proceeded into the refectory with her daughter still on her hip, a vase of flowers in one hand, and her son, terrified, still sitting on the cool linoleum floor.

Later, when she replayed this memory at the library in Omaha and even again afterward, she wasn't certain of much of it. She was pretty sure that Patience had recoiled when reminded of Johnny's age; she was pretty sure that her father had reprimanded her appearance even though he was the one who had modified the rules; she was pretty certain Patience had soft pink nail polish on. But trust, even in herself, was slippery, a minnow in a porous net. Maybe none of that had happened. Maybe her trauma and her sleeplessness had turned her brain inside out, embedding memories that were actually fiction.

At the library, Google landed on Julian's obituary. She didn't know what she expected, like she or Sybil or Zeke would be mentioned, but it was short and concise. She thought he would like that: the brevity. Clean lines, no fluff. Most important, it was confirmation that she hadn't panicked, that reality wasn't blurring into something vaguer. Julian had been struck by a car near his apartment.

The walk to the hostel took forty-five minutes. She tried Levi again along the way. She'd swapped out the sim card of her phone as soon as she left New York, so she didn't expect him to pick up any more than she expected him to answer when she tried him at Thanksgiving. He'd been crystal clear: use the flip phone; anything else he blocked or would assume was too risky to answer. But in her haste to leave, she'd left the flip phone, their only meaningful lifeline for six years, at Zeke's.

She kept trying; he kept not answering.

She reached the hostel, home for the next few nights while she regrouped, showered, tried to rest, whatever that meant these days. She stood beneath the glow of the vacancy sign for a long beat, turned around once more to be triple-certain no one had followed her. Then she stared up at the vast, star-filled sky.

He was out there somewhere underneath the same expanse of galaxies. She was getting closer.

53

NIGHT TWENTY-TWO

SYBIL

January 12th

SYBIL HADN'T REALLY expected Mark to follow through with the list of landmarks, so she spent the next few nights falling down rabbit holes online in an attempt to track down the sites that matched the postcards, but she was frustratingly coming up short. Nothing about Wheaties at all. So when that proved fruitless, she couldn't stop herself from googling Zeke and reading an article in *The Arizona Republic* about his move to Phoenix in preparation for spring training. Timothy was quoted, as was the manager of the Mets, all prophesying optimism, a roaring return, a sure thing in the lineup by opening day, but notably, Zeke was absent in any line, any word of the article. There was a picture of him in the training room at the Mets' facility taken by the paper's photographer, so Zeke had signed off on the piece, but when Sybil zoomed in on his face—and she zoomed and zoomed and stared and stared—he looked stony, the Zeke she had witnessed the night of their fight. Not the Zeke she'd known all the nights before that.

She lingered on the photo longer than she should have. He

hadn't reached out in a week, and Sybil knew that was more about him than it was about her, but still, it stung. She had thought they were friends. For a while there, maybe even more than friends. In Georgia, yes, his assistant had booked separate hotel rooms, but when they checked in, he had lingered at the front desk, the question forming, an unusual uncertainty between them. She got so flustered that she blurted out, "Reservation for Rodriguez, two rooms," and she saw, out of the corner of her eye because she absolutely could not look anywhere but straight ahead, Zeke deflate ever so slightly.

Or maybe she wanted to see if he would deflate ever so slightly. It was dawning on her that she was going to be single for the back half of her life, and the thought of meeting someone new, of casual sex, was less thrilling, more daunting than she'd considered when she'd announced to the kids at Thanksgiving that Mark was fucking Vivian.

She stood. Poured herself a glass of white wine from a bottle that Natalie had dropped off when she told her about Mark's drop-in. Natalie hadn't had to ask if Sybil was reconsidering the divorce because that wasn't what this was about. She took only one look at her and said, "Bastards, who needs them."

It had started to snow outside, and Sybil could tell by the way her excess frenetic energy was radiating through her that it was going to be an entirely sleepless night. She'd adjusted, as much as a human could, to a few hours here and there, to drifting off at one A.M. and waking at four A.M. Tonight, she already knew even that was out of the question.

She opened the patio door, grabbed two logs from the stack that Mark had brought home from the hardware store earlier in the fall at the first hint of chillier weather. She started a fire with ease, one stroke of a match on the kindling and newspaper. Her mother had taught her self-sufficiency, and she nearly laughed out loud at how her self-sufficiency had hardened, then morphed into something akin to loneliness. She considered that maybe this was why she was so dogged in finding Betty, in helping her. Maybe Betty's own self-sufficiency had also hardened; maybe Betty was lonely now too.

She folded herself in front of the fire with Pluto stretched in his dog bed, snoring, then drained her wineglass. Just as she rose to pour a refill, her phone pinged with a text.

Mark: hey, sorry this took so long,
Jasper's been in Switzerland

Sybil: naturally

Mark: still nursing that grudge?

Sybil: no grudge, he just
refused to call me Dr all
through our residency

Mark: that's a grudge, syb

Sybil: he's a misogynist, so
then yes

Mark: no wonder Eloise turned to
women's studies, she got it from
her mom

Sybil muttered, "Fuck off," but smiled because he was right. Eloise wasn't going to pursue medicine, but maybe Sybil had imbued her with the exact right amount of self-sufficiency.

Enough to tell her meddling mother that she needed to chart a course of her own, but not so much that she didn't see the bigger picture. Sybil didn't know how you could be a women's studies major and not consider the bigger picture. Now that she thought about it, and yes, it could have been the glass of wine warm in her belly, she was utterly delighted at Eloise's decision.

Sybil: i'll text her, tell her that I expect her to be a supreme court justice

Mark: sybil

Sybil: i'm joking

Mark: i have to head to the hospital—on call—but here's the list.

An attachment landed in the text box.

Mark: It wasn't Wheaties, sorry, my bad. It was Fodor's. Remember how we were fanatical about that guide for our honeymoon? Anyway, I'd forgotten, Jasper told me, how Fodor's had a contest with National Geographic where if you took pictures in front of each landmark and sent them in, they were doing a giveaway of free guides for life. So not postcards either. My bad. Memory is going in our old age, I guess.

Sybil wasn't surprised that he'd gotten it wrong. But she was a little surprised that he admitted it.

Sybil: so you entered?

Mark: no, we totaled the car, remember?

Of course they had. She'd forgotten some of Mark's stories, as if once he vacated her life, she was able to open up a little more space for new information.

She clicked on the attachment, sent it to her printer.

Mark had been right about some of it though. She held the list up against the wall of postcards. She and Zeke had sorted them by postmark, but now that she had an actual road map, she could see that this was more than just a nomadic brother who sent a postcard every four months or so from a new state. This was a brother who was telling her where she could find him. Or at least that's how Sybil would have done it. Send a coded message, let her know he would stay for a while, let her know that he was one beacon shining in the darkness if she needed it.

But why go to such lengths? Sybil knew about their draconian father. She knew about the fire and Patience and Matthew. Were Betty and Levi running because they had started it? No, Levi was long gone by then. To confirm, she stripped the postcards from the wall, flipped each of them over. They dated back six years ago, starting in Washington, DC, the National Mall. Sybil traced through the next few and landed on Niagara Falls, early June of 2021. She already knew the date of the fire but retrieved Annabeth's article from *The Macon Telegraph* anyway. Overlooking details could be the difference between life and death on the operating table. Or on a *Dateline* episode. How many cases had gone cold because investigators were three degrees too sloppy? Sybil had never been three degrees too sloppy, unless she considered her feelings for Zeke, which weren't so much sloppy as they were reckless. How foolish she was, how stupid she felt.

The fire destroyed the church and killed four people on June 11th. The postmark from Niagara Falls was June 8th. Ostensibly, Sybil realized, Levi could have made it home to Georgia. Sybil fought the urge to text Zeke and tell him that maybe they got everything wrong. That they hadn't considered that Levi and Betty could be running because they conspired to burn it down together.

54

NIGHT TWENTY-TWO

ZEKE

ARIZONA WAS MISERABLE. Zeke hated that he was being trotted out to the press as some sort of comeback king. He hated that the team had put him up in a cookie-cutter condo with the rest of the training staff in same building, that every single thing he did day in and day out revolved around his recovery, and if he wasn't doing something involved with his recovery, he had multiple sets of eyes on him to course correct so that he *was* doing something that revolved around his recovery. Timothy had set up camp for the time being at the Four Seasons and made daily check-ins, and when Zeke snapped that he didn't need a babysitter, Timothy said that Zeke's attitude was maybe half of the problem. So they added in an extra day with the sports psychologist, who was also housed at the condo complex, which meant that every time Zeke left the apartment, he risked colliding with someone who was on the team's payroll.

When his bloodwork came back with sky-high cortisol, he finally told the sports medicine doctor that he never slept, and a prescription was written on the spot. Zeke didn't think that a sleeping pill had cured the rot that caused the problem—and he resented that no one stopped to ask *why* his cortisol, the stress hormone, had blown through the roof. But at least for the past four nights, it meant that he wasn't staring at the ceiling and thinking of how he fucked things over completely with Sybil. And how Betty might be, at best, in trouble, at worst, in danger. He would wash the white pill down with a custom-blended electrolyte drink each night and wake up five hours later, disoriented that he had actually managed to sleep. The first thing he would do, in the darkness of his bedroom before the sun rose, was check to see if Sybil had texted, emailed, called. He would have taken a stupid Sudoku at this point. He considered that he could be the one to bridge the divide, but he'd been brusque, overly harsh the night of their fight. He knew she'd want an explanation, and he also knew he'd feel like a fool when he couldn't offer one. Sybil was not the type of woman to shrug her shoulders and accept half-formed apologies. He thought about that night in the hospital, with a knife literally impaled in her toe. How she still managed to keep her head on straight when Mark and his girlfriend appeared.

No, Zeke was now coming apart at the seams, and he didn't want to drag Sybil into his open wounds. Georgia. That would have been the time to do something. To let her know how he felt. To kiss her. Maybe if he'd kissed her in Georgia, he wouldn't be down here in Arizona without her.

He stepped out of the condo. It was still dark outside, and Zeke hadn't adjusted to the snap of the cold desert in the morning. His arm was sore from yesterday, and the air, even with his team fleece, seized his elbow like a vise. He exhaled, and a plume of condensation from his breath dissipated. The clock on his phone said 4:37 A.M. He realized that he had about two hours to steal away before anyone on his team would rise. They reported to breakfast at 7:15 A.M., were at the weight room by eight. Then it was swimming and cardio and massage and more weights, then some throwing time, then repeat repeat repeat. Zeke was a cog in the wheel. An extremely well-paid cog in the wheel but still a cog.

He took a right out of the condo's driveway. The streets were empty, but he stayed on the sidewalks, a luxury of this particular spot of Arizonian suburbia. He thought again about that trip to Georgia, but this time, about Betty. He'd started listening to a book about how people get sucked into cults. He couldn't remember the last time he'd read a book that didn't have to do with anatomy or kinesiology or nutrition. Timothy had spotted it on his phone on the plane, and said, "Jesus Christ, Zeke, you're not in a fucking cult. It's called the major leagues."

At the time, Zeke had been a little embarrassed. Maybe that he wasn't intellectual enough to solve any of this. Maybe Timothy was right in the implication that he was just an athlete whose brawn outmatched his brains. In their partnership, Sybil had always been the brains, and maybe he'd gotten a little ahead of himself, thinking he could understand the psychology behind what Betty was running from.

It was ironic, Zeke thought now, what Timothy had said. It hadn't even occurred to him that *he* was indoctrinated, but maybe, in some ways, he was. He'd been told that this was the only thing he was good for, made to believe that he had to dedicate his life to a cause that he wasn't even sure he believed in anymore. Or maybe no one had told him that. Maybe that wasn't fair to his parents and Lani, who probably would have been fine if he coached Little League and worked as a UPS driver. He was the one who had convinced himself this was the only place he had any worth, not anyone else.

He took a left down a street with oversized new builds. He thought about Betty. How so few people are able to extricate themselves from situations such as hers; how maybe she did burn that fucking church down, and if she did, it was a triumph that she had freed herself. He thought about that dickhead, Matthew, her sister's husband, and how he expected reverence from a stranger in Georgia, when Zeke was always the one who had been revered. Maybe that's a little fucked up, too, Zeke thought, that he and Matthew weren't all that different, but also, he and Betty weren't either.

But something about all of it didn't make sense. Zeke couldn't pin it down, and if he had the guts to call Sybil and apologize, surely she could. He'd spent his entire career fine-tuning his instincts—when to wave off a pitch, when to brush the batter on the inside, when to go a little wild—and his instincts here said that Betty ran because she was scared, not because she was guilty. Or maybe he was just a fool who had deluded himself into thinking his instincts counted for something. Maybe they counted for jack shit. He hadn't moved out of the way of Schmidt's line drive when he could have. So.

The sun was coming up by the time he got back to the condo. Back to being a cog in the wheel. But whatever clue he was missing still pricked him, a splinter in the sole of his foot. If Betty didn't do it, he thought, who did?

55

NIGHT TWENTY-THREE

SYBIL

January 13th

SYBIL HAD NARROWED down Levi's location to just three possibilities. There were only twelve postcards, leaving three landmarks on the Fodor's list remaining. The last postcard had been sent from Mount Rushmore eight months ago, May, back before any of this started between the four of them. Sybil could barely remember the time before she'd hopped online, posted to the forum, found *Beartown* and *KingofQueens,* before they met at the diner on the Upper West Side and became inextricably linked to one another in a way that felt permanent.

Sybil had texted Simone earlier that morning. She wondered if Julian's partner—*Richard,* according to his notes, which were scattered across her kitchen island—might have any insights. Simone had replied with Richard's cell number. He picked up on the first ring, and after Sybil assured him repeatedly that she wasn't a telemarketer and that she was calling about the Revivalist Church, and that Simone had given her his number, he sighed and said he didn't remember many of the details.

"Could you look?" she asked. "It's sort of important. I think Julian wasn't settled with how it ended."

"You have to understand, Julian and I dealt with dozens of bad operators over the years. Once we closed a case, we closed it," he said. "Although Jules always had a harder time moving on than I did."

"Do you think his . . . accident, uh, the car that hit him, could be retaliation for a case?" Sybil was surprised to hear herself pose the question. As if the notion only just presented itself in her brain and then it flew out of her mouth.

"Possibly," he said.

"Actually?"

"No one could dismiss that. What we do, what he did, I should say, before he retired, was dangerous work. You know he nearly dropped dead from this case, right? We forced him into retirement. Simone and me."

She heard him shuffling some papers.

"Right, but in this case, the guy we were investigating, he's been ruled as dead," he said.

"Aaron Jones?"

"The one and only."

"The newspaper articles said it was quasi-inconclusive." Sybil grabbed a pen and made a note to follow up with Annabeth.

"Yeah, the determination came out a few months after the fire department cleared the place for the rebuild. DNA remnants, his wedding band. No signs of any bank account usage. They could only identify his wife by dental records. It was . . . oh, here's a photo of the scene . . . right, it was gruesome. Did you know the human body burns at about seven hundred degrees?"

"I—I did not," Sybil stuttered. She thought about it. She remembered something vaguely about burn victims from medical school, but Richard was a man who knew more than she did. And she was learning to accept this.

"Right, well, the main explosion occurred . . ." Sybil heard him reading his notes, and she reached for Julian's folder, a road map to what Richard was saying. "The main explosion occurred off the kitchen, by the boiler, just off the dining area where dozens of congregants had gathered for dinner. In a confined space like that, the explosion could easily reach a thousand degrees upon combustion."

"I see," Sybil said. She stared at the photo of the aftermath. Bodies that had turned to dust.

"Yep, it became an incinerator," Richard said, with the passivity of a man who had seen too much.

"So Aaron Jones is declared dead, and the case against him is dropped?"

"No, ma'am, we didn't have a rock-solid case, at least nothing that was indictable yet. That's not what Jules and I did. We gathered evidence to make the case. And we didn't have any reason to believe that anyone else, at least who was still alive, in his . . . clergy, I guess you could call it, was involved in the questionable financial issues. It wasn't that we didn't want to nail Jones, it's just that when he died, there wasn't much else to chase down. Whatever he was doing seemed to die with him."

"But Julian may have disagreed?"

"Did you know him well?" Richard asked.

"Fairly," Sybil replied. She didn't know how well anyone could have known Julian.

"Then you know that Julian disagreed with just about everything. I fucking miss that bastard but 'agreeable' was not a word you'd ever use to describe him. And anyway, we were partners because I was more of the numbers guy, he was more of the personnel guy. He reviled the scheme that Jones was pulling—"

"Scheme?"

"Well, yeah, I mean, I don't know, I'm not religious, but it seemed to be basically a pile of bullshit. An entire grift. And Julian really had a problem with that. Which, since you knew him, I'm sure you don't have problems imagining."

"And Levi? Any thoughts on him?"

More papers being shuffled.

"Oh, the son. One of the sons. No thoughts on him, he was never a suspect. We confirmed—" He paused. "Yep, we confirmed that he was out of the state. Had gotten a job selling tickets at Niagara Falls."

"Right." Sybil hesitated. "But when you say 'suspect,' I thought it was ruled as an electrical fire."

"It was. But we check out everything else just in case. And in this situation, there were some just-in-cases." He sighed. "Look, ma'am, I know you mean well. I know that every person now fancies themselves amateur sleuths." Sybil's ears burned pink. "But I remember saying to Jules at the time that Aaron Jones was a bad motherfucker, and though we couldn't shut down the church, we could rest easy that this slippery fuck was dead. And I honestly haven't given it another thought since."

How lucky, Sybil thought now. To be so unburdened. She knew that in Richard's line of work, he must carry plenty of burdens. But not the way Julian did. Not even the way that Sybil did, feeling as if she had to carry everyone else on her shoulders. Even now, trying to help Betty when Betty hadn't asked.

Based on the list and the postcards, Levi was either in San Francisco (the Golden Gate Bridge), Los Angeles (the Hollywood sign) or Arizona (the Grand Canyon). Part of Sybil hoped he was in Arizona, which might give her a reasonable excuse to call Zeke, but part of her wanted to solve this all on her own. Show him what he had missed out on. That she was a mastermind of sorts, that she was dogged, that she would do anything at all for the people she loved.

She was googling "Levi Jones" in the state of Arizona and coming up with no real leads when she remembered the flip phone. She found it in the Bankers Box, dead again. While she waited for the charger to revive it, she typed out a text to Eloise, apologizing for how badly Christmas break had gone, and thanking her for telling Mark to apologize.

Sybil: El, I don't need you to worry about me though or get involved with stuff between your dad and me.

Surprisingly, Eloise wrote her back immediately.

Eloise: mom, I do

Sybil: no, that's not your job, I should have done a better job keeping you out of it

Eloise: mom, for real, I'm an adult now.

Sybil: sweetheart, I know that

Eloise: no, what I mean is that you have to let someone look out for you too. we r studying that in

abnormal psych. Care has to be
reciprocal.

Sybil's eyes welled in seconds.

Before she could thank her daughter for her thoughtfulness, however, the flip phone sprang to life, vibrating and skittering across the counter.

Sybil snapped it open and gasped.

There was a new message from Levi.

56

NIGHT TWENTY-THREE

BETTY

BETTY PROBABLY WOULDN'T have run if Sybil hadn't told her about Julian that night. Even now, five weeks later, with sharpened cheekbones and still-jet-black hair, on a thinning sheet at the hostel a few miles from the bus depot, Betty found herself right back outside the diner, with Sybil's voice echoing on the other end of the line. Breaking the news.

Betty had thought maybe she was imagining someone following her at Grand Central the night she met Caleb, spinning something out of nothing. So she'd ignored her intuition that she had run out her clock in Manhattan. But Julian's death? Betty didn't have the luxury to believe in coincidences, not anymore. About a year before Levi left—was kicked out—he started tiptoeing into her room late at night. They were the only two kids left in the house; the other three were married; offspring abounded. Betty had eight nieces and nephews by the time she was sixteen, her siblings taking seriously her father's edict that marriage was intended for procreation.

For those few years, just the two of them, they were lucky to each have their own bedroom. And if her dad caught Levi in hers, that would be the end of it. No fraternizing between genders, even siblings, was allowed in private. Her father had gotten even more fanatical about that recently, inventing new rules whenever one struck him.

"You know one day, he's going to either kill me or boot me," Levi said. He was stretched out on her bed, his legs extending a foot past hers.

"Shhh," Betty whispered. Her dad was prone to popping up in doorways these days, his eyes lingering on her, his face a mix of something like consternation and wistfulness, if wistfulness had a knife's edge to it.

"Dad's not even here," he said. "You know he goes back out at night, right, once Mom is asleep?"

Betty did know. She tried not to think about it. Not because she didn't think that her dad was capable of being deceitful. But because she worried that he would see through her, see into her heart, which was rotting on the edges and turning black with rage, and then he'd punish her the way he punished Levi.

"You also know that I'm leaving soon, right?" He turned his head to the right, and she turned hers to the left.

"Maybe not. Maybe he'll let you stay."

"I don't *want* to stay, Bets. And you shouldn't want to either."

"I don't," she whispered.

"Then we need to come up with a plan."

Every few nights, he slipped into her room and prepared her.

When you have a chance to run, *take it*.

Stow money.

Be inconspicuous.

Don't stay anywhere too long.

Be careful who you trust.

And when you can, *find me.*

"He might just let me leave," she said. "All on my own."

"You're his youngest daughter, the last of his creations, the one who is supposed to carry on his promise in the name of God," he whispered. "Or whatever. Something like that."

"Patience can do that," she said. She felt him shake his head.

"You haven't been listening in to his sermons lately, have you?"

Admittedly, she had not. She sat in the pew and thought about how increasingly absurd her father looked at the pulpit, red-faced and shouting with spittle flying from his mouth. He was almost cartoonish, almost like *he* was the one possessed by demons, not the rest of them.

"He's been preaching more and more about the sanctity of the children, their path to righteousness in the name of their father."

"He's always done that," she said.

"No, not like this, not about daughters being carved out of their father's rib, not about them paying homage to their fathers to get to the gates of heaven. Don't you see the way he looks at you now? How whenever you are in the same room together, he never lets you out of his sight?"

Betty had only recently gone through puberty, a late bloomer at fifteen. Now, on the cusp of sixteen, she unavoidably did catch her dad eyeing her, even in her itchy, modest clothing, the way her breasts couldn't be tamped down, the way her dress hugged the curve of her hips. He wasn't leering; he was instead irritable, like her womanliness offended him. Betty had been too naïve to make the connection.

"You think he's speaking to me?"

"Well, I don't think he's speaking to me," Levi said.

"I don't want to get married," Betty confessed. "Not at eighteen, not to someone Dad has chosen."

"You won't have to," he said with such assurance that she believed him completely.

Six weeks later, she found the flip phone under her pillow. Two months after that, Levi was gone.

Betty had gotten sloppy in New York, falling a little bit in love with the Insomniacs, falling a little bit in like with Caleb. Shooting that stupid commercial. Even if it had been local. Even if it had been for five thousand dollars. Now, someone could turn on their television, see her face and easily trace her back to New York. To the casting agency. Who knows what from there. She wasn't sure how Julian was involved, how he'd gotten wrapped up in her mess, but she knew in her bones that it wasn't a coincidence.

Betty showered at the hostel, the water lukewarm, and found a diner down the block. She hadn't treated herself to a warm meal in days, partially to conserve money, partially because she thought she had seen someone with a shadowy resemblance to her dad in St. Louis, and even though she knew it was her brain again, playing a trick, she raced back to her motel, grabbed her bag and hoofed it to the bus station. Glancing over her shoulder the entire time.

She forked the eggs, marginally better than the ones from her former place of employment. She sat at a booth with an expansive window by the street, so she could see all the passersby, and thought about St. Louis again. It couldn't have been him. It *wasn't* him. She snapped a piece of bacon between her teeth. But the seed of doubt had rooted itself.

It was untenable, living like this forever. She could alter her hair color, give herself a new nickname, switch jobs, change cities. But it wasn't *tenable* to do this forever. She was weary in a way that she felt on a cellular level. Her purple welts beneath her eyes were puffy and protruding; her skin was sallow, her brain misfiring on occasion, which could have been the leftover trauma, but could have also been that your body can sustain a level of fear for only so long before it collapses.

She checked her phone again. She knew Levi wasn't going to call her back on this line because he was too disciplined. But she had to check anyway. Her fingers floated over Caleb's number, then Sybil's, then Zeke's. But she worried they were angry with her, at how she had left, and more critically, she worried that reaching out to any of them could draw her into more of a trap, as with Julian. She'd ignored or deleted all of their initial texts and calls, and eventually, they stopped calling. She told herself this was for the best, for their own sake, but she wanted to just this once think about *her* sake. She couldn't be an island forever.

She left a twenty-dollar bill on her table, a luxury she couldn't necessarily afford, but she'd once been a diner waitress too. Now she was an anonymous traveler moving through the city, like anyone else.

But she wasn't like anyone else.

She was her father's daughter. Her brother's sister.

Elizabeth Jones was ready to live life on her own terms, tired of being that anonymous traveler wafting through cities, through life, always looking behind her. She was ready to end things so that she could start looking forward, shoulders straight, face toward the sun.

57

NIGHT TWENTY-FOUR

ZEKE

January 15th

TIMOTHY WAS DRUNK and sprawled on the couch in Zeke's condo. Zeke wanted to nudge him, tell him to go back to his suite at the Four Seasons, but he was feeling gregarious and didn't want to kill the vibe. For the first time since his injury, he'd had an excellent day of training. He threw a fastball that was *almost* on par with last season; he showed laser-like placement; he got through what would have been a full batting rotation without surrendering much velocity or control.

Timothy had wanted to celebrate, and Zeke figured why the fuck not. His arm was throbbing, on its way to a bruising soreness tomorrow, despite an ice bath, despite a massage, but in the moment, on the mound at the spring training facility, it had felt worth it. He threw and he threw and he threw, and he didn't have to think about Sybil or Betty or Julian, and he resolved that this really *was* his purpose in life. He'd been given a once-in-a-generation arm, and who was he to be selfish and greedy and squander it?

"I knew we'd get you back," Timothy slurred. "I knew we

just had to bring you down here, get you focused, train the shit out of you. Remove all the distractions."

Timothy always shot his mouth off when he was drinking, but still, Zeke bristled.

"I'm not a rescue dog who needs training," Zeke said. He thought of Pluto and the dog's rancid breath that he had grown to love. Was it possible he'd just never speak with Sybil again? Could he live with that in pursuit of a World Series?

"Sometimes everyone is a rescue dog who needs a little training," Timothy said.

"I wasn't distracted either." Zeke rose, found the electrolyte drink in his fridge, swigged from the bottle. His nutritionist had banned alcohol, so forced sobriety with his intoxicated agent was the only option.

Now Timothy snapped open his eyes.

"I saw you playing detective with that woman. I watched that documentary on the Zodiac killer on HBO, you know; I saw what you guys were doing."

"We weren't playing detective," Zeke sighed. "And she's not *that woman*, she's a friend of mine." He paused. "And Jesus Christ, we were not trying to solve, like, the Zodiac killer."

Timothy raised his eyebrows and shrugged. "I knew it was the right thing to bring you down here. This is why you pay me," he said. "You have to trust me. Ten days in Arizona and you're already seventy-five percent there."

Timothy closed his eyes and started humming. Zeke suddenly felt a wave of nausea, that he was trapped in his cookie-cutter condo with this man whom he paid 10 percent of his earnings, and for what? He didn't have Zeke's talent. He didn't have Zeke's drive. He didn't have to do the physical therapy, the grueling workouts, the regimented diet, the emotional isolation that Zeke imposed upon himself so he could be the *best best*

best. He wanted to tell Timothy to shut the fuck up with his humming, to get the fuck up and get out.

"Her name is Sybil," Zeke said, and Timothy fluttered his eyes open, looked confused, then settled.

"Okay, that's cool."

"And the other girl you met, her name is Betty."

"The more the merrier." Timothy shrugged. "As long as they're consenting adults. Don't make me pull in legal."

"Fuck you, Timothy. They're my friends."

Timothy eased his way into sitting, wobbled a bit. "All right, all right, I'm glad you have friends, Zeke. Everyone always says you need to get laid, but in this case, I'll take the friendship."

"No one says I need to get laid."

"No," Timothy said, and reached for an open beer bottle on the coffee table. "They do. I just keep all that shit away from you because your job is to focus."

"My job is playing a sport that I happened to be good at as a kid."

"That makes you lucky," Timothy said. He drained the beer. Stood, wobbled a little more. "I think you've forgotten in all of this that this makes you exceptionally lucky." He found his keys by the front door. Zeke knew he should stop him from driving back to the hotel.

"I'm not lucky anymore," he said to his agent's back. "I've earned it."

"That is true," Timothy said, a hand on the doorframe. "You've earned everything. And you can be pissed at me for forcing you down here, for not calling you out five months ago when we both know you were fast enough to dodge that hit."

Zeke's chest rose and fell. There it was, someone said it. Someone else knew his secret too.

Timothy turned toward him. "I'm the only one here, Zeke.

Those girls, women, whatever. They're not here. Your family, they're not here. Your teammates? As I said, they think you need to get laid, then maybe you'll be more fun. I'm down here in Arizona for you. Be glad you have someone in your corner, someone who will burn everything down in service *to you.*"

Zeke sat with that long after he left. Not the getting-laid part and not the part about his family, because Lani probably would have punctured Timothy's tires if she heard him speak that way to Zeke. But about how far someone would go to protect the person they loved. He'd thought he could come to Arizona and silo himself off from his life, from Sybil and Betty and the loss of Julian. What he had missed is that his attempted laser focus had partially rendered him impotent. Timothy hadn't been wrong about everything.

A puzzle piece slid into its notch, and he jumped off the couch. He found his phone charging in the bathroom.

He went to her voice mail.

"Annabeth, uh, hey, it's me, Zeke Rodriguez. The pitcher? Anyway, could you call me back when you have a second? I have some questions about Matthew."

58

NIGHT TWENTY-FOUR

SYBIL

LEVI'S TEXT WAS six days old. Sybil was furious at herself for not thinking to charge the flip phone sooner, for thinking that just because it hadn't been particularly fruitful when she and Zeke first excavated it, that it couldn't help them down the line. Now she was a week behind chasing Levi.

> I got your msg from Thanksgiving. Sorry so slow. My old phone busted. Tougher than you'd think to get a replacement with the same number paying cash. Didn't mean to worry you. I'm fine. Hope you're fine? Love you, Bets.

Sybil had thought of a million ways to reply to him, but none of them seemed like what Betty would say, so her thumbs hovered over the phone's keyboard until eventually, she gave up. If she were part of one of those crime podcasts, one of her cohosts would probably prod her into texting, tell her just the right thing to convince Levi she was an ally. But without Zeke or without Julian, Sybil was, for once in her life, paralyzed with uncertainty. Worried that she would spook Levi. Worried that she would lose this thread to Betty, the only one they had, permanently.

She spent the day trying to put the pieces together—she was pretty certain he had already departed the Grand Canyon if the timeline of the postcards held steady—a move just about every four months, and the last postcard from Mount Rushmore was eight months old, which meant a stop at the Grand Canyon, next on the Fodor's list, had likely come and gone as well. She realized that Levi may well have sent a now-outdated postcard to Betty's old address, the one with Mallory, but she couldn't imagine that Mallory saved her old roommate's mail. According to Betty, she couldn't even preserve her yogurts. So Sybil, citing logic, wrote off the Grand Canyon. This left San Francisco or Los Angeles. Technically, the contest ended at the Golden Gate Bridge. Which meant Levi should be in LA. But the postmarks also told the story of a man who didn't entirely follow directions: He swapped the Liberty Bell in Philadelphia with the Lincoln Memorial in DC, and the four-month intervals weren't entirely predicable—an extended stay in the French Quarter of New Orleans several years ago, a shorter stint in St. Louis, where a postcard was sent with the Arch.

Sybil tried to think of what Betty would do but realized that she didn't have any idea. She'd spent two months trying to mother her, and here Betty was still a stranger to her. She tucked herself into bed—aspirational, no doubt—then thought of Eloise. She reached for her phone, and surprisingly, though it was past midnight, her daughter picked up on the first ring.

"I need some advice," she said.

"Oh my god, Mom, you're calling *me* for advice?"

"It turns out that I don't know everything," Sybil said, and the way Eloise laughed nearly got her high. "I'm sorry for winter break."

"Sometimes you just get tunnel vision," Eloise said. "I know you thought I would make a great doctor. Honestly, I would have." She laughed again. "I am my mother's daughter."

Tunnel vision. That felt like exactly Sybil's problem right now.

"Can I pick your brain about Betty, the girl you met at Thanksgiving?"

"Sure?"

"Not really about her, actually, about her brother."

"Did I meet her brother? Oh god, are you trying to set me up with her brother?"

"No," Sybil said. "Oh goodness, definitely no. I just—you're better with people than I am. If you needed to gain someone's trust, I guess I'm curious how you would go about it."

"One second," Eloise said. The line went quiet, and then Eloise was back and said, "Charlie, I've patched you in with Mom. She needs our advice."

"Hi, Mom," Charlie said.

"Oh! Hi, honey, how are you?" Sybil hadn't heard a peep from Charlie in over a week, and yet Eloise got him on the phone within seconds. She was beginning to suspect her closeness with her children was a one-way, situational relationship.

"Fine," he said, and she heard him swallow down a burp. She stopped herself from asking if he were out drinking, because he was a college freshman and that wasn't any of her business anymore.

"Well, as I was saying to Eloise," Sybil said, "you are both . . . well, people like you more than they like me." Sybil thought of Mark. People liked Mark more than they liked her too. For all of his failures, even despite his mediocrity, Mark was likable, winning even. Sybil was fastidious and organized and razor-sharp. But this also meant that she was highly strung, occasionally inflexible and usually convinced that she was right. (She was usually right, so there was that.) "And I'm in a predicament because I very much need to convince someone to trust me, to like me, even when he has no reason to give me the time of day or the benefit of the doubt."

"Oh Jesus, Mom, is this about Zeke Rodriguez?" Charlie asked. "I am not prepared to weigh in on your dating life, even if it's with Zeke Rodriguez."

"No," Sybil sighed. "It is not about Zeke Rodriguez."

She still hadn't heard from Zeke, and she couldn't lament that for another minute. She was a forty-six-year-old woman going through a divorce who had some delusional fantasy about a hot younger man. When she left Zeke's apartment that night, after Timothy had torn down their evidence wall and after Zeke started throwing his clothes onto his bed next to the suitcase with the jammed zipper, she was convinced that he would call her. Text her. She hadn't thought it was a *fight* fight. Not a split. She and Mark used to bicker all the time, but you woke up, forgave each other and took another step forward. Her argument with Zeke hadn't been the sort of argument, so she'd thought, that shattered everything. First a day passed, then another one, then another, and after a few, she asked Natalie what to do, and Natalie told her that Zeke sounded like an emotionally immature dickwad. Sybil didn't think that was quite fair, but then her phone remained dormant, so what did she know.

Maybe she shouldn't have been so surprised. In Georgia, after Annabeth dropped them at the hotel, Zeke said a brusque good night by the elevator bank. She knew that his arm was hurting from when Annabeth swerved off the road, but she lay flat in her bed, staring at the stucco ceiling, trying to figure out if she'd done something wrong. Said something wrong. The next morning, he was silent in the car to the airport, and though he signed a few autographs at the gate and took a few selfies, he wasn't himself. Could barely meet her eyes. Then came Timothy's pop-in, and the next thing Sybil knew, it was as if Zeke had been yanked from her life so quickly, the whole thing nearly felt like a mirage.

"Middle-aged women don't have to put up with this shit, you know," Natalie said.

Natalie was right. And Sybil was prepared to snap out of it.

"It's about something else. Nothing romantic, okay?" she said to her children.

"Thank god," Charlie said.

Eloise snapped, "Oh, shut up, Charlie. You don't get to shame Mom for being a *woman*."

Sybil wanted to crawl under her covers, because she was pretty certain her kids were now talking about her sex life.

No one said anything until Eloise spoke back up.

"I think the only way to go, Mom, is to just be totally honest. People respond to transparency, they don't want to be pushed into something they aren't comfortable with—"

"Right, so you didn't want to be a doctor," Sybil said. "I got it."

"Well, yeah, but more than that, people like Charlie and me because we meet them where they are. Like, we're friends with everyone—the math club and the football team and the robotics kids and the quiet ones and the weed kids. Everyone just wants to be seen, you know?"

"Even better," Charlie said. "Everyone wants to be heard."

Sybil was a little astonished that she had raised two children who were so much smarter than she was.

"Say whatever you need to," Eloise said. "But be honest, no bullshit. Meet him where he is."

Sybil had taken up enough of their time. Pluto hopped up onto the bed, sighed, plopped at her feet. She opened the flip phone, decided that she was just going to be honest. Explain who she was, how she knew Betty, how much she cared for her and how profoundly worried she was about his sister. How she found his postcards—she included pictures of them tacked up to her wall as proof in case this all sounded preposterous—and that she thought Betty was trying to find him, in Los Angeles or San Francisco, wherever he might be at his penultimate or very last stop on this voyage of his.

She fell asleep around three A.M.

When she woke up, there was a message from Levi.

59

NIGHT TWENTY-FIVE

ZEKE

January 16th

ANNABETH RETURNED ZEKE'S call while he was in the whirlpool bath in his condo. The day's training had gone as well as yesterday's, and he could see the fever pitch rising in the coaching staff, in his management team, all of whom were now in Arizona, turning up at practice today. They stood to the side, arms folded, in khaki pants, fleece vests and Nike hats from Zeke's endorsement deal, reminding Zeke of little matching Lego men. Created brick by brick in his name.

Zeke punched the button to stop the jets in the bath and put Annabeth on speaker.

"Sorry it's late," she said. "The news in Macon, Georgia, never sleeps. But I pulled up all my files on Matthew. I can email them?"

"Sure, yes, thanks," he said. "Do you mind giving me a brief overview? In the interest of time?" Zeke knew he probably didn't have the discipline to read all the fine print. That was Sybil's department. He closed his eyes, dipped his head back against the ceramic lip of the tub. He missed her in a way that reverberated in his bones.

"Well, the CliffsNotes version is that Matthew showed up at the Revivalist Church about fifteen years ago, in his early twenties. Pastor Aaron—" She stopped and cleared her throat. "Sorry, force of habit from growing up in the church. Aaron Jones hired him to build a new wing of the building. As I showed you, what Matthew rebuilt after the fire is pretty jaw-dropping, easily the biggest church compound in the area, but Jones was pushing the limits of what was thought of as impressive at the time."

"Where'd he come from? When he showed up in Georgia."

"Excellent question," Annabeth said. Zeke heard her clicking her mouse. "Right, according to government records, he was born in Florida, finished high school there, then there really isn't a solid trail of addresses." She paused. "Do you mind me asking why the interest in Matthew? I don't think anyone ever thought he had anything to do with the fire. If . . . I mean, if that's what you're implying."

"Didn't you feel like something wasn't right with him?"

"You're talking about a man who is leading what is considered by most to be a doomsday cult, so I think the answer to that is clear."

"Right, right," Zeke said. He wasn't sure what he meant to say, and he hated this about himself—his instincts could lead him right up to pressing his nose against a window, but once there, he didn't always know how to ask for someone to open it. "I mean . . . it's as simple as he gave me the creeps."

"If it helps, his brother, Silas, has a notoriously even creepier reputation."

"He has a brother?" Zeke sat up a little straighter in the

bath, the water sloshing around. He hoped Annabeth didn't hear it.

"A few years younger. He joined Matthew not long after Matthew started working for Jones. My understanding is they were hard workers, excellent at construction. But Matthew was even better at prophesizing, and I think he was elevated to Jones's number two pretty quickly. It didn't hurt that two other elders were killed in the fire. This is all conjecture, sort of church gossip from my notes, but I think Jones's grown sons were pissed off. They stayed at the church because to leave it, like Levi or I guess like Elizabeth—Betty," she corrected, "you had to take pretty drastic measures. But there was always a grudge there from the Jones boys."

"And how did Patience end up with Matthew? She seemed . . ." Zeke drifted. He didn't know what she seemed. Kind at first. Hardened minutes later when her husband descended.

"Oh, she didn't have anything to do with that. Pastor Jones made all those choices. Patience was his eldest daughter, so it made sense that she would marry his right-hand man."

"In the twenty-first century? He's arranging marriages?"

"The church, or, I mean, *that* church, the Revivalists, isn't run like it's in the twenty-first century," Annabeth said. "Especially when it came to the pastor's daughters."

"And did anyone ask Patience or Betty how they felt about that?"

"That's outside my purview, not really a reporter's beat," she said. "But I do know that Levi thought for himself. From what I saw of Betty, she did too. I think Patience was thought of as pretty headstrong, which is why she has a spot on Matthew's council now."

"What does that mean?"

"She took care of some of her dad's policing, the dirty work. Not with men really, but keeping the other women in line. Dress codes, courting, showing up for Bible study, all of that." She half laughed. "I actually like Patience because sometimes she's just totally normal, and then you see her in action, and she's sort of a psychopath. But under the guise of doing it in the Lord's name. Or more accurately, Matthew's." She quieted. "Do you mind me asking . . . is this still about Betty? She hasn't turned up?"

"No," Zeke said. "She hasn't turned up, and something about this whole thing, the fire, is nagging at me. Who set it. It has to be part of this, why she ran from home. But it seems like a lot of people were plenty happy to get rid of Jones."

"Oh. Yeah, no one disputed that, even at the time. Actually, Matthew cried a lot. I remember in the days afterward, trying to get him on record, and he couldn't hold it together. But also he struck me as a performative narcissist, so who knows what was real and what was for show."

"And you believe the findings, that it was an electrical fire?" Zeke wasn't sure why he kept poking around this. He wasn't an expert in these things. He wasn't a detective. He didn't even listen to true crime podcasts or watch *Dateline* like Sybil. His fingers were pruning now, and the bathwater was lukewarm. He should get out, start his evening stretching routine. He considered it; there was almost nothing he wanted to do less than his evening stretching routine. Even if the water turned to ice, even if his lips turned blue and his fingertips peeled off.

"You know," Annabeth sighed. "I don't know if I do or I don't. I think the local investigators, certainly, were happy to put it to rest, if I'm honest. Down here, a lot of them didn't want to ensnare themselves with the Revivalists, even with Pastor

Jones gone. The church has long tentacles. When the FBI left town, because my reporting showed they were really just there for the pastor, I think the local cops wanted to tie it in a bow."

"Justice had been served?"

"You didn't hear that from me," she said, and Zeke could tell she was stifling a yawn. "But certainly, plenty of local residents thought so."

60

NIGHT TWENTY-FIVE

BETTY

BETTY HAD GOTTEN used to traveling by night by now. She wished she had the luxury of peering out the window of the bus at sunset or in the midday sun. She was jealous of Levi and how he'd seen the country, just as he said he would do since the time he'd torn the advertisement for that contest of United States landmarks out of an old magazine from the school library. Betty had been terrified that they would get in trouble for vandalism, but he said, "Seriously, Bets, this was published in"—he flipped it over and searched for the date on the cover—"oh my god, this magazine is a decade old. You think they're going to notice a page missing? No wonder we're all such idiots here, the magazine collection is ancient. How are we supposed to actually learn anything?"

She wanted to tell him not to use the Lord's name in vain, not because she cared, but because if anyone heard him and reported back to her dad, Levi would be shunned to his room again for a week minimum with only one meal a day and no contact with the rest of them. The first time it happened, the school called once asking about his absences, but the assistant principal had recently become a member of her dad's church, and then no one called again. She also wanted to tell him that he wasn't an idiot. He had an actual *plan* for getting out. That made him the smartest one in the family.

There wasn't much to see at night now anyway. A long stretch of deserted land. If it had been daytime, she'd probably see pockets of tumbleweeds, some cacti. She purposely chose indirect bus routes, going north, switching stations to go south. She hadn't seen anyone trailing her this past week at the hostel, but then, Las Vegas was nearly as crowded as Manhattan had been, and look what happened there.

Run.

Last night, when she couldn't sleep, she finally googled Julian. Not just the obituary, though that, distressingly, was the first link that popped up. But deeper, into some of the back pages. No one had ever taught her how to be a citizen of the internet, and as ridiculous as it sounded in 2026, Betty honestly was just not good at it. All the other girls her age were on, like, seven different apps posing in bikinis and with ornate manicures, and Betty was still half scared that she'd stumble down a link that could lead her straight to hell. She didn't really believe that, but also, eighteen years of her father's sermons didn't just evaporate. She thought that the farther she got from Georgia, the safer she would feel. But actually, the farther she got from Georgia, the more she realized how little she knew. And that she would never be truly safe.

Run.

There was very little on the internet about Julian. A donation from him and his wife to a police fund; a donation from him and his wife to his daughter's middle school, and she found that only by clicking on the school's newsletter archives. His wife's obituary caught her eye. Nothing identifying about Julian other than what she already knew, but she scrolled down to the comments, the *memory book* as the funeral home put it.

There were over twenty comments in the memory book. Most innocuous. *RIP!* And *Deepest Condolences!* But one, from a Richard Watkins, stood out.

> *Simone—your mother was a superstar. She always sent your dad into the office with a fresh packed lunch because she knew he would skip it otherwise; she always checked in with us when the cases were tough and the hours were long. She never held it against me when I needed your dad in the middle of the night or when a two-day trip stretched into a five-day one. She raised you because your dad was off fighting bad guys too often to be around, but she made sure to let you know how much he loved you. I'll miss your mom, and I'm so sorry for your loss. I have your dad's back always, and now I have yours too.*

On the thin twin mattress at the hostel, Betty's heart felt like it was going to detonate, like she already knew what she was about to uncover. She curled herself into a fetal position, her face illuminated by the glow of her phone, and typed "Richard Watkins" into Google.

Her hand covered her mouth when she pulled up a news article about a triple homicide outside Baltimore. He was quoted in it. Richard Watkins was FBI. Julian had been FBI.

Betty had never believed in coincidences, and now she was sure. Julian had been killed because of her. She bolted upright in bed, packed her bag. Checked the bus schedule and reformulated her plan. She sped up her itinerary, got the hell out of Vegas and onto a bus that night.

All of this had to end. She couldn't keep on running. It had to end immediately.

She was going to be the one to do it. Not just for what had been taken from her. But for Julian too.

61

NIGHT TWENTY-SIX

SYBIL

January 17th

LEVI'S TEXT WAS one sentence long. An address.

Sybil hadn't been to Los Angeles in years. She and Mark had come out to Beverly Hills for a medical conference half a decade ago, but she didn't know the city well enough to orient herself at night, as her car from the airport wound through the streets of Beverly Hills. She was startled when they pulled into the hotel driveway. She was so discombobulated that she hadn't expected to arrive so soon.

She checked in, dropped her bag in her room and caught a glimpse of herself in the bathroom mirror. Even with the soft lighting of a five-star hotel, she looked undeniably wrecked. Puffy eyes, splotchy skin. Her highlights had grown out, leaving an inch of muddy brown roots; her Botox was totally gone now, and that crease between her brows made her look somewhere in a state between bitchy and furious. She rubbed in two pats of cream blush and dotted her lips with gloss. It was the best she could do for now. How delusional had she been? Hoping Zeke Rodriguez would make a move in Georgia! She looked every day of her middle age. She stepped back to get a better look in the mirror. She thought even her boobs looked saggier than they had just a few days earlier.

Levi lived on the second floor of an apartment building in Ocean Park. One of those cute retro buildings with a shared pool that reminded Sybil of *Melrose Place*, even though she knew the reference dated her. His door was a lime green that needed repainting, and before she could knock, it swung open as if he had been staring out the peephole waiting for her.

"Levi?" she asked. Like it would have been someone else.

"Come on in."

The apartment was nicer inside than the door implied. Pristinely clean, inexpensive furnishings that had been well maintained, attempts at decor with framed black-and-white photographs, a rich emerald green rug, a pretty gold lamp like something that Eloise would rustle up at a flea market.

He sat on an upholstered armchair and gestured for her to do the same on the gray fabric couch facing him.

"I—first, thank you for agreeing to meet me," Sybil said. She had a long speech prepared, about how worried she was about Betty, how grateful she was that he answered her text, but Levi's intensity spooked her, the way his eyes bored into her but were also wholly aware of everything around them, like if he needed to bolt at any second, he'd disappear before she could even realize what was happening.

"I wouldn't normally," he said. "But I believed you in your text. And . . . I remember Bets called me from your house, left me a message. Thanksgiving. She liked you, I could tell. And that you figured out the postcards"—he shrugged—"I realized that you were smart. If Bets trusted you, *and* you were smart, I figured I could trust you too." He cleared his throat. "I normally block all unknown numbers on my phone, even hers—if I don't have your cell number, then you don't need to have mine. But I left home the week after Thanksgiving, so, um, I was feeling lonely, nostalgic, I guess, and I decided to check my messages. Sometimes I give myself, like, an hour to wallow." He shook his head, like he wasn't sure if he'd made a mistake or wasn't sure that he should admit such vulnerabilities to a stranger. "Still, I wasn't certain if I was being played." He sighed. "When you reached out over the flip phone I'd given her—I mean, I realized then it really was her calling me that night. I still have a lot of residual trust issues, I guess. Obviously."

Sybil glanced around.

"So . . . she's not here? With you? I was hoping you texted me on her behalf, that she'd be in LA. Safe."

His brow furrowed. She saw the resemblance between them now, if Betty had dark brown hair and a square jawline. Their eyes were the same, the straight slope of their noses too. Levi still looked a little bit like a kid who had to dress up as a man for a job he didn't like, in a button-down shirt and khaki pants that needed an iron.

"No," he said. "And what she did—calling me at Thanksgiving, was stupid. She knew better than that, to use her cell phone; I told her in no uncertain terms: She has to be smarter than that. It's why I didn't, couldn't, call her back, couldn't trust the message until I was sure." He dipped his head, then raised it. "I'm sorry if you thought you'd find her here. That you came all this way."

"I don't mean to . . . pry," Sybil said. She did mean to pry, but she didn't want him to throw her out of his apartment. "But I don't really understand what is going on. We went down to Georgia—"

At this, Levi jolted up in his chair.

"You went down to Georgia with Bets?"

"No, I'm sorry. I went down with, well, do you know the baseball player Zeke Rodriguez?"

"Sure, yeah, of course. I'm a child who escaped a cult, but I did not just land here from Mars."

Sybil hadn't meant to insult him, so she talked faster, like that could mask her embarrassment. "Right, well, Zeke and I went down there. He's friends with her too." She watched Levi's eyes narrow in confusion. "I know your general story. The church, your dad, the fire, that Betty was orphaned."

His eyebrows rose now, but he didn't interrupt.

"Our other friend Julian, he . . ." Sybil sighed, stared up at the ceiling and tried to think of what to say that didn't make this sound absolutely ridiculous. Whenever she lost herself to her true crime podcasts, she never once thought how preposterous it all sounded. What an absurd confluence of events had to unfold for these stories to be real, to be told, to be believed. "I know this sounds like a lot, but he was killed."

"I'm sorry," Levi said.

"He was close with Betty, and the night it happened is the same night she disappeared."

"You don't think Betty did—"

"No, oh god, no," Sybil said. "I think she got spooked. It turns out, Julian was investigating your dad or, I mean, the church."

"Oh fuck."

Sybil passed him her phone. "Julian had been sent this photo of her the same night. I can't help but think—" She stopped when the blood drained from his face.

"Levi?"

"Someone sent this photo to your friend?"

"Yes, why?"

"And you trust your friend Julian?" Levi dropped her phone on the coffee table between them, then was on his feet, twisting the rod that closed his blinds. Then four long steps later, he crossed the apartment and locked the door. Sybil's heart began to thud so loudly she could hear it throbbing in her ears. Was Levi the one who started the fire, casually killing four people—even if they were very bad people—then running? Was he about to chop her up, dispose of her body? She grabbed her cell, typed in a frantic message to Zeke before she could think clearly. She wasn't naïve enough not to recognize that she was totally out of her depth here.

Sybil: I found Levi, in LA. If you never hear from me again, it was him!!!

He sat back down in the leather chair, dropped his head into his hands.

"Fuck," he said. "Fuck fuck fuck. I spent four, no, six years warning her to be careful."

"I don't—" Sybil felt foolish. Not at all the smartest person in the room. "I'm sorry, Levi. I don't understand." Then: "Are you about to murder me?"

"What?" Levi looked so stunned that Sybil wanted to slink out of his apartment and forget she ever contacted him in the first place. "What? No! Oh my god." His eyes floated over to the locked door, the shuttered blinds. "Oh shit, I'm so sorry. I do all of that whenever I panic. Oh god, oh Jesus, I apologize."

Now Sybil was triply embarrassed.

"No, no, I'm the one who should apologize," she said. "I overreacted. I'm not . . . I'm not always a people person." And *shit,* she'd texted Zeke, like a damsel in distress. She couldn't now text him and say to ignore the first text, because that just drew even more attention to the fact that she'd texted him in the first place. *Shit shit shit*. She breathed in, breathed out. Like she was at a yoga class she used to take that felt like it was of utmost importance, how long she could hold her crow pose, how many calories she burned. Still, now, her breath slowed, calming her. "I don't keep meaning to say that I don't understand, but this picture . . ." She gestured to her phone. "What just happened?"

"Shit," he said again. "Give me a second." He disappeared behind a closed door, and she heard his muffled voice on the phone. Then he emerged, grabbed his coat from a hook on the back of the front door.

"Come on," he said. "I'll drive. We need to hurry."

62

NIGHT TWENTY-SIX

ZEKE

ZEKE WAS ALREADY at the airport when Sybil's text came in. His ASU hat was slung low, and he kept his eyes down so hopefully no one recognized him. He'd thought about just flying private, but the impulse to get back to New York, back to Sybil, struck him so suddenly that the fastest thing was just to get on the next flight out.

Los Angeles? He reread her text.

"Actually," he said to the ticket agent. "Change of plans. I need your next flight to LA."

"Absolutely, Mr. Rodriguez." She smiled at him, and he knew she knew who he was.

He hated that Sybil had been the one to break their standoff, that he hadn't been mature enough to apologize for being such a petulant dick in New York. He thought he could surprise her. Board a flight, show up at her house with roses or something maybe less predictable because Sybil would appreciate whimsy, and sweep her off her feet. And now he'd gone and blown it.

"Here you go," the ticket agent said. Then whispered, "And go Mets!"

He forced a grin and said, "Thank you." He hadn't told anyone that he was ditching town, so he didn't even know if he'd be on the team after tonight. Or after tomorrow, when his trainers and managers woke up and realized that he was gone.

Earlier, he'd had one of the best practices of his career. Every pitch was faster, more precise than the last one. Like abandoning his life in New York and singularly lasering in on his game really was the antidote to all that ailed him. He'd taken an anti-inflammatory before he got out there, and his pain was abating in the way that a long, slow tide would; his throws were nearly, though not quite, what he'd been hurling before the injury. The coaching staff was elated. Timothy wouldn't stop pumping his fist. When the trainer called it for the night, these people who profited off his arm gave him a standing ovation. He should have been bouncing, high on serotonin, coasting on euphoria. The doctors hadn't been able to say if the great Zeke Rodriguez would fight his way back, but he could, and he *had*. And yet when he retreated to the locker room and stood under the scalding water for so long that it turned into more of a sauna than a shower, he felt none of that. There was no pride at his accomplishments anymore, just . . . emptiness. A windup toy who had been repaired and was entertaining the children again. He missed Sybil. He missed Betty. He missed Pluto and the way that he shed all over Zeke's couch and left little stains from his drool on the cushions. He texted Lani after his shower, a towel around his waist, alone on a bench in the locker room and said: do you think I could just move home and become a UPS driver? And she texted him back and said: I hear FedEx pays better, but yeah, absolutely. Come home. We got you. Just come home.

He'd been poring over his conversation with Annabeth all day. As he did his stupid laps in the pool. As he lifted his stupid weights. As he threw at his target again and again. Part of why he'd crushed it might have been his rehab, but part of it might also have been that he was so focused on something else that he forgot to be worried about his arm, his accuracy, his future.

He churned the information about Matthew and Pastor Jones over and over with each throw. About how far someone would go to get out. About who would protect you when you couldn't protect yourself.

Matthew was the one who benefited from Pastor Jones's death.

Throw.

But Jones was the one who was up to his neck with the FBI.

Throw.

Levi was already gone, but he knew what Betty was up against.

Throw.

Come home, Lani had said. *We got you. Just come home.*

He hadn't realized that he was close to an answer until startlingly and all at once, it came to him. Zeke had never been the first to solve a formula. Half the time, he didn't even think he understood the problem well enough to figure out which formula to use. Everyone around him was solving for *x*, *y* and *z*, and he was still flipping through his cheat sheet for the equation.

Intrinsically, in his bones, reverberating in his gut, he knew he'd done it. Just like he could see where the batter was going to swing before the bat even began its rotation, he could see this now. All his life, Zeke Rodriguez had been told he was good at one thing and one thing alone. But it turned out that everyone had gotten his narrative wrong. He wasn't *just* a pitcher. Being a pitcher meant detecting things right in front of you that no one else could see. This is why Timothy knew that Zeke could have avoided Schmidt's line drive, and this is why Zeke now realized that he should have given himself more credit than he'd gotten for something other than his arm. You needed guts, you needed intuition to go head-to-head with a guy armed with a bat and a hell of a lot of power.

After he got back into the condo, he packed a bag and slid into the SUV the team had hired for him, then directed his driver to the airport. He passed his driver two hundred-dollar bills not to say anything to anyone until the morning. He'd be back in New York by then, and they could chase him down at his apartment and argue with him there.

Then Sybil's text landed while he was at the check-in counter, and she was just a ninety-minute flight away.

He settled into his first-class seat. The doors closed, wheels were up.

Zeke needed to find Sybil and tell her.

He'd figured out who started the fire.

63

NIGHT TWENTY-SIX

SYBIL

THEY CROSSED THE border into Nevada two hours into the drive. Cell reception was spotty, coming in and out over the stretch of miles, and Sybil tried not to think about how Zeke had reacted when her text came in. When she'd asked Levi where they were headed, he'd said only:

"If this goes to shit, the less you know the better."

Sybil wondered if this is what it felt like—when you were duped into a car by an ax murderer who passed himself off as congenial, only to have him dump your body in a ditch. Or if that's just what consuming too much true crime had led her to believe. The women on those podcasts were always too trusting. Sybil would hear the initial episodes and think: *Who could be so stupid?* But it turned out, maybe she could! Maybe Sybil Bowman Foster, top-ranked at Harvard Medical School, was actually just a fucking gullible moron.

"Sorry," he said, as if her anxiety was radiating off her. "I'm not trying to be creepy."

"You are being creepy though." She tried to laugh, but it didn't come off as funny.

He sighed. Gripped the wheel. A large bug smacked the windshield, which was now polka-dotted with various insect innards, and he flipped on the wipers, which mostly just spread their guts around.

"I've spent half a decade relying on myself, more than that if you count my childhood," he said. "It's not personal. I've just found, from, uh, like, lifelong trauma, that trusting anyone else tends to backfire."

"Ironically," Sybil said, "I am much the same."

"I'm not trying to freak you out. I just know what I'm doing, where we're going and how."

Sybil eased back in the passenger seat. Levi did not appear to be a serial killer, so either she was going to end up on a podcast episode as a Jane Doe or they were going to find Betty. There weren't many options to get herself out of this anyway.

"And what are we doing and where are we going?"

Levi laughed. "That was a good effort, a different way of asking the same question. This is old history, with me and Bets."

"So trust you?"

"Something like that." He bounced his head, and Sybil was struck by how young he was. He wasn't much older than Charlie. A boy who had been abandoned years ago, who had to grow up with only himself for guidance. Sybil hadn't been cast out of her home, but she'd had to raise herself too. Here they were, semi-lost souls on a dark highway in the dead of night, bugs splattered on their windshield. The jury was still out on if they'd raised themselves effectively.

"I had to try to pry for information," she said, and he nodded again, kept his eyes on the road. "Okay, how about . . . twenty questions? Whenever my family would take road trips, we'd play twenty questions."

"And I'm sure you know enough about my family to know that we did not."

"Did you take road trips at all?"

"Only to, like, indoctrination events. They used to do something every few years at the Greenbrier. West Virginia. I only went once though—they realized I was too young to see what I saw; not sure if Bets ever did."

"Indoctrination?"

"You don't just get to show up for my dad's church and start praying. Have you ever heard of very fine Christians throwing what was essentially a key party?"

"You mean, like, from the seventies?"

"More or less."

"I thought part of your dad's whole thing was . . . um, purity?"

"What applies to me does not apply to thee," he said.

"And you didn't play twenty questions with your dad afterward, on the way back? Talk about a missed opportunity."

At this, Levi managed a half grin.

"I don't think I needed to ask questions, to be honest. I understood from pretty early on that none of it was for me."

"But your brothers? And Patience?"

"My brothers are, what I would say kindly, fairly stupid. The church set them up with money and prestige within the community that they'd never have a shot at otherwise. They're not in charge of anything really. They sit on the council, and that makes them feel important, so, you know." He took a hand off the wheel, batted it. "In some ways, even though they propped up my dad and still serve under Matthew, they're harmless. Complicit, yes, but neutered."

"And Patience?"

"Not fairly stupid," Levi said, then went quiet.

"Meaning . . . ?"

"Is this the start of twenty questions?"

"It can be. We're up to three."

"Fine, Patience was a good older sister to Bets and me. She didn't have a say in whom she married, and she seemed to tolerate Matthew well enough. I think she is the smartest one of us, or at least the most adaptable. She watched my dad for years, learned how to avoid triggering him, figured out how to appease him. In a different life, I think she'd have gone to college, become a doctor maybe, or a scientist, something like that."

"I was told that she did some . . . disciplining? On behalf of your dad? And Matthew." Sybil tried to remember exactly what Annabeth had told them down in Georgia. *Defanged but not toothless.*

"That's question four, and she's complicated."

"Explain please," Sybil said.

"When you're in that . . . bubble, which is actually a very gracious way to say *cult*, you figure out how to survive. Patience was always the best at surviving."

"But you and Betty got out."

"I was kicked out, which probably saved my life, though I never knew if he would change his mind about me, either, so I stayed inconspicuous, tried not to be found. Betty had to run. My dad . . ." He paused and flicked on the wipers again to clear the bugs. "My dad never would have let her go. The older she got, the more possessive he became of her. Started giving sermons aimed at her. Started changing all of his rules at a whim just because of her. So we planned for it for almost a year—me, teaching her how to get out." A car crossed the other side of the highway, and its headlights illuminated the wince on Levi's face. "He was not . . ." He considered. "He was the worst combination: erratic, possessive and willing to do anything to maintain control."

"And now you think Betty's in danger?"

"Yes. Possibly." He blinked quickly. "I don't know how dumb she is being. So maybe."

"Do you know where she is?"

"Also yes, maybe. But I also don't know what else she knows."

"Extremely vague answer," Sybil said. "Technically, these are supposed to be answered yes or no."

"Nothing about my life has ever been black or white. If that's the case for you, you're extremely fortunate."

"Your decision to leave home, that wasn't black or white?"

Levi's jaw twitched. "Actually, it wasn't. I knew I could never become an elder in my dad's church like my other two brothers had, but leaving all of it behind wasn't clear-cut, no."

"Because of Betty?"

"Because of Betty. I knew she wasn't meant for the church any more than I was. But ultimately, I couldn't protect her. If you'd known my dad, you'd understand."

"So you *didn't* start the fire?"

He turned to face her, the tires overcorrecting just a bit, and they swerved on the empty highway. Sybil thought of Zeke down in Georgia, at his obvious pain when he'd rammed into the armrest. Maybe she shouldn't have been surprised when he left for Arizona. He had a whole big life outside of their little Insomniacs quartet. She was embarrassed now, two weeks after their fight, that she had expected that she was enough for him to reconsider, to prioritize finding Betty. She checked her phone again, still no signal.

Levi steered them back into the middle lane without answering one way or the other about the fire.

"All right. Well, I found all of your postcards. Please explain."

"I thought twenty questions were yes or no answers?"

"And I thought you'd never played before," Sybil said.

"The postcards were some old lark that I'd told Bets about when we were kids. I'd torn a page out from an ad in an old *National Geographic*. Had it hidden under my bed, told Bets we'd do it, get out and see all the places, even though the contest was obviously over."

So Mark had been right. Sybil made a mental note to thank him.

Despite everything, particularly the anesthesiologist, she found that she no longer resented Mark. Maybe they did the best they could in the circumstances they found themselves in and had raised two brilliant kids who gave fantastic advice, without which, she would not be in this car with Levi, who hopefully was not going to murder her. And who hopefully was taking her to Betty. Maybe life was all interconnected like that. Mark and her kids and Levi and the Insomniacs and Zeke and Julian and Betty. Maybe there were invisible strings tying them all together, and the best thing anyone could do was be tugged along and appreciate the journey in retrospect. She reconsidered. Not just in retrospect. That was like saying she loved a surgery only after the patient was in recovery. In the middle of it, too, that was juicy and exciting and yes, uncertain and sometimes catastrophic, but thrilling all the same. Maybe Sybil had forgotten in the middle years of her life that she could still be thrilled by the simple fact of being alive.

Her phone, resting between her legs, vibrated with a notification. They must have been driving through a spot with service.

Zeke: tell me where you are in LA,
I just landed
Zeke: and I'm sorry about before
Zeke: not that I should apologize
over text, I know

Three dots appeared as he was typing, and then the cellular bars disappeared from her phone again.

Sybil typed in a reply: Not in LA anymore!

She tried to send it three times, but it kept getting bounced as undelivered.

"Do you know when we will get cell service again?"

"Is this part of twenty questions?"

"No," she said.

"Usually outside Reno," Levi replied.

So they were headed to Reno.

She typed: meet me in Reno??? Hit send, held her breath hoping it would go through. Finally, after a long gap, she heard the whoosh of a sent text.

"Oh!" she said, just remembering something. She should have written down all of her questions, been better prepared. The old Sybil Foster wouldn't have arrived at Levi's doorstep anything less than over-overprepared. "Betty's Bible."

"Betty's Bible?"

"Yes, we found it in a flour tin. In Zeke's bathroom cabinet. It's a long story."

"You found *Betty*'s Bible in a flour tin in a bathroom cabinet?"

"Yes, but that's not my question. My question is . . . I haven't asked: Are you sure she didn't set the fire? I know you want to protect her but, isn't it possible—"

Sybil's phone vibrated, then dinged, and she lost her train of thought.

Zeke: I'll be on a flight to Reno in an hour. Tell me where to meet you.

"Zeke is meeting us in Reno," Sybil said to Levi. "Can I give him a meeting spot? An address?"

"I'll tell you when we get closer."

"Okay, not to be overly dramatic, but I want to confirm that you haven't kidnapped me?"

"No, I haven't kidnapped you."

Another text:

Zeke: also, I know who started the fire

Sybil started to type back, but an SOS appeared in lieu of reception bars. She raised her cell to the roof of the car but still nothing. All she could do was dip her head back and exhale. Sybil had never been good with patience, but now the only thing to do was wait.

64

MORNING

SYBIL

January 18th

SYBIL WOKE UP disoriented, her head resting against the car window, a spot on her shoulder damp from drool. Her shoulder and neck were throbbing, as if sleep hadn't been what they needed, or at least, sleeping in a clunky sedan for a couple hours wasn't what she needed. She was parked in a strip mall parking lot in front of a dicey-looking Mexican restaurant with a shattered window. A donut shop with a half-illuminated sign was next door, a shoe repair on the other side. Her neck ached, her temples throbbed, and it took her a moment to recalibrate. Levi was gone, and when she reached between her legs for her phone, that was gone too. She unclipped her seat belt, tilted upside down and checked under her seat, in her purse, in the cup holder.

Is this what Betty felt like? Alone? Untethered? She tried not to panic. One of Sybil's pride and joys was that, had she ever had the chance to be Chief Resident, to be one of America's Best Doctors, she would never panic. *She* was the person she wanted in her foxhole.

She was unprepared for the biting air outside, and her skin prickled in rebellion. She'd packed for Los Angeles. Not for—she checked the plates on the car next to hers—Nevada. So they really had landed in Nevada, and she had slept on the way. If the circumstances weren't so bizarre, so nerve-racking, she'd be elated. Maybe she just needed to plop herself in a moving vehicle overnight, like a baby in a stroller, and at last she would rest. She could pay an Uber driver, ride the subway, start taking Amtrak.

The sun was dull behind a thick blanket of clouds. She reminded herself that Levi hadn't murdered her. So that was good. He probably would have done so already if he planned to. Sybil squinted, pulled the hood of her sweatshirt over her head. The bell clanged as she entered the donut shop, and an older woman with a poof of gray hair and fuchsia lipstick appeared from the back.

"Excuse me," Sybil said. "Do you mind if I ask where we are?"

"You're in Nevada, honey!"

"Right, but . . . are we in Reno?"

"About twenty miles outside, give or take." The woman narrowed her eyes. "Are you okay? Do you need me to call someone?"

Sybil wouldn't even know whom to call. She hadn't memorized anyone's number in years, and what could she even say? That she was in a donut shop twenty miles out from Reno on a wild-goose chase with a former cult member to find his missing sister? And the star pitcher from the New York Mets was supposed to be joining her as part of their daring detective duo? That she'd fancied herself an armchair detective who got herself stranded at a dilapidated strip mall and had her phone stolen?

"Let me get you a coffee," the woman said, then poured from one of those old-fashioned glass pitchers with an orange rim that Sybil hadn't seen since the 1990s.

"Do you happen to know how long that car"—Sybil took the coffee, then gestured to Levi's Honda—"has been parked there?"

"I come in around back," she said. "This is the first I'm noticing it."

The coffee was better than Sybil had expected, so she asked for a powdered donut, which was similarly delicious.

"I'm surprised you're not busier on a weekend morning," Sybil said. "This is excellent." She had sugar all over her fingertips, which she dipped in her mouth to ensure she got every ounce into her bloodstream.

"Weekend mornings are slow." The woman shrugged. "Half the county is getting ready for church lunch. Pray on Saturday, commune on Sunday. Or something like that."

Sybil felt her face fall, her pulse race.

"Saturdays for church?"

"Oh, I know. A few years ago, a new church set up shop, one of those aspiring megachurches, you know? Anyway, the pastor keeps Sabbath, and like sheep to the slaughterhouse, all of the parishioners fell in line." She shook her head. "I don't know how he did it. It's like he arrived one day, and everyone decided that he was the second coming of Jesus. From what I understand, he basically claims that he is." She blew air out of her nose. "Can you imagine? Claiming that you are the second coming of Jesus?"

"No," Sybil said. "I cannot."

She needed to reach Zeke. She was desperate to reach Zeke. She closed her eyes, leaned back against the wall. What was she doing here? She was a middle-aged empty nester who had mistakenly thought that she could somehow turn into an amateur detective because she had too much time on her hands and had watched too many depressingly bleak documentaries. She got into a car with a stranger who drove her eight hours across state lines, then absconded with her cell phone. She was divorcing her husband of twenty years and fantasizing about sleeping with one of the most famous men in the country who had been on *People*'s Sexiest Man of the Year short list, and all of it—*all of it!*—felt suddenly absolutely ridiculously preposterous. Betty hadn't asked her to find her! Betty hadn't asked her to help her! She'd embarked on this wild-goose chase because she mistakenly thought Betty needed saving, and she hadn't even considered that *she* was the one she should have thought about saving.

"Here you go, honey." The donut lady placed a plate of three on the table. "You look like you could use a few more."

Sybil fished around in her purse for some cash and didn't hear the bell ding when the front door pushed open.

"Syb," a voice said, and when she turned, there was Zeke.

65

MORNING

ZEKE

I GOT A TEXT with this address," he said. "I was waiting at the airport, then drove straight here." She looked worn down and strands of her hair defied gravity. Part of him hoped she'd leap into his arms, like they hadn't spent two weeks in a silent fight. She did not.

"Levi," Sybil said.

"I don't understand?"

"Levi took my phone. He texted you from it. Which, I mean, I guess it's good that we have confirmation that he's not a kidnapper. Just a thief."

He took a step toward her, willed her to do the same toward him, but when she didn't, he closed the distance between them. "I'm sorry about before."

She raised an eyebrow.

"I'm sorry about being self-centered and crabby and rude before," he tried again. Now she nodded, a tiny spark of a smile hinting at the edges of her lips. "I had to sort some things out. But I have. I did." She nodded a second time. "And before you tell me anything else, before we get into whatever this mess is . . ." He drifted because he was nervous. Jesus, he was fucking *nervous!*

He'd rehearsed all of this in the car, what he would say, how he would stride toward her with the confidence of an All-Star, hold her face in his hands and kiss her until her knees went weak. But now, standing in front of her, he felt like a kid in eighth grade, screwing up the nerve at the middle school dance. She blinked, and he snapped out of it. This was Sybil. He had nothing to be nervous about.

"Syb," he said. "I'm really fucking sorry. And I really fucking missed you." Then he dipped his head toward hers, tilted her chin up to meet his and kissed her. He'd kissed enough women to know that he caught her by surprise. Not just her, though, him too. The way his blood ran hot, the way his heart thumped in the best of ways, the way his brain stopped with any singular thought except *her. Her.* After a beat, Sybil gave into it, too, her body relaxing against his, and he wondered if this was what he needed, they both needed, to finally have some peace. To finally get some rest.

She pulled back first. "Hi."

"Hi," he said. "I've been wanting to . . ." He shook his head. "I've needed to do that for weeks." He dipped his head down again, kissed her one more time as if he needed proof. He wanted to tell her that they should get out of here, that they should go somewhere private, that he needed to take off all of her clothes and kiss every last inch of her, but, well, he knew her better than that. He knew that she was here for Betty, and he also knew the best way he could prove himself to her right now was to honor that by helping.

"Excuse me," the lady behind the counter said. "Can I get you some coffee?"

She had absolutely not a single look of recognition in her eye, and for that Zeke was more than a little grateful. At the airport, he'd taken selfies and written autographs. The rental-car lady checked his driver's license, then said, "*Holy shit,*" and he stood there and had to make small talk about how her eight-year-old nephew might be destined for the majors. He just wanted to be normal for a moment, just wanted to be normal with Sybil for more than a moment.

"That would be amazing," he said. "And a dozen donuts for the road." He reached for Sybil's hand: "Do we . . . should we . . . do we need to speed it along?"

"I thought your team had you off sugar and refined carbs?" Sybil asked. "And yes, we do." She bit her lower lip, looking a little stunned, like she couldn't believe what he'd just done but in a good way. Zeke's belly stirred with joy. "I just need to finish my coffee. Though I think I probably need to quit."

"Quit what?" He sank into a booth, and she sank right next to him. He braided his fingers through hers beneath the table.

"All of this. I'm not the intrepid detective I thought I was; I'm certainly not intrepid, and I don't know why I ever imagined I was a detective. So . . . can we have five more minutes to sit here?"

"Five minutes to sit here and feel sorry for yourself? Absolutely. I could use some coffee too."

"I feel as if you're mocking me," she said.

"Then you would feel correctly."

"That's not very nice. Mocking an old lady when she is down."

He leaned over. Kissed her again quickly.

"I'm giving you five minutes of pity. I never thought Sybil Bowman needed more than five minutes to accomplish anything. Also, not old." She rested her head on his shoulder.

"Anyway, to your question—I might be off more than just sugar and carbs," he said. "I might be off the roster."

It wasn't quite nine A.M. in Arizona. Someone at the training facility would have noticed his absence. Timothy probably thought he overslept and was on his way to pound on the condo's front door. In an hour or so, all hell was going to break loose.

Sybil nodded, just once. "Want to talk about it? We have four minutes."

They untangled their hands, and he sipped the coffee, which was black and hot and felt like gasoline for his bloodstream, in a good way.

"Not particularly," he said. "But I do want to apologize again."

"Look," she sighed, "you do have a right to prioritize yourself. No one can blame you for that."

"But there are better ways I could have done it. I'm sorry I was cold, that I took it out on you."

"I told my kids I was leaving their dad by announcing he was fucking his coworker at Thanksgiving," she said. "Maybe we both need a little reprieve."

Zeke dipped his head back and laughed, his abdominal muscles seizing, like they had atrophied from lack of happiness in Sybil's absence.

"Okay," he said. "But still."

"Since we're on the clock, the big bit of news is that there's a new megachurch in the area," Sybil said.

"A new . . ." Zeke started.

"Yes, exactly," she answered, because they could speak each other's language now, nearly finish each other's thoughts. Zeke felt something joyful bubble up in him again, not lust, but . . . was it contentedness? What he had been missing, he realized, as Sybil nudged her half-eaten plate of donuts toward him, all through his career, was a sense of connection. Being the best in the league was fantastic until it was no longer particularly interesting to him. You challenge yourself until you run out of challenges, and then, evidently, you freeze in front of a line drive that both you and your agent well know you could have dodged, and you use it as an excuse to quit. Because you don't have the emotional tools to say: *Hey, I could stand a little help here, a little support, a little friendship, a little love. I want to do something else with my life, but self-destruction is the only visible path out of it.*

"So Betty . . ." he said, putting the pieces together.

"And Levi," she answered.

"Their dad is maybe not so dead after all?"

"I think she came all this way to stop running away from him, to end his pull on them. Levi said"—she stopped, sighed—"Levi said that their dad would never let Betty go if he had a choice in the matter. So maybe Betty is going to leave him with no choice in the matter."

"And Levi is going to stop her?" Zeke asked.

Sybil drummed her fingers over the faux-wood table. "Stop her, help her, I'm not clear. He is somewhere between a savior and a lunatic, and I'm not sure that I have figured it out."

"Well, I'll help you figure it out," he said. He reached under the table, linked his fingers into hers again and squeezed. When she squeezed back, he felt like it was the first time on the mound the night of his major league debut. All nerves and electricity.

"Your arm?" she asked.

"Oh yeah, good as new. Sore after training but in a good way."

"Modern medicine," she said.

He stood. "Come on, time's up." To the donut lady, who had a box waiting for him, he said, "This new megachurch? Can you give us directions?"

When they were nearly there, Sybil turned to him.

"The fire, I forgot. You didn't tell me who started it. And how you figured it out."

"Levi didn't tell you?" Zeke asked. They were on a wide-open two-lane highway. Yellowed grass, barren trees, an occasional cow zipped by.

"I didn't ask," she said. "To be honest, I'd forgotten that the fire mattered. I only wanted to find Betty."

"The fire has to matter," he said. "Because that's what set this whole thing in motion."

Zeke's GPS announced that they'd be making a turn in a thousand feet, then their destination was half a mile down the road. He veered right around the bend, and that's when they saw it. Zeke was so stunned that he nearly careened the car onto the shoulder of the road into the aluminum guardrail.

"Zeke!" Sybil. "Oh my god."

He slammed on the brakes to get his wits about him and turned to face her, but she was as pale, as stunned as he must have been.

"Go!" she shouted. "Don't stop, we need to go!"

"Is it . . . is that a building?" he asked. "Is that . . ."

"Just go!" she said again. "*Go.*"

He startled out of his stupor and rammed his foot on the accelerator, so hard that Sybil's head jolted back against her headrest.

There in the distance, a plume of smoke snaked into the air, rising up like a pox, like a curse that would trail Aaron Jones no matter where he ran.

66

NIGHT ZERO—THE FIRE

BETTY

Four Years Ago

BETTY WAS PISSED off at Patience for sending her home to change for the Sabbath. She liked how she looked, in Levi's green sweater, in the jeans her mom had bought. When her dad relaxed the dress code, her mother, in a rare moment of independence, had told Betty to get into the minivan and taken her to the local mall. They'd eaten at the food court and bought two pairs of jeans, a pink sweater and a striped button-down at the Gap, and when they pulled back into their driveway, her mother met her eyes and said, "Don't tell your father, okay? But it's your senior year, and I wanted you to have a few new things. To look pretty. Not *too* pretty. But pretty."

Betty walked back to their house from the church. The sun was starting to set, the summer humidity that would choke the region by August only beginning to take hold. She kicked rocks, thinking of all the ways she could hold this against Patience at the Sabbath dinner, but if she did, if even a hint of unruliness crossed her face, her father would see it. Whatever he decided next, for her punishment, wasn't worth it. She was almost eighteen now, and she'd overheard Matthew and her father discussing Matthew's younger brother, how he would be a suitable match. Then, of course, the formal official introduction, where her dad squeezed her arm hard enough to leave a bruise, as if he didn't want to let her go and also didn't want to let her run. From him. From Silas. What was the difference at that point? Betty thought Matthew's brother was a beady-eyed idiot, who laughed too loud at her father's jokes and seemed to take seriously only the Bible verses that suited his needs. Not that Betty took any of the verses seriously, but she'd heard enough of the women in church murmuring about the way that Silas ogled them, how he drank too much wine at the congregants' dinners, how Matthew had hired him to do construction work for the new building her dad had commissioned, but he mostly just bossed other people around.

Betty wanted to tell Patience to convey that she wasn't interested, that she refused to be courted by this man. But Patience, the Patience whose spine straightened and tone turned chilly when her dad or Matthew entered the room, didn't feel like the same sister who spent their childhood whispering in the dark to her, teaching her how to protect herself. Their father had gotten even more ardent, more controlling as Betty approached eighteen; she could see it in how he leered at her, hear it in how he called her into his office whenever she was at the church to ensure that Betty was being a good girl, that she was fastidious in her prayers, mostly that she was fastidious in abiding whatever new rule he had invented of late. By then, though, Levi was gone, and Patience was gone. She was the only person who could protect herself now.

She tossed the jeans and green sweater on her closet floor, pulled out a dress that had been her sister's, so she knew Patience would approve. She brushed her hair, applied Vaseline to her lips, and was happy to see that the June sun had given her cheeks a bit of a glow. She was running late by then, and her dad punished people in front of the entire church for being late—she knew he would happily make an example of her, so she grabbed Levi's old bike, pedaled down the same rocky road she'd come from.

Now it was dark, and dinner had definitely begun.

She pedaled harder, but she couldn't make up for time that had already been lost.

She turned the corner onto the paved street of the church, and she wasn't sure if she saw the fire first or felt it. The rush of heat against her face, the way that the flames rose up and danced, like it was a celebration. There were people huddled in small pockets, some screaming, some running around like they didn't know what else to do. She saw Patience on the outskirts, kneeling in the grass, an arm around each child, a hand covering their eyes.

Her hands clenched the bike's handlebars.

She thought of Levi and his advice. When you get your chance to go, *take it*.

She spun the bike in the other direction.

And that was when, out of the corner of her eye, she saw him. Unmistakable. He had a runner's gait because he'd run cross-country in high school, and a ramrod spine because his father used to spank him when he slouched. She watched her dad disappear into the woods behind the church, and before she lost her nerve, she biked like hell in the other direction.

67

MORNING

BETTY

BETTY HAD SIX weeks to prepare for this morning. Six weeks of planning to confront her father, tell him that she was calling the FBI—she had memorized Richard's name and title from the *Washington Post* article—and planned to use it as a threat. *Leave me alone forever. I am not your daughter forever. You will never tame me forever.*

Levi had made the mistake about a year ago, just before she got the job at the diner, when he sent that postcard from Las Vegas, and Betty had inadvertently thought he was in Paris. She'd missed him so urgently that she'd used the flip phone to call him, ask if maybe she could join him. His voice turned stony, and he said no, absolutely not, not in Vegas. She'd assumed for a while it was because Vegas was so, at least from what she could glean from the internet and *Ocean's Eleven,* sinfully outrageous, and Levi simply didn't think she could handle it. She was googling where else she could go in Nevada, just to be close to Levi, when a message board about Reno mentioned the three-year-old church that was becoming a phenomenon.

She skimmed the post, then reread it twice in case her brain was malfunctioning. To be sure, there were plenty of megachurches popping up all over the United States, and Betty probably could have stuck a thumbtack on a map and been in the vicinity of one. But the poster mentioned a new charismatic pastor named Aaron, no last name—"like Cher!" the poster had said—who claimed that he was one of Jesus's disciples. There were other men who pulled off this sort of fraud, certainly, but almost no one did it as well as her dad. She clicked on the user's profile, found their full name, searched them on Facebook, and there, buried in a sea of posts with Bible quotes, was a picture of her father with his arm slung around two parishioners.

Betty had to run to the bathroom to throw up.

She'd been willing to let the repression of her childhood go, to live in a world where her dad occupied his corner of the earth, and she occupied hers. As far as she knew, he hadn't tracked her down yet. Levi had always warned her, though, at least before he left, that as the youngest, their dad would never willingly relinquish his grip on her, like she was his vessel built from his rib. Like he owned her, really. She thought of how he looked at her as she approached adulthood, how he squeezed her arm until it bruised when he introduced her to Silas, how he lectured her from the pulpit in front of his entire flock. And Betty knew that Levi was right.

She'd obviously been careful, but careful was exhausting, and she stared at the picture of the man who for eighteen years of her life made all decisions on her behalf—how she dressed, how she learned, what she read, whom she befriended, and worst, whom she was set to marry—and she seethed until rage practically radiated off her. Mallory knocked on her door and said, "Betty, are you okay?" and then opened it and said, "You just screamed, and I'm trying to sleep, so do you mind keeping it down?"

She never told Levi, and she knew he was only trying to shield her, so she didn't blame him either. She dyed her hair another color and got a job at the diner instead of Bloomingdale's, and one day, three insomniacs wandered into her shift, and then everything was different. She met Caleb and did a commercial, and maybe, yes, she was getting sloppy, or maybe she was just tired of being so wary and wanted this all to be over. Because as long as he was still out there, as long as the threat of him forcing her back under his wing still loomed, nothing about her could ever be normal.

This morning, with dew still coating the acreage surrounding her father's church, what she wanted most was to just be normal.

She'd hitchhiked from the bus station in Reno and was now sitting under a tree staring at the compound, which looked like a renovated farmhouse with adjoining quarters. She would threaten him first, and if that didn't work, she would dial Richard Watkins and say that she'd found her father, the man who started the fire that killed her mother, and if that still didn't work, well, then she was prepared to . . . she didn't know what exactly. Then she remembered that her dad somehow discovered that Julian was looking out for her, protecting her, on standby to alert her if her dad or one of his goons got too close, close enough to grab her, bring her back to him. And that the pious pastor then sent someone to hurt him for doing so.

Betty stood. She would do whatever she had to this morning to buy her freedom. But also, to deliver payback for Julian.

She was halfway down the hill when there was an explosion and a burst of fire, then smoke erupted from the back part of the building. She jolted and ran back toward the protection of the tree, and when she turned, she saw Levi slip out the front door. But Levi wasn't alone. A woman, somewhere in the middle of her pregnancy, trailed him.

And even from her perch under the tree, she recognized her sister's voice, yelling, "Run!"

68

MORNING

SYBIL

WHEN THEY GOT a little closer, Zeke stopped the car, and they walked until the smoke congested their lungs, and the air alone felt flammable. They stood in the middle of the road, their hands on their hips, gaping until finally Sybil said, "Shit. Betty. Shit!"

Then she broke out into a sprint.

Zeke took an extra beat, seeming to have a better scope of the situation and called, "Sybil, *Sybil!* Look!"

She turned, and he pointed.

Betty—was that Betty with black hair and a bob?—was flying down the slope of a small hill, and that's when Sybil saw two people racing toward a parked car on the far end of the road.

Zeke cupped his hands around his mouth and shouted, "Betty!"

She didn't stop.

"Betty!" Sybil shrieked, and maybe it was the high piercing tone that would have reached dogs miles away, but Betty stopped, turned and squinted. The other two running did as well. Levi. Sybil could make out Levi, and . . . was that Patience? She blinked, reopened her eyes. That was Patience. Levi and Patience made a beeline toward their sister.

Zeke took off, and Sybil ran lagging behind him.

Zeke got to her first, then Levi. Sybil had a cramp in her side and a cough that was building from the ash.

"You can't be here," Levi said to Betty. "What are you *doing* here?"

"I came to tell Dad that I was done with him forever. To leave me alone forever."

Sybil wanted to pull Betty into her, assure her that she was okay. But she didn't know if Betty *was* okay. She didn't know if any of them were. This whole thing was meant to be a quiet cadre of friends who could calm each other's anxieties. Now Julian was dead, the fire was growing, and Betty and her siblings may have been complicit in arson. None of this was at all what she imagined it would be.

"We need to go. Right now," Patience said. She had only just made her way up the hill and appeared both unbothered and wild, like the flames below that could take their time but also destroy everything in the path. "*You* need to go," she said pointedly to her sister.

Sybil caught Zeke's eye, and he mouthed, *Patience*. Then he mimicked an explosion with his fingertips. It took Sybil a long beat to intuit what he meant. *Patience had started the fire.* Back then. And now. Patience had always started the fire.

How? Sybil mouthed back.

"I realized what my sister would do for me," he said. And Sybil nearly lost her breath, at how easy the puzzle piece actually was. Family. How far we would go.

"Levi," Betty said, her voice breaking.

"I know," he said back, and she walked into his arms.

She pulled back and said, "You never called me. I would have been here, I would have done this with you." She looked at Patience, a little mystified. "With both of you. You don't have to fight my battles."

"Your battles are *our* battles," Patience said.

"You're our little sister, Bets," Levi said, a shoulder rising and falling. As if it was that simple. Maybe it really was that simple.

Patience took a long look at Betty, then clutched her by both cheeks. "You need to go. You aren't any part of this."

"I have to tell him—to leave me alone, that I'm not *his*, that I never was," Betty said, the hitch in her voice gone, the steely resolve returning. "I want this over. For good."

"You don't need to tell him," Levi said. "It *is* over. For good."

Betty's eyes flared wide, and Sybil felt her own chest heave with a gasp of air.

"He was alone," Levi said. "Before anyone else arrived for the day." He paused. "Just him." He reached into his pocket, passed Sybil back her phone. "Sorry. I couldn't use mine, and I couldn't risk you being there. It wasn't personal. I knew he would come get you." He nudged his head toward Zeke.

In the distance, Sybil heard the wail of a siren. The fire alarm must have triggered.

"I'm leaving," Patience said. She tilted forward and kissed her sister on the forehead. "I always told you that I had you. I have you."

"Patience—" Betty started.

"If he makes it out alive, tell him I did it for both of us, for all of us," she said over her shoulder just before she ran toward the other side of the incline. "But I want him to know that it was me."

69

NIGHT ZERO—FOUR YEARS AGO

PATIENCE

June 11, 2021

PATIENCE HATED SETTING up for Sabbath, but her father had determined that it was her duty, even though she was twenty-four and should have aged out of parent-mandated chores years ago. She hated being pregnant again when the other three kids were still so little; she hated that Matthew thought her father could literally walk on water, and if for some reason he couldn't, if he slipped under the water and drowned, that Matthew would happily accept his fate as lead pastor.

Betty was turning eighteen next week, and their father had selected Silas to be Betty's husband. Patience snapped off flower stems and put them in vases. Patience hated Silas. Never mind that he had a drinking problem, never mind that he liked to gamble. Silas was stupid and more often than not, unkind, and liked to comment on Patience's breast size when she was pregnant or nursing, which was basically all the time.

In high school, Patience had been part of the chemistry club. She never told her parents and begged her teacher not to put her name in the yearbook. But she was good at science, and she liked the rational way that experiments unfolded. The exact opposite of what her dad preached, of faith. She found that she could live with both, as if the contradictions between the two made each more interesting. Her sophomore year, they were tasked with exploding balloons. Nothing harmful, nothing too large. "I don't want to lose my job, get on an FBI watch list," her teacher had joked.

Most of the ingredients for explosives were found right in the kitchen. Patience was also an exceptional baker, which pleased her mother and seemed to validate her father, as if he'd been right by telling women that their place was in the home, subservient to men. When it was her turn to blow up her balloon in the science lab, her explosion was so loud and so fierce that the fire department showed up, and the school was evacuated thinking there had been a bomb.

Which gave her two ideas.

She asked her dad if she could start holding bake sales around town and at church, with the donations going to the tithe. She donated half and stuck the rest in a FLOUR tin in the back of the pantry. Her mom had delegated nearly all the baking to her by then, and she knew the money was safe. When she had enough, she'd run.

The bake sales were the first idea.

The explosion, the fire, was the second.

When she turned eighteen, however, her dad surprised her with a wedding the night of her birthday. She knew Matthew from around the church, and though he was charismatic and handsome, he was also ten years older and a fanatical opportunist. Within a month, Patience felt nauseated, and then she peed on a stick, and she was pregnant.

Sixteen months later, she was pregnant again. She thought of the money in the flour tin, she thought of her growing resentment toward Matthew and her father, who had now roped her into monitoring the behaviors of other women in the church—including Betty, a task she reviled but did all the same, and one day, in a fit of rage, she dumped her personal Bible in the tin and slammed the top shut. On the Sabbath, when Matthew asked her why she hadn't brought her Bible, she lied and said she donated it to a homeless woman at the shelter. Her dad teared up. She wanted to scream.

Three kids later, the flour tin and the plan had all but been forgotten. And then her dad asked her what she thought of Silas. For Betty. Levi was already gone, and she knew that he'd prepped Betty for the moment an opportunity to escape presented itself. Patience couldn't abandon her kids, not now, not with Matthew, not with her dad. Maybe one day it would be *her* chance to get out, but for now, she could keep pretending because pretending meant she could at least do this much for Betty.

The night of the Sabbath, when she was snapping off flower stems, Betty showed up underdressed and unprepared for what her father was planning with Silas. Once they were married, it would be exponentially harder to leave. Patience well knew this. Patience had lived this.

She barked at her little sister, chiding her for her appearance, sending her home to change. She knew she had one shot, one chance to do this. So she tucked the flowers into a dry vase and placed a balloon filled with her chemistry formulation between the stems. Matthew had only recently allowed for nail polish, and nail polish remover, Patience knew, was flammable enough to burn the place down. She carried the balloon out of the kitchen and into the maintenance room, set it down right by the boiler, which was faulty, emitting steam and shooting off sparks every so often. Earlier that week she'd heard Matthew tell her dad they needed to call a repair guy. Her dad had told him that he'd try to fix it himself first, his way of saving money, which was absurd because Patience knew her dad was squirreling away fistfuls of cash with shady accounting and likely a lot of illegality on his taxes, not to mention the suspicious carbon monoxide poisoning of the treasurer a few years back. She dumped nail polish remover all over the floor.

She feigned a terrible case of morning sickness, and since the kids were her responsibility, too, planned to bring the three of them home with her as soon as she walked out the boiler room door. She hadn't meant, honestly, to blow up half the building and start a fire that would reduce the entire place to ash, but she hadn't been devastated when it happened either. She mourned her mother, who had never stood up to her husband, only briefly. She grieved her dad not at all.

She gave Betty a chance to run, and Levi had trained her well. She did.

A few weeks later, Levi called. She might have been the scientist, but he was always the disbeliever. So, of course, he would be the one who discovered that their dad wasn't dead after all. They agreed that as long as he left them alone, left Betty alone, then they could live with this tenuous tightrope. It worked for four years. And then her dad, a narcissist who could never ease his grip on his youngest, a girl, who dared defy him, decided that she needed to come back to him.

Levi called again yesterday, last night. She walked out of her home in the woods and got on a red-eye flight. They had a plan.

"I want him to know it was me," she said to Betty, just like she'd vowed in her Bible years back.

You can never tame a woman into submission, she would say to him if he made it out alive, though she suspected that he had not. This was what happened when you tried.

EPILOGUE

MARCH

ZEKE'S PRESS CONFERENCE announcing his retirement made the front page of every newspaper, which was saying a lot, considering the world was going to shit, and there were more important things to cover. Betty was relieved that these headlines were significantly more positive than the ones about her father. Like a cockroach of doomsday evangelicalism, he had made it out alive, though barely. She made good on her promise and called Richard Watkins, who sent a squad to the Reno hospital and cuffed him to his bed. The fire department had been racing down the road while Levi and Patience drove in the other direction, and Betty, Sybil and Zeke passed the fire engines in the opposite lane, holding their breaths, as if breathing meant the authorities could trace any of this back to them. No one did. The fire was ruled inconclusive, and since her dad was the only one on-site, an insurance investigator was sent out, and Betty stopped paying attention to those details since Richard Watkins made it clear there were other charges, the ones that mattered, pending. And then Watkins followed through.

Her dad pled not guilty for the deaths of three parishioners in Georgia court and was denied bail; everyone believed he was guilty—he ran, he abandoned his family, a second fire occurred on his watch. It was an impenetrable case. Sybil and Betty flew down to Georgia to witness the arraignment. Betty didn't think she'd have the stomach to step inside the courtroom, but with Sybil beside her, with a hand guiding her, she walked in with her shoulders back, head high. Her dad wobbled to his feet and declared his innocence, and Betty knew she could speak up to clear him, but he was guilty of so much else that she thought this was poetic justice. He'd confessed to hiring someone to spook Julian but insisted he'd never agreed to murder. Unfortunately for him, the hired gun had disappeared like the smoke from the fires: gone, poof, no one to verify that her dad was telling the truth. "I just wanted that FBI goon to back off my daughter," he said. "I had plans for her. To reunite. I was just getting them in order. I needed him to lay off. To let me bring her back into my flock."

Betty didn't know if she believed him, but that was beside the point. Richard didn't, Richard hadn't, and even if her dad weren't prosecuted in Georgia for the fire that Patience had set, he'd likely spend the rest of his years in jail for the hired hit. The sentencing for the church fire was just an added bonus. Annabeth Collins, the reporter, was in the courtroom too. She wanted Betty's story, she told Sybil, to tell the full truth of the church, to expose it for what it was. Betty wasn't yet ready to crumble the house of cards while Patience was still embroiled in it, but maybe in time she would. She could. Only when that would be of service to her sister who had been of service to her for so long, in ways Betty was only beginning to grasp. And not before and until it was safe to deliver Patience's own message to their father: that it had been her this whole time. One day. Soon.

Once the judge denied her father bail, she found herself on her feet, and her dad, as if he still believed he was her keeper, turned and met her eyes. Patience couldn't be there, for obvious reasons—Matthew had sided with their father, and whatever came next would take time—so Betty would have to do this on her own. Not on her own, she remembered suddenly, as Sybil rose to her feet beside her.

"I was never yours," she said, and she could hear her voice trembling. Her dad cocked his head. So she reached into her guts and said it with her full chest. "I was *never* yours. Not then, not now, not *ever.*" Her dad heard her this time, she could tell by the way his lips formed a thin line, how his chest rose and fell as if he were trying not to combust. She reached for Sybil's hand and spun around, bolting from the courtroom. If he had something to say in return, she didn't want to hear it. No, she didn't *need* to hear it. They pushed open the doors to the courthouse, and the cool Georgia sun hit their cheeks, and for the first time in a long time, Betty thought she might believe in something like a higher power, even if that was just a belief in herself.

This morning, before Zeke's press conference, they'd trekked north to the diner. It was an unseasonably warm day in New York, and Sybil proposed they walk, the trees showing off their new buds, the fever that infects Manhattan on bright spring mornings palpable. They ordered the pancakes, which Sybil laughed about because Julian never ordered pancakes, but none of them wanted the dried-out fruit plate he used to get, and they raised their coffee cups to him. Betty sometimes dreamed about him now, how a stranger changed the course of her life by protecting her because her own parents couldn't, and she said this aloud at the booth by the window where the Insomniacs first gathered. Sybil got teary, and Zeke massaged her shoulder, and Betty thought that it was amazing, how strangers could become family, even when you didn't ask for it. Sybil liked to talk more and more about their plan Bs, how you had to accept it when plan A went to shit, so after they toasted to Julian, Betty also toasted to plan B. What a marvel it was: to take the alternate route and have it lead you to a place you didn't even know you were looking for.

Later, at Zeke's press conference, Sybil and Betty sat in the last row, and when it was over, Zeke's driver deposited them back at Sybil's house, where Zeke could have a little privacy. Pluto greeted them all like he hadn't seen them just a few hours earlier.

In the months since her father's arraignment, Betty had grown a little itchy—she still wanted to return to Georgia, extract Patience and her children from Matthew's clutches, give the interview to Annabeth Collins, but Patience, as communicated through Levi, had been clear: She was going to detonate things from the inside. She didn't want her younger sister entangled again, and it had to be done on her terms, cleanly, so her kids and her pregnancy—she was due in four weeks now—remained unscathed. Before Patience disappeared with Levi that morning, she'd promised Betty she could handle it. Would handle it.

"She will, Bets," Levi said. "We will." She hadn't communicated with Patience since. She knew better than to risk her sister's safety with Matthew; and she knew better than to risk the fact that her sister had been there that day in Reno. Betty had told Richard the fire started spontaneously, a coincidence upon her arrival. She didn't think he believed her, but he didn't much care. "I'll call Simone," was the only thing Richard had said. "She'll want to know that we caught the guy who did this to Jules." Then Betty called Levi from the flip phone and told him to go out and buy a regular phone like the rest of them. He didn't have to cover his tracks anymore, didn't have to worry about their fanatical father. Levi finished his trek and decided to stay in San Francisco now, try to plant some roots, and they texted and called freely, a relief, a gift, after so many years of covert back-and-forths.

Today, Zeke propped himself up on Sybil's marble kitchen island. "I'm genuinely exhausted," he said. "It turns out that being unemployed is extremely tiring."

"It's been, like, half a day," Betty said. "You've literally been officially retired for five hours."

Zeke had been offered a coaching position on the Mets and a broadcasting deal with the networks, but he'd turned them both down for now. *Maybe I want to drive a UPS truck,* he'd said last night. *Maybe I just want to coach Little League,* he'd mused. Sybil had rubbed the spot between his shoulder blades and nodded and said, "Yes, absolutely, all of that sounds wonderful."

"Okay, but it's been a very long day," Zeke said, tilting his head up, winking. "Also, once athletes slack off, the cliff between healthy and sloth is a steep one."

Betty rolled her eyes because Zeke Rodriguez turned out to be irresistibly charming now that she wasn't running from everything. She watched Sybil delight in his ridiculousness, a smile building at the edges of her mouth that wasn't too different from the one that Betty knew she wore when she would see Caleb waiting in Zeke's lobby to pick her up for a date. When she got back in town from Reno, she called him and tried to explain, but Caleb already intuited most of what she needed to say. She liked this, the ease between them. She had no idea where any of it would go, but for once, she tried to simply be in the present, live for the moment. It was terrifying. And exhilarating. And she had earned it.

She called Natalie, too, apologized for blowing off the national commercial, but Natalie had seen the news about the man she now understood was Betty's father and waved her apology off. "We'll use this as emotional fuel," she said. "You'll be able to cry on cue. You really will be an actor's actor!" Betty had two auditions lined up next week. She wasn't sure she really wanted to be an actor, but she'd been training for it all her life, it turned out. She might as well monetize it for now. Plan B. Maybe there would be a plan C, eventually.

"I'm exhausted too," Sybil said, refilling Pluto's water bowl, giving him a treat for no reason other than he was a very good boy. "I might head up to bed."

It was strange now, the good kind of strange, how once they got back from Nevada, sleep found them in fits and starts, but found them all the same.

"I might head up too," Zeke said, and his eyes wandered toward Sybil.

Betty had her suspicions about what was building between them. Whenever they crashed at Sybil's, Zeke slept in Charlie's room, but Betty thought they were just trying to be proper around her, like two parents who didn't want their kid to know they still had sex. She knew Sybil's kids were teasing her, asking if they had a new famous stepdad yet, but Sybil just kept laughing at their texts because, Betty supposed, she'd been constrained by a man for twenty years and wasn't ready to officially declare herself tied to another one. Even a very good man. Not just yet. But eventually, Betty surmised, she would be. She loved this for everyone involved.

"I'm heading up too," Betty said, and made her way to the stairs toward Sybil's guest room.

Downstairs, Sybil would wipe down the counters, tuck Pluto in, turn off the lights and shut down for the night. Then, when for so long, it felt like an impossibility, the three of them would slip into dreaming, soundly, restfully. Maybe they just needed each other, Betty would think before slumber took over. Maybe they just needed to know they weren't alone, that they were tethered to something greater than themselves. Maybe this was its own sort of family, the one you choose, the one that finds you.

Because after so many months when their bodies betrayed them, at long last, they finally slept. Sometimes, when dawn broke through their windows, they would even remember their dreams. That they dreamt at all now felt like a little miracle. That, Betty would think, was how she knew she was finally living; that, she would believe, was how she knew she was actually free.

ACKNOWLEDGMENTS

Every author thanks their agent and editor at the end of a book, but when I give credit to Kerry Donovan, my editor, and Elisabeth Weed, my agent, for this book, it is more than a generic platitude. I was cranky and stubborn and grouchy while writing *The Insomniacs*; this is the first book where I woke up and thought simply: *I don't think I can do this*. Kerry and Elisabeth, to their enormous credit, held my hand as they encouraged me to write outside my comfort zone, to hurdle over my imposter syndrome, to trust that I could pull this off. When I sent in my draft and didn't hear from them immediately, I was in a complete state of panic that they were going to tell me that I had to start over. (After having started over several times already.) When, instead, they called me to tell me that I had pulled it off, I genuinely almost fell over. I didn't do it alone: They were by my side every chapter. I am tremendously, *tremendously*, grateful. Trying something new can be both terrifying and exhilarating. I'm so appreciative that they pushed me past my terror to get to the good stuff.

The team at Berkley is unparalleled, giving me room to grow and putting their faith in me as I pivoted to something new. Claire Zion, Christine Ball, Craig Burke, Danielle Keir, Anna Venckus, Tawanna Sullivan, Kalie Barnes-Young, and Genni Eccles, I love collaborating with every last one of you.

Laura Dave remains my first and most trusted reader, and

she provided sharp and insightful notes that strengthened the entire book. Julie Clark and Rochelle Weinstein are author friends who always answer a text when I need to whine. Berni Barta and Michelle Weiner at CAA, thank you for always being on my team. My niece, Lexi Winn, much better at science than I am, made the pivotal suggestion of how the fire could have started. (Keeping that one vague for all you who read the acknowledgments before the book. 😊) My mom read this manuscript with a figurative fine-tooth comb and proved to me once and for all that I have no idea where and how to use a comma. My son indulged me and read for continuity holes and emerged from his room to tell me that I'm a pretty good writer.

Like Sybil, I am at midlife and struggle with turning my mind off when I tuck into bed. In fact, the idea of *The Insomniacs* struck me in the middle of the night a few years back when I was staring at the ceiling at three A.M. How lucky I am to have a family who lets me go to bed late and sleep in when I need to. Perhaps the greatest gift a mother can be given. Rest.